RACHEL VINCENT
ROGUE

MIRA®

MIRA®

ISBN-13: 978-0-7783-2914-5

ROGUE

Recycling programs for this product may not exist in your area.

www.MIRABooks.com

Printed in U.S.A.

This is for Number One, who puts up with me on a daily basis. Who is patient when the line between fiction and reality blurs. Who remembers when I forget. And who does hundreds of little things to keep me healthy and happy, because we both know I'd rather be working than sleeping or eating. I'm still up and running because you take care of me.

ACKNOWLEDGMENTS

I owe more than I could ever express to my critique partner, Rinda Elliott, for the use of her eagle eyes and for her willingness to tell me when I'm not living up to my potential. I only hope I'm half as much help to her as she is to me.

Thanks to my Dad, for the native Texan's perspective.

Thanks to Livia Rosa, for double-checking my Portuguese, and for making suggestions. To Elizabeth Mazer, for more work on my behalf than I can begin to list. And to D. P. Lyle, M.D., whose medical expertise kept my corpses realistic. Any medical mistakes in this book are mine, not his.

Thanks to my agent, Miriam Kriss, for late-night, last-minute reads, and for all those times you must wish the Easy Button really worked.

And finally, thanks to my editor, Mary-Theresa Hussey, for patience, guidance, wisdom and encouragement. Your enthusiasm is contagious, and I'm so happy to have caught it.

One

"Catch and release, my ass!" Grunting, I shoved the stray facedown over the trunk of Marc's car, snatching back my free hand just in time to avoid his teeth as they snapped together. The bastard was half again my size, and thrashing like a…well, like a scared cat, determined to shred anything he could get his hands on—including me.

Several feet behind me, Marc watched, no doubt mentally noting every aspect of my performance so he could recreate it later for my father. So far, I hadn't given him much good to report.

Beating prowlers senseless to teach them a lesson was one thing; I'd easily mastered most of the common scare tactics. But this whole chase-them-down-and-haul-them-out approach? That was bullshit. Complete and total idiocy. What was my father thinking?

The only stroke of luck I'd had all evening was that the stray had fled to a deserted make-out spot on the outskirts of Dumas, Arkansas. If he'd headed *toward* the town lights instead of *away* from them, I'd never have caught him. I wouldn't even have tried. We couldn't risk human passersby seeing an average-size young woman like me haul around a man who outweighed me by at least forty pounds. And the truth was that if the stray had known how to fight, I probably couldn't have caught him.

Not that the capture had gone smoothly, even so. Marc had made no effort to help.

"Can you give me a hand, here?" I snapped at him over my shoulder, slamming the stray's head back down on the trunk as he twisted, trying to break free of my grasp.

Masculine laughter rang out from behind me, unaccompanied by footsteps. "You're doing just fine, *querida.*"

"Don't…fucking…call…me…that," I growled through clenched jaws. With my free hand, I seized one of the trespasser's flailing arms and pinned it to the small of his back. His other hand escaped me, clawing grooves into the paint. Not that it made any difference on Marc's oft-abused car.

Marc laughed, unmoved by my threat.

Leaning forward, I draped myself across the intruder's back to hold him still. His heart pounded fiercely against the thin, shiny material of a red blouse I'd had no plans to fight in.

His free hand flailed, still out of reach. I squeezed the wrist I'd captured. His bones ground together. Howling in pain, he bucked beneath me. I held on, determined not to screw up my first solo capture. Not with Marc watching. He'd never let me live it down.

"Let me go, bitch," the stray growled, his words distorted with his face pressed into the car.

Behind me, Marc chuckled again. "I think he likes you, Faythe."

"Either help or shut up." With my free hand, I dug into my back pocket for my new handcuffs, fresh out of the package and still shiny. It was time to break them in.

Metal clinked against metal as I opened the first cuff, and the stray's thrashing intensified. He threw his head back and tossed his free arm up at an awkward angle. His hand smashed into mine. My fist opened.

For one agonizing moment, the open half circle of metal dangled from my index finger, the other end swinging like a pendulum. Then the cuff slipped from my grasp and landed across the toe of my prisoner's left shoe. Tightening my grip on his wrist, I bent to grab it, hauling him backward in the process. He kicked out. The cuff sailed beneath the car, skidding across the gravel.

"Damn it!" *So much for shiny and new.* I jerked us both upright and slapped the back of the stray's head. He growled. Marc laughed. I barely held back a scream of frustration. This was *not* how my first catch-and-release was supposed to go.

Shoving aside my irritation, I slammed the stray back down on the trunk, but it was too late to regain the upper hand. I'd screwed up, and he'd rediscovered his balls.

Grunting, the stray threw his elbow back, into my left side. Pain tore through my chest and abdomen. My breath escaped in a single, harsh puff. His arm slid through my fist, and I nearly lost my grip.

Screw this. He'd blown his shot at nice-and-easy, which only left quick-and-brutal—my favorite way to play.

I sucked in a deep breath. Fire raced up my newly bruised side. I shifted my weight onto my left leg and slammed my right knee into his groin.

The stray made a single, pain-filled gulping sound, as if he were swallowing his own tongue. For a moment, I heard only Marc's steady breathing at my back and the crickets chirping all around us. Then my prisoner screamed. He hit notes that would have made Steven Tyler wince.

Satisfied that he couldn't stand, much less run, I let him go. He crumpled to the ground at my feet, shrieking like a little girl.

"Well, that's certainly *one* way to do it." Marc stepped up to my side. He looked a little pale, and not just from the moonlight.

I smoothed more hair back from my face, eyeing the pathetic form on the gravel. "Give me your damn cuffs," I snapped at Marc, not the least bit ashamed of myself for dropping my opponent with a knee to the groin.

Marc pulled his own handcuffs from his back pocket. "Remind me not to piss you off," he said, dropping them into my open palm.

"You still need to be reminded?" Kneeling, I pulled the stray's arms behind his back and cuffed them. He was still whimpering when I hauled him up by his elbow and half dragged him to the passenger side of the car. At the door, I spun him around to face me. "What's your name?"

Instead of answering, he leered at the low neckline of my blouse. It wasn't the smartest or most original response, but it was a definite improvement over the guy who'd tried to take a taste. Still, I was in no mood to be ogled. At least, not by him.

I let my fist fly, and my knuckles smashed into his rib cage. His eyes went wide, and he clenched his jaw on an *oof* of pain.

"This is the last time I'll ask," I warned, focusing on his closed eyelids. "Then I'll just knock you out and call you Tom Doe. Your choice. Now, what's your fucking name?"

His eyes popped opened, staring into mine as if to determine how serious my threat was. Whatever he saw must have convinced him. "Dan Painter," he said, the end of his own name clipped short in anger.

"Mr. Painter." I nodded, satisfied that he was telling the truth, based on his expression and the steady, if quick, beat of his pulse. "To what do we owe the displeasure of your visit?"

His eyebrows rose in confusion.

I rolled my eyes. "What the hell are you doing here?"

The wrinkles in his forehead smoothed out as comprehension spread across his face. "Just doin' my civic duty," he insisted. "Chasing a piece of ass, not that it matters now. Bitch gave me the slip."

Marc stepped forward. "That must have been some piece of ass, to tempt you into south-central territory."

Groaning inwardly, I held my tongue. It would have been poor form to yell at my partner in front of the prisoner. Again.

"You got no idea." The stray looked at Marc over my shoulder. "Or maybe you do." His eyes slid back to me, and I ground my teeth as his gaze traveled down my blouse and snug black slacks. "This one's kind of plain in the face, but she's got it where it counts, huh?"

I felt Marc tense just behind me, and heard his knuckles pop. He was forming a fist. But he was too late.

"Consider this your only warning to stay out of our territory." My fist flew in a beautiful right hook. My knuckles slammed into the stray's left cheek. His head snapped back and to the side. And for the second time in four minutes, he collapsed—this time unconscious.

Already flexing my bruised hand, I let him fall. What did I care if he scraped his face on the gravel? He was lucky I hadn't broken his cheekbone. At least, I didn't *think* I'd broken anything. Except possibly my own knuckles.

Behind me, Marc made a soft whistling sound, clearly impressed. "That's not standard procedure," he said, his tone entirely too reasonable as he leaned over the stray's body to open the back passenger-side door.

"Yeah, well, I'm not your standard enforcer." The rest of my father's employees had more respect for the rules than I had. They also had much more testosterone and two fewer ovaries. None of them really knew what to do with me.

Marc grinned, pulling my injured hand into the light from the car's interior bulb. "I won't argue with *that*." He tilted my wrist for a better view, and I winced. "It's not broken. We'll stop for some ice on the way to the free zone."

"And some coffee," I insisted, already dreading the hour-long drive east to the Arkansas-Mississippi border, where we would release Dan Painter in the free zone on the other side of the Mississippi River. "I need coffee."

"Of course." Bending, Marc grabbed the stray's shirt in his left hand and the waist of his jeans in the other. He picked up the unconscious werecat and tossed him headfirst onto the backseat. "That was one hell of a right hook." Marc produced a roll of duct tape, apparently from thin air. He tore off a long strip and wound it around Mr. Painter's ankles, then bent the stray's legs at the knees to get his feet into the car. "I don't remember your father teaching you *that*."

"He didn't."

Marc slammed the door and arched one eyebrow at me in question.

Smiling, I knelt to look beneath the car. "Ultimate Fighting Championship."

He nodded. "Impressive."

"I thought so." On my hands and knees in the gravel, I felt

around beneath the car, searching for my handcuffs. I'd lost my first pair diving into the Red River in pursuit of a harmless but repeat offender a month earlier. If I came back without the new set, my father would have my hide. Or dock my paycheck.

My fingers scraped a clump of coarse grass growing through the rocks and skimmed over the rounded end of a broken bottle.

"Need some help?" Marc reached down to run one hand slowly over my hip.

I grinned at him over my shoulder. "You're not going to find anything there."

"That's what *you* think." His hand slid up my side as my fingers brushed a smooth arc of metal. I grabbed the cuff and backed out from under the car, and Marc pulled me to my feet. He turned me around to face him as I slid the cuff into my back pocket, then he pressed me against the side of the car. "Let's take a break," he whispered, leaning in to brush my neck with his lips.

"Like you've been working," I said, but my hand reached automatically for his arm. My fingers brushed the lines of his triceps, my nails skimming the surface of his skin, raising goose bumps. I loved drawing a reaction from him. It gave me a sense of power, of control. And yet the feeling was mutual; I couldn't say no to him, and he knew it.

"So why don't you put me to work?" he purred against my ear, pressing closer to me. His fingers edged between me and the car, moving slowly to cup my rear, his grip firm and strong.

I leaned forward to give him better access. "Do we have time?"

"All the time in the world. Unless you have a curfew I don't know about."

"I'm grown, remember?"

"Oh, I remember." His tongue trailed lightly down the side of my neck, hesitating slightly at the four crescent-shaped scars, leaving a wet trail to be caressed by the warm September breeze. "You're very, *very* grown." His tongue resumed its course, flicking over my collarbone before diving into my cleavage. The sweet spot, he called it. With good reason.

"What about our unwilling guest?" My fingers trailed over his chest, feeling the hard planes through his T-shirt.

"He can find his own date." Marc's words were muffled against my skin, his breath hot on the upper curve of my breast.

"I'm serious." I pulled him back up to eye level. "What if he wakes up?"

"He'll be jealous." Marc leaned in to kiss me, but I put a hand on his chest. Breathing an impatient sigh, he glanced through the car window over my shoulder, then back up to meet my eyes. "He's out cold. Besides, we never have any privacy at the ranch, anyway, so what does it matter?"

Privacy. It had become our most precious commodity, and the supply was never enough to meet the demand in a house full of propriety-challenged werecats—noisy, overgrown children with supernatural hearing and no lives of their own. Marc was right: middle-of-nowhere Arkansas was about as private as we were going to get. Ever. For the rest of what passed for our lives.

I nodded, sliding my hands slowly beneath the front of his shirt. "Okay, but you'd better have a blanket in there." I tossed my head toward the trunk. "'Cause I'm not lying down on this gravel."

He frowned, and his nose met mine as he bent down for one more kiss. "Who said anything about *lying*—" his cell phone rang out from his hip pocket, just as his lips brushed mine "—*down*."

I smiled, not a bit surprised. Timing was everything, and in that regard, my father was a force to be reckoned with.

Marc stepped back, pulling the phone from his pocket, and my hands fell from his chest to rest on my hips. "Damn it, Greg," he muttered, glancing at the backlit screen.

"Tell him what we were about to do, and he'll probably leave us alone," I said, pulling open the front passenger-side door. Unlike most fathers, mine was…*enthusiastic* about my relationship with my boyfriend. So was my mother. They loved Marc as if he were a son, and would have done anything to make an honest couple of us, including gluing the ring to my finger. It was kind of creepy, if I stopped to think about it for too long.

"That's not a conversation I particularly enjoy having with your father." Marc scowled as the phone continued to ring. "And if I get one more *tip* from Michael, I'm going to throw him right through the living-room window, even if he is your brother."

I flinched. "He didn't."

Marc raised his eyebrows.

Damn. He did. Marc wouldn't have to kill Michael; I'd do it myself. I just could *not* make people understand that my private life was exactly that: private.

Smiling now, Marc pressed the on button and held his phone to his ear. "Hi, Greg. What's wrong?"

My father's reply came through loud and clear. "I just checked my messages and found something interesting. An anonymous call about a dead cat. I hope you have your shovel."

Of course Marc had his shovel. Because what better way

was there to end a date than by burying a corpse in the middle of the night?

It's official. My job sucks.

Two

"An anonymous call?" Marc said, his brow furrowed. "That's...unusual. What time did it come in?"

"Shortly after seven." Thanks to my werecat's enhanced hearing, my father's voice was easily audible, even though I was several feet from the phone.

I pressed the button on the side of my watch, illuminating the face. It was just after ten. The message was three hours old.

"Where did the call come from?" Marc asked.

Over the phone, my father cleared his throat. "A phone booth in southern Arkansas. You and Faythe are closest, so keep your eyes open, because whoever made the call could still be around." Silence settled in over the line for a moment. "I need you to identify the corpse and take care of the body."

Marc glanced at me, and I shook my head. *Hell no.* We'd already detoured from a much-anticipated weekend road trip to take care of some random trespasser, and were just about to take care of each other. That was enough for one night. The body could rot, for all I cared.

Except that we couldn't really let it rot. At least, not where a human could find it. Humans tended to get uptight and curious around corpses, and were generally adamant about pinning down the source of the problem. Which, of course, was us. Well, not my Pride specifically, but likely a member of our species. So, Marc and I would take care of the body, whether we wanted to or not. For the good of the Pride. Because that was our job.

Marc frowned at me, and I nodded reluctantly. "Yeah, we'll take care of it as soon as we get rid of the stray in the backseat," he said.

"Did she do it on her own?" my father asked, and I ground my teeth together. I couldn't help it. I'd called to report the intruder like a good girl, and was rewarded with an order to take him unassisted. It was my father's idea of a test.

Most aspects of my training didn't agree with me. There wasn't as much bossing around as I'd hoped for, and there was way too much following orders. Fortunately, there was also ample opportunity to vent my frustration in the guise of protecting and defending our property boundaries. That part wasn't too bad.

"Let's just say your daughter has one heck of a right hook," Marc said, laughter bubbling up behind his words.

"I'm not surprised." Our esteemed Alpha gave Marc directions to the exposed corpse as we settled into the car, and by the time we turned left out of the empty lot, he'd hung up the phone.

"So, what are we supposed to do with the body?" I asked, pretty sure I already knew the answer.

"Bury it. Unless you'd rather take it to school for show-and-tell?"

"Smart-ass," I snapped. Burial was what I'd expected. Unfortunately, we hadn't come prepared with a backhoe. Or a coffin. All we had was an emergency kit and a couple of shovels Marc kept in the trunk, for just such an occasion.

Huffing in irritation, I glanced at my clothes, selected with our weekend getaway in mind. But our trip had been canceled. There would be no quiet dinner in a nice restaurant with cloth napkins. No popcorn in the dark theater. No private hotel room, far from the inescapable eyes and ears of our fellow werecats.

Instead, we'd be working. All night. For no overtime.

Most of my friends had returned to school the week before and had probably spent their night gathered around textbooks and boxes of pizza. I, on the other hand, had chased down a trespasser, in three-inch heels, and would soon be digging a grave by hand in the middle of the night.

I felt my mood darken just thinking of school, and of not being there. Of not completing my master's degree, or even using my brand new BA in the foreseeable future. But I'd bargained with my father for the next two years and three months of my life, to be spent serving the Pride and training for a future I wasn't even sure I wanted.

"Definitely a broken neck."

"Hmm?" I murmured, staring hard at the line of trees twenty feet to the east. If I focused on them, on the way the moon cast ever-shifting shadows of the branches as they swayed in the early-morning breeze, I wouldn't have to look at the corpse. And I *really* didn't want to look at the corpse.

We'd found him just where the informant had said we would, in an empty field about half an hour south of Little Rock, near a tiny rural town called White Hall, which boasted some six thousand residents. From what little I could see of it in the dark, White Hall seemed like a decent place to grow up. A place that did *not* deserve a middle-of-the-night visit from us.

Marc turned his flashlight to my face, and I winced, squeezing my eyes shut against the sudden glare. "Pay attention, Faythe," he snapped, his earlier playfulness gone. He was all business now, kneeling next to the dead man who lay facedown in the grass. "I said it's definitely a broken neck. Come feel this."

"No thanks." I shoved his flashlight aside and blinked impatiently, waiting for the floating circles of light to fade from my vision. "I can see it fine from here."

"Yes, but you can't *feel* it."

I glanced down to see Marc's fist around a handful of the corpse's hair, using it to rotate the poor man's head, which obviously provided no resistance. "The bones kind of…*crunch,* when you turn his neck. That means his vertebrae are fractured."

"Fascinating. Really." I swallowed thickly, and Marc continued to twist the man's neck, his ear aimed at the ground. Maybe he could actually hear the bones grinding together. *Ewwwww.* "Could you stop that, please? Leave the poor man alone."

"Sorry." He dropped the head, and it hit the grass with a nauseatingly solid thunk. "It's weird, though. Not a bite or fresh claw mark anywhere."

"How do you know? You've only seen his neck." With a resigned sigh, I stared down at the body, scenes from the latest *CSI* rerun flashing through my mind. "Shouldn't we turn him over, or check for wounds beneath his clothes, or something like that? What if he was killed somewhere else, then moved here to keep us from finding the real crime scene?"

"Crime scene?" Marc laughed, and I gritted my teeth, uneasy with the fact that he was so comfortable around corpses. "You watch too much TV," he said, refocusing the light on the werecat's neck.

Only it wasn't just any werecat. It was a stray—a human initiated into our secret existence by violence rather than by birth. At least he *had* been a stray. Now he was dead, and his social standing no longer mattered.

Lucky bastard.

"It's research." I dragged my gaze from the corpse to Marc's face. His gold-flecked brown eyes glittered in the moonlight.

"Whatever." Marc shrugged, and the flashlight's beam swung off into the grass. "My point is that he wasn't bitten or clawed. I don't smell blood."

Pushing damp strands of hair from my face, I sniffed the air, flushing in annoyance when I realized he was right; if there had been any blood present, fresh or old, we would have smelled it. And if there was no blood, there had been no fight. No werecat—even one in human form—would fail to draw blood with a bite or scratch.

How was I sure the murderer was a werecat? Simple. No human had the strength to break a man's neck one-handed, and judging from the bruises on the back of the dead guy's neck, that was exactly what had happened to him. Sure, in theory it could have been a bruin, or one of the other shape-shifter species, but the chances of that were almost nil. What few other breeds existed weren't interested in us, and the feeling was mutual.

"Oh," I said, glancing again at the trees as I conceded his point. What else could I say? Marc was the expert on dead bodies, and in spite of having…um…*made* one a few months earlier, I knew almost nothing about murder victims. And I liked it that way.

Marc sighed. "Fine. If it'll make you happy, I'll check for other wounds." With an Oscar-worthy grunt of effort, he tugged up on the dead guy's T-shirt, exposing a tangle of old scars reaching toward his spine from both sides of his chest.

I frowned at the long-healed marks. "You're right. I admit it. There's no reason to undress him."

Marc shot me a cocky smile and lowered the poor man's shirt.

Biting my lip in frustration, I glanced at my watch, pressing the button on the side to illuminate the face with a soft green glow. Almost one in the morning. *Great.* I should have been curled up next to Marc in bed, exhausted but satisfied. Instead, I was digging unmarked graves by moonlight, exhausted but creeped-the-fuck-out.

We'd dropped off the unconscious Dan Painter in a thick stand of trees just east of the Mississippi River and north of Arkansas City, still bound and now gagged, to teach him a lesson. Then we'd backtracked two hours northwest, on a predominantly two-lane highway. Or rather, *Marc* had backtracked. I'd recited the prologue to *Canterbury Tales* in my head. In Middle English. Backward. Marc had his special skills, and I had mine. Of course, his came in far handier than mine in our line of work. Bad guys were hardly ever intimidated by a stirring recitation from *Hamlet.*

Gritting my teeth, I clung to the last of my dwindling supply of willpower and gave up all hope of seeing my bed before dawn. If I was going to be awake all night, I might as well get something done.

"Okay, a broken neck, but no other obvious wounds," I said, tugging on the hem of my snug white T-shirt.

Of course, if I'd known I would be handling a corpse, I would have worn something…darker. Or disposable. As it was, I considered myself fortunate to be wearing jeans and a T. If not for the bag I'd packed for our weekend getaway, I'd be digging in expensive black slacks and a red silk blouse.

"So, we're probably looking for another stray," I continued, brushing imaginary grave dirt from my shirt. "Maybe one with a grudge, or a history of violent behavior?" I could feel the fine layer of grit all over me, like a ghostly dusting of death, somehow itching and burning *beneath* my skin.

Or maybe I was overreacting.

Marc shrugged, oblivious to my discomfort as his face smoothed into an unreadable expression. "That describes nearly every stray I've ever met. But it doesn't matter, 'cause we're not looking for anyone. We're here to dispose of the body, not investigate the murder."

I nodded and glanced away. I'd known better. The Territorial Council, nominally led by my father, would never tie up its resources investigating the murder of a single stray. They would almost certainly view the dead cat as one less flea in their collective fur.

"It doesn't matter what he was doing here, or who killed him," Marc whispered, kneeling next to the body. "No one gives a damn."

He would never have voiced such a concern to anyone else, and my heart ached for him, knowing what it had probably cost him to say it in front of me. I knew he cared not because he'd known the stray, but because he *hadn't*. Because no one had. And because, like the dead cat we'd come to bury, Marc was a stray. He was facing what I knew to be one of his worst fears: a quick burial in the middle of the night, without a single friend to remember him kindly.

As long as I was alive, that would never happen to Marc.

He had me, my whole family, and our entire Pride to miss and remember him. Yet the injustice of a secret burial for the anonymous cat still bothered him. Righteous anger burned bright in his eyes when he looked up at me, and there was nothing I could do to put out the flames.

Marc glanced away from my sympathetic look, but before he turned back to the body, his expression hardened into its usual business face, cold and unreadable. It was a defense mechanism I had yet to master.

He pulled a brown leather wallet from the stray's back pocket and thumbed through the contents: two credit cards, a few folded receipts, a single wrinkled twenty, and at least two dozen crisp new one-dollar bills. Marc slid a driver's license from its plastic cover and passed it up to me without even glancing at it.

I looked at the photo, and immediately wished I hadn't. Until I saw his face, Bradley Moore had just been a body, a nameless corpse to be disposed of quickly, so I could get on with my night.

But now that I'd seen his license, I knew that Moore lived in Cleveland, Mississippi, and was licensed to drive a motorcycle. He'd just celebrated his thirty-fourth birthday, was six foot two and a half, and weighed two hundred and twelve pounds. And he had the most beautiful, hypnotic bluish-gray eyes I'd ever seen.

"Do you smell that?" Marc asked.

"Smell what?" I slipped the license into my front pocket and knelt beside him, eager to forget Mr. Moore's haunting eyes.

"The killer, I assume. I smell another cat on him. On his clothes, and here, on his neck." He bent to sniff where he'd indicated, and my stomach churned. I understood his sympathy for the unknown stray; I really did. And after seeing Moore's face, I couldn't help but share it. But three months earlier, I'd had to rip out a tomcat's throat in order to free myself and Abby, my kidnapped cousin. And impractical as it might sound, considering my line of work, I'd had no plans to ever again share such intimate contact with a corpse.

I could handle wrapping the cadaver in plastic and dumping it in a hole in the ground, though that might have been easier if I'd never learned the victim's name. But sniffing a corpse's neck went way past my definition of decorous behavior. It was macabre, and disturbing.

"I can smell it from here," I said. Marc hadn't asked me to come closer, but I wasn't taking any chances.

"Does it smell like a stray to you?"

I inhaled deeply, mentally sorting through the smells I already knew. The strongest was Marc. Musky and masculine, his scent was as familiar as my own. It was also *blended* with mine, the result of every kiss and embrace we'd shared since my last shower. Which we'd also shared, come to think of it.

Next, I filtered out the scents from the field around us, so pervasive I barely noticed them without conscious effort. I identified trees, grass, dirt, fresh dew, and several small rodents, mostly rabbits and mice.

On the body itself were several more scents, including Mr. Moore's cologne, the oppressive stench of cigarette smoke, and a strong, minty breath spray. What was left after I'd sorted out all of those smells was the one Marc meant. It came from the stray, but was not his personal scent. It was something else. Something definitely feline, and rich, and pungent. Almost spicy…

Shock jolted up my spine, cold and numbing. Terror ripped

through my chest. For one long moment, my heart refused to beat, and I could do nothing but stare at the corpse. I knew that scent. One aspect of it, anyway.

"Well?" Marc asked, staring at me as I stared at the body, my eyes narrowed in concentration.

"Foreign cat." I stood and stumbled back a step, too horrified to form a complete sentence.

"What?" Marc glanced up at me sharply, then back down at Moore. "No. It can't be. Luiz is long gone. We would have heard about him by now if he were still around."

Luiz was one of a pair of jungle strays who'd invaded our territory three months earlier, kidnapping and raping at will. I'd fought him once, and won, but he got away and we hadn't heard from him since, a fact that scared me more than I was willing to admit out loud. And fucking pissed me off.

"It's not Luiz." I was certain of that much. The scent was very faint—meaning the murderer had only briefly touched the victim—but I knew two things without a doubt. The scent was not from a native cat, and it did *not* belong to Luiz.

"There's barely a trace of a scent." Marc shook his head slowly, but his stare never left Moore's neck. "I don't see how you can tell a damn thing about it."

"I can tell." I'd only met Luiz once, but that was plenty. If I lived to be two hundred, I'd still remember his scent on my deathbed. It was permanently imprinted on my brain, alongside such innocent memories as the taste of my first kiss—Marc—and the flavor of my first snow cone—blue raspberry.

"Fine." Marc nodded, glancing up at me. "It isn't Luiz. But is it a stray?"

Against my better judgment—and in spite of an irrational urge to run, or at least find a weapon—I knelt for a stronger whiff of the scent. It didn't help. "I don't think so. There's something…weird about the smell. It's a foreign scent, but it's also…more. If that makes any sense."

"It doesn't," Marc said as I stood and backed away from Moore's corpse. "But you're right." He still knelt by the body, looking at it rather than at me as a light breeze ruffled tall blades of grass against his jeans. "There's an element to it that I can't quite place." He leaned back on his heels, frowning in frustration. "What's his name?"

"Bradley Moore." I slipped my hand into my pocket, feeling the slick surface of the plastic card, now warm from my own body heat. "He's from Mississippi."

Marc nodded, as if he'd already known that last part. It wouldn't be too hard to guess. Mississippi was the nearest free territory, unclaimed by any Pride. And because it had the mildest climate of any of the free territories, it was home to the largest concentration of strays in the country, mingling with the human population like the proverbial wolves in sheep's clothing.

We were less than forty miles from the Mississippi border, where interstate travelers were welcomed across the state line by a seedy-looking strip club, at which Moore had no doubt planned to spend the bundle of ones in his wallet. At least that much of his plan for the evening was clear. Unfortunately, a stack of one-dollar bills did nothing to answer the other questions pinging around my brain like the little silver balls in a pinball machine.

"Well, let's get going." Marc stood and brushed his palms against his legs, as if he could wipe the feel of dead flesh from his hands like road dust. I knew exactly how he felt. "It's a shame the son of a bitch didn't have the courtesy to give him

a decent burial," he said. "We do that much even for tres-
passers, and this asshole couldn't be bothered to bury a
friend."

I blinked at Marc's tone, so low and gravelly. And angry.
Then his meaning sank in. "You think Moore knew whoever
killed him?"

"How else could the killer have gotten so close to him?"

I thought about that for a moment, still rubbing the license
in my pocket as I stared at the ground near poor Mr. Moore's
head. "No defensive wounds," I said finally. I took another
deep breath, again searching with my sensitive nose for any
sign of blood. I still found none. "No blood beneath his nails
or in his mouth. He didn't fight back." Marc was right. They'd
probably known each other. But how was that even possible?
How could an American stray have become friends with a
foreign cat who had no business in the United States, much
less in the south-central territory? And what were they both
doing on *our* land?

Marc nodded again, interrupting my silent confusion. A
hint of a smile showed me he was pleased that I understood
what he was getting at.

I wasn't pleased. I didn't *want* to understand death and mur-
derers. Unfortunately, what I wanted mattered no more then
than it ever had. Alphas aren't big fans of free will. In fact,
our social and political structure is more of a monarchical
system, in which the monarch is invariably the strongest male
in the territory. Power passes not to one of the Alpha's several
sons, but to the tomcat who marries his only daughter. This
son-in-law and future Alpha must be strong enough to lead,
protect, and ultimately control the entire Pride, or the entire

system falls apart. And the system—along with the continuation of the species itself—must be protected at all costs.

My father was a bit of a rebel among the other Territorial Council members, Alphas of each of the nine other territories. Rather than passing the south-central Pride on to my future husband—Marc, if my parents have any say in the matter— he wanted to hand the reins over to *me*. That very concept was sending shock waves of anger and impropriety throughout certain elements of the council. If my father's scandalous scheme ever came to fruition, I would someday have an opportunity to change the system from the inside.

It was the "inside" part that bothered me.

A chill went through me at the very thought of ever being in my father's position, and Marc mistook my shiver for one of sympathy for the dead stray.

"He probably never saw it coming." Marc shook his head in disgust. "The bastard just reached over and snapped his neck from behind."

My phone rang into the silence following his words, rescuing me from the fact that I had no idea what to say next. I fumbled in my right front pocket, digging for the phone. Squinting at the tiny display screen, I was relieved to recognize the number for my father's private line. "It's my dad."

Marc nodded and bent to pick up the roll of black plastic in the grass at his feet.

I pressed the yes button as he spread the plastic out on the ground beside Moore's body. "You rang?" I said into the phone, turning away from Marc as he prepared to flip the corpse over.

"Did you find it?" my father asked.

"Yeah." I grimaced at the heavy thunk and the crinkling of thick plastic at my back. "I think we need to look into this one." Marc went silent behind me, and I knew he'd frozen in surprise. He would never have voiced such a request.

"Faythe…" A chair creaked in the background as my father leaned back. "You know we don't have the resources to investigate every stray who dies in a brawl. We'd just be chasing our own tails. Bury him and come on home."

I exhaled slowly, wondering whether I was trying to satisfy Marc or set my own mind at ease. "It's a little more complicated than that."

"How so?"

"There's a scent on the body. It's very faint, and it's only on his neck, so we're ninety-nine percent sure it's the killer." I hesitated when the next words seemed to catch in my throat, threatening to choke me. Then, finally, I spat them out, grimacing at the bitter taste. "It's a foreign cat."

A sharp, near-silent inhalation was my father's only reaction. He was as worried and pissed off as I was at the news of an outsider in our territory. Thank goodness.

"Are you sure?" he asked, his voice frightfully calm as Marc went still again behind me.

"Completely."

Silence stretched out over the line, and I knew exactly what he was thinking. I'd come to recognize that particular pause over the past three months; everyone close to me lapsed into it often enough. He was thinking about Miguel, debating whether or not to ask me if I was okay. Like the rest of my family, my father was afraid of upsetting me with reminders of the bastard who'd kidnapped, caged, and beat the living shit out of me. Apparently he thought I was sturdy enough to chase down intruders and bury dead bodies, but too delicate to withstand the assault of my own memory. Go figure.

What my father didn't realize, what *none* of them seemed to realize, was that just reporting for work every morning reminded me of Miguel, the jungle stray whose disregard for personal liberty and a woman's right to say "no" had changed my life forever. I'd agreed to work for my father in exchange for the opportunity to go after Miguel. To take my pound of flesh from the sadistic bastard who'd murdered one of my childhood friends and raped my teenage cousin. And who'd tried to sell all three of us as personal property to a jungle Alpha somewhere in Brazil.

Though no one seemed willing to believe it, thinking about Miguel didn't so much upset me as inspire me. It reminded me of my new purpose, of why I was willing to forgo a weekend with my boyfriend to kick the shit out of one stray and bury another. And every now and then I really needed that reminder, so I wished my father would quit stalling and just spit it out. And finally he did.

"Miguel's dead, Faythe. He's not coming back."

"Damn right." But I shivered in spite of the balmy breeze. Marc laid a warm, heavy hand on my shoulder, clearly having heard both sides of the conversation.

"Are you okay?" My father's voice was hollow-sounding, the way it got when he cradled his head in one hand, in spite of the telephone.

In the distance, a whip-poor-will sang, unconcerned by our presence. "Yeah. I'm fine." *And if I'm not now, I will be soon.* "Really," I added, before he had a chance to ask if I was sure. "Let's just get this over with."

"Good." Over the line, he cleared his throat and tapped a

pen against his desk blotter, and I couldn't stop a smile. My father was gone; the Alpha had arrived. "Okay, so you're pretty sure the killer is foreign. Is it a jungle cat?"

I inhaled again, but was rewarded only with frustration. "I don't know. It's too faint to tell for sure, but that's a definite possibility. And there's something weird about the scent. It's definitely foreign, but it's also…*more*. If that makes any sense."

"Not *much* sense, I'm afraid," he said. "Would you recognize it if you smelled it again?"

"Absolutely." I nodded, though he couldn't see me.

"Me, too." Marc bent to pick up a shovel mostly hidden by tall grass. I didn't bother passing his answer along; my father could hear him just fine.

"Good. That's a start."

"Any word yet on who called it in?" I asked, shuffling my feet in the long grass.

"We're still working on it, without much luck." Metal springs squealed and I pictured my father leaning forward again in his desk chair. "The only thing we know for sure is that the caller was male."

That was pretty much a given. Female cats—tabbies— were few and far between, and we were never unattended for long enough to stumble across a dead body in an empty field.

"And that he isn't one of ours," my father continued. "He sounded young, but that isn't specific enough to be of any help. Owen's compiling a list of strays living closest to the Arkansas border."

"Did Bradley Moore come up on your list?" I asked, glancing over my shoulder to see Marc sliding a pair of scissors through the plastic, on which Moore now lay faceup.

"Just a minute…" Papers shuffled and my father cleared

his throat as my gaze slid back toward the trees. "Yes. Bradley Moore. You have reason to suspect him?"

"Nope." From behind me came a dull ripping sound as Marc tore strips from a thick roll of duct tape. "I have a reason to cross him off your list. He's dead."

"We usually have to work much harder to identify corpses not of our own making."

By which, of course, he meant Marc's making. Marc was my father's de facto executioner—the enforcer charged with carrying out death sentences for any werecat guilty of one of the three capital crimes: murder, infection, or disclosure of our existence to a human.

"Well, this one was easy. He still had his wallet." I curled my left hand into a fist to keep it from sneaking back into my pocket to feel Moore's license.

"That's unusual. They're typically stripped of their ID and anything valuable."

"Yeah, well, it gets even weirder." I brushed my hair back from my face, making a mental note to wear a bun or a ponytail on my next burial run. "His neck is broken, but he wasn't bitten or scratched at all, and he has no defensive wounds. Marc thinks he knew his attacker."

"Does he have any lumps on his skull? Do you smell any strange chemicals?"

I shook my head before I realized he couldn't see me. "No, no bumps that I've seen. Um…hang on." I turned to Marc with an upraised eyebrow. He frowned and handed me his flashlight, then squatted to rip a strip of duct tape from one end of the long black bundle. Sheet plastic fell away to reveal Bradley Moore's face, his beautiful eyes staring up into nothing.

Marc lifted Moore's head gently, and I grimaced at the ease

with which it rolled on his broken neck. Mouth set in a grim, hard line, Marc moved his fingers quickly but thoroughly over the stray's skull, examining every inch of it as I watched, fending off nausea by sheer will. Finally, he lowered the head back onto the plastic and looked at me, eyes glittering in the beam of the flashlight. "No bumps. And that odd element to the scent is biological, not chemical."

"Okay." My father sighed in frustration. "Just get him buried and come home." He paused, and I could feel the lecture coming, even as I heard the tired smile in his voice. "And if you make Marc do all the digging, I'll give him all of your paycheck."

Hmm, there's an idea. What was I supposed to do with my meager income, anyway? I lived with my parents, owned no car, and had no bills. And I hated shopping. Marc could *have* my check, especially if he'd dig the damned hole himself.

I grinned, glancing at Marc from the corner of my eye as I spoke into the phone. "Thanks for the warning. I gotta go bury a body."

"Make it at least five feet deep," my father said, and very few other people would have heard the exhaustion in his voice. Then he hung up. No "Thanks for giving up your weekend to do my grunt work, Faythe." No "Have a safe drive home." Not even a goodbye. The Alpha was all business.

A little miffed, I shoved my phone back into my pocket and met Marc's eyes. He frowned sternly at me, but his lips held a hint of a smile. "Don't even say it," he warned. "I'm not digging this grave by myself. Not even for your *annual* salary. So quit looking at the dirt like it's going to stain your soul, princess, and get to work." Openly smiling now, he tossed me the shovel one-handed.

I caught it, though I'd literally never held a shovel before. Cats have great reflexes, which isn't always a good thing.

He grinned, gold-flecked eyes sparkling in the moonlight. "First one to hit five feet wins."

"Wins what?"

"A nap on the way home."

I groaned, my good humor beginning to fade. Nothing good could come from such a wager. If I lost, I'd have to drive for the entire five-and-a-half-hour trip home. But if I won, Marc would drive, which was much, much worse. With him in the driver's seat, I'd be afraid to blink, much less sleep. Marc's favorite travel game was highway tag, which he played by getting just close enough to passing semi trucks to reach out his window and touch their rear bumpers. Seriously. The man thought the inevitability of death didn't apply to him, simply because it hadn't happened yet.

Marc laughed at my horrified expression and sank his shovel into the earth at the end of the black plastic cocoon. With a sigh, I joined him, trying to decide whether I'd rather risk falling asleep at the wheel, or falling asleep with *Marc* at the wheel.

It was a tough call. Thankfully, I had three solid hours of digging during which to decide. Lucky me.

Three

Marc hit five feet first, naturally, and as he grinned in triumph, completely covered in grave dirt, I dropped my shovel in defeat. I was done, and not a single threat from him could pry my tired, grimy ass off the ground. My formerly white T-shirt forgotten, I lay sweating on dew-damp grass as Marc rolled Bradley Moore into the hole, then shoveled dirt in on top of him. Then I took the keys Marc held out to me and snatched my shovel from the ground, my mood growing more foul with each step I took toward the car, in spite of my relief to be leaving the unmarked grave behind. This was *not* how I'd planned to spend my time off.

I stopped for coffee five times on the way home, and had to use the restroom at each stop. Marc slept the whole way, and his obnoxious snoring did more to keep me awake than the caffeine did during the drive from White Hall, Arkansas, to the Lazy S Ranch. My family's property—devoid of domestic animals in spite of the title *ranch*—sat on the out-skirts of Lufkin, Texas, sixty miles from the Louisiana border.

Yes, at twenty-three years old, I still lived with my parents. But so did three of my older brothers, and four of my fellow enforcers, though they technically lived in a guest house on the back of the property. The concept of a group dynamic is different for werecats than it is for humans. Pride members are very close, both emotionally and physically, especially the core group, consisting of the Alpha, his family, and the enforcers. We've always lived in large, mostly informal groups for protection, comfort, and social interaction. And because one of the primary duties of an enforcer is to protect and assist the Alpha, which we couldn't do if we weren't *with* him most of the time.

Fortunately, the advantages balanced out the drawbacks of being forever under my father's watchful eye. Most of the time. And the number one benefit—other than free food and freshly folded laundry—was the fact that my family's mostly wooded property backed up to the Davy Crockett National Forest and its 160,000 acres of woodland. Which made one hell of a big— and convenient—playground for a houseful of werecats.

It was nearly 10:00 a.m. when I turned Marc's car onto the quarter-mile-long gravel driveway. I parked in the circle drive, as close to the front door as I could get and heat hit me like a blast of steam from a furnace as I opened the car door. The 102-degree-heat index was our own personal inferno, a September-in-Texas specialty, guaranteed to melt tourists where they stood. But I was a native, and all the searing, blacktop-melting blaze drew from me was a weary sigh.

My boot heels sank into the gravel as I stood, and I glanced at Marc, where he still sat snoring against the passenger-side window. *I should wake him up,* I thought. But then, he should have offered to split the drive with me.

I was too tired to go to war with my conscience, and more than a little irritated with Marc. So, I cranked down the driver's-side window to keep him from baking and closed the door gently, smiling to myself as Marc shifted in his seat, then resumed snoring, still out cold in spite of the heat.

My boots clomped as I trudged up onto the porch, and when I opened the front door, cool air rushed out to meet me. I sagged in the doorway for a moment, one hand on each side of the frame, letting the artificial breeze dry my sweat and chase away the heat that had been slowly draining my vitality.

In my room near the end of the long central hallway, I stripped completely, tossing my dirty clothes into a pile by the door. I considered putting them in the hamper, but since I had no plans to ever wear them again, going through that much effort seemed pointless.

I glanced around the room, happy to find everything just as I'd left it. My books—hundreds of them—were crammed two rows deep into my only bookshelf, the extras stacked horizontally wherever they would fit. My bed was unmade, because I hadn't made it, and because I'd refused to let my mother into my room to clean since my first week home, when I'd realized she was using housework as an excuse to spy on me. *That* could not continue. Besides, I was damn well old enough to clean my own room. Or to *not* clean it in peace. So I'd told her to stay the hell out. She'd frowned at my language, but complied.

At my dresser, I paused to take off my watch and caught sight of my own reflection. I looked like shit. Dirty, sweaty, tangled, and…still wearing the diamond stud earrings I'd put on in concession to my original plans for the night before. It was a miracle I hadn't lost them both—along with half my earlobe—to Dan Painter's temper and desperate, flailing fists. Or his teeth.

As much as I hated to admit it, even to myself, I'd been completely unprepared for my run-in with Painter. After we dropped off the stray, Marc had laughed at my bewildered expression as he'd pulled item after item from a trunk emergency kit, the likes of which I'd never seen because I'd never had reason to use one. The kit included two shovels, a roll of 3 mm black plastic, duct tape, black jeans and a black T-shirt, a pair of old sneakers, and an ax.

I didn't ask what the ax was for, because I doubted its uses involved fallen tree branches and cozy campfires. Regardless, Marc was nothing if not prepared. He was like an overgrown Boy Scout. A Boy Scout with gorgeous gold-flecked brown eyes and glossy black curls crowning a physique solid enough to stop a fucking freight train. A Boy Scout who could bring a girl screaming with a single lingering glance…

Okay, he really had little in common with the Boy Scouts, other than the whole overpreparedness thing. And his damned emergency kit hadn't kept me from letting him bake in his own car, now, had it?

Thoroughly satisfied with my revenge, I dug out a change of underwear and a nightshirt and tossed them onto my bed, then plodded into my private bathroom and straight into the shower. Ten minutes later, I stepped out into the suddenly frigid bathroom, soaked but smelling of lavender-scented soap, rather than sweat and dirt. To a cat's sensitive nose, smelling good is very, very important, especially in human form, where body odor, unlike personal scent, isn't socially acceptable.

I was reaching for my robe when the first few grunts of

Pink's "U + Ur Hand" rang out from my cell phone. I pulled my robe from its hook and shoved my arms through the sleeves on my way out of the bathroom. In the middle of my bedroom floor I glanced around for my phone, my focus sliding over my dresser, bed, nightstand, and wall shelf before finally landing on my desk. *There.* Only lower.

My gaze dropped to the clothing I'd kicked off to the right of my door. Squatting in front of the pile, I searched my jeans pockets frantically, wondering who the hell would be calling me at 10:00 a.m. on a Thursday. Unfortunately, I no longer had much contact with the world outside of the Lazy S, and my fellow enforcers wouldn't bother knocking on my door before barging in, much less calling first.

Maybe it was Abby. She'd spent most of the summer on the ranch, recovering from her ordeal at Miguel's hands with a fellow survivor—me. And she'd called me at least a dozen times in the three weeks she'd been home, with little to say except that she was fine. She seemed content to hear that I was fine, too, and to listen to me prattle on about my endless, exhaustive training.

But Abby should be back in school by now, so who…

Sammi. A smile formed on my face in spite of my fatigue as I thought of my college roommate, and how long it had been since I'd spoken to her.

My fingers closed around the phone and I flipped it open without bothering to look at the caller ID. "Hello?" I said, fully expecting to hear Sammi's perky, full-speed chatter from the other end of the line.

"Miss me?" The man's voice was sharp with hostility, obvious even in just those two words.

The unexpected voice—and the angry question—surprised

me so much that I fell on my tailbone, smacking the back of my skull against the edge of my desktop. Confused, and still rubbing the new bump on my head, I held the phone at arm's length to read the number on the screen. I didn't recognize it.

"*Should* I miss you?" I asked finally, pressing the phone against my ear.

"I guess that's a matter of opinion, Faythe. My idea of what you should do obviously has little in common with your own."

Irritation flared in my chest like heartburn. "Who the hell *is* this?" I demanded, half convinced that my judgmental caller had the wrong number, even though he knew my name.

Deep Throat clucked his tongue in my ear, and I gritted my teeth against the intimate sound and feel of his disapproval. "How soon they forget," he whispered, and the enmity in his tone chilled me.

Bewildered, and now truly pissed off, I glanced at the phone again, hoping to identify the number on second glance. I couldn't, yet the caller obviously knew me. In fact, he spoke as if I should have been expecting his call. As if we were picking up an old, unfinished conversation…

And suddenly I knew. *Andrew.*

Shock knocked the breath from my lungs. The phone slipped from my hand and landed in my lap, then cartwheeled to the floor with a carpet-muffled thud. Miraculously, it remained open.

I'd never heard my human ex speak a word in anger before, and the rage in his voice rendered it completely unrecognizable.

For a moment, I simply stared at the phone, too astounded to move. I hadn't spoken to Andrew in three months, since before I'd quit school and agreed to work for my father. Hearing from him now was odd and uncomfortable, especially considering how mad he obviously was.

But then, that last part was at least partially my fault.

After surviving a beating from Miguel, taking a life in defense of my own, and becoming the country's first and only female enforcer, I was no longer the same girl Andrew once knew. The entire college experience—including the exotic-because-he's-normal human boyfriend—seemed really *tame,* and much less relevant to my new life. Which was actually my precollege life on steroids.

I'd tried to tell Andrew I was leaving school, and that Marc and I had gotten back together, but Andrew hadn't answered his cell phone, and his roommate didn't know where he was. And honestly, I thought it would be easier for all concerned if I let my efforts rest there, so we could all move on in peace.

Clearly I was wrong.

"What, all of a sudden you have nothing to say?" Andrew said, breaking into my thoughts. "*That's* certainly new."

So is your attitude. I picked up the phone and held it to my ear, unsure what I was going to say until the words came out of their own accord. "Andrew?" I asked, the gears in my brain grinding almost audibly as I tried to reconcile this bitter, sharp-tongued man with *my* Andrew, who was sweet, and funny, and…*nice.* I couldn't do it.

"So you *do* remember me?" His sarcasm was every bit as sharp as my own claws.

"Of course I do."

"I haven't forgotten you, either." He didn't sound very pleased by that fact, and at the moment, the feeling was mutual.

Before I could reply, a harsh rustling sounded in my ear, as if he'd covered up the phone on his end of the line. Then I heard indecipherable angry words, and the line went silent. No static, and no breathing. He'd hung up.

The words *end call,* printed across the screen on my phone, confirmed it.

At least a minute later, my bedroom door swung open to smack against my knees, and Marc stuck his head around the edge to see what he'd hit. He found me still staring at my phone, my robe gaping open across one thigh. "You have to push the buttons to make that work," he said, his expression completely serious.

"Thanks, smart-ass." I shook my head to wake myself up. Fatigue and the shock of hearing from Andrew had pulled me past the end of my energy reserve.

Marc offered me his hand as he stepped into the room. I took it, and he hauled me up. He would have pulled me into an embrace, but I aimed a pointed glance at his grime-covered clothes and stepped back, banging my hip on the corner of my desk. "Something wrong with your phone?"

"Nope. I was just checking the charge." I trudged over to my dresser and dropped the phone next to my watch, going for nonchalance as I opened the top drawer and grabbed underwear at random. But my faux casual gesture was pretty much ruined when I realized I already had a clean pair waiting on the bed.

I couldn't tell Marc about the phone call, because he'd assumed from the beginning that I'd ended things with Andrew properly. I hadn't lied, exactly. I just hadn't corrected his assumption. And really, was it my fault he'd made an ass out of us both?

"Oh." Marc pulled his shirt over his head and dropped it on top of my pile of clothes.

"You have your own shower." I crossed my arms over the front of my robe to hold it closed. I couldn't concentrate on being irritated while he was half-naked, and he damn well knew it.

Marc gave me a sly grin and kicked the door closed with his foot. "I'm borrowing yours. It's the least you owe me after leaving me to sweat to death in that crematorium of a car."

I shoved the extra pair of underwear back into the drawer. "Serves you right for sleeping through the entire trip."

"I'll make it up to you." His jeans fell to the floor, and my eyes trailed after them helplessly, hypnotized by the golden-brown color of his skin. No fair tempting me while I was too weak to resist.

Fortunately, I knew how to play that game, too. I let my robe fall open, framing my body with lavender terry cloth. Marc came forward with his arms outstretched, lust in his eyes and impatience in his step.

I held him at arm's length. "Not while you smell like an enforcer."

He groaned and backed toward the bathroom, his eyes holding mine captive. "I'll be back in two minutes. Time me. Two minutes."

I laughed. "Two minutes, or you're out of luck." I let the material slide off slowly. The shower was running by the time my robe hit the floor, but I was too tired to chuckle as I pulled a nightshirt over my head and stepped into my underwear. I slid beneath my covers with thoughts of Marc in the shower, slick with soap and water, and scented by my shampoo.

I'd already forgotten about Andrew's phone call by the time I fell asleep, and the last thing I heard before surrendering to exhaustion was Marc's groan of frustration when he opened the bathroom door to find me already curled up. Without him.

Four

"Faythe, watch out!"

I whirled instinctively toward the sound of Ryan's voice the instant I heard it. I should have known better. In the far corner of the basement, my second-born brother stood gripping the steel bars of the cage, staring over my shoulder with his eyes wide in warning.

Shadows shifted on the wall in front of me. Clothing whispered behind me. A foreign heartbeat echoed in my ear. Hot breath stirred hairs on the back of my neck. I spun to face my foe. I was too late.

My eyes found his as his foot hit my ankle. He swept my feet out from under me. My ass hit the thick blue mat with a muted thud. My teeth clicked together, one side of my cheek between them. Sucking on the wound, I glared up at my opponent.

Ethan grinned down at me, peering through green eyes a shade brighter than my own, and my frown melted. I'd never been able to stay mad at the youngest of my brothers; he was too damn cheerful. But such was not the case with the black sheep of the family.

"Damn it, Ryan," I snapped, twisting to glare at him over one shoulder. "Your stupid warnings do me more harm than good. Quit trying to distract me and keep your worthless mouth shut next time."

"Fine." Ryan's hands fell from the bars, and he slid them into his pockets, where they usually stayed hidden. "Keep practicing in total silence. So long as the bad guy's mute, you'll be prepared." He seemed inclined to say more, no doubt with a healthy dose of sarcasm, but a single look from our father silenced him. Thin lips pressed firmly together, Ryan shuffled across bare concrete to the cot in one corner of the cage.

My father turned from his prodigal son to face his life's true challenge—me. "I'll admit I've considered muzzling Ryan, but this time his interruption raises a good point." He strolled across the floor toward me, smoothing down the front of a pressed white dress shirt as he walked. In spite of the heat and the grimy, unairconditioned basement, my father looked un-ruffled and flawlessly well pressed, as usual.

"And that point would be…?" I left my question hanging as I accepted the hand Ethan offered. He hauled me up with no visible effort, then smacked me on the back. I glared at him, irritated to realize that though I was soaked with perspi-ration, he had yet to break a sweat. It didn't seem fair that he was both older *and* stronger. Okay, he wasn't really that much stronger than I was, but he definitely had more endurance, in spite of our father's best efforts to stretch mine to its limits.

My father stopped with the tips of his polished dress shoes touching the edge of the mat. "Yes, Ryan is arguably worth less to the Pride than the money it costs to feed him—"

At that, my incarcerated brother growled deep in his throat, but another glance from the Alpha shut him up. Ryan might have been vocal in his dissatisfaction over his meager accommodations, but he wasn't about to make his situation any worse. He was wise in matters of self-preservation, if in nothing else.

"—however, his interruption *is* typical of the kinds of distractions you'll face in a real fight." My father adjusted his silver wire-rimmed glasses and stared hard at me through the lenses. A lecture was coming. I could feel it. "You can hardly expect a confused, out-of-control werecat to oblige you with silence just so you can concentrate on putting him out of his misery, can you?"

I frowned, unhappy to hear that we'd dropped any pretense of these lessons being about self-defense. I was hired muscle for now, whether I liked it or not. Sighing, I repositioned the wide shoulder straps of a black sports bra I no longer completely filled out. "No, but—"

He held up one thick, worn hand to silence me. "You have to practice as if every fight is real, as if the danger is not only to you, but to those under your protection. You owe it to the rest of the Pride to give everything you have. All the time. You can't win a real fight if you're easily distracted."

Grinding my teeth together, I fought the urge to remind my father that I'd *been* out in the real world, that for the past three months, I'd been chasing down interlopers, hand-delivering warnings, and patrolling the territory boundaries. I'd been supervised, of course, but not two days earlier, I'd apprehended Dan Painter on my own. I wanted to say that and more, but I didn't, because I knew how he'd answer. He'd ask why, if I was capable of more, was I not showing it now. I didn't have an answer for him. So I kept my mouth shut.

That was one lesson I'd learned well over the summer. And since it was apparently the *only* thing I'd learned, I nodded curtly, sending my ponytail into a harsh bob behind me.

"Try it again." With that, my father backed into a dark corner of the basement, his clothes fading into the shadows as the darkness seemed to consume him, but for the shine in his bright green eyes.

I took a deep, calming breath, ready for round four. Or was it round five? I couldn't remember, but it didn't matter, because Ethan was already coming at me again.

This time I was prepared.

I squatted, feet and knees spread, so that my center of balance was closer to the ground and my stance more stable. Ethan loped toward me, impossibly nimble. He lunged the last few feet. I bounded to my left and out of his path. He skidded past me. I whirled around to keep him in sight.

Ethan spun in midstep, showing off a lithe feline grace and flexibility. He landed on his knees facing me. His hand shot toward my leg. I darted out of reach and kicked out with my right foot. My sneaker connected with his jaw. His head snapped back.

He growled as I backpedaled, and both his depth and volume put Ryan's puny attempt to shame.

Ethan rubbed his jaw. I smiled sweetly. Fresh sweat glistened on his back in the light of the bare bulb hanging from the ceiling. He dropped to all fours, fingers splayed on the mat. His back arched. My smile vanished. He was going to pounce.

I barely saw him move. Beads of perspiration hit the mat. Ethan's sweatpants were a black blur as he flew toward me. I dropped to the pad, rolling onto my back. I tucked my elbows in at my sides and pressed my knees into my chest. Feet flexed, I pointed the soles of my shoes at the ceiling. Ethan landed exactly where he'd aimed: on me. His weight crushed my legs into my torso. Air burst from my lungs. Fingers scrambled for a handful of my hair. Grunting, I shoved my legs away from my body.

Ethan flew backward across the basement, still several feet off the floor when he passed the edge of the mat. He twisted in midair, like a house cat falling from a fence post. His scuffed sneakers hit the ground. His hands followed almost instantly. Ethan hissed in pain as his momentum drove him forward, skinning his palms on the rough concrete. He jumped gracefully to his feet, his back to me, shoulders hunched. When he turned to face me he was smiling.

"Damn, Faythe!" he cried, rubbing two angry red shoe-prints on his bare chest. "Where'd you learn that?"

Standing, I opened my mouth to answer, but my first syllable ended in a string of vowels as something crashed into my left shoulder, driving me to the mat. I landed on my right side, pinned by something hard and heavy. Air whooshed from my lungs for the second time in as many minutes. With the first of my recovered breaths, I took in the scent of my new attacker, even as I recognized his laugh.

My temper flared. I hadn't even heard him come down-stairs. Why couldn't our basement steps creak like everyone else's? *Stupid high-quality construction.* That's what comes of being born to an architect.

"Get—" I paused, shoving at the form draped over me as I twisted onto my back "—off. Get the hell off me."

Marc smiled down at me, propping himself up on his

palms as his knees moved to straddle my hips. "Give me one good reason."

Frowning, I stopped struggling to glare up at him. "What I'll give you is five seconds to get up before I end what little possibility you have of ever siring children—with me or anyone else."

Instead of heeding my threat, he laughed again and leaned down to steal a kiss. I hissed and lunged off the floor with an ugly grunt of effort, my palms shoving on the front of his dark T-shirt. I didn't make it to my feet—in fact, I barely moved Marc at all—but anger must have been obvious in my eyes, because my father cleared his throat, and we both stopped to look up at him. "Marc, get up."

My mouth opened in surprise and my hands fell to rest on my stomach. The Alpha was backing me up? Instead of Marc? Were the roads of hell slick with ice? Had pigs taken to the skies? I smiled at my father, pleased by his support, even though I didn't need it. I could throw Marc off on my own. I'd certainly done it before.

But then my father had to go and ruin what might have been an unprecedented father-daughter bonding moment. He met Marc's eyes, a smile claiming the lightly wrinkled corners of his mouth. "I want grandchildren."

Of course. I rolled my eyes in frustration. Just because I'd lost sight of the big picture didn't mean *he* had. Or that he ever would.

Marc took one look at the exasperation on my face and slid onto the mat on my right side, between me and my father. The gesture, though clearly unconscious, was more than appropriate. Marc was always coming between us, though it was hard to tell which of us he was trying to protect.

"Grandchildren, huh?" I said, sitting up in a single jerky motion. My father's joke wasn't funny, because it wasn't really a joke. It was yet another reminder that no matter how good an enforcer I became, I couldn't escape my primary duty, and no amount of sugarcoating could make that pill go down easily.

I gained my feet, and Marc took a step back. Ethan's smile vanished, his hands dropping to hang loose at his sides. On my left, Ryan's shoes shuffled away from me on the floor of his cell, and I could almost feel the tension in the room spike. They thought I was going to start yelling; I could see it in their faces.

I met my father's eyes and forced a laugh. "You don't even know what to do with Ryan. What on earth would you do with a bunch of grandchildren running underfoot?"

Our Alpha smiled, and Marc exhaled in relief. He was a big fan of my new effort to be agreeable, because as my father's right-hand man and my potential other half, he was usually caught in the middle of our fights and forced into the role of moderator. And Marc was a rotten moderator, which was just as well. Alphas typically got their own way, and thus had little need for lessons in compromise.

"What would I do with grandchildren?" My father adjusted his glasses again, probably to hide the relief in his eyes. Or maybe that was amusement. "I'd do exactly what I did when you and your brothers were little—let you crawl all over your mother until you were toilet-trained." He paused for a beat, his eyes sparkling. "And for Ethan, that was quite some time. Nearly five years, if memory serves."

"Thanks, Dad." Ethan snatched a towel from the old bench-press machine and used it to wipe sweat from his face and chest.

Ryan snorted, and Ethan glared at him. In spite of very

close family ties, and the fact that all but one of my siblings still lived with me in our childhood home, none of us had much sympathy for Ryan's extended stint in the cage. Not even me, though until Ryan took up residence in the basement, I'd held the Pride record for consecutive days spent behind bars. I hadn't seen daylight for two straight weeks once.

Ryan was nearing the end of his ninety-first day, with no end in sight, and he deserved every single second of his punishment. Actually, he deserved worse, but our father consistently refused my request to have him neutered. It must have been a guy thing.

"Watch it, jailbird, before I forget to empty your coffee can," Ethan snarled.

Ryan opened his mouth to reply, then closed it with a click of teeth against teeth. His gaze traveled to the corner of the cage, where his makeshift toilet sat, empty—for the moment.

"That's what I thought." Ethan dropped the towel on the bench press and stepped back onto the mat. Ryan glowered at him but kept his mouth shut. He'd been pathetically well behaved over the past thirteen weeks, apparently hoping to get time off for good behavior. But our father was no state prison warden. He wouldn't let Ryan out until he knew what to do with him. Unfortunately, short of skinning him alive, we had yet to come up with a single more appropriate punishment for the part Ryan played in the hell Miguel put us all through. Except for the kitchen shears I kept sterilized and ready to go.

"Okay, let's try it again." My father backed slowly away from the mat. "Marc, would you care to join them?"

"Love to." Turning his back to the Alpha, Marc favored me with a teasing smile, emboldened by the heat in his eyes. "It would be my pleasure to take her to the mat. Again."

I pushed past Marc to glower at my father. "Two against one? That's hardly fair."

Ethan snickered, but I ignored him, already wishing I'd kept my mouth shut.

"Only children speak of life in terms of fairness, Faythe." My father's face was expressionless, his mouth a firm, straight line. But his eyes reflected the ghosts of more painful memories than I could possibly guess at. "Life is neither fair nor unfair. It is what it is, and our responsibility is to deal with whatever comes our way. Including opponents who don't fight honorably. You have to be completely aware of your surroundings. Be prepared to deal with the unexpected, such as Marc jumping you from behind." He came a step closer to the mat, driving his point home by his very presence.

A lump formed in my throat as I realized he was right. If I'd been paying more attention to my surroundings three months earlier, I would never have been kidnapped.

I nodded, feeling like the kindergartner I'd once been, accepting a well-deserved scolding for coloring on the leather upholstery in his office. "So, you're saying two against one *is* fair?"

"No, I'm saying that *fair* doesn't matter. You do whatever you have to do to survive. We all do. Now, give us your best." With that, his gaze flicked pointedly over my shoulder.

I turned to face Marc, preparing to go again, whether I was ready or not. But Marc was gone. I spun to my right, and Ethan was gone, too. *Damn it,* I thought, comprehension sinking in a moment too late.

I whirled toward the whisper of a soft sole on concrete. Marc was on me before I could react. He shoved me backward with one hand. His foot swept my legs out from under me. Air exploded from my lungs as I hit the mat on my back.

Again. Marc straddled my hips, his hands pinning my shoulders to the mat. My hands encircled his wrists trying to push him away, but he didn't budge.

Adrenaline scalded my veins, prompting me into action. I struck out. My right fist slammed into the left side of his head, just above his ear.

His eyes widened in surprise, and his smile vanished in a grimace of pain. Before he could react, I shoved him in the chest with both hands. He fell onto the mat on his left hip, one hand pressed to his head. I leapt to my feet, pleased with my performance.

Marc stood, rubbing his skull.

"Damn, Faythe." Ethan whistled. "Dad, I don't think we need to see her best during practice anymore. We all know what she's capable of."

From the corner of my eye, my father nodded, his expression caught between surprise and pride.

Hinges creaked overhead, and we all looked up. "Greg, you have a phone call."

Blinking, I made out Victor Di Carlo standing on the top step, his bulky form dark against the background of afternoon sunlight shining from the kitchen behind him.

"Take a message," the Alpha said, without a moment's hesitation.

Vic frowned. "Um, you should probably take this one. It's Parker. They found another body."

Five

My father paced back and forth in front of the sturdy oak desk in one corner of his office, the telephone pressed to his right ear. His stride was characteristically long, smooth, and confident, in contrast to the tension clear in the lines of his face. From the telephone receiver came the steady cadence of Parker's voice, calmly explaining what he'd found.

I sat on the leather love seat with Marc, listening in on my father's phone call.

We weren't just being nosy, though; it was expected. If my father hadn't wanted us to hear, he would have kicked us out of his concrete-walled, and thus virtually soundproof, sanctuary. Most humans would have used the speaker phone, but we didn't bother.

Ethan and Vic sat opposite us, on the matching leather love seat. Covering the hardwood at the center of the seating arrangement was an Oriental rug in rich shades of silver, jade, and black, across which my father paced as he listened to Parker's report.

What I'd gleaned from the conversation so far was that Parker and Holden, his youngest brother, had found the body of a stray in an alley behind a restaurant in New Orleans—in broad daylight. Parker had left the Lazy S the day before to drive Holden back to campus for his senior year at Loyola, after a month-long visit to the ranch. Holden had talked him into staying for a late lunch at his favorite Cajun restaurant in nearby Metairie. After their meal, and probably a couple of drinks, if I knew Parker, the Pierce brothers had gone outside to catch a cab back to campus. Instead they'd caught the scent of an unknown stray.

New Orleans and the surrounding communities were on the edge of the south-central territory. *Our* territory. As one of my father's enforcers, Parker was honor bound to find the tres-passer and escort him across the border into Mississippi, as Marc and I had done with Dan Painter two days earlier. But as the search for the stray in New Orleans led them to the alley behind the restaurant, the scent grew stronger rather than weaker. The stray wasn't running from them, which meant that he was either looking for a fight, or he'd already found one. And lost.

After a few minutes, Holden spotted a foot sticking out from beneath a pile of trash, and they knew why the stray hadn't run. Shoving aside several garbage bags, most already torn open by neighborhood dogs, they uncovered the corpse of a Caucasian male in his midtwenties. He was definitely a stray, and he was definitely murdered. Unless your definition of natural causes includes a snapped neck. Mine doesn't.

"Please tell me you didn't leave the body exposed," my father said, one thick hand massaging his temples as he paced. His glasses lay on his desk blotter, looking abandoned and useless.

Parker's voice carried over the line, surprisingly clear. "Don't worry. We covered it back up with garbage, and we're still in the alley. It's not like we can walk around Metairie smelling like day-old crawfish. What do you want us to do?"

My father's silence caught my ear, and I looked up to find him standing still, his eyes closed in concentration. While we didn't bury bodies on a daily basis, disposing of a corpse was nothing new for an enforcer, and generally required little more than a phone call to the Alpha to report the situation.

Unfortunately, this case couldn't be handled quite so simply; the body was found in the middle of the day, in a very well-populated place. That hardly ever happened, because even most strays had the sense to take care of werecat business in the dark, and in complete isolation from human society. To do otherwise was to risk revealing our existence to the human world. It was an issue of self-preservation, which—unlike humans—most members of our species seem to understand instinctively.

Still, every now and then we came across a werecat—be he stray, wild, or Pride—who showed no interest in hiding his activities, and thus our very existence, from the rest of the world. While public exposure would be most threatening to strays, who had no network of protection, ultimately we all stood to lose everything we had. And we weren't about to stand back and let that happen.

Disclosure—the council's term for the failure of a werecat to keep his existence secret—was a capital crime, and leaving a body unburied fell well within the definition of disclosure. The Territorial Council's policy on capital criminals—called rogues—was to eliminate them as soon as possible, using any means necessary. Enter my father, Alpha of the south-central Pride and head of the Territorial Council.

The fate of the rogue who'd killed the Metairie stray was already sealed. My father was his judge, and Marc his executioner. And there would be no appeal.

However, before we could worry about catching and eliminating the murderer, we had to figure out what to do with his victim, a rather interesting dilemma. How do you dispose of a murdered werecat in the middle of the day, in the outskirts of New Orleans?

Ethan shifted on the couch, and his movement drew my attention. He scratched one bare shoulder absently as he stared at our father, clearly as intent on listening in as I was.

Finally, my father stopped pacing. He stood in front of his desk with his back to the room, the phone still pressed to his ear. "What other businesses open into the alley?"

"Um…hang on," Parker said. Holden's slightly higher-pitched voice came through, muffled and indistinct, then Parker was back on the line. "It looks like…a florist, another restaurant, a print shop, an antique store, a hardware store, and…I think that's a dry cleaner. Why? What do you have in mind?"

"Where did you leave the van?" the Alpha asked in lieu of an answer. Parker had taken our old twelve-passenger van, loaded with Holden's luggage.

"On campus, about four miles away."

"Have you already unloaded it?"

"Yeah, last night," Parker said.

"Okay, listen carefully," my father began, and an attentive silence descended in the office, as well as over the line. "Send Holden into the hardware store for two pairs of painter's coveralls and two pairs of work gloves. When he gets back, you put on one set of coveralls and gloves, then give him the keys to the van and some cash. Tell him to take a cab back to campus, empty several of his moving boxes and throw them in the back of the van, to give you both a reason to be in the alley. While he's gone, you stay with the body, just in case.

"When Holden returns, back the van as far into the alley as you can without drawing attention, while he puts his gear on. Then, get the plastic sheeting and a roll of duct tape from the emergency kit in the van. Lay some plastic in the bottom of my van. Use a double layer. If you get rotten food in the carpet, you'll spend all night scrubbing it out."

I frowned, disturbed by the realization that my father was more worried about the carpet of his fourteen-year-old van than about the body whose disposal he was planning. But that was one of the things that made him a good Alpha. He did what had to be done. And he thought of everything. *Everything.*

My father plucked his glasses from his desktop, wiping the lenses on a handkerchief from his pocket, the phone propped on his shoulder. "I assume you're alone in the alley?"

"At the moment," Parker said. "A guy came to dump trash from the restaurant a minute or two ago, but he went back in. He didn't even notice us."

"Good." My father balanced the glasses carefully on his nose and began pacing across the hardwood floor again, from the front of his desk to the back of the couch where Vic and Ethan sat. "Put the body in the van, close the doors, wrap him in more of the plastic, and tape it up. Do it quickly, and do it in that order. Then take off the coveralls and wrap them up separately. Drive Holden back to school. Obey the speed limits and draw no attention to yourself." That was standard practice, the reminder of which Parker didn't need, but Marc couldn't hear often enough. "After you drop him off, come home, and we'll handle the disposal from here."

I turned to face Marc, my eyebrows arched at him in question. "Why?" I mouthed silently, hoping he understood an Alpha's thought process better than I did. After all, he'd been an enforcer for more than a decade.

Marc held up his index finger, motioning that he'd explain it to me in a minute. Or maybe that I could ask the question aloud in a minute. Regardless, I'd have to wait. I *hate* waiting.

My father made Parker repeat his instructions word for word, which was also unnecessary. But our fearless leader was not a risk-taker, which was why I didn't understand his order to bring the body home.

Never shit where you sleep. That was rule number two for disposing of a corpse. Of course, my father's phrasing was a bit different, but the point remained; corpses were always disposed of far from the Lazy S, and I knew of at least two burial sites between New Orleans and East Texas, neither of which had been used recently. So why would he want the body brought home? Unless he wanted to see it. Or maybe smell it. But why?

The answer hit me almost as soon as I'd thought the question. We'd found two bodies in three days, which was unusual, but not that big of a deal. Violence, like everything else in life, seemed to come and go in cycles. Sometimes we'd go a year without a problem, then deal with several bodies not of our own making in a single month.

What had obviously piqued the Alpha's interest in this case was the fact that both of the victims had died of a broken neck, which meant the killers had acted in human form. That was almost unheard of. Most homicidal strays killed in cat form, by biting through the back of the victim's skull, ripping out his throat, or—my least favorite—by eviscerating the poor fool.

But these victims had both been killed in the same, very rare manner. They were related. They *had* to be. Which meant the foreign cat we'd smelled on Moore was still roaming free in the south-central territory, apparently exercising his own brand of population control—and in the process, breaking more of the council's laws than I could even begin to list.

Not that this particular rogue gave a damn about our council's laws. Especially if it *was* a jungle cat. Jungle cats are to Pride cats what wolves are to the domestic dog. They're feral. Brutal. Governed by instinct, instead of logic or law. Rather than convening to debate the best course of action, jungle cats converge to fight, and what the victor says, goes.

Such behavior has only escaped notice by humanity because—unlike Pride cats the world over—jungle cats live in…well, the jungle. They're native to the Amazon, the deepest, darkest, least-explored wilderness on the face of the planet, where people go missing without explanation on a regular basis. Where humanity is, for the most part, still afraid to build its concrete roads and cell towers, the universal security blankets of the modern era.

But this jungle cat—if the worst-case scenario was accurate—had stepped out of the jungle, and here, his uncivilized behavior would not go unnoticed by the human authorities. Not without our help, at least. And we would help him, all right. We'd help him right out of this life and into the next one.

I swallowed thickly, still watching my father. Fear chilled my blood at the thought of confronting another jungle cat, even as anger curled my hands into fists in my lap. Sweaty, nervous fists.

When he was satisfied with Parker's recitation, my father said goodbye and dropped the cordless receiver back into its cradle. For a moment, he stood with his back to us, his still form framed by the sides of the glass-shelved display cabinet behind his desk, where his plaques and trophies gleamed beneath recessed lights my mother had positioned strategically.

The Alpha turned, releasing a weary-sounding sigh, then made his way across the room. When he sank into his armchair facing us all, I noticed for the first time how stiff he seemed, as if the action hurt, and I realized with a jolt of shock that my father was growing *old*. Too old, possibly, to deal with another jungle cat leaving his mark—and his corpses—all over our territory.

When he continued to stare at the rug beneath his feet instead of speaking, I glanced at Ethan, who shrugged at me. Marc was first to break the silence. "Did you want me and Faythe to get a whiff of the body, Greg?"

My father nodded, his green-eyed gaze flitting from Marc to me. "We need to connect the murders, if possible," he said, confirming my suspicion. He cracked one knuckle, an old habit that sometimes meant he was angry, but in this case indicated deep thought. "But you might not find anything. This latest body may simply be the result of a careless new stray who hasn't learned to control himself, or to cover his kills."

Ethan frowned. "How do we know that's not the case with Moore?"

Vic shifted in his seat, and leather creaked beneath him. "From what Marc told me last night, Moore's attacker wasn't new. Nowhere near."

I whirled on Marc, wondering what he'd caught that I'd missed. "How do you figure that?" I hadn't known there was a difference between the scent of an old stray and that of a new one.

"Moore's scars. Most of them were old and faded."

My eyes were drawn to Marc's chest, where I knew similar marks lay hidden beneath a vintage Van Halen concert T-shirt. His scars were old and faded, too. Marc had been scratched—and thus infected—fifteen years earlier, when he was barely fourteen. "So, Moore wasn't new." I shrugged, still staring at his chest. "What does that matter? We're talking about the killer being new, not the victim, right?"

Marc crossed his arms over his pecs, as if he knew what I was thinking. "Moore had dozens of healed wounds. He'd obviously been in several brawls, and I'm guessing he won most of them, since they didn't kill him. There's no way a new stray could take out someone with as much experience as Bradley Moore clearly had."

Oh. That made sense. "Okay, but that's sort of a moot point," I said, my hand hanging over the end table to my right, my fingers brushing the back of a pewter cat reared to pounce. "Whether the killer is newly infected or not—whether he's even a stray—doesn't really matter. What matters is that Moore may have been killed by a jungle cat. And this new one probably was, too."

"Jungle cat? We're looking for a jungle cat?" Ethan glanced back and forth between me and Marc. "When were you guys going to enlighten the rest of us?"

"We aren't sure about it yet." My father frowned, displeased by my loose tongue. "And you're on a need-to-know basis. I saw no need to alarm everyone without further proof of a problem."

"Well, now we have proof," Ethan muttered, drawing a stony frown from our father.

The Alpha folded his arms over his chest. "No, we don't. And we won't, until Parker gets back with the body."

"Okay, that'll tell us about the new body. But how sure are we that *Moore* was killed by a jungle cat?" Vic asked.

"Not completely," Marc admitted, patting my leg. "But it's certainly possible. The scent was definitely foreign."

"Yeah, but that doesn't make sense, either." I brushed his hand off, distracted by the thoughts swirling through my head like colors in a kaleidoscope. "Jungle strays usually rip their victims apart." We knew that for a *fact,* after cleaning up the mess Luiz had made of a couple of college girls at the beginning of the summer. "Neck-snapping seems a little too neat and orderly."

"And too easy," Marc added. "Moore didn't fight back, which means he probably never saw it coming. He must have known his murderer and trusted the bastard." He paused, frowning at no one in particular. "Why would he trust another stray, especially a jungle cat?"

Vic arched his eyebrows. "Why would he even *know* a jungle cat? We executed the only one *I've* ever met." Not for being a jungle cat. For kidnapping, rape, and murder—the unholy trinity of crimes.

My father cracked another knuckle and we all turned toward his chair, where he'd sat quietly for the past few minutes, content to let us discuss the situation on our own— no doubt another aspect of our training. When he had our full attention, the lines around his mouth deepened. "That seems to be the bottom line. With any luck, knowing how Moore and his killer are connected will tell us how to find the rogue." He stood, signaling the end of the impromptu meeting. "We'll know more when Parker gets back with his corpse."

Ethan snickered, then swallowed his laughter at a stern look from my father. I hid my own smile against Marc's shoulder. My dad had a weird way of referring to every dead body by the name of the person who found it. Or the person who rendered it dead in the first place. His habit was nothing short of macabre, and as a child, I'd flinched each time he'd made such a reference.

The guys thought it was hilarious. They kept a running total of all the corpses attributed to them by my father, as if it were a point of pride. I hadn't been a bit surprised to find out a month earlier that Marc held the lead by a comfortable margin. I *was* disturbed by that fact, however, because I happened to know that he'd never actually *discovered* a single body. What that said about his kill count was enough to give me nightmares. And enough to make me seriously consider requesting a new field partner.

"Parker should be back by nine-thirty, so I want everyone in the barn at a quarter to ten. And I need a couple of volunteers to man the incinerator when we're done with the body." My father's gaze settled on Marc automatically, and Marc in turn stared at Vic.

"No way." Vic shook his head vehemently, short brown waves bouncing. "Owen and I just got back from patrolling."

Marc blinked at him. "Faythe and I disposed of the last body."

"Digging a hole's one thing. Cremating a corpse, then grinding up the solid chunks, is something else entirely." Vic closed his eyes briefly, no doubt remembering the one time he'd run the incinerator. "That smell stays with you."

Ethan sighed, glancing from one to the other in irritation. "It's not like the body's going to sit up and yell boo, you big babies." He turned to face our father with a contrived look of stoicism—his best shot at appearing serious. "Jace and I will do it." No one bothered to ask if he wanted to consult his partner before volunteering them both. Jace Hammond would follow Ethan into hell and back, if he thought there'd be a decent per diem and a cold bottle of beer in it for him.

"Where is Pretty Boy?" Marc asked, his hand going stiff in mine. A quick glance at his face revealed a mask of tension stretched across the familiar strong, dark features, and I exhaled in frustration. I'd spent all summer waiting for the delicate truce between Marc and Jace to fail, and so far they'd both surprised me, but that fact had the fragile feel of transience.

"Jace went to the liquor store," Ethan said, searching my eyes quickly before running a hand through his thick black hair. "It's his turn to restock the supplies."

"Okay," my father said in his Alpha voice, bringing us back on topic as all eyes turned his way. "Spread the word. Nine-forty-five in the barn. Anyone more than a minute late takes a dock in pay. That means you, Ethan." He headed for the hall with my brother right behind him, trying to talk his way out of his latest tardy fine.

"But, Dad, if you'd *seen* that waitress, you'd *totally* understand…."

My father rolled his eyes. "Don't embarrass yourself with excuses." He stopped and turned to face Ethan, his expression even more stern than usual. "And while we're discussing your social life…are you *properly prepared* for your date this evening?"

I nearly choked trying to hold back laughter, and both Vic and Marc shook with their own efforts.

"Yeah, I'm good. Thanks for asking." Ethan slapped my father's shoulder, as if he were talking to one of the other guys, rather than the Alpha. "I'm glad we could have this little talk."

"I'm serious, Ethan." My father's expression darkened. "The world isn't ready for your offspring. And neither am I."

"I know, I know. I've got it covered." With that, Ethan headed down the hall toward his room. My father followed, shaking his head silently. As soon as they were gone, Vic fell on the couch in laughter, holding his stomach as if it hurt. Marc and I collapsed onto the love seat, laughing until tears formed in our eyes.

Birth control was not a topic werecats discussed very often. Most tabbies *wanted* children, and until recently, we'd thought toms couldn't impregnate human women.

We'd been wrong. Toms could, in fact, produce children with human women. Rarely. The proof was…well…strays. *All* strays.

According to Dr. John Eames, a geneticist from one of the northern Prides, every single stray he'd tested over the course of a ten-year study turned out to have a half-human, half-werecat genome. Or something like that. The layman's version was that strays, according to the good doctor, already had werecat genes *before* they were infected. Genes they'd inherited from an unknown werecat ancestor somewhere in the branches of their various family trees.

His conclusion was that normal humans—without these recessive werecat genes—cannot be "infected." But that those *with* the genes can have their werecat halves "activated" by a simple scratch or bite.

I didn't pretend to understand all the details, and neither did most of the toms I knew. Especially Ethan. All he cared about was that his social life had been disrupted by what he saw as a microscopic risk. The procreational equivalent of hitting a bull's-eye with an arrow from a mile away. But my parents were taking no chances, and I found the irony as frustrating as Ethan did. From *me,* they wanted children. From my brothers, they wanted prevention.

Still grinning, Marc leaned back against the arm of the love seat. "We still have three hours until dinner," he said, running one hand slowly up my thigh.

I smiled. "Oh yeah? Whatcha cookin'?"

My mother served a sit-down dinner five nights a week, because that's what her mother had always done. But on Saturdays, it was fend for yourself or starve. And tonight—Monday—was my parents' date night every week that my father was home, as it had been since before I could remember. When he was out of town, Michael "Atlas" Sanders, my oldest brother, took her out to dinner, eager as always to carry the weight of the world on his shoulders, for all to see. The big suck-up.

Marc put his hands around my waist and twisted to lift me into his lap. I straddled him, my knees pressed against his hips while my fingers played along the hard lines of his chest. Leaning forward, he pushed aside my hair with his nose, purring into my ear. "If you cook, I'll make it worth your while."

"You'll do dishes?" Grinning, I pushed him back gently, my fingertips trailing down to his stomach, to skim over each firm ripple through his shirt. With each bump, I felt his pulse spike, and mine responded in kind. He licked his lips and his eyes roamed down from my face, lingering several inches south of my collarbones.

Promising chills raced across my skin as his hands slid slowly up from my waist. His fingers brushed the sides of my breasts through my workout bra, and my breath caught in my throat. Marc smiled at my reaction, but the look in his eyes was more heat than humor.

One hand cupping the base of my skull, he pulled me toward him and his lips grazed my cheek. "I had something else in mind, though my idea did involve something hot and wet."

Behind me, someone snorted, and I jumped. My head whipped around fast enough to make my neck pop. Vic sat on the couch across from us, his arms crossed over a chest only slightly less well defined than the one beneath my hands. I'd forgotten he was there, and judging by the look on Marc's face, so had he. Embarrassed, I twisted around to sit on the couch, my leg pressed against Marc's.

"You know, no one likes a voyeur," Marc said, the hint of a smile ruining any attempt to sound serious.

"Not true," Vic insisted. "Some people get their kicks from being watched. I know this chick in Atlanta…"

I rolled my eyes, and he laughed, then changed tactics. "Anyway, I'd only be a voyeur if I'd invaded your privacy." He spread his arms wide to indicate the office around us. "If you didn't want an audience, you should have taken your show off the stage and into the bedroom."

I let my forehead fall to rest on Marc's shoulder, my ponytail tumbling forward to hide my flaming cheeks. "I think he's got us there."

"So." Vic grinned. "Who's cooking?"

I did a mental inventory of the other members of our household, searching for someone else to saddle with the chore. Parker was still on the road, and Ryan was locked up, and thus less than worthless regarding household labor. "Where's Owen?" I asked, my mouth already watering at the thought of our resident cowboy's chicken-fried steak.

"He took the tractor to Livingston to be repaired and won't be back for a couple of hours. And Jace and Ethan have a double date with a set of twins they met at Sonic." Vic crossed his hands over his chest and tried to hide a smile. I frowned, sure he was kidding, but his expression said otherwise. "Seriously. And they can't even tell the girls apart."

I winced in sympathy for the twins I'd never met. "So, we're back to Marc and his world-famous mac and cheese with hot dogs," I said, rubbing Marc's shoulder.

He shrugged out from under my hand. "I'll race you for it. Loser cooks. And cleans," he added as an afterthought.

"To the tree line?" The sparkle in my eyes reflected back at me in Marc's pupils. He knew I loved to run.

He shook his head. "Too easy. Make it the stream."

I nodded. "But you have to stop and Shift once you hit the trees."

"Fine." Marc turned to face Vic. "You in?"

"For a free meal?" Vic grinned, his blue eyes shining with more pure joy than I'd seen in them in the three months since his sister was murdered. "Hell yeah."

"On the count of three." I glanced from one to the other, and leather creaked as they prepared to jump to their feet. "One…"

"Two-three," Marc finished for me. I frowned, but before I could cry "foul," he hoisted me into the air by my waist and tossed me across the rug, without so much as a grunt. "Catch," he shouted to Vic, who'd just bolted up from his seat on the couch.

Vic's eyes went wide as I sailed toward him, unable to stop or even change my trajectory. My arms flailed in the air, and I landed on him with all the grace of a hippo dancing the *Nutcracker*. My momentum drove us both back onto the couch, where he plopped down sideways, and my knee nearly hit his groin. My forehead smacked the back of the couch over Vic's shoulder, and my front teeth clicked together sharply. By the time I'd recovered enough balance to stand, fury no doubt glinting in my eyes, Marc was nowhere in sight.

Growling, I launched myself toward the hall as a screen door slammed on the other side of the house.

Damn it, Faythe, I thought, as mad at myself as I was at Marc. *Will you never learn?*

Six

Vic's footsteps thumped rapidly behind me on the tiled hallway floor. I ran full-out, racing after Marc with my heart pounding in my ears and adrenaline pumping through my veins. A litany of colorful phrases chased one another in my head as I tried to decide which would best express my outrage at Marc. I'd crossed out "worthless scratch-fevered tomcat" and was leaning toward "future eunuch" when I reached the end of the hall.

I shoved the storm door open, and the heat hit me instantly, humidity and intensity giving it an almost solid presence. It was like trying to inhale damp cotton. Pushing through the initial obstruction of warmth, I jumped over the back step and took off, leaving the door to slam shut at my back. But instead of the rattle of glass and the metallic click I expected to hear, the door closed with a solid thunk and a nasal-sounding moan of pain and surprise.

Barely slowing, I glanced back over my shoulder. Vic stood behind me, holding the storm door open with one hand, while the other covered his nose. Blood ran down his right arm, dripping from his elbow to land in a spreading crimson puddle on the back step.

Damn. I'd slammed the door in his face.

"Sorry!" I yelled, already turning back to face what little I could see of Marc as he ducked beneath a low-hanging branch at the tree line. Vic mumbled something so low and muffled that even with a cat's enhanced hearing I couldn't make it out. But I could guess, and it wasn't pretty.

My eye on the goal, I sprinted with a new surge of speed, powered by determination and irritation at Marc. Blood raced through my veins. My lungs expanded with each deep, exhilarating breath. My entire body was alive in spite of the heat, reveling in the thrill of exertion and the glory of the outdoors.

I pulled my sports bra over my head as I passed the guesthouse, where Marc and the guys lived. The warm wind tore the lightweight material from my fingers, and it snagged on a clump of holly bushes growing along the back porch of the guest house. As I ran, I worked the ponytail holder free from my hair and let it fall to the ground. At the tree line, I kicked off my shoes and stripped from the waist down.

In a small clearing just inside the forest, I dropped to all-fours, pleased to see Marc in the same position several feet away. He was almost done Shifting, and I hadn't even started, so I did an abbreviated version of my usual silent meditation routine. As I focused on the rhythm of each slow inhale and exhale, my Shift began on its own, a convenience which was the result of years of practice and a conscious effort to put my mind and body at ease.

In Shifting, one rule holds true: the more anxious you get, the more pain you experience. But I'd learned quickly, following my first Shift at the onset of puberty, to relax and go with the pain. And eventually I came to welcome it. My mind was never so clear as when pain forced me to concentrate and internalize my focus. Each searing, stabbing sensation sharpened my thoughts, and each agonizing ache lubricated the grinding gears in my brain. My learned ability to think through pain had come in handy on more than one occasion, and had saved my life at least twice. That made pain my friend. A very good, love-to-hate kind of friend.

As my back bowed and my joints popped in and out of their sockets, movement to my right caught my eyes through lids squeezed almost shut in concentration. Marc had finished his Shift. He stood before me on four powerful feline legs, long muscles bulging beneath a gorgeous coat of glossy, solid-black fur. He stared back at me through eyes the same gold-flecked brown they were in human form, though the shape was entirely different.

Unlike lions, tigers, and the other breeds of large cat, which have round pupils similar to that of a human, in cat form, we have the distinctive oval pupils of a house cat—vertically oriented black slits. And because it was daytime, Marc's pupils had narrowed almost completely out of existence to protect his sensitive feline retinas.

I blinked at him, and he licked his muzzle in return, flashing a mouthful of pointed, slightly curved teeth. He was mocking me. He could already have been halfway to the stream, but he'd stuck around to watch my Shift because he knew he could afford to. Marc was flaunting his anticipated victory, and in that moment, my new goal in life became making him pay for his arrogance with a mouthful of bitter dust raised by my paws as they flew past him.

Marc watched me carefully, waiting for the onset of the final phase of my Shift, which would be his signal to leave. If he hung around until I finished, he wouldn't stand a chance.

Fresh pain lanced through my face as it began to ripple over a sickening current of elongating bones and protruding teeth. Marc huffed through his nose and slunk gracefully toward the far edge of the clearing. Toe pads nestled on a soft bed of ivy, he turned back for one more glance, just as the first undulating wave of fur sprouted on my back, flowing down from my spine to cover my torso.

With a silent, powerful shove against the earth, Marc was gone, soaring over a three-foot-high clump of undergrowth to land soundlessly on the other side. By the time sharp, curved claws erupted from the ends of my new cat toes, I could no longer hear him running through the forest. But that didn't mean much. Cats can be absolutely silent when they want to. And Marc wanted to.

His nose still dribbling blood, Vic shoved aside a low-hanging branch and ducked into the woods. I paused long enough to give him an apologetic glance, then followed Marc through the forest toward the stream.

Trees flew past as I ran, launching my newly lithe form over moss-covered logs and around bushes. My body resisted such strenuous exercise at first, because I hadn't taken the time to properly stretch my new configuration of muscles. But soon the act of running eased my residual stiffness and alleviated that I-don't-fit-into-my-own-skin feeling that followed a Shift. With those kinks worked out, I was free to enjoy the exhilaration of racing through the forest at a speed no human could possibly experience without the benefit of an engine and at least two tires.

From all around me came the sounds of the forest: nature's residents, busy even in the midday heat. My practiced ears had little trouble weeding through the myriad croaks, squeaks, chirps, hisses, and the rhythmic rustle of leaves as I searched for any sign of Marc.

Marc had truly disappeared, but I'd only been running a few minutes when the gurgle of running water met my ears. Even if I hadn't known the way by heart, I could have followed the sound to its source. Rather than tracking by smell like dogs, cats use their sensitive hearing to locate prey, one another, and anything else that makes noise.

I turned toward the sound, and a couple of minutes later I could smell the water. Or rather, I smelled the minerals, plants, and creatures *in* the water. And suddenly I could smell Marc. We may not use our noses to track, but we use them regularly to identify one another, and my nose was telling me Marc was somewhere just ahead.

The race wasn't over yet.

Encouraged, I scrounged up a fresh burst of energy. Small animals darted out of my path. Thorns tugged at the fur on my legs and stomach. With each bounding step, my paws sank into a soft layer of ivy, moss, and last year's leaves. I ran directly into the breeze, stirring the branches over my head, and only the occasional twig cracking beneath my paws betrayed my presence. And as I drew closer to the stream, I heard a faint huffing noise.

Marc. And he was close.

I sprinted around a thick patch of raspberry briars to find him directly in front of me, headed straight for the stream. He was almost there. But so was I.

A growl rumbled from deep in my throat. Instead of

stopping at my warning, Marc sped up. I did the same, my muscles burning in protest. Cats are sprinters, not long-distance runners. But I was so close!

The distance between us narrowed. My claws gripped the earth as I ran, providing traction on a slick bed of moss that grew thicker the closer I got to the water. My lungs burned from exertion, demanding that I win, that I not put my body through such torment in the heat of the day for nothing.

But I couldn't win. Marc's tail was only inches from my nose, but I had no more speed to offer, no more energy to spend. Marc had cheated, and he was going to win.

Unless I cheated, too.

After an instant's hesitation, I sank my teeth into the tip of Marc's tail.

He yelped and tried to stop instantly. Instead of the graceful halt he'd no doubt intended, he tumbled forward, stumbling over his own front paws. His muzzle hit the ground, buried in a patch of moss, while his hind legs kept going, propelling the rest of him forward. He looked like a pig rooting in the mud.

I dropped his tail without slowing, and huffed in Marc's ear as I passed him. It was the closest I could come to laughing in his face.

He recovered quickly. I glanced back to see him running after me, moss stuck in his front teeth. He was too late. I splashed into the stream up to my shoulders, snorting and tossing my head as I inhaled too much water.

Before I could clear my nasal passages, Marc bounded into the water after me. He hissed and slapped the surface with one front paw, spraying me with a backlash of water.

I'm sure you are *pissed, you cheating son of a bitch,* I thought. But all I could do was grunt at him. And splash him back.

For the most part, stories about cats hating water are exaggerated. About us, they're an outright fabrication. Like most large cats, we love water. The guys and I had been known to waste entire summer afternoons splashing around in the stream, treading water at the deepest parts. We'd catch fish when we got hungry, and when we grew tired, we'd stretch out on the banks to dry in the sun before bounding off into the woods for more recreation. And with the national preserve bordering our land, we had plenty of forest in which to play.

While the woods were usually thick with humans during the tourist season, none of the backpacking trails or campgrounds were anywhere near our private wilderness. We'd seen very few hikers, and on those rare occasions when we had, the noise of their approach gave us plenty of time to hide in the trees before the two-legged wanderer came into view.

Marc and I played in the water for several minutes before Vic, now in cat form, padded to the edge of the stream, announcing his presence with a low-pitched yowl. His nose looked better, from what I could tell. It was swollen, but straight, and the bleeding had stopped.

Though it hurts like hell, Shifting shortly after receiving an injury can reduce healing time by as much as half. The best explanation I'd heard for the phenomenon was that since muscles, ligaments, and bones are torn apart and rearranged during a Shift anyway, injuries begin to heal automatically as our parts are reattached in new positions.

I'd experienced this personally twice, and had welcomed the accelerated recovery time in spite of the extra pain.

Vic growled at us from the bank, clearly chewing us both out. Though I couldn't understand his exact phrasing, the gist was clear enough: we'd both cheated, and he had no intention of cooking either of us dinner. Ever.

That said, or growled, in this case, he jumped into the water between us, draping one heavy black paw over Marc's shoulders and hauling him beneath the surface. They both came up sputtering, each batting playfully at the other's muzzle as they tried to dunk each other.

I backed away to watch from the edge of the stream, and to slake the thirst I'd worked up during my long sprint. But even sloshing with water, my stomach wasn't satisfied. Hunger gnawed at me, my belly demanding compensation for the calories burned during my Shift.

Shifting takes a lot of energy, which must be replaced quickly with both food and water. Water, I had plenty of. Food was another story.

My stomach growling, I turned to recruit Marc and Vic for the hunt I was already planning. But again, Marc was gone. Vic paddled alone in the middle of the stream, beckoning me forward with a playful splash and a toss of his head. Wondering vaguely where Marc had wandered off to, I pushed off from the bank and swam toward Vic, intending to dunk him as he'd dunked Marc. But as I extended one paw beneath the surface, my sheathed claws only inches from his head, something heavy dropped onto my back. I plunged to the bottom of the stream, my limbs flailing in the weak current.

For a long moment, I panicked, sucking water in through my nose in bewilderment. My paws scraped uselessly at loose, smooth stones, scrambling for purchase. My tail stirred the water fast enough to create a light foam. Then the weight was gone, and I floated to the surface, sputtering and hissing with my first gulp of air.

Rachel Vincent

Marc bobbed in front of me, treading water. The gold specks in his eyes sparkled in delight. He seemed to be laughing at me around a muzzle full of sharp, pointed cat teeth. The bastard.

I growled at him in mock anger, swatting his ear with my paw, claws unsheathed. But I didn't hit him hard enough to hurt him, or even to break his skin, because we were just playing. And because I'd get him back later, when the time was right. When I had the advantage of surprise. When he'd completely forgotten I still owed him…

After Marc's champion pounce, we played in the stream, swimming and splashing each other, until my stomach renewed its demand for food with cramps instead of gurgling chatter. But by then I was too tired, from our play and from hunger, to even think about hunting. I jumped up onto the bank, signaling to the guys that I wanted to Shift back by tossing my head in the direction of the ranch.

Marc climbed the northern bank of the stream and took off through the woods with Vic trailing close behind. Evidently they still had far more energy left than I did. But then, they hadn't spent all afternoon sparring with Ethan.

I trudged after them, not bothering to keep up. Surely by the time I made it home and Shifted back, someone would have started cooking. Or at least ordered a few pizzas. But as I made my way through the forest, plodding around tree stumps instead of leaping over them, something raced across the left edge of my vision. My head turned instinctively to follow the movement, ears arching forward as the rest of my body froze.

At first, I saw nothing but the great outdoors: trees, dead leaves, underbrush, and fallen twigs and branches. But then something moved again, and my focus shifted. And that's when I saw the other cat.

My pulse spiked, and my jaws clenched. My paws flexed, claws digging into the dirt out of instinct. It was just a brief glimpse, a flash of slick black fur between two trees at least forty feet away. But it was enough to put me instantly on alert.

I'd made no effort to be quiet on my trek back from the stream, and neither had Marc or Vic, so any other cat in the woods would certainly know we were there. If he were one of ours—even my one nonresident brother, Michael, who came over a couple of times a month to make use of our excess of wilderness—he would have made his presence known out of courtesy. With the exception of Ryan, who wasn't allowed out anyway, we were all very close, and none of us would have snubbed the others by walking by without a greeting.

The mystery cat wasn't one of ours.

On alert now, I tensed, going completely still in a tangle of honeysuckle. I had to call for help. I had no delusions about my ability to take on a trespasser in cat form alone. Not with my energy reserve tapped by an afternoon of sparring and an un-fueled Shift.

But what if I was wrong? What if the cat *was* one of ours, just out for an odd solitary stroll? If I bellowed a roar of alarm and everyone came running to find me stalking one of our own cats, the guys would never let me live it down. I had to be sure.

I took off after the other cat, my steps silent and confident, my ears alert for any sound to tell me which way he'd gone. Unfortunately, the short glimpse I'd gotten of black fur did nothing to help me narrow down the list of possible suspects. All werecats are solid black in feline form, regardless of their hair color and skin tone on two legs. Black fur is part of our heritage, even for newly initiated strays. To identify the unknown cat, I'd need either a good whiff of him or a much closer look.

After less than a minute of careful stalking, keeping my eyes, ears, and nose on alert, I heard leaves crunch to the west and adjusted my direction accordingly. Minutes later, I heard the crack of wood splintering. The sound was much closer that time, and just to my left, on the other side of a thick clump of briars.

I padded silently to the edge of the brush and peeked around it. At first I saw nothing but more trees and bushes. But then I heard him breathing, slowly and evenly, and near the ground. The suspicious werecat lay stretched out peacefully beneath a cedar tree with his eyes closed, almost asleep. Except he wasn't a he. He was a she.

It was my mother.

I huffed sharply in surprise and stepped back from the edge of the briar patch, hoping she hadn't heard me. In my entire twenty-three years, I'd only seen my mother in cat form twice, because since she became a mother, she only Shifted when she was really upset. The first time I'd seen her with claws and a tail was the day her mother died, when I was ten years old. The second time was the night Ryan left the Pride to live as a wildcat, breaking her heart. That time, she'd stayed alone in the woods for three days, and my father had forbidden any of us to go after her. Brow creased in worry, he'd said she needed time to mourn her loss, and that we should be willing to give our mother whatever she needed. So we had.

Ryan, I thought, trying to jerk my left rear paw free from a tangle of ivy without making any noise. *This is about Ryan.* My mother had been spending large blocks of time alone all summer, even during Abby's stay, which just wasn't like her. Normally, she'd have used a fellow tabby's visit as an opportunity to show me how I *should* be living my life. But this time, she'd turned my teenage cousin over to me several times a week, claiming Abby needed plenty of distractions to help her recover from her ordeal at Miguel's hands.

I happened to agree, and since she let me teach Abby the basics of self-defense during her stay—after all, nothing puts repressed rage to better use than kicking the shit out of a big punching bag with a scary face drawn on it—I didn't think to question what my mother was doing during our "therapy" sessions. I'd assumed she was in her room, knitting something for one charity auction or another. Evidently I'd been wrong.

It started the day we'd returned from Missouri with the body of Vic's younger brother, Anthony, along with the remains of Miguel and Sean, his accomplice. I'd assumed my mother was trying to deal with what had happened, with the loss of one tabby and the near loss of two more, including me. After all, our very existence had been threatened, our collective vulnerability exposed. But I should have known better. My mother was stronger than that. She was the silent backbone of our family and a former power on the Territorial Council. As such, she could deal with threats and disasters on a large scale, because they weren't aimed at her personally.

But she couldn't deal with Ryan.

Ryan was her Achilles' heel. He had wounded her twice now, the first time when he left us, and the second when he teamed up with Miguel to save his own fur. But there was more to my mother's personal crisis, to the guilt that drove her into isolation in the woods, than everyone else knew.

My mother had a secret, and it was eating her alive.

Seven

I snuck back through the woods as soon as I was sure my mother was asleep, and during the entire twenty-minute walk back to the ranch, I debated whether or not to tell her I knew her secret. And that I wasn't the only one.

To my knowledge, only two others knew, and I was sure neither of them would ever tell. Ryan's motivation for keeping his mouth shut was the same as always: to save his own hide. Our father had agreed to let him live against the wishes of most of the rest of the Territorial Council. In fact, our father was the only thing standing between Ryan and a very slow, very painful death. Ryan would never do anything to piss off the one man keeping him alive, and nothing would put his existence in greater peril than telling our father that he'd used our mother to spy on the Territorial Council.

The only other person who knew that my mother had unwittingly fed our abductors privileged information was Abby. She'd been locked up in the basement cell across from mine when we found out about Ryan betraying his family to save his own life, and she'd been just as disgusted with him as I was. But she'd promised me never to breathe a word about it to anyone. For my mother's sake, not for Ryan's.

In the clearing just inside the edge of the forest, I stopped to Shift back, my mind still on my mother.

I'd never really questioned my decision not to tell her what I knew. Technically, it was none of my business, but more important, I didn't want to be the cause of problems between my parents. She had meant no harm. On the contrary, she'd been trying to mend the rift between Ryan and the rest of the family.

Shortly after Ryan left, when I was thirteen, my mother became secretly obsessed with tracking him down to talk him into rejoining the Pride. After two years of searching, she found him, and though he eagerly accepted her money, he steadily refused to come home. In retrospect, I think that was the closest he ever came to standing up for something he believed in.

When Ryan got tangled up in Miguel's kidnapping scheme and began using her to spy on the council, my mother never had a clue. I could only assume she figured it out when Owen dragged Ryan home in shame, not to mention shackles. I couldn't be sure, though, because I'd never asked either of them. But as far as I knew, she hadn't spoken one word to Ryan since the night my father locked him up.

My Shift complete, I forced thoughts of my mother and brother from my mind as I stepped into the backyard to find my clothes.

Normally I wouldn't have bothered dressing until I'd showered. Werecats are accustomed to seeing one another in all variations of undress, as well as all stages of mid-Shift. But hopefully there would be a delivery boy on the property soon, for whom we'd have to make allowances. Walking around nude in front of humans was *not* a good way to keep a low profile with the local community. It was an excellent way to make new friends, though.

Unfortunately, Marc didn't like new friends.

Dressed, except for my bare feet, I crossed the yard and stepped into the back hall, shoes dangling from the fingers of my left hand. Before I reached my room, Ethan stepped out of the kitchen with a stack of cheddar Pringles cradled in one hand. He smiled, extending his snack toward me. "Bite?"

I hesitated, then shrugged. "Actually, yeah. Thanks." We met halfway, only a few feet from my open bedroom door, and I snatched the entire stack from his hand, grinning as I danced out of reach. I was still dodging my brother's long-armed grasp when my father's office door opened and he appeared in the threshold.

"Karen!" he bellowed to the house in general. "We're supposed to be there in an hour."

Clearly expecting an answer, he paused, glancing down the hall in our direction. But no response came.

"Karen?" he called again, stepping into the center of the foyer. Still no answer. My father's eyes locked onto mine, and my heart started to pound. Surely he could hear it. He knew I knew something. I barely resisted the urge to hide behind Ethan. "Have either of you seen your mother?"

"Yeah," Ethan said, and my heart actually skipped a beat.

He knew Mom was in the woods? If so, why hadn't he mentioned it? He knew as well as I did that she only Shifted when she was upset about something.

But I should have known Ethan was joking. "Slim lady. Blue eyes and a gray pageboy," he continued, his eyes glistening in appreciation of his own humor. "Answers to the name, 'Mom.'"

Our patriarch frowned, his eyes darkening. Fortunately, he thought Ethan was answering for us both, which was fine with me. I tossed another chip into my mouth and started to duck into my room before my father could question me separately. But my foot froze in midair when my mother's voice rang out from my parents' bedroom.

"Gracious, Gregory," she called out. The door opened, and my mother stepped into the hall with a towel wrapped around her hair, tying the sash of a pale pink bathrobe. Her feet peeked out from beneath the robe. Two entirely human feet with neatly polished toenails.

My jaw dropped open, and I was glad no one was watching me. *How the hell did she get past me?*

"What on earth are you shouting about?" my mother demanded, and for a moment, I thought she'd read my mind. But then she propped her hands on her hips and glared in irritation at my father. "Have I ever made us late?"

"There's a first time for everything," Daddy said. But as stern as his voice was, his eyes were gentle when he looked at my mother. His eyes were *always* gentle when he looked at her, as if something about her melted his heart, even when she was second-guessing him or slapping his hand for trying to sneak a bite of raw cookie dough. And that was probably a pretty good assessment. She thawed him out. It was a damn good thing someone could.

"Well, I'm still waiting for the first time you let me get ready in peace." Her mouth twitched in an effort to keep from smiling. "Meet me in the car in twenty minutes." She backed into her room and closed the door gently. I followed her example.

In my room, I stripped for the third time that day and headed straight to the bathroom for a quick shower.

Clean, dry, and lavender-scented, I pulled a brush through my still-damp hair and dressed in a pair of short denim shorts and my favorite green stretchy-T. I paused at my dresser to put my watch on, then glanced up at the mirror.

Not too bad, I thought, brushing clinging strands of hair from my neck. But with my throat exposed, my eyes caught on my first and only battle scars: four small white crescents running down the left side of my throat. No one else ever noticed. But *I* did. All the time. And each time my gaze focused on them, I remembered Miguel's fingernails popping through the surface of my skin and sinking into my flesh.

Miguel had cut off my air for less than two seconds, but they were the most terrifying two seconds of my life. Even worse than the memory was the fact that he'd left his mark on me. Permanently. I couldn't help but see that as a mark of shame, a daily reminder that I hadn't been able to keep his hands off me.

"He's dead." I said it aloud to comfort myself, but it didn't work. *Miguel may be dead, but Luiz is still out there somewhere. Lying low. Waiting.*

I was sure of it. He'd disappeared too easily. It was too good to be true. And if the new body gave us evidence of another jungle cat in the territory, the rest of the council would have to listen.

Shaken by thoughts of nightmares not yet over, I pulled my hair back over my shoulder, covering the scars. Then I brushed it back again, angry at myself for being so squeamish. The guys bore their scars with pride, as evidence of the work they'd done to keep the rest of us safe. Why shouldn't I? Even if the sight of them did make my stomach churn…

"You get lost?"

I jumped, then whirled to find Marc leaning against my door frame, arms crossed over a deeply tanned, well-toned chest. "Quit sneaking up on me," I said, mentally cursing a werecat's stealth. But I couldn't summon a sharp edge to my voice. He looked too damn good to scold.

Marc smiled and stepped over the threshold, pushing the door closed with his foot. He sauntered across the room to plop down on my unmade bed, the soles of his feet grazing my cream-colored Berber carpet. My pulse spiked just watching him. "Vic ordered pizza."

I laughed as I came toward him; I'd guessed as much. "What did he get?"

Marc leaned forward to grab my wrist as soon as I was within reach. He pulled me into his lap, nuzzling my chin, just below my right ear, sending tingling sparks to smolder in very promising places. "A meat-lovers, a cheese-lovers, and a supreme. All large."

"That'll be enough for *me*," I whispered, trailing my fingers down the side of his face. His chin was rough, and the stubble tickled my fingers, a delightfully masculine texture. I liked chin stubble. Especially on him. "But what are the two of *you* going to eat?"

Marc laughed, and I pushed him back on the bed, where he rolled us over until I lay looking up at him. Light from the fixture overhead made a halo around his head, but he was no angel. His next words confirmed it. "I have an idea," he murmured, pinching my earlobe lightly between his front teeth. "But Vic's out of luck." His tongue trailed from my ear down my throat.

"Mmm," I purred as my arms snaked around his waist,

my fingers playing lightly over the muscles of his back as they bunched and rolled beneath my hands. "I might need a snack, too."

"That can be arranged." He hooked his right hand beneath my knee and wrapped my leg around his waist. His hand skimmed slowly up the length of my thigh to cup my rear beneath my shorts. He squeezed, and my breath hitched. He slid his hand beneath the hem of my shirt, and my pulse leapt. He ground his hips into me, and…

My phone rang, Pink singing "U + Ur Hand" from across the room.

Exhaling in frustration, I planted one hand against his chest and tried to push him up, but he only growled and refused to move. "Let it ring," he moaned. Which I found ironic, considering the title of the song.

I let my head fall back against the rumpled covers and sighed, enjoying the feel of his weight pressing me into the bed. "What if it's important?"

"What could be more important than this?" His hand trailed up my stomach, and I squirmed beneath him. But the song played on, and I wasn't one of those people who can just let the phone ring. I'm too curious. And yes, I know what curiosity did to the cat.

"I have to get it, Marc," I said, stroking the hair at the base of his skull. "It'll only take a second."

"Fine." But he refused to move, so I squirmed out from under him, which gave me some very interesting ideas for later….

Smiling to myself over the naughty images in my head, I grabbed my cell phone from my desktop, glancing at the number on the display.

My smile withered instantly, leaving my expression hollow. It was the same number I'd seen a day and a half ago. When Andrew called.

"What's wrong?" Marc asked.

"Nothing." My thumb hovered over the yes button as I tried to calm my pounding heart. If he heard it racing, he'd know I'd lied. Then I'd have to explain, and he'd know it wasn't the first time. I hated lying to him. I really did. But if I told him an ex-boyfriend was bothering me, he'd insist on fixing the problem for me. And not only would that offend my pride— I was hardly your typical damsel in distress—it would probably involve an unpleasant road trip, an overdose of testosterone, and a major cleanup effort, which would only make things worse for everyone involved. Most of all, Marc himself. So really, I was lying to him for his own good.

Or so I told myself as my mouth opened, intent on digging me even deeper into my proverbial hole.

"It's Sammi," I said, cringing inside even as the lie came out smoothly. "Why don't you go make a salad to go with the pizza? I'll be right there, okay?"

Marc frowned. "Fine. But we're not done here," he said, gesturing toward the bed with an unmistakable spark of mischief in his eye. I nodded, and he left to make me a salad. Sometimes he was too sweet for his own good. And for mine.

I closed the door behind him and pressed the yes button, cutting Pink's song short before the phone could switch over to my voice mail. But I didn't speak, in part because I knew that since I could still hear Marc's footsteps, he could hear anything I said. But the other reason, of at least equal importance, was that I had no clue what to say.

"Have you been thinking about me?" Andrew said into the empty static over the line.

Shit. Until he spoke, I'd clung to the sliver of hope that I'd been wrong. That it wasn't his phone number on my screen. But that hope was now as real as the Easter Bunny. "I know you're there, Faythe. I can hear you breathing, so answer the fucking question."

I opened my mouth, yet I had no idea what I was going to say until the first word slipped from my lips.

Eight

"Yes."

Frustrated with my own answer, I let my head fall to thump against the door, then held my breath until I was sure Marc wouldn't turn back to investigate the sound. He didn't. Instead, from across the house came the barely there sound of the magnetic seal breaking as he opened the refrigerator door.

"Really?" Andrew sounded suspicious, almost as surprised by my answer as I was. But it was the truth; I *had* been thinking about him. In fact, I'd had trouble *blocking* him from my thoughts. I felt guilty about the way I'd left things between us, and about how ugly the whole situation would get soon if he didn't stop calling.

I sighed silently. Why did I feel compelled to be honest with Andrew, but not with Marc? Did I owe Marc any less than I owed Andrew?

No. The truth was that I owed them both an explanation. I'd left each of them—albeit five years apart—without saying goodbye. But Marc was like me. He was strong, and stubborn, and…one of us. Resilient. Andrew was human, and thus fragile in a way I could never really understand, and Marc could no longer remember. Honesty was the least I owed Andrew—up to a point.

"Yes, really," I said at last. I snatched the remote from my desktop and aimed it at my stereo. Music blared to life from the speakers mounted in the corners of the room. The All-American Rejects, "Dirty Little Secret." Frenetic, taunting tempo and all.

Figures.

Counting on the music to cover my voice, I turned my attention back to Andrew and exhaled slowly in anticipation of a very awkward conversation. "I was thinking that I should have tried harder to get in touch with you in June."

"How right you are. Fortunately, you're going to have the opportunity to make that up to me. Soon."

What? My pulse spiked. *No.* He was coming to see me.

Andrew *couldn't* come to the ranch. There was no possible way for a meeting between him and Marc to go well. Or even a meeting between him and my father, who also assumed my human *indiscretion* to be a thing of the past.

"What does that mean?" I asked, my voice soft with horror I couldn't quite disguise, but he only laughed. "Andrew, how do you want me to make it up to you? You want to talk? We can talk. Let me explain what happened." One version of it, anyway…

He snorted. He actually snorted into my ear. "Oh, let me guess. It's not me, it's you. I just don't fit into your life anymore, right?" The bitterness in his voice stung.

"It's not like that." But it was. It was exactly like that—in no way he could possibly understand.

"Oh? What is it, then? Your parents? You're scared to introduce me to your parents?" I started to answer, but he spoke over my protest. "They don't even know about me, do they? You never told them." His accusation was sharp and pointed. But this time he was wrong.

"Of course I did." My words came out rushed; I was eager for something legitimate to deny. "They know." Did he honestly think my parents thought I was a virgin? That I was afraid to tell them I'd gone off to college and had sex? Sure, my mother *looked* like she belonged in a fifties sitcom, but my parents were neither stupid nor naive. Which was no doubt one of the reasons they'd sent the guys to watch over me.

"You told them?" He didn't believe me; that much was obvious. "And they're okay with it?"

I shrugged, though he couldn't see the motion. "Well, I doubt they're *thrilled* by it." They were no more pleased with my perceived promiscuity than any parents would be. But their real problem was not that I'd let a guy into my bed, but that I'd let a *human* guy into my bed. A guy I could have no future with, who could never marry me and give them grandchildren.

None of which I could tell Andrew, naturally.

"You're lying," Andrew shouted into the phone, and I could actually hear his teeth grinding together as he spoke through them. "You're *fucking* lying, and we damn well know it."

"We?" I frowned in confusion. "Who's w—"

"You didn't tell them about me. You didn't tell your family any more than you told *him*."

"Andrew…" On the radio, the All-American Rejects gave way to an announcer rambling on about the weather and the traffic, and I lowered my voice, hoping no one would walk by my room before the next song came on. "Andrew, what the hell are you talking about?"

"You owe me, Faythe. I know where you are, and I know who you're with. And when the time comes, that won't make one fucking bit of difference. He won't be able to prote—"

Another voice barked in the background, pounding through Andrew's fury like a hammer through a block of ice—quick and violent. And effective. I couldn't make out what he said, and before I had a chance to think about it, Andrew was back. "I'll see you soon, Faythe. Tell Marc I'll see him, too. I think he and I have a lot to talk about."

Oh, no. Oh hell *no.* Alarm shot through my limbs and I stood so fast my chair fell over on the carpet in front of me. "Andrew!" I whispered into the phone, glancing at my bedroom door, just to be safe. "You have no idea what you're—"

But he was gone. He'd hung up on me. Again.

Furious, I snapped my phone shut and tossed it onto the desk behind me, then bent to pick up my chair. *What the fuck is wrong with him?* I slammed the chair on the floor, but that did nothing to help burn off my anger. Andrew and I had only dated for four months and we'd now been apart almost as long as we were together in the first place. So what the hell did he hope to gain by coming here and confronting Marc?

Oh, shit. Marc. I sank back into the chair, facing my desk this time.

Marc would never attack a human, and under most circumstances would make no offensive moves even if assaulted by one, so I wasn't really worried about him hurting Andrew. But my father would never trust me again when he found out I'd kept the first call to myself. And neither would Marc.

I'd meant no harm by keeping my secret. But seriously,

how was I supposed to know that one little human ex-boyfriend could be so much trouble? That not breaking it off with him in person would turn a calm, rational, *nice* individual into the bitter, angry man I'd just spoken to?

The thing I'd liked most about Andrew was how very *normal* he was. How incredibly even-tempered and predictable. He was almost boring, which I loved because of how well it contrasted with my claws-and-kicks home life.

The most daring thing I'd ever done with Andrew was, well...*him,* in broad daylight. In his apartment. Beneath the covers. With the door locked. Andrew wasn't a daring sort of guy—at least not when we were a couple. Even during our one nooner, only hours before I'd left campus, he'd complained when I nibbled too hard on his earlobe. I'd barely broken the skin, but he jumped as if I'd tried to pierce his ear.

Instead of protesting, Marc would have upped the ante. He was always up for more. Faster. Harder. Anytime. Anywhere.

If Andrew came to the Lazy S, disaster would be hot on his heels.

How does he even know where I live? I wondered as I flipped my phone back open and navigated to the call history screen. I'd never told him, specifically so he couldn't visit. But it wouldn't be too hard to find out, even with nothing but my name and an Internet connection.

I pressed the call button and stood again as Andrew's phone rang in my ear. It rang four times, and by the time his voice mail answered—in a woman's mechanical voice—I was already pacing. When the beep sliced through my thoughts, I stopped, one hand propped on my hip.

"Andrew, it's Faythe. Stop hanging up on me! And do *not*

come here! I'm sorry about leaving like that, but it's over now. You can*not* come here. Please."

I hung up and threw the phone at the wall this time, glad only in retrospect that it didn't break. How did Andrew even know about Marc, anyway?

Sammi.

No one else from school knew about Marc, but Sammi had met him. She must have told Andrew. My heart pounding again, I snatched the phone from the floor and dialed my college roommate. But she wasn't home, either, so I left a message on her machine asking her to call me back as soon as she could.

Then I sat on the end of my bed and forced my heartbeat to slow, my breath to come evenly. If I went out in my current state, Marc would know something was wrong the minute I entered the kitchen. I couldn't keep doing this. It was unfair to Marc and bad for my own health. If Andrew called again, I would tell Marc the truth. I'd rather have him mad at me for a few days than taken by surprise when Andrew showed up at the gate.

At the front of the house, the doorbell rang, and I listened as Vic answered the door, exchanging pleasantries with the pizza guy as he paid for our dinner. When anger and frustration no longer pulsed through my veins, I pressed the power button on my stereo remote, shoved my phone in my pocket, and ran a brush through my ponytail, reminding myself one last time that I'd been talking to Sammi, just in case Marc asked. Then I prayed that he wouldn't, and headed for the hallway.

In the kitchen, Marc and Vic stood guard around three open and steaming boxes of pizza, a slice in each of their hands. Marc saw me and swallowed his mouthful. "There's your salad," he said, barely pausing before stuffing the pointed end of another slice into his mouth.

"Thanks." I looked where he'd pointed with a chunk of pizza crust and found a single cereal bowl full of limp wet lettuce. I laughed. I should have known. Even on two legs, Marc was a carnivore, with little use for the food groups unrelated to meat, fat, and dairy. He probably didn't even know what else went into a garden salad. Luckily, like the rest of us, he had great metabolism.

I'd just popped open a chilled can of soda from the guesthouse when the clicking of heels on tile echoed from the foyer. My mother paused in the kitchen doorway wearing a simple but elegant calf-length black dress, accessorized only by the pearls at her throat and the matching clutch purse in her right hand. "We'll be back in a couple of hours." Her voice was low for a woman's and smooth. Like butterscotch, it was sweet and deceptively soothing, which was part of what made her nagging so annoying. It was terribly hard to tune out such a beautiful speaking voice, even when it was telling you what you should already have accomplished by this point in your life.

"We'll be at Mansion on the Hill, in case you need to get hold of us," she continued, clearly speaking to me as her eyes roamed the junk food contaminating her pristine kitchen. "And, of course, your father will have his cell phone on."

"Aww, Mom," Ethan said, stepping up behind her to lay a heavy arm across her shoulders. "She may be a spoiled brat, but she's old enough to take care of herself for a couple of hours."

"Yes, of course you're old enough," my mother continued. She smiled at me and patted Ethan's hand affectionately where it rested on her shoulder. "Old habits die hard sometimes."

My mother was a study in contradiction. Petite, prim, and delicate, she was the embodiment of feminine grace, with a backbone of pure steel. She was both overbearing and soft-spoken, hiding the power she'd once wielded on the Territorial Council behind the facade of a cultured 1950s model housewife.

"Come on, Ethan, we're going to be late," Jace called from the hallway, his footsteps clomping toward the front door. He was dating again, and would smile back at me if I smiled at him first, but we were never alone together anymore, and he'd stopped teasing me entirely. Things between us had not been the same since I told him I was in love with Marc, and as sad as that made me, it seemed to be a necessary sacrifice for the peace of the household.

"Don't forget, your father wants you both in the barn by nine-forty-five," Mom said, trying to brush the wrinkles from Ethan's shirt.

He frowned and swiped at her hand. "We'll be there. Eventually."

Jace stepped into sight behind them both and smacked Ethan's head, sending straight black locks flying. "We'll be early." He pulled Ethan toward the front door by one arm, never quite making eye contact with any of the rest of us. "Save me some pizza."

"Get your own!" Vic yelled as the front door closed.

"Pizza again?" Mom came closer to inspect. "You know, it wouldn't hurt the three of you to take a bite of something green every now and then."

Grinning, I grabbed my "salad" from the counter behind me and popped a piece of lettuce into my mouth, crunching it loudly as I chewed. "There." I set the bowl down and crossed my arms beneath my breasts, leaning against the counter to smile at her. "Happy now?"

"It's a start," she conceded, refusing to rise to my bait. "But next time add some tomatoes and carrots."

"But I didn't make—"

"Karen!" my father bellowed from across the house, cutting off my protest.

"There's no reason to shout, Greg. I can hear you even when you whisper." My mother shot me a conspiratorial eye roll, as if we shared some kind of special experience by virtue of tolerating the male sex.

I took another bite of Marc's pizza, ignoring her. I refused to willingly bond with her unless she could pick an activity that didn't require me to use my feminine wiles. I'd misplaced them sometime during adolescence.

My father appeared in the kitchen doorway, wearing a black three-piece, which showed off the tall, athletic figure he'd kept even in his midfifties. The silver vest and tie brought out streaks of silver in his hair. His eyes, the same vibrant green as Ethan's, contrasted brilliantly with the monochromatic formality.

"You look great, Dad," I said, wishing I could hug him without getting pizza grease all over his clothes.

"I agree." My mother wrapped her arms around him, resting her head on his shoulder as her hands snuck beneath the material of his jacket to snake around his back. My heart ached as I watched them, recognizing a pose Marc and I had struck countless times. But surely we'd never looked as in love, as picturesque, as they did.

In that moment, I was absolutely sure I'd done the right thing by keeping my mother's secret. They should look like that forever, and her secret, while it probably wouldn't end their marriage, would end the possibility of any more embraces like that.

"Where are you two going all dressed up like movie stars?" Vic asked.

My mother shot us a tight, suffer-in-silence smile. "We're meeting with the head of the Dallas City Planning Commission."

"You'll never be back by nine-thirty," Marc said, vocalizing almost my exact thought. "We can always meet in the morning, instead."

"No." My father didn't even hesitate. "We are not going to leave a corpse to rot in the barn because of a business dinner. *Any* business dinner."

I smiled at my father's resolve, wiping pizza grease from my chin with a paper towel. His career depended upon him making and keeping the right connections, but he would let nothing get in the way of Pride business.

"Your mother will develop a migraine around eight, and we'll have to excuse ourselves to take care of her. So don't risk being late because you think I won't make it. I will."

None of us doubted it. My father didn't make plans he couldn't keep. Nor did he bluff. He was a horrible poker player, but one of the best Alphas in the entire world. I should know. I'd been on the receiving end of his wisdom and guidance more often than anyone else in the Pride. He was hoping some of it would rub off.

I wasn't holding my breath.

Nine

Three and a half hours later, the pizza was gone, the kitchen was clean, and Parker was back from New Orleans, having stashed the van in the barn without bothering to remove the body first. Not that I could blame him.

The guys and I sat in the guesthouse in the dark, passing around two huge bowls of popcorn as *The Howling* played on their obscenely large flat-screen television. The movie was a house favorite, and the basis for a time-honored south-central territory drinking game—a shot for every howl in the film. Hollywood couldn't resist a good werewolf flick, and neither could we.

Marc, Parker, Owen, and I had piled together on the old brown-and-yellow plaid couch, me on Marc's lap, facing the television, with my legs stretched across the others' laps. Ethan sat on the floor at our feet, his legs splayed across the scarred hardwood floor, his head resting against the side of my thigh.

Across the room Vic lay stretched out in his recliner, and Jace was folded into a lumpy, overstuffed armchair all by himself. He wasn't obviously pouting, but neither was he happy or relaxed, in spite of the fact that he and Ethan had returned from their double date half an hour earlier in very good spirits, both reeking of fruit-scented lotion and recent sex.

"There she goes." Parker shook his prematurely gray head in disgust as the on-screen heroine pulled on her robe in preparation to leave her bungalow. Alone. In the middle of the night. "Off to check out strange sounds coming from the woods, armed with nothing more than a flashlight and a pretty smile."

"A flashlight's better than nothing," I mumbled, remembering a night three months earlier when *I'd* left the guesthouse alone in the middle of the night, completely unarmed. Of course, I hadn't been following some ominous howl, thus had no idea there were bad guys waiting for me in the woods. I'd just been looking for a little privacy in which to think.

"There she goes, the moron!" Vic said, leaning forward in his recliner, full shot glass pinched between his thumb and first two fingers.

I smiled. I couldn't help it. Bagging on the film was part of the tradition. The best part, in my opinion. Someone would make fun of the outdated effects, and someone else would scoff at the heroine's startling naiveté and conveniently repressed memory. And inevitably, during one of several low-budget Shifting scenes, one of the guys would yell at the victim du jour to *attack,* for fuck's sake—after all, shapeshifters are most vulnerable in mid-Shift. No werecat worth the cost of his own upkeep would ever Shift in front of an enemy. There was no faster way to die.

Well, there was *one* faster way to die, though the movie industry got that part all wrong, too.

Silver bullets. Ha. Still, you gotta love Hollywood for convincing the world that shape-shifters are damn hard to kill. How disappointed they'd probably all be to find out any ordinary lead slug would do the job just fine.

I leaned back against Marc's chest and relaxed into the arm he wrapped around me. But then we both tensed as a long, piercing howl erupted from surround-sound speakers mounted all over the room. Marc's eyes lit up and Ethan stiffened against my leg, going completely still as he sucked in a huge breath. Then, all at once the guys joined in, throwing their heads back in sync and baying at the moon. Or rather, at the screen. They were pretty good, too, considering that cats don't howl. At least not like dogs howl, as a primal cry of victory. Or of warning.

Looking around at them, I couldn't help but laugh. They were all dorks. Big, muscle-bound, furry dorks. But they were *my* dorks.

As the last sharp, baying tones faded from my ears, Marc twisted to grab two full shot glasses from the scratched and tilted end table on his left. He pressed one of them into my hand and lifted the other to his lips. All around me, the guys did the same, tossing back shots as they had each time one of the TV werewolves howled. If they were human, they'd all be seeing double by then. But thanks to their carefully maintained tolerance to alcohol and their werecat's metabolism, the guys were nowhere near drunk. At least, not yet.

"Throw it back, Faythe!" Parker ordered, refilling the shot glass Ethan handed him.

I hesitated, staring at the tiny glass in my hand. We were supposed to meet my father in the barn in twenty minutes to inspect the body of a murdered stray. To me, drinking seemed to be a very poor way to start such a meeting. But the guys saw the New Orleans corpse as a reason to indulge, rather than a reason *not* to. It was one of the ways they coped with the less-pleasant aspects of their job. A strict regimen of alcohol, anonymous sex—excluding Marc—and denial. They were keeping themselves sane.

Or maybe they were creating their very own brand of crazy.

Either way, they were determined to make me one of them, and I was less and less inclined to resist….

"Drink it!" Parker said, refilling Owen's glass.

I glanced at Marc, my eyebrows raised. He shrugged, so I opened my mouth and drained the shot glass—my first of the night. Tequila burned like hell going down, but it was better than whiskey. Marginally.

Smiling, I handed my glass to Parker. He traded the whiskey bottle for tequila and refilled my glass. It was official. I was one of the guys, for better or for worse.

"Now, see, that's why werewolves didn't make it in the real world." Vic leaned down to set a half-empty bottle of Jäger-meister on the floor to one side of his recliner. "They were too damn fond of the sound of their own voices."

"What?" I gulped from Marc's can of Coke, trying to squelch the flames scorching my throat. "Werewolves are just stories. Hollywood cash cows. They were never real."

"The hell they weren't." Vic was still smiling, but his eyes were serious. "They were as real as we are, and a damn sight more prolific than the fucking bruins."

"He's messin' with you, Faythe," Owen said, laughter shining bright in his dark eyes as he shifted on the couch beneath my calves.

Vic shook his head, brown waves flying. "I'm dead serious."

"So where are they now?" Parker drained his new shot, apparently for the hell of it.

Vic shrugged. "'Survival of the fittest' turned out *not* to refer to them. Werewolves had no stealth, and little common sense. The damn fools started howling every time they got excited, like a pup pissing himself over table scraps. Got themselves mistaken for real wolves and hunted to extinction more than a hundred years ago, before humans ever had a chance to figure out that some of their bedtime stories were true."

On screen, Karen White had abandoned bravery for a brief bout of common sense, locking herself into the relative safety of her bungalow. In the guesthouse, skeptical silence descended.

"Yeah, right!" Ethan scoffed, as usual, the first to voice an opinion.

"I'm not kidding," Vic said. "Ask your dad."

"Speak of the devil…" Owen said, twisting to glance at the front window. Light flashed across his face, bathing the room in the glow of my father's headlights as his car pulled into its customary parking spot, alongside the main house.

"Last one to the barn unloads the body!" Ethan cried, and the guys leapt into action. Ethan turned off the TV, and Parker began screwing caps on bottles at random. Vic vaulted from his recliner, kicking the footrest into place. Owen gathered a handful of shot glasses and dumped them on the kitchen island, unwilling to leave a mess in a house he didn't actually occupy.

I stood as the guys scurried around the living room, but Marc pulled me back onto the couch next to him. The gold specks in his irises sparkled with mischief. His hand slid up my rib cage, thumb brushing the low swell of my breast.

Ethan thumped across the floor toward the door without sparing us a glance. Parker was at his heels.

Marc leaned in, his gaze focused on my neck. I tilted my head back to oblige him. His lips trailed from just below my ear to the base of my throat. My hands reached for him automatically, finding their way beneath his shirt, playing across the ridges and valleys of his stomach.

"I'm not unloading that body," I whispered as his teeth grazed my collarbone.

"You won't have to." He leaned in for a kiss, and my lips parted, welcoming him. He pulled me back onto his lap so that I straddled him, my mouth still on his. My fingers trailed up his arm to his neck. I pulled him closer, tilting his head to better accommodate my tongue.

Marc groaned into my mouth. His thumb brushed my nipple and I gasped.

Glass shattered behind me, and the sharp scent of whiskey rolled across the room. Pulling away from Marc, I twisted on his lap to see Jace standing in a puddle, the broken bottle at his feet. His eyes were fixed on me. On *us*.

Shit. I'd thought he was already gone. "Jace…?"

"I'm fine," he snapped, snatching a dish towel from the counter. He dropped it on the pool of Johnnie Walker and stomped across the kitchen for a broom.

I got up to help him, but Marc put a hand on my shoulder and shook his head, watching Jace in frustration and obvious sympathy. He was right. Offering to help Jace would only have further embarrassed him. So we left Jace to his mess and crossed the western field well behind the others, heading for the big, red, prairie-style barn dominating the landscape.

After a couple of minutes the guesthouse door slammed at our backs and we heard Jace walking behind us. He made no attempt to catch up, and we refrained from looking back out of common courtesy. Jace would be okay. He always was. And

I would make a more concerted effort not to flaunt our relationship in front of him.

We caught up with everyone else as they stood gathered in front of the barn, waiting, their collective mood sobered by the task at hand. When my father saw us, he nodded and stepped toward the entrance.

Old, rusty hinges squealed as he pulled open the huge double barn doors centered beneath the gable of the steeply pitched roof. A waft of air rushed out to meet us, oppressively hot, though the temperature outside had already begun to drop from melt-you-where-you-stand to almost-tolerable.

The interior of our picturesque old barn was just as quaint as the exterior. Empty stalls stretched down the left and right sides, leaving a wide, empty space in the center, running the entire length of the building. The dirt floor was scattered with loose, fragrant hay, as was the loft overhead. On either side of the doors, wooden ladders led to the loft, where several bales still sat, left over from the year before. In a couple of months, both levels of the barn would be stacked full of hay bales, until my father sold them to the neighboring ranches, which, unlike ours, kept animals.

My father's van sat in the center aisle, looking out of place in a barn built nearly a century earlier. Dented, with peeling blue paint and spots of rust sprinkled like a scattering of red freckles, the van had seen lots of action in its fourteen years, and had carried more than its fair share of bodies.

Our Alpha herded everyone inside, then closed the doors, shutting us in with the heat. And with the dead stray. "Okay, Parker, let's take a look."

I glanced at my father as he spoke, and blinked in wry amusement. There he stood, sweating into a three-piece suit, his dress shoes dusty from the dirty floor, asking to see a cadaver Parker had brought home from New Orleans. Life couldn't get much weirder. Surely.

Parker opened the van's rear doors and Vic came forward without being asked to help remove the black-wrapped bundle from the floor of the cargo area. The stench was strong and immediate, but it wasn't the smell of rotting flesh. It was the smell of rotting food, from the garbage the body had been buried under.

Together, Vic and Parker lowered the bundle to the straw-strewn floor, then pulled strips of duct tape from the plastic, unwrapping the giant burrito and exposing the body beneath a smattering of putrefied lettuce, tomatoes, olives, and noodles.

Inhaling deeply through my mouth, I forced all traces of disgust from my expression and made myself look at the victim.

He was about my age, maybe a couple of years older, with freckles and nearly black eyes, which I could see because no one had bothered to close them. Or maybe the eyelids had simply refused to cooperate.

At a glance, I couldn't tell that his neck was broken, but I was more than willing to take Parker's word for it.

My father wasn't. He knelt next to the man's left shoulder and grabbed a handful of soiled brown hair, then gave the head a tug to the right. It moved with no visible resistance, and chills crept up my spine at the faint scraping of bones grinding together. His neck hadn't just been broken. It had been broken in *two*. As in a completely severed spinal cord. He'd never stood a chance.

Our Alpha stood, brushing straw and dirt from his knee. "Ethan, check his ID."

Ethan dug in the man's back right pocket and came out

with a thin black leather wallet, folded into thirds, which he handed over without opening.

My father took the wallet and rifled through the contents. He didn't pass it around, nor did he remove anything. "Robert Harper. Twenty-three. From Picayune."

Mississippi. He'd lived in the free territory, which was no surprise.

"So what was he doing in New Orleans?" Owen asked. I'd been wondering the same thing.

"He could have been doing anything," Parker said. "Or *anyone.* But whatever he was doing, it must have been pretty important for him to risk trespassing on south-central territory."

"Not necessarily." All eyes turned to Marc, who stood leaning against the van, his arms crossed over his chest and one foot propped on a rear tire. "Picayune's less than an hour from New Orleans, and we only have, what, two Pride cats living there other than Holden? What are the chances that either of them would get close enough to sniff him out? He's probably made countless trips without us ever knowing. It wouldn't be much of a risk for him."

My father nodded in agreement. "Unfortunately, we can't be everywhere all the time, and Harper obviously knew that."

"Well, someone sure as hell sniffed him out *this* time," Jace said.

"Evidently." My father turned to me, and I held my breath. I dreaded catching his attention the way a child who hasn't done her homework fears being called out by the teacher. "How does Parker's body compare with yours?"

Great. A pop quiz, I thought, recognizing his transition into lecture mode.

"How does Parker's body compare with mine? Hmm." I

gave Parker a quick, theatrical once-over, and he smiled, clearly catching on to my line of thought. "Nice legs and killer biceps. But I have better boobs. No question."

My father frowned, but not before a flicker of amusement flashed across his face. If I hadn't been looking for it, I never would have seen it. "Faythe…"

"Oh, fine." I barely resisted the urge to roll my eyes, gathering my thoughts for the test he'd just presented. "There don't seem to be many differences at a glance."

Our esteemed Alpha nodded, and I continued, walking slowly around the body as I spoke. "The only difference I see at the moment is their respective ages. Harper was twenty-three, and Moore was about a decade older. Each apparently died of a broken neck. Both men are Caucasian, and both are strays. Both are sturdy in build, which makes me wonder how an attacker could get close enough to either of them to break his neck without suffering so much as a scratch." Okay, technically Marc had pointed that out first, but if he could borrow my shower, I could borrow his wisdom. Right?

Squatting on the ground next to the corpse, I made myself examine the fingers. "And based on the lack of blood and tissue beneath their nails, I'm going to assume I'm right about that."

I glanced up at my father, and he nodded for me to go on, his face carefully devoid of any expression. Behind him, Marc beamed at me, obviously pleased. I smiled at him and stood, rubbing my hands on the front of my shorts out of habit, though I hadn't actually touched the corpse.

"Both bodies were found on our territory, but near the Mississippi border, each less than an hour from his own home." I paused, closing my eyes in thought as the gears in my brain whirred fast enough to make me dizzy. "Oh, wait. I just thought of another difference." A second pause. "No, two."

"Go on." Though my father's face remained unreadable, I thought I detected a hint of encouragement in his tone.

"Assuming they died where they were found, Robert Harper was killed in the middle of New Orleans, but Bradley Moore died in an empty field in Arkansas, miles from anything but empty fields and a small patch of woods."

"And the other difference?" Marc prompted.

"Moore's murder was reported, albeit anonymously, but Harper's was not. In fact, it's a miracle Parker and Holden found him before anyone else did."

For a moment, no one spoke. Then the boss had to go and ruin my good mood. "Does anyone see any flaws in her logic?"

Glancing around boldly, I silently dared them each to speak. I'd ruined the curve in my college logic class with a perfect score on the final, and I was pretty confident in my deductions. So it came as a complete slap in the face when Ethan spoke up.

"Sure, no one called to report the body in New Orleans, but that doesn't mean it *wouldn't* have been reported. For all we know, the killer was on his way to a pay phone when Parker and Holden found the body."

"That's certainly possible," Daddy said as I stuck my tongue out at Ethan, well aware of how immature I was being. My brother reciprocated, as I'd known he would. "Anyone else?"

Vic cleared his throat. "Well, this isn't a flaw in Faythe's logic, since she mentioned it, but there's always the possibility that one or both of them were killed somewhere else, then moved."

"Yes, but without a forensics lab, we have no way of

knowing, so I'm going to suggest we concentrate on what we *do* know. Or what we can smell." My father's eyes came to rest on me, then flicked to Marc, who now stood behind me, his arms wrapped around my shoulders.

Marc's chin brushed the back of my head. "I'm guessing you want us to get up close and personal with Harper's trace fragrances."

The Alpha nodded.

"I can smell him fine from here, thanks," I said, doing my best not to wrinkle my nose. While a human probably would have found the stench of rotten garbage offensive, for us it was virtually unbearable. At least in human form. As cats, we were more accustomed to nature's less-pleasant scents, most of which were a normal part of life in the wild. But things were different on two legs.

My father frowned, and his face hardened, but before I could make things any worse for myself, Marc gave me a little shove and followed me toward the body.

Kneeling by Harper's shoulder, I turned to look up at my father, who was wearing his Alpha face. Again. "I assume you want to know if he has the same weird smell as the last one."

Daddy nodded. "And anything else of interest that you notice."

Following Marc's lead, I leaned closer to the body, struggling to swallow the gorge rising in the back of my throat. I breathed in deeply through my nose, and felt my stomach churn. Trying to ignore the nausea, I clamped a hand over my mouth and took another deep breath. Behind me, Ethan snickered, and I made a mental note to accidentally kick him somewhere sensitive next time we sparred.

Marc looked at me with his eyebrows raised, and I nodded

to tell him I was okay. I leaned down one more time. This time I concentrated on classifying the smells to distract myself from my urge to vomit. To my surprise, it worked. I detected several variations on the theme of rotting vegetables, and three or four kinds of moldy meat. *Cooked* meat. Harper hadn't been dead long enough to start smelling on his own, mostly because he'd spent the majority of the day in an air-conditioned van.

After the food, I identified several biological scents, probably from emptied bathroom trash cans. And under all that was *the* smell. The one I was looking for. It was faint, and I would never have noticed it beneath the other, stronger smells if I hadn't already known what to look for. But it was definitely there.

I glanced at Marc, my eyebrows raised in question. He nodded. He smelled it, too. The murders were connected.

Turning back to the body, I closed my eyes in concentration. Bracing my hands on the floor to the left of the corpse— I was *not* going to end a perfectly good day by falling face-first onto a dead man—I followed my nose, moving to the right as the smell grew faintly stronger. When it began to fade again, I moved back to my left until my face hovered— eyes still closed—over the point at which the scent was most noticeable, though it was faint even then.

I opened my eyes. I was inches from Harper's broken neck. The smell was strongest in the one place we were sure the killer had touched him, and that could only mean one thing: I was smelling the killer's scent.

Standing, I turned to face my father. "It's the same as the scent on Moore. It's definitely a foreign cat, but it's…*more,* somehow." Ethan snickered at my unintentional pun, but I ignored him. "Different. And it's strongest on his neck."

"It's on both his hands, too," Marc said, rising to stand next to me.

Instead of replying, our Alpha knelt beside the body, heedless of the dirt floor, and closed his eyes as he inhaled deeply just above the corpse's neck. He exhaled, then inhaled again. His forehead wrinkled and his eyes opened. He stood and pulled a clean handkerchief from his jacket pocket. "I don't smell it. I smell rot, and his personal scent, and cheap cologne, but nothing else." He frowned deeply, cleaning his lenses out of habit, and his next words were softer than he usually spoke. "I guess this old nose isn't quite what it used to be."

Parker came forward then, and Owen followed him. They knelt side by side, inhaling with almost comic expressions of concentration. Several seconds later, they stood, shaking their heads in unison. The scent was too faint, and completely overwhelmed by the stench of garbage.

The others each took a turn, but none of them could detect the scent. Still, it was almost funny to watch the parade of beefy men take their turns kneeling on the dusty barn floor to sniff the refuse-strewn corpse. And by the time Vic stood, chestnut waves flopping as he shook his head in disappointment, I'd decided that they couldn't smell the scent because, having never smelled it before, they didn't really know what they were looking for. Marc and I had probably only been able to pinpoint it because we'd gotten a good whiff of it earlier on Bradley Moore.

Marc shrugged. "Well, I guess you'll just have to take our word for it."

My father shook his head, frowning down at Harper, as if the victim were to blame for the faintness of the mystery scent he carried. "That's not good enough. This same cat is responsible for murdering both strays. On *our* territory. We can't let that continue, nor can we let it go unpunished, and if we're going to stop him, we have to know who he is. Or *what* he is. I have to smell his scent."

Resolute now, his jawline firm, my father turned sharply and marched away from us. I watched him go, noting the determination in his stride and the final-sounding thump each time his heels hit the ground. But I didn't understand what he had in mind until he turned into the last empty horse stall on the right and dropped out of sight.

He was going to Shift.

In cat form, all of his senses would be heightened, even above the elevated sensitivity he had on two legs. My father wanted to give his feline nose a chance to succeed where the human version had failed.

As we stood around looking at one another, waiting for our Alpha to finish Shifting, my gaze returned to the body, and my thoughts to the scent in question. The smell was strongest on Harper's neck, where he would have been gripped by his murderer. That made sense. What *didn't* make sense was the fact that the smell was also noticeable—at least to me and Marc— on Harper's hands, yet we'd found no defensive injuries.

"Hey, guys?" Six heads turned my way. "Harper has the killer's scent on his hands, so he must have touched the bastard. But he has no blood or obvious tissue beneath his nails, and no defensive injuries." I paused to give them a moment to digest what I'd said. "Why would Harper touch his killer, yet make no attempt to protect himself?"

In the back of my mind, I noted the whisper of claws scraping hard-packed dirt as my father neared the end of his Shift on the other side of the barn.

"The most obvious answer is that he trusted his murderer," Owen drawled, shifting his cowboy hat back and forth on his head with one rough, tanned hand. "Knew him personally."

I nodded. Marc had drawn the same conclusion about Moore in Arkansas. "Yeah, that makes sense—for a Pride cat." My brothers and fellow enforcers were very close. They'd been friends and housemates for years, and in a Pride, a connection that strong came with a lot of physical contact. "But both Harper and Moore are strays. Loners," I continued. "They were born human, and human men don't touch one another much. They may shake hands, but that would only put the scent on Harper's *right* hand. Right?"

Jace nodded, clearly following my train of thought. "So why would Harper touch his killer with both hands, if not to fight him off?"

"Exactly."

A huffing sound drew our attention toward the rear of the barn and I turned to see my father padding toward us, his paws silent on the packed-dirt floor.

Even in his midfifties, my father was impressive and physically intimidating as a cat. He wasn't as long as Owen or Marc, but he was bulky and solid, and obviously powerful. Like all werecats, Daddy's fur was sleek and solid black, with no spots or rosettes. But unlike the rest of us, he was easy to identify from a distance, even with the wind blowing his scent the wrong way. As he'd aged, my father had developed a streak of silver fur behind each ear, the exact shade and placement of the two most prominent streaks of silver in his hair.

As he slunk toward us, moving gracefully across the floor, I thought about the difference between the life of a Pride Alpha like my father and that of a stray like Harper. My father had everything: respect, responsibility, power, and more friends and family than he knew what to do with. By contrast most strays were socially isolated and constantly at risk of losing everything to a faster, stronger stray. Which raised a very important question: Who the hell would a wary loner trust?

Someone he has no reason to fear, I thought, surprised by how obvious the answer seemed in hindsight. But who was that? Who didn't a stray fear?

My father paused at the edge of the ring we'd formed around the corpse on the floor. He took us all in with a single, sweeping glance, then padded directly to the body, bending to place his nose less than an inch from Harper's neck. His long tail swished slowly behind him, and his nostrils twitched as he inhaled, sniffing to isolate the scent none of the rest of us could identify.

And still the gears in my brain spun furiously. I was on to something, and I couldn't let it go, even when my father raised his head from the body, huffing in triumph.

Who's strong enough to break a stray's neck, yet seems harmless enough to put him at ease? Who can get close enough to touch a stray tomcat without setting off his inner alarm? And just like that, I knew the answer: *I* could.

The killer wasn't a tomcat at all. *She* was a tabby.

Ten

My father reemerged from the empty horse stall on two legs, wearing a satisfied, cat-who-ate-the-canary look—and little else. He'd taken the time to pull on his pants, but the remaining parts of his suit—including socks and tie—lay draped across his left arm, his shoes hanging from the fingers of his right hand. We were getting a rare glimpse of our Alpha at his informal best, and I couldn't help but smile.

"The scent was definitely there," he said, walking toward us from the other end of the barn in long, confident strides. "It was faint, but unmistakable once I caught it. We're not looking for a stray after all." He paused dramatically, and I was amused to realize my father was dragging the moment out to prolong the tension. It was working. All eyes were on him, and Ethan actually leaned forward in anticipation.

The Alpha opened his mouth to make his grand revelation, but I beat him to the punch. I just couldn't resist.

"We're looking for a tabby."

I'd whispered, but they all heard me clearly in the eager

silence created by our Alpha's theatrical pause. At the edge of my vision, Marc gaped at me, but my eyes were on my father, whose face registered first surprise, then annoyance. Then pride. He was *proud* of me for figuring it out on my own.

I grinned, relishing what felt like a rare moment of competence. But my father kept watching me, as if waiting for more. My smile faded as I wondered what I was missing. Was he irritated at me for one-upping him on purpose? Instead of answering my unspoken question, he smiled and glanced from me to the rest of the guys. Whatever was on his mind, he didn't want to talk about it in front of everyone else. At least, not yet.

"How did you know?" he asked at last, moving on as if he'd never paused.

"Deductive reasoning." Beaming openly now, I glanced from face to astonished face, unbothered by the knowledge that they were reacting to my news, not my skill in deducing it. "There's no way the average stray would let someone else get close enough to hurt him without going on the defensive. Unless that someone was a girl. Specifically, a tabby—the tomcat's Achilles' heel."

Ethan frowned, skepticism etched into every line on his face at the thought that a *girl* could ever be his downfall. I was more than happy to burst his sexist bubble.

"Tell him, Dad. Harper and Moore got their tickets punched by a *girl.* And it could just as easily have happened to *you,* Ethan." Self-defense would have been the last thing on my youngest brother's mind if he'd met a strange tabby on the street. He'd have been more concerned with getting his hands on her than with keeping hers off him.

"No way." He shook his head, short black hair falling across his forehead.

I sighed. Tomcats aren't threatened by tabbies. I'm proud to consider myself the exception to that rule, but generally speaking, male werecats see nothing to fear in the female of the species. Even as a member of the not-so-gentler sex, I'd made the same mistake. The truth was that we'd all been trained from birth to underestimate women. Some of us, to underestimate ourselves.

While human society had made wonderful progress in the struggle for gender equality, the werecat community was still decades behind the times. Irritating though that fact was, I understood the reason. Tabbies are very rare, averaging only one out of every six or seven Pride births. Once you add in the strays, who are all male, the ratio of tabbies to toms becomes even smaller.

Since technology has yet to eliminate the necessity of a womb in the process of procreation, female werecats are not only rare, but very valuable.

How do people treat rare and valuable treasures? With great care and respect. And with a single-minded determination to eliminate all possible dangers. For that reason, most tabbies grow up to be full-time moms, like my mother. As such, they can remain under the watchful eyes and protective arms of their husbands and teams of enforcers, who would gladly give their own lives to protect the woman who will someday bear the next generation of werecats.

Frustrating, and frighteningly archaic, but true.

And when I thought about it that way, it wasn't really much of a surprise that none of us had considered that the killer could be a woman. Or that Harper and Moore had let her slip through their personal defenses. Fear for his life was probably the last thing on either man's mind when he saw the mystery tabby. The first was no doubt lust. On second thought, that might have been the *only* thing on either of their minds.

"Think about it," I said, enjoying my moment in the limelight. "You guys have been falling for that one since the beginning of time. Remember Adam and Eve? Samson and Delilah? Need I go on?"

Apparently not, judging by the less-than-friendly looks on their faces. And I had serious doubts they'd recognize references to Calypso, Circe, or Scheherazade. Maybe Lorena Bobbitt…

"Whatever." Ethan glanced from me to Marc, then back to me. "If you're so sure it's a tabby now, why didn't either of you recognize the scent in the first place?"

Shrugging, I crossed my arms over my chest. "The smell is very faint, and just like the rest of you, we went into this *expecting* to find a tom's scent. So that's exactly what we found. Or what we *thought* we found. Besides, I can't speak for Marc, but I was blindsided by the foreign aspect of the scent. That surprised me—" and *scared* me "—so much that I didn't think to analyze any further."

Marc nodded in agreement, threading his warm fingers through mine. I squeezed his hand in response, thanking him silently for backing me up. If we'd *both* missed the cat's gender, I didn't come off looking like such an idiot.

"Well, she's not a jungle cat." My father's voice rang into a silence broken only by the crickets chirruping outside, and I felt a small measure of tension ease from the cramped muscles in my neck. "She lacks that distinctive Amazonian scent. But she's definitely from somewhere south of the equator."

"Holy…crap." Vic glanced at our Alpha as he altered what he'd been about to say. "A South American tabby? We're looking for a serial-killing *foreign tabby cat?* In our territory? How is that even possible?"

In spite of the frustrated feminist in me who insisted that women were capable of anything men were—including murder—I had to admit to having similar questions. To my knowledge, I was the only other tabby who'd ever killed anyone, and I'd done it in self-defense. Mostly. But there were no signs that either Harper or Moore had tried to hurt the tabby in question.

And beyond all of that, there was an even bigger question…

"Who the hell *is* she?" I asked, my attention on my father even when someone grumbled softly over my language. No one else ever cussed around our Alpha; it was considered disrespectful. I didn't do it to be rude; I did it to remind him that even though he had me where he wanted me—for the moment—I wasn't completely malleable. And, honestly, sometimes it just slipped out. My mother was right: bad habits die hard.

"I don't know," my father said, surprising me with the honest bewilderment in his voice. Of *course* he didn't know. There was no reason he *should* know. But I was kind of accustomed to his having all the answers…

"How on earth did she get here?" Parker wondered aloud. "And where are her enforcers? Why would her family let her come here alone? She has to be alone, doesn't she?"

"Yes." Marc nodded firmly. "We'd know it if there were an entire contingent of foreign cats in our territory. It's one thing for a single cat to evade detection for a little while. But a whole party?" His tone went up in question on the end. "No way."

Jace brushed a strand of short brown hair back from his face, and his cobalt eyes sparkled with sudden excitement. "Maybe she doesn't have any family or enforcers. Maybe she's a stray."

Vic snickered, and even Parker smiled at the thought of a female stray. There weren't any, and to my knowledge, there never had been. Not even in legend.

The theory generally accepted by the council was that human women were too weak to survive either the initial infection, or the transition period itself. To my surprise, that theory had survived Dr. Carver's recent revelation about the recessive werecat genes, by virtue of the fact that we'd never once found a female stray. But with no proof of the impossibility, I was no longer willing to accept the old theory as fact. Women really *could* do anything men could do, and our mysterious tabby was proof of that.

Still, while the possibility of a female stray *did* exist, at least in my mind, our murderer didn't fit the bill.

"No." Marc and I spoke in unison, and I gestured for him to continue. The spotlight was starting to make me sweat, and he was more than welcome to it. "She's not a stray," he said, and I nodded in agreement. This second whiff of her scent had verified that she was a natural-born cat. A natural-born *South American* cat, apparently.

"Then that brings us back to my questions," Parker said. "If she belongs to one of the *South American* Prides, where are her fellow Pride members? Why on earth would they let her off on her own?"

"Maybe she killed them all," Vic suggested, morbid humor shadowed behind his eyes.

Ethan crossed his arms. "Then they probably won't mind if we keep her." His cocky smile clearly showed his confidence that he could tame any tabby.

I frowned, un-amused. "Ethan, she's a murderer, not a stray puppy. You can't be serious." But he only smiled, and most of the others suddenly found the straw at their feet fascinating. I looked to my father for help, but he simply gestured at my fellow enforcers, telling me to take my complaint to the general assembly. Frustration rumbled up my throat in the form of a mild growl. "Guys, come on!" I couldn't believe them! We were talking about a cold-blooded killer, and they acted like she was a lost kitten they wanted to adopt.

"What would you suggest, Faythe?" Owen asked gently, peering at me from beneath the brim of a stained and faded cowboy hat. "You want to execute a tabby?"

Did I? My uncertainty stung like salt rubbed into the open wound that was my own indignation. Whoever the tabby was, she was a murderer. But she was also a tabby-cat. The species needed her just as badly as it needed me. Did that mean she should literally get away with murder?

Based on the expressions around me, the guys had come to an unspoken, unanimous conclusion: yes. She should get a walk—at least from the death penalty—because of her gender. They thought they could reform this murderess, whoever she was. Or they at least thought it was worth a try. Even Marc, who met my eyes unflinchingly.

My father cleared his throat, effectively cutting off the retort I hadn't even thought of yet. All eyes turned toward him, and I noticed idly that no one was looking at poor Harper anymore. Our interest had shifted from the dead guy to the girl who'd introduced him to his current state of rigor mortis.

Our Alpha eyed each of us in turn. "We'll cross that bridge when it crumbles beneath our feet. For now, I believe the most important question is, *Who is she?* While I seriously doubt she killed her entire family, the fact remains that she's running around the southern U.S. killing strays, so I'd say there's a very good possibility she's no longer on good terms with her Pride. But without more information, or a stronger scent, I couldn't begin to guess which Pride that is."

My father dropped his shoes on the ground in front of his feet and glanced around the barn. "I don't know about the rest of you, but I've had enough excitement for tonight, and we need some time to think about all this. I'm going to bed, and I suggest the rest of you do the same. Except for Jace and Ethan, of course."

Ethan nodded, and he and Jace came forward to wrap the body for its date with the industrial incinerator.

I turned to Marc, intending to ask if *I'd* get away with murder just because I had ovaries, but before I could even open my mouth, my father popped his knuckles. Several at once.

My eyes closed in dread. Knuckle-cracking was never a good sign.

Marc elbowed me and I opened my eyes to find the Alpha watching us both. As I'd expected.

"You two pack your bags before you go to bed." My father leaned against the van and pulled on one black dress sock, then stepped into his shoe. "I want you both on the first flight out in the morning from Houston International."

"Where to?" Marc asked, pulling me toward him. I let myself melt into his chest, pulling his arms around me as my head fell back to rest against his shoulder. I didn't want to go anywhere. We'd only been home for two days, and I'd rather spar with Ethan twice a day for the next month than go out on another assignment.

"New Orleans. If memory serves, Kevin Mitchell still lives there. I want you to meet up with him and find out what you can about Harper. Check out the restaurant and the alley, and see if you can figure out what he was doing there. Then drive out to Picayune and look around his apartment. I'll get you the address."

My father paused to put on his other sock and shoe, then stood and gathered the rest of his clothes. "Talk to his neighbors. Be discreet, of course, but find out if any of them saw him with a woman who could be the tabby. Get a good description. While you're doing that, I'll work on her identity from another angle. I have a contact in Venezuela who should be able to tell us who's missing a daughter, and why."

My mouth dropped open, and I clamped it shut before anyone noticed. "You have a contact in Venezuela?" How could I not have known that?

"Faythe, I'd been to six different continents before you took your first step. When will you stop sounding surprised that I bring a bit of worldly experience to my position?"

"I'm not surprised, Daddy. I'm just ready to accumulate a little of my own."

He raised one brow. "Fine. Start with New Orleans. And, Faythe?"

"Yeah."

"Be careful what you ask for. Life has a way of giving you what you want, whether you're ready for it or not."

I frowned. "Why do you say that?"

With a cryptic smile, the Alpha strolled past me and through the barn doors. A moment later, his voice floated out of the darkness. "I got you, didn't I?"

Eleven

Kevin Mitchell met us at baggage claim. I didn't recognize him until he stepped into my path and stuck his hand out, his broad smile brightening an otherwise ordinary face.

"Faythe Sanders, you look amazing!" he said, brown eyes shifting upward as his gaze slid over my denim shorts before stalling at the low neckline of my shirt. His leering appraisal made me wish I'd opted for painter's coveralls instead of the snug black tank top. Or maybe a big paper sack. Rather than shaking the hand I extended reluctantly, he used it to pull me into an intimate hug, as if we'd known each other for years, when really I'd only met him once before.

Bristling, I broke free from the involuntary embrace and bent to pick up my bag, determined to get Kevin's brain focused on business and keep it there. He was only a few years older than Marc, but my gut had labeled him a dirty old man the minute he'd made eye contact with my breasts. If that's where he thought my eyes were, I didn't want to know where he'd look for my brain.

But I was pretty sure where to find his.

"Hi, Kevin." I glanced at Marc and started to take his hand out of habit. But then I stopped. I didn't want either of them to think I was using Marc to shield myself from unwanted attention. Instead, I gripped my bag in both hands, though it wasn't heavy, and met Kevin's eyes candidly as I introduced him to Marc.

"Marc Ramos, Kevin Mitchell."

"We've actually met before, but it's been a while," Marc said, extending his hand. His expression remained admirably neutral, in spite of the possessive growl I knew he held ready deep in his throat.

Kevin studied the offered hand for several seconds, as if inspecting it for grime, and my grip on my bag tightened as I watched Marc's eyes harden and his shoulders tense. This wasn't going to be pretty. I could already tell.

"Of course." Kevin finally accepted Marc's hand, but instead of shaking it, he squeezed it, and to my horror, Marc squeezed back. "Who could ever forget Greg's pet stray?"

Marc's hand tightened visibly around Kevin's fingers, his digits going white. Again. Both men clenched their jaws, Kevin in pain, and Marc in an obvious effort to control his temper and keep from breaking Kevin's hand. *Off.*

Why couldn't guys find a more original way to test each other's manly prowess? Arm wrestling might have been more subtle. Or maybe comparing the length of their…*canines.*

I elbowed Marc in the ribs, and he let go. Then he turned an insincere smile on me for a moment before aiming it at Kevin. "I guess this is your big chance."

Kevin raised one eyebrow at Marc. "For what?"

"To prove yourself. Isn't that why you're here? You think

if you impress the boss's daughter, he'll finally make you an enforcer."

His verbal jab jarred loose an old memory and I realized I'd actually met Kevin not once, but twice, the first time nearly eleven years earlier. I'd been just a kid when Kevin applied for a job as one of the south-central territory's enforcers. My father accepted him into our Pride from his birth Pride, but turned him down as an enforcer, along with four other tomcats, including my brother Ryan.

Though Marc hadn't quite been eighteen, he'd gotten the job. And apparently he wasn't above lording that over Kevin, though I could hardly blame him after the stray comment.

"Actually, I just want to help." Kevin swallowed thickly and made an awkward attempt at a smile.

Marc nodded, wearing his business face, nearly expressionless and impossible to read. "Good. Keep that in mind, and we'll be fine. But if you forget your altruistic intentions, we're going to have a serious problem. Got it?"

For a moment, Kevin said nothing, and I could almost see the possible answers cycling through his brain as expressions flitted across his face. "Look, I'm just doing Greg a favor," he finally said, settling on an arrogant I-don't-know-what-you're-talking-about look as he tried to imply that he and my father had a much closer relationship than they actually did.

No one was fooled.

Marc threw his backpack over one shoulder, snatched his overnight bag from the floor, and took off toward the parking lot, without even a glance back to make sure we would follow him.

I scowled at Kevin, then raced to catch up with Marc.

In the parking lot, as the muggy Louisiana heat settled in

around us, Kevin stormed past Marc, and we followed him to a green four-door sedan with a dent in the rear bumper and a four-inch scratch on the driver's-side door. Kevin came around the car to unlock the front passenger-side door first, holding it open for me with an inviting smile. I almost admired his tenacity. Marc did not. He took my bag from me and tossed it onto the front seat along with both of his own, then reached through to the back door and unlocked it himself.

He held the back door open for me as I climbed in, then slid over to sit directly behind the driver's seat. Marc settled onto the seat next to me and slammed the door on Kevin's irritated pout. By the time our driver had stomped around the car and unlocked his own door, his resolute smile was firmly in place once again. He was resilient; I had to give him that.

"Where to?" Kevin adjusted the rearview mirror so he could see my face. I read him the name of the restaurant and the Metairie address my father had written down, and Kevin pulled out of the parking lot without another word. And without readjusting his rearview mirror.

I rolled down my window to relieve the locked-car heat, then unbuckled my seat belt and snuggled up next to Marc in spite of the temperature, content to know that now Kevin couldn't stare at me without seeing Marc, too. In the mirror, our reluctant chauffeur's eyes crinkled in a frown, then shifted to look at the road.

Including Holden Pierce, there were two other Pride cats living near New Orleans, both of whom were more courteous, more polite, and infinitely more pleasant to be around than the one behind the wheel. Yet my father had insisted that Kevin Mitchell be our guide for the day, probably just to test my self-discipline. I was pretty sure that if I made it home without

Kevin's detached head in tow, I'd get a gold star on my permanent record. Or maybe one of those little smiley faces.

Kevin's father was Alpha of one of the northern Prides, and beating the shit out of an Alpha's son, even if he was a real prick, wouldn't be very good for inter-Pride relations. In fact, it would be really *bad*. Anyone looking for a reason to oust my father from his position as head of the Territorial Council—and there were several people on that list—would have plenty of ammunition if either of us lost our collective temper with Kevin without ample justification. For that reason, on the plane, Marc had rattled off some crap about this assignment being an assessment of my diplomatic skills. But it was really a test of my patience.

And I was willing to bet Marc would lose his before I lost mine.

After baking for forty-five minutes in the back of Kevin's clunker, we pulled up in front of a long strip of connected storefronts, each housing a different business. Kevin parallel-parked at the curb and we got out, staring around like the tourists we practically were as brass-heavy jazz music poured from an open doorway nearby and strangers bumped and jostled us on the egg-fryable sidewalk. This part of town had obviously recovered nicely from the infamous hurricane.

The first thing I noticed was the Closed sign in the door of the Cajun Bar and Grill. According to a plaque propped in the front window, the restaurant didn't open for lunch until eleven o'clock, which gave us nearly half an hour to stand around like idiots before we could speak to the employees inside.

"Let's check out the alley while we wait," Marc suggested. We went with his idea rather than mine, for obvious reasons.

The restaurant was in the middle of the block, so we had

to walk past a florist and a hardware store, then around a dry cleaner to get to the mouth of the alley. Once there, we discovered that though the restaurant didn't open for thirty more minutes, the staff inside was already hard at work crafting a jumble of spicy aromas that made my stomach growl in anticipation of dishes I'd never even tried.

How did we know this? The back door of the Cajun Bar and Grill was propped open, spilling laughter, the sharp clang of pots and pans, and piquant, lyrical accents into the alley.

"We can't leave without eating there," I told Marc, gripping his arm with one hand as I pointed to the open doorway with the other. "I'm starving."

He grinned. "We'll order extra and take it home."

"You're hungry?" Kevin asked from my other side. "There's this great Italian restaurant near my apartment. You like manicotti?"

"Thanks, Kevin." I was trying my hand at tact and discretion. And manners. "But I'm going to try some of the local favorites. Right here." I paused to glance at Marc, then continued, though I hadn't seen what I'd been looking for in his expression. "You're welcome to join us."

Kevin frowned. "Thanks," he said, but I wasn't sure if that was a "Thanks, but no thanks," or a "Thanks, I'd love to."

"Okay, now what?" I mumbled under my breath, eyeing the row of widely spaced Dumpsters as I concentrated on the epicurean aromas to block out the other, less-pleasant smells originating from farther down the alley. Parker had said he found Harper's body beneath the overflow from the one nearest the Cajun Bar and Grill. But what exactly were we looking for?

As we approached the Dumpster, my progress hindered

momentarily when I put my sneaker through a rotten plank in an old pallet, a feeling of dread settled into my stomach. The Dumpster looked pretty clean, as far as Dumpsters go. It sat on bare, if slimy, concrete, absent of the overflow of garbage Parker had described. Trash collectors had clearly come and gone, taking any evidence we might have found to the city dump, wherever that was. And I was in no hurry to find out.

Marc climbed a stack of wooden crates to peer into the trash receptacle, tossing the heavy lid open without so much as a grunt. "It's nearly empty," he said, glancing down at me. "And what's in here smells fresh."

Behind me, metal hinges squealed as a door opened across the alley and down a few feet from the Cajun Bar and Grill. I whirled around to see a short, slender man wearing black jeans and a hot-pink T-shirt. He nudged a broken brick into the threshold to prop the door open, and when he stepped into the alley, I could see that the block printing in black across the front of his shirt read Forbidden Fruit.

"Hey, you can't be back here," he said, his fist tightening around the top of a bulging garbage bag.

Marc grabbed my elbow and I looked up to find something intense and imploring in his eyes. He was trying to tell me something, and I wasn't getting it. Maybe he wanted me to pound the guy? Seemed a little extreme to me, but definitely effective.

The little man in the doorway reached for a wireless radio hanging from his belt. I curled my hands into fists and started to step forward. Marc pulled me back by that same elbow, and I glanced up to see him roll his eyes at me in exasperation.

Oops. Not the right time for a pounding, apparently. Kevin glanced from me and Marc to the man, then stuck his hands into his pockets, making no effort to help.

"My sister left her cell phone in there yesterday, and no one turned it in," Marc said, lacing his voice with a healthy dose of bored irritation as he nodded at the restaurant behind us. "The guys in the kitchen said we could look through the garbage."

Actually, the guys in the kitchen hadn't noticed us yet. They probably couldn't hear us over their own racket. But the little man bought Marc's lie with no hesitation. His hand moved away from his belt and his posture relaxed. He seemed more than willing to believe I was just some dumb chick whose most dangerous trait was an inability to keep hold of her own stuff. I couldn't help being insulted by how readily he accepted that thought.

"Good luck." Shrimpy nodded at the Dumpster as he walked toward it, passing less than two feet from me without so much as a shiver of fear. *Damn it.* We were going to have to do something about my harmless-looking exterior. "The garbage truck came first thing this morning," Shrimpy said, tossing his bag into the Dumpster. "You'd have better luck finding the Holy Grail in there." He strolled back across the alley, making no attempt at all to avoid me, though he steered noticeably clear of Marc, and even Kevin. Pausing in the doorway of Forbidden Fruit, Shrimpy held the door open with one hand and pushed his brick back inside. Then he turned to look me up and down. But mostly up, because I was at least two inches taller than he was.

"I can't help you find your cell phone, miss," he said, meeting my eyes much more boldly than I would have thought possible for such a small man. "But if you decide you want a job, come see me. Go to the bar and ask for Jeff."

Before I'd recovered from surprise, he disappeared into the dark interior of the building.

Kevin's raucous laughter filled my ears, as Jeff's meaning sank in. "He just offered you a job as a stripper. Sounds like a lot more fun than your current line of work, and *I'd* sure as hell pay to watch you take off your clothes."

No, casual nudity wasn't a big deal for werecats; it was generally unavoidable. But stripping wasn't casual nudity, and an unwelcome pass at me—especially in front of Marc— was a *very* big deal, to which Jace could readily attest.

My right hand formed a fist, but before I could put it into motion, Marc's arm soared past me. His fist slammed into Kevin's stomach. Kevin's laughter ended in a sudden whoosh of breath rushing from his lungs. He flew ass-first into the wall at his back, then crumpled into a heap of denim and cotton on the ground.

Ha! Marc lost his temper first, and suddenly I was in very good spirits. Of course, my mood was also elevated by watching Kevin struggle not to vomit.

I held my hand out to Kevin, but he slapped it away and pushed himself up on his own, glaring at Marc over my shoulder as he stood. I wanted to tell him that he'd be singing soprano if Marc hadn't beaten me to the punch, but he looked like his pride was in pretty poor shape without hearing what might have been. Pity.

One hand pressed into his stomach, Kevin took several deep breaths with his eyes on the ground, clearly mentally assessing his injuries. When he finally looked up, he seemed angry but surprisingly calm.

If Marc had just been thrown into a wall by a single

punch, he'd have come up spittin' and swingin'. For that matter, so would I.

Kevin looked past me as if I weren't there, glaring at Marc. "You know, *I* wasn't the one who just suggested your girlfriend take her clothes off for cash." Although, actually, that's exactly what he'd done. "Maybe you should have taken your irritation out on *that* little prick."

"He's human," Marc growled, his fists still clenched. "He gets an automatic walk. Once. And since I don't plan to see him again, he'll probably live. But this is *your* last warning to watch your mouth—if you want to keep your canines."

A weak, hot breeze blew down the ally from the end opposite us, fluttering several scraps of paper and bringing with it the unmistakable stench of mold. When one of those scraps failed to settle into the shadows, my attention centered on the door Jeff had come through. A single sheet of paper flapped against the dented metal surface, hanging from a long strip of Scotch tape.

"Um, Marc?" I stepped carefully over a splintered crate on my way toward Forbidden Fruit's rear exit. "You're going to have to see the little prick again. Soon."

"What?" Glass crunched behind me as Marc's boot came down on a broken bottle. He stopped at my side, following my gaze to the homemade poster printed in black on hot-pink paper.

In the center of the page was a black-and-white photo of a stereotypically buxom blonde, smiling with her beautiful, thickly lashed eyes as well as her mouth. The caption at the top read, "Have you seen me?" Beneath the photo was the name "Kellie Tandy" and a list of her vital statistics. Below that, the poster read:

KELLIE VANISHED DURING HER SHIFT AT
FORBIDDEN FRUIT ON THURSDAY, SEPTEMBER
11TH, 2008.
IF YOU HAVE ANY INFORMATION REGARDING
HER WHEREABOUTS, PLEASE CALL 555-7648.
$$ REWARD $$
FOR ANY INFORMATION THAT HELPS US FIND
HER.

"Remember the bundle of ones in Bradley Moore's wallet?" I asked Marc, still staring at the poster. "The only building within five miles of that damn field was a strip club. Do you believe in coincidence?"

Marc shook his head slowly, and when his frown deepened, I knew he was thinking the same thing I was. "Harper wasn't at the Cajun Bar and Grill. He was at Forbidden Fruit."

Twelve

September 11th. The stripper had been missing for three days, since Thursday, the day we'd buried Bradley Moore in Arkansas. Then yesterday—Saturday—Parker and Holden found Robert Harper's body in the alley behind the missing stripper's place of employment. I saw no obvious connection, but like Marc, I didn't believe in coincidence.

Kevin focused on the picture of the missing girl, and his forehead crinkled in confusion. "Wait," he said, his voice rising in pitch as his words rushed out. "Greg said your men found a dead stray here. Guy named Harper. So who's Bradley Moore, and what does he have to do with some psycho killing Robby Harper? And what the hell does all *that* have to do with a missing stripper?"

My father had given Kevin only the information he needed to know, which included nothing about the foreign tabby or the body we'd buried in Arkansas.

"*Robby* Harper?" I asked, turning to watch Kevin through narrowed eyes as his familiar use of the dead stray's name sank in. I ignored his questions in favor of one of my own. "You knew him?"

Kevin shook his head as if to clear it. "Only by reputation. He…uh, used to sneak across the boundary line every so often to party in the Big Easy. Guess there's not much to do in rural Mississippi."

"And, of course, you reported him for trespassing, right?" I asked, already well aware that he hadn't.

Marc took a threatening step toward him, and Kevin shrugged, slouching back. "It didn't seem important enough to bother Greg about. Especially considering all the trouble he was having keeping tabs on *you*." He shot an accusing glance my way before turning his attention back to Marc, who represented the biggest threat. So far as *he* knew, anyway.

Kevin's last statement rang in my ears, and the hairs on the back of my neck bristled. My immediate impulse was to correct his misconception with my fist, but a slow, deep breath brought my temper back under control. See, I really was growing up. Mostly.

"He was *not* having trouble with me," I snapped. "And *you* should have reported Harper the minute he set *foot* in the south-central territory."

"Come on, Faythe." Kevin crossed his arms over his chest, as if unaware that Marc was prepared to maim him if he couldn't justify his failure to report the trespasser. "We all know you have your father over a barrel. You won't settle down with a decent tom, for no reason anyone else understands, and he can't make you, so the best he can do is try to keep tabs on you until you listen to reason and give him some heirs."

A grinding sound met my ears, and it took me a long moment to recognize it as the sound of my own teeth gnashing together. I was struggling to keep a grip on my rage, but that wasn't easy to do with Kevin flaunting the fact that my personal life was about as private as a celebrity sex video.

"Rumor has it your dad's had you under round-the-clock surveillance for the last *five years* just to keep you safe and in one place. If that's true, he's not only been consistently one man short, but he had to break up a team of enforcers to keep one man free to watch you prance around campus with all your college buddies. Greg hasn't had the manpower to check out every trespassing report in years. Because of *you*."

Even as I shook my head in denial, fury sending sparks of indignation up my spine, part of me wondered if he was right. Had I kept my father from doing his job? Had I forced him to divide his loyalties between me and the rest of the Pride? Had I compromised the security he worked so hard to give us all?

I hadn't meant for any of that to happen, for my decisions to affect everyone else so drastically. Yet they had. I'd just wanted a little freedom, but the entire Pride had paid for my liberty. If an ass-clown like Kevin Mitchell had seen that, why the hell hadn't I?

Fortunately, Kevin was so consumed in his own defense that he noticed neither my fury nor my self-doubt. "I was doing your father a favor." He crossed his arms, as if determined to make himself believe the load of cow shit he was shoveling. "I'm perfectly capable of keeping an eye on the odd stray who wanders across the border without having to bother Greg. If there was a real problem, I'd have given him a call. But there wasn't. I had it under control."

Marc took another step forward, and Kevin mirrored him with another step back, flinching and uncrossing his arms when he bumped into the Dumpster. Marc stared down at him, gold-flecked eyes glittering in rage and unspoken challenge. "Then how do you explain Harper winding up dead in an alley?"

Kevin held up his hands, palms out. "I had nothing to do with that. I wasn't here yesterday. I have no idea who killed him."

Stunned, I blinked at Kevin, and from the corner of my eye I saw Marc stiffen. He'd heard it, too. "You weren't here *yesterday?*" he growled. "Meaning you *were* here on other days? With Harper?"

Kevin stuttered as comprehension surfaced in his eyes. Finally, he understood how deep his pile of shit was. And he had no idea how to dig himself out of it.

"Spit it out, Kevin." I made no move to intercede as Marc closed in on him. Marc was the better bad cop, anyway—not because I couldn't carry it off, but because he wasn't believable as a good cop. "Did you and Harper go to Forbidden Fruit together? Were you strip-club buddies?"

"Don't bother. The answer's obvious," Marc spat, his voice dripping with disgust. He watched Kevin the way a cat watches a mouse he plans to play with, rather than eat. "The only thing I don't understand is why a prissy little snot like you would hang out with a scratch-fevered stray."

Kevin glanced at me around Marc's shoulder, having evidently decided I was the lesser threat. I saw no reason to disillusion him. "He paid me."

I cocked my head in mock confusion. "He paid you to hang out with him? Isn't that a little 'desperate-schoolboy'?"

Kevin glared at me, shaking his head as sweat dripped down his hairline. "He paid me to keep my mouth shut. To let him cross the lake and hang out in a city that doesn't roll up its sidewalks at 9:00 p.m."

"And you went with him?" I asked, prodding him on.

"Yeah, to keep an eye on him. So what if I got paid? Your dad should be paying me, anyway."

"Why weren't you with him yesterday?" Marc asked.

Kevin stared at the ground, nudging a broken bottle with one foot. "My boss called me in to work, so I couldn't go. I had no idea he was dead till Greg called last night."

Marc lunged forward, and his fists slammed into the Dumpster on either side of Kevin's head, leaving two deep dents in the metal. "If you're lying, you'll walk with a limp for the rest of your life."

Kevin glanced anxiously at Marc, then around him at me, and his left eyebrow began to tic. "It's the truth." Though he was clearly angry, his voice came out in a high-pitched whine. "You want to see my fucking check stub?"

Satisfied, Marc took a step back and dropped his hands to hang at his sides, but even then he was no less of a threat. He seemed to tower over Kevin, intimidating the smaller man with his very presence. "Do you know Kellie Tandy?" Marc's question lent credence to my own suspicion that the missing stripper was somehow involved.

"Only by sight. She's hot." Kevin paused and shrugged, looking at me over Marc's shoulder. "Well, I assume she's dead now, but she *was* hot."

Nausea rolled through me at his complete lack of sympathy for the missing girl. Diplomacy be damned, Kevin was inches away from stepping past my point of no return.

"You think Robby killed her?" he asked, completely unaware of my mounting irritation.

But his question gave me pause. I pushed damp strands of hair from my face, considering. I had no intention of answering him, but it would have been nice to actually *have* an answer. Did I think Harper had killed the stripper? Because if he'd attacked her at all, the only possible result would have been her death.

Okay, that wasn't the *only* possible result, but definitely the likely conclusion. But did I actually suspect him?

I wasn't sure. I couldn't see how Kellie Tandy fit in at all. Not yet, anyway. And if Harper had killed her, was it mere coincidence that *he'd* been killed only two days later?

"Have you ever seen any other cats in the strip club, stray or otherwise?" Marc asked, when I failed to respond to Kevin's question.

"Nah. There're only two others in the area, that I know of. The youngest Pierce boy goes to Loyola, but the college kids don't hang out around here. And Jamey Gardner lives near Baton Rouge, but I haven't seen him in nearly a year."

I nodded toward Forbidden Fruit's back door. "Do you know Jeff the pip-squeak?"

"Yeah. He's one of the bartenders. His brother owns the place."

"Did he know Harper?" Marc asked.

"I don't think Jeff knows either of us by name, but he'd probably recognize a picture. Or a description."

"Good." Marc stepped back from the Dumpster and from Kevin, gesturing toward the end of the alley. "Let's go find out what the pip-squeak saw yesterday."

I stood between Marc and Kevin in the foyer of Forbidden Fruit, bathing in the cool current of air flowing from the vent overhead. The artificial gust was quickly turning the sweat dripping down my spine into ice-cold rivulets, a transformation I welcomed.

We'd had to walk around to the front door in the one-hundred-three-degree heat, made worse by relative humidity hovering around the ninety percent mark. Luckily, the front door was unlocked, probably because the employees couldn't get in through the back door, either.

The interior of the strip club was visible through a wide archway, and the sticky vinyl floor, collection of cheap tables, and room-length bar were pretty much what I'd expected—minus the naked women. The club wouldn't actually open for ten more minutes, so the elevated dance platform was dark and empty. Thank goodness. The last thing our farce of an investigation needed was Kevin in a hormone-induced moronic frenzy.

Though the dancers had yet to shake their well-proportioned hindquarters into action, Jeff and another, taller man in an identical hot-pink shirt were hard at work behind the bar, drying glasses and counting cash register drawers. And judging from the smell of fried food, someone was busy in the kitchen. The sign out front had advertised a lunch special of "hot wings and hot girls," served with the drink of your choice.

And though my mouth felt dryer than a sand dune, the drink of my choice was any kind not served in the Forbidden Fruit.

As I watched Jeff-the-pip-squeak pour peanuts into a bowl on the bar, a short, busty woman walked past the foyer, barely dressed as a slutty version of Little Red Riding Hood. If she was looking for the Big Bad Wolf, she was out of luck.

"Sorry, boys, we're not open yet," Red said in a sultry Cajun accent, flashing a mouthful of small, bleached-white teeth at Kevin before she dismissed him entirely in favor of Marc. Only Marc. She hadn't even glanced at me. *Bitch*.

"I hate to ask you to leave, sugar," she said, batting her eyelashes at *my* boyfriend, her hands propped on the hips of a short, scarlet Lycra skirt. "But rules are rules. Come back in ten minutes, and I'll give you a show. Then I'll let you buy me a drink." She cocked her head to the side and tapped her full lower lip with the end of one long red fingernail. "Oh, hell, I'll buy *you* a drink."

Marc stared down into her eyes, and his lips curved up in a slow, seductive smile. "As tempting as that sounds, I'm not here for pleasure. Exclusively," he added, as if it were an afterthought. "My friend's here to see Jeff about a job."

My chin dropped into the cradle of my cleavage. Seriously. I nearly dislocated my jaw. And, of course, Kevin snickered, knowing he was safe for the moment because Marc wouldn't hit him in public. And because I stood between them.

"Your friend?" Little Red Riding Whore asked, her gaze sliding in my direction for the first time.

I snapped my jaw shut in a hurry and did my best to wipe the astonishment from my face. It went willingly, but anger swooped in to take its place. I was *not* applying for a job as a stripper. Not even to find out what happened to Robert Harper. And especially not in a club that couldn't account for all of its employees.

My teeth ground together as Red's eyes boldly roamed my body. I'd never been checked out by a woman before—that I knew of—and wasn't sure how to respond gracefully. Or if I should even bother.

Finally, she nodded, apparently satisfied by my appearance.

"So glad I meet your approval," I said, my voice thick with irony. Marc was the only one who caught my tone, and I was only sure about that because he kicked my sneaker when Red turned to glance over her shoulder at the bar.

"You shouldn't have much trouble convincing him to give

you a chance," she said, turning back to look at Marc, though she spoke to me. "We're short-handed right now, anyway."

"That's right," Marc said, as if he'd just remembered. "We saw the flyer about your missing dancer." Taped to the front window were three more posters identical to the one on the back door.

"Yeah, that was weird," Red said, her fake accent vanishing as genuine concern filled her eyes. Even her stance changed. She wrapped her arms around herself and bent one knee, balancing all of her weight on one red spiked heel.

"What was weird about it?"

She reached beneath her oversize, drooping red hood and withdrew a long strand of deep brown hair, twisting it around one thin finger. "Well—"

"*Vite,* Corinne! Five minutes!"

Red, whose name was evidently Corinne, glanced over her shoulder at a tall, thin man in another hot-pink T-shirt standing on the now well-lit stage.

"*Je viens!*" she called out, then mumbled, "Gimme a damn minute," under her breath as she turned back to face us. And by us, I mean *Marc.* "Honey, why don't we talk some more after my set, 'kay? Sit down and save me a seat, and I'll find you after I dance. *Oui?*"

"I guess I can spare a few minutes," Marc said, flashing a dazzling smile.

My hands curled into fists as she spun on her stupid, dangerously high heels and sashayed—yes, *sashayed,* swinging ass and everything—into the main room, curling a finger over one shoulder at Marc to beckon him forward.

How the hell does he do that? I thought as we followed Corinne to a booth against the back wall. Somehow, Marc had gotten a potential witness to *beg* him to question her. Over drinks. Without losing even a shred of dignity.

Yet I'd have to pretend to want to take my clothes off for money in front of a room full of strange men, just for a chance to drag some information out of the bartender. Fat chance.

Marc slipped into the curved booth, and Corinne bent to whisper something into his ear, her hand resting on his shoulder. Only she didn't really whisper anything. If she had, I'd have heard it. So whatever she did must have involved her tongue, rather than her voice box.

A warning look from Marc kept my mouth shut, but it didn't keep my fingernails—my short and unmanicured but very practical fingernails—from digging into my palms.

"Jeff, bring these gentlemen something to drink," the red-clad whore, excuse me, *exotic dancer,* called out on her way to a door marked Employees Only on the other side of the room. "And I think the girl with them wants a *word* with you." Somehow, she made that sound dirty, in spite of the fact that I was supposed to be applying for the very job she already had.

I shoved Marc over and sat next to him, repressing the over-whelming urge to express my displeasure aloud. Unfortu-nately, we were in public, in a manner of speaking, and I had no choice but to stick to the story Marc had made up for me. But he would pay later. Boy, would he pay.

"What'll it be?" Jeff called out, leaning on the bar with both palms flat against the polished surface.

"Whiskey and cola," Marc called, raising one eyebrow at Kevin, who'd taken a seat across the table from us. We had no rules against drinking on the job, because it takes a great deal of alcohol to impair a cat's judgment or coordination. And that was pretty damn convenient, considering that teetotalers didn't stand a chance in hell of blending into the crowd at a strip club. Especially a New Orleans strip club.

"Michelob," Kevin said, just as hidden speakers crackled from somewhere near the painted-black ceiling and grungy background music blared to life.

Only once the music was playing did I realize it had been missing before. That accounted for the uncomfortable, *exposed* feeling I'd had since walking through the front doors. Well, that, and the fact that I was in a strip club.

Not that the nudity bothered me. But the blatant advertisement for sex with perfect strangers made me a little uncomfortable, and while I knew there was a difference between nude dancing and prostitution, I was a little fuzzy on the legalities. And hoped to stay that way.

Less than a minute after the music began, the first real patrons came through the front door, a gaggle of men about my age, in neat civilian clothes with identical military haircuts—clearly a sample of our country's finest on leave from the nearby naval air station. They chose a table near the raised dance platform and sent an emissary to the bar to order their drinks.

As the bartender reached beneath the bar for a bottle, the background music screeched into silence, and bright lights burst to life at the foot of the stage. Seconds later, new music came over the speakers, louder and faster than the previous sample, and within four beats, Corinne pushed through a heavy black curtain and pranced onto the platform, almost completely covered by her red hooded cape. For the moment.

Immediately, the young men up front began hooting and laughing, daring one another to call Little Miss Hood closer.

"Here you go," Jeff-the-bartender said, less than a foot

from my left shoulder. I jumped, startled by his sudden appearance. I'd been so distracted by the spectacle of the only striptease I'd ever seen that I hadn't noticed a *human* approach. That was just sad.

Jeff set a short glass full of dark liquid in front of Marc, and a foaming mug of beer in front of Kevin. "Enjoy the show, guys," he said, then turned his attention to me. *All* of his attention. He dismissed Marc and Kevin the way Corinne had dismissed me. Selective vision must be contagious.

"You change your mind about that job?"

I glanced at Marc to see whether he intended to make me go through with the fake interview. He did. He shoved me half off the bench with a not-so-subtle thrust of one hip.

"Uh, yeah," I said, standing awkwardly to keep from falling to the floor.

Jeff grinned and took a second opportunity to appraise my…um…*qualifications*. He nodded, much as Corinne had, and gestured toward the bar. "Step into my office."

From the corner of my eye, I saw Marc tense, and knew he would watch me wind my way among the tables to make sure I wasn't actually going into another room. He'd make me play along, but he wouldn't let me out of sight. Or out of earshot.

I followed Jeff to the bar and took a seat on the backless stool he pulled out for me. To my surprise, instead of returning to his post behind the bar, he sat on the stool next to mine and swiveled to face me, his smile broad and a little too eager.

"The best part about my job is the preview of coming attractions. You're not shy, are you?"

I blinked at Jeff, then turned to face Marc, anger no doubt blazing in my eyes. "I'm going to kill you," I mouthed, but he only chuckled.

The joke's on you, I thought, swiveling to face the bar again. *It'll be a long time before I feel like taking my clothes off after this....*

Thirteen

Jeff's eyes wandered down from my face as he waited for my answer, and to my extreme frustration, I didn't feel justified complaining, because my assets were a legitimate part of the application process. So I said the first thing that popped into my head, just to draw his gaze back up.

"I need the money."

"Then you're in the right place, um…. I'm sorry, I didn't catch your name?"

"Julie." *Better than Jane Smith, right?*

"Okay, Julie…" Jeff grabbed a clipboard from the bar and slid it toward me along with a pen. "Let's get the paperwork out of the way first."

Paperwork? For strippers? My eyes widened as he peeled back the layers of documents to reveal an application, a W-4 form, a release form in case of personal injury, and an official-looking page outlining what the customers were and were not allowed to do, some of which were transgressions I'd never even *considered,* and flushed just thinking about.

After a lifetime of casual, nonsexual nudity among my fellow werecats—after all, I was *related* to most of the members of our household—I found the idea of flaunting my body for cash…*distasteful,* to say the least.

Jeff noticed my shell-shocked expression, and possibly the awkward way I held the clipboard, as if the metal clip might bite my fingers off. "First time?" he asked, forehead wrinkled as if in concern.

I nodded, lifting one thigh from the now-sticky vinyl, so I could cross my legs at the knees. It felt like a cross-your-legs kind of moment.

"Well, then I'll need to see you dance, of course. Do you have your own costume?"

I shook my head, and he smiled at the bewildered look on my face. "That's okay. We'll put our heads together and come up with an act for you. Are you allergic to feathers or double-sided tape?"

My blank look must have clued him in to my confusion.

"You know, personal adhesive?" His eyes wandered back down to my breasts, and suddenly I understood.

Personal adhesive? Eewww! Spinning around on my stool, I leveled a furious gaze at Marc from across the room, but he just smiled and waved. *You're gonna pay,* I mouthed, and he laughed, clearly enjoying my humiliation. Vicious bastard.

"Is that a 'no' on the feathers?" Jeff asked, and I nodded mutely. "Okay, we can do fur. You don't mind fur, do you?"

It was all I could do not to laugh in his face. "No, I don't mind fur, and I'm damn fond of claws," I said, more for Marc's benefit than Jeff's. In the booth, Marc spewed whiskey out his nose, spraying Kevin from the forehead down.

"Claws…" Jeff mumbled, clearly picturing an outfit I had

no urge to ever see. "I never considered putting claws on the cat costume. Kellie never thought of that."

Kellie? I shuddered at the realization that they were not only preparing to replace the missing stripper, but that they were ready to give away her outfit. I couldn't put on a dead girl's costume, much less dance around in it.

Jeff went on, oblivious to my reaction. "But then, she had long nails, kind of like claws. But for you—" he took my left hand in his and examined my ragged nails "—fake claws might be just the thing. Not too long or sharp, though. You want to turn the customers on, not scare them off."

That's what you *think....*

"Okay, go ahead and fill these out," Jeff said, standing as he glanced over the growing crowd in the club. "When you're done, we'll go back to my brother's office and you can show us what you've got." He grinned. "Normally we'd do that first, but something tells me you know exactly how to keep a man's attention."

Indeed I did. Get a tight grip on his balls. A man's attention never wandered far from his crotch, especially when it was in mortal jeopardy.

Stifling a smile, I nodded and picked up the pen, and Jeff went back behind the bar to help the other bartender keep up with a rush of drink orders.

What the hell do I do now? I thought, twirling the pen between my fingers. Marc would have already known Jeff's full name, rank, and serial number, whatever *that* was. At least, he would have if Jeff wore a skirt. Or a G-string.

A change in the music caught my attention, and I glanced at the stage to see a tiny Asian woman dancing in a brightly colored dragon costume that could, at best, be described as abstract.

Across the room, I found Marc and Kevin seated on either side of Little Red Riding Hood, now wearing a mostly see-through red nightie. She sat sideways on the semi-circular booth, angling her back to Kevin to give her full attention to Marc. Kevin didn't seem to care. He sipped his beer while he watched the dragon lady shed layer after layer of shiny scales.

By all appearances, Marc seemed glad to have Corinne's attention all to himself, and if I wasn't already certain of his disinterest in human women in general, I'd probably have fallen for his performance myself. After all, enforcers typically dealt with violent, angry strays, not beautiful, willing women.

I'd never seen Marc flirt with anyone else before, but he did it well. *Very* well. Fortunately, I was secure enough in myself and in our relationship to know that he was just doing his job. Marc thought of his appearance—his beautiful face and sculpted physique—the same way he thought of his teeth and claws: as just two more weapons in his personal arsenal. And he would never hesitate to use any weapon at his disposal if he deemed it necessary. Which made me wonder how far he'd be willing to go....

As far as it takes, a soft, treacherous voice spoke up from deep within my heart. *He'd do anything for the Pride, and you know it.*

Corinne had one hand on his bicep and one foot hooked around his calf beneath the table, and Marc seemed to be eating it up. He looked directly into her eyes, a courtesy I was pretty sure strippers rarely got at work, and leaned close to her, as if to better hear what she was saying over the loud music. That was just for show, of course. He could hear her perfectly well. Hell, *I* could have heard her if I'd concentrated. But I didn't, because while I knew he was only acting, doing his job for the good of the Pride, I had no desire to hear another woman tell my boyfriend how hot he was.

If I wanted him to know, I'd damn well tell him myself.

Then, as I tapped my pen on the bar, Marc began questioning Corinne. I knew when that moment came, even without listening for it, because her hand fell from his arm and her eyes dropped to the bright red drink on the table. As she spoke, presumably answering his questions, Corinne picked at the fingernails of one hand, her forearms resting on the table. Her expression had gone from cheerful and flirtatious to sad and worried. Which meant Marc was doing his job.

Inspired by his success, I glanced at the clipboard in front of me, considering my next move. How was it that Marc had gotten information out of his source, while I'd only gotten paperwork?

Fortunately, it wasn't too late to play the boob card against Jeff. Surely that would be easier than testing a patch of my skin for an allergy to double-sided tape.

But I couldn't do it. I couldn't flash my flesh in exchange for information. For my life, yes. I'd been down that road three months earlier, and vowed never to travel it again. And I wasn't willing to break my vow for mere information. I didn't fault Marc for flirting in the name of duty, but neither could I follow his example. That would be demeaning myself, and using Jeff, and I just couldn't do either.

I'd have to find another approach. An approach that left me with my clothes—and my self-respect—intact.

Slowly, an idea began to form. I'd already made up a name, so why not make up a story to go with my new character? What if Julie hadn't really come to Forbidden Fruit looking for a job? What if she'd come for something else?

When the rush was over and Jeff came back, I was ready.

"You forget how to spell your name?" he asked, nodding at the blank application as he set a bottle of spring water on the bar in front of me.

"Thanks." I stared at the bottle as I opened it and took a long drink, intentionally—and hopefully obviously—avoiding his eyes as I recapped the bottle and set it back on the bar.

"Something wrong?" he asked, ducking his head into my line of sight to catch my eyes.

I gave him a hesitant, self-conscious smile. "I, um, I'm not really here for a job."

Jeff arched one eyebrow and grabbed a handful of peanuts from a bowl on the bar. Leaning into the corner formed where the bar turned at a ninety-degree angle, he popped one of the nuts into his mouth, chewing while he watched me. "Okay, I'm intrigued. What *do* you want?"

Smiling, I let genuine relief show on my face. I'd been counting on his curiosity, which wasn't really such a risk. Most guys will take any chance to prolong a conversation with a pretty girl. Jeff wore no wedding ring, and I'd already gathered that he liked women, so the odds of him showing interest were in my favor.

Score one for *my* approach.

"Information," I said as I let my smile fade into a serious expression, with just enough anger to lend authenticity.

"Information? That's a new one." He paused to chew on a few more nuts, and I kept my eye contact bold to show determination. "What kind of information?" he asked, his mouth still half-full.

"I want to know who my husband is fucking."

Jeff choked on his mouthful, coughing to clear his throat. When he could breathe again, he laughed out loud, admiration showing in his eyes, hopefully for me, and not for my "husband." He dropped the remaining peanuts back into the bowl and brushed salt from his palms, glancing pointedly at my left hand. "You're not wearing a wedding ring."

"Would you, if your wife were screwing someone else?" I spat, maintaining eye contact to reinforce my sincerity. "Besides, I seriously doubt Robby wore his when he was here. Turnabout's fair play, right?" I shrugged, and tilted my water bottle back for another drink.

"So, who's your husband, and why do you think he's cheating on you?" he asked, leaning back to work on another handful of peanuts.

"My husband." I sighed, as if settling in for a long story. "Robby Harper, computer programmer and wanna-be stud. We've been married less than a year, and he's already looking for a little something extra on the side." I paused and gave a bitter laugh. "Well, as of last night, I guess he's not just looking anymore."

"And you know this because…?"

I glanced up sharply, letting a little bite seep into my tone. "Because he didn't even bother to shower before he came home. I could smell the bitch on him." *Oops.* "Her perfume," I added quickly, as it occurred to me that humans probably couldn't smell one another's personal scents the way cats could. "I think he met her here, and I want to know who she is." I made a show of glancing around the room, eyeing the dancer strutting around onstage in a Princess Leia bikini before turning back to Jeff.

He nodded in understanding. "I don't know many of the regulars by name, so you'll have to tell me what he looks like. But I can tell you right now that he probably wasn't with one of *our* girls. My brother runs this place by the book, and girls who break the rules don't last long."

I dismissed his opinion with a careless wave of my hand. I already knew I wasn't looking for a stripper. But Julie Harper didn't. "He's about five ten, with short brown hair and dark eyes. They're nearly black, actually."

Jeff frowned and shook his head. "I don't usually get close enough to the customers to notice their eye color, and other than that, you've just described a good third of our regulars. Anything else about him I might remember?"

I chewed on my bottom lip as I thought. "Yeah." I shifted on the bar stool, where my bare thighs were stuck to the vinyl again, and turned to face the booth where Marc and Kevin still sat with Corinne. "See those guys sitting with Little Red Riding Hood?" I turned around to see Jeff squinting into the dimly lit main room.

"Yeah."

"The one on the left is a friend of Robby's. They usually come in here together. Until last night, I thought they were going to the gun range."

Jeff nodded and popped another peanut into his mouth. He chewed, then swallowed while I waited, growing more nervous with each passing second. Then he nodded again. "Yeah, I remember your husband. He comes in a couple of times a month. Usually gets a lap dance from Ginger, the redhead in the coconut bra and grass miniskirt." I glanced around the room, trying to locate "Ginger," as Jeff continued. "But Ginger doesn't work the day shift, and yesterday your hubby was here for lunch. First one through the door. I remember because he left with the only female customer we've had all week. We get a few who come in on Friday and

Saturday nights with their husbands and boyfriends, but we hardly ever get women in for lunch. And they almost never come alone."

My heart pounded. He'd seen the tabby. And he remembered her. "Robby left with this woman?"

"Yeah. Maybe…an hour after we opened? Something like that."

I leaned over the bar, fighting not to appear too eager. "Do you know her name?"

"Nah. I'd never seen her before yesterday. She drank a club soda, though. Ordered it with this really thick, sexy accent. Spanish, maybe."

"Do you remember what she looked like?"

Jeff frowned, as if I'd just asked him if sugar was sweet. "I'll *never* forget what she looked like. She was *hot.*"

I rolled my eyes, prepared for a bit of exaggeration in his response. After all, he'd offered *me* a job as a stripper. How high could his standards be? "Got anything more specific than 'hot'?"

"Yeah, sorry." And he actually looked sorry. Or at least sheepish. "She was about your height, maybe a little shorter. Dark, exotic skin. Long, curly hair, not quite as black as yours, but still pretty dark. Pale gray eyes. Weird-pale, but beautiful. *Her* eyes I noticed. I remember when she left because I'd been about to offer her a drink on the house, then I looked up to see her heading out the door with…well, with your husband." Jeff shrugged apologetically. "Did that help?"

"Yeah. Thanks." I stood, already turning to go.

"Hey, what are you gonna do when you find her?"

I answered him beneath my breath. "I'm gonna use up a few of her nine lives."

Fourteen

I thanked Jeff for his help and caught Marc's eye from across the room. He raised one brow at me in question, and I tossed my head toward the entrance to tell him I was ready to go. He gave me a single, brief nod and tapped Kevin on the shoulder. Together, they stood, and Corinne slid out of the booth behind Marc. He offered her his hand, but she hugged him instead, standing on her toes to whisper something in his ear. Her lips actually moved that time, but I didn't want to know what she was saying, so I turned and wound my way through a jumble of tables, heading toward the door.

We had lunch at the Cajun Bar and Grill, where Marc and I exchanged information over spicy jambalaya, doing our best to ignore Kevin's interruptions. He was working overtime to get on our collective good side, but he might as well have saved his breath. We'd be reporting him to my father even if he'd been able to hand over the murdering tabby bound and gagged.

After lunch, Kevin drove us across the Mississippi border into Picayune, where we found Robert Harper's apartment with little trouble. He lived on the second floor, next door to Mrs. Grady, a friendly—and obviously bored—senior citizen who would have been more than happy to help Robby's best friends and his little sister, Julie, make up the guest list for his surprise birthday party. Unfortunately, she didn't know the names of any of his numerous lady friends.

According to Mrs. Grady, Harper'd had frequent overnight guests in the four years he'd lived next door, but none had stayed more than one night, and none of them came even close to fitting the tabby's description. Evidently big brother Robby had a thing for redheads, and while he'd settle for a blonde in a pinch, he'd never shown any interest in brunettes.

However, according to Jeff's description of the woman seen with Harper the day before, it was obvious that species trumped hair color any day of the week.

When we'd gathered everything we could from Mrs. Grady, Marc and I left Kevin in the hall listening to her party-menu suggestions while we used Julie's key—which had actually come from Harper's own pocket—to check out the apartment. We discovered nothing more interesting than a massive pile of dirty laundry and an unhealthy fondness for SPAM and SpaghettiOs.

We rescued Kevin from Mrs. Grady, reluctantly, and he drove us back into New Orleans, where we made a short stop for beignets and cafés au lait before heading out to catch our flight home. At the airport, Kevin pulled into a space in short-term parking and popped the trunk without getting out. I got out on the passenger side and circled around to grab our small bags from the back while Marc knelt to have a final word with Kevin through the lowered driver's window.

"Stay close to home and keep your phone within reach."

Marc's voice was low and amazingly professional. "You'll be getting a call from Greg very soon."

"Hey, it doesn't have to be like that," Kevin whispered. "There's no reason to involve Greg in this. I'm sure we can work something out, just between the two of us."

"No," Marc said. "We can't." He stood and turned his back on the prick behind the wheel, accepting the bag I handed him.

"…think you're so much better than me," Kevin hissed at Marc, when we were several feet from the car. "*Faythe's* the only reason you're even here. Without her, you're just another stray cat licking the Alpha's boots, one false move away from the wrong side of the river."

"What did he say?" I demanded, turning back to face our idiot of an escort. But by the time I had him in sight, Marc was already beside the car, swinging a rare left-handed punch, because of the angle of the open window. His fist smashed into Kevin's nose. Blood spurted all over the steering wheel, the windshield, and the front of Kevin's shirt.

Kevin was too busy spitting out his own blood to scream, and Marc turned back toward me calmly, already wiping blood from his fist with a wet wipe from his backpack. He threw the wipe in the nearest trash can, and we continued on into the airport without another word.

I finally thought to turn my cell phone ringer back on and check my voice mail at the gate, as we waited to board the plane. There were two. Messages, not planes.

The first was from my father, telling me he'd sent Vic and Owen after yet another body, following a second tip by the same anonymous informant. They'd gone to Pickering, a tiny Louisiana town near the western edge of the Calcasieu Ranger

District of the Kisatchie National Forest. Marc had a similar message on his own voice mail.

My hand began to shake when I saw the number the second voice mail had come from. *Andrew.* Shit. I waited to listen to the message until Marc ducked into the men's room nearest our gate.

"I got your message, Faythe. If I didn't know any better, I'd say you—" His voice was interrupted by a series of loud pops or explosions, followed by the distinctive *thwup, thwup, thwup* of blades beating the air, like the rotors on a helicopter, only older and more rickety-sounding. And when silence settled in again, he went on, as if he'd never been interrupted. "—you don't want to see me. But I'm looking forward to seeing you. Won't be long now." His next words were swallowed by another series of booms, just as Marc came out of the men's room, heading right for me. Smiling, I flipped the phone shut and shoved it into my pocket as he sank into the molded plastic airport chair on my right.

This had gone too far. I would have to tell both Marc and my father about Andrew; there was no getting around that now. But I couldn't do it in the airport, or on the plane. Marc was *not* going to react well, and shouldn't be cooped up on a plane full of humans when he found out.

I'd tell him later, when we were alone together. Then my father.

It was going to be a long night.

By nine o'clock that evening, Marc and I were back at the ranch. My mother had held dinner for us, so the entire household—minus Vic and Owen—sat around the eight-foot dining-room table, eating baked halibut and listening to our report.

"So, Harper left with the tabby voluntarily?" Jace asked, stabbing two spears of asparagus with his fork.

"So it would appear." I stirred sugar into my tea as I continued. "According to Jeff-the-bartender, she was more than adequately equipped to lure any man away from his favorite stripper. Or his wife. A regular siren on two legs. Jeff didn't know her name, but he gave me a good physical description. She's my height. Maybe a little shorter. Long, dark, curly hair. Pale grayish eyes. Dark, exotic skin. And he said she was hot, which I assume means she's curvy." *Or maybe that she's all ready to burn in hell for her crimes.*

Ethan's eyes lit up, and I rolled my own. I should have known he'd care more about the tabby's build than the fact that she'd already murdered at least two toms. I occupied my mouth with a bite of fish to keep from telling him exactly how screwed up I thought his priorities were. He wouldn't listen to me, anyway.

Ignoring my hormone-challenged brother, I looked toward the end of the table, where my father had sat for the past fifteen minutes, chewing quietly as he listened to my informal report. "What did your Venezuelan contact have to say?"

He set his fork on the edge of his plate and wiped his mouth with a cloth napkin. "Nothing yet, but I expect to hear something soon. Until then, all we have to go on is your description."

"Wonderful." I frowned down at my halibut.

"It's a start, which is more than we had before," Parker said, cutting into a slice of scalloped potatoes with the side of his fork. "But I can't believe Kevin Mitchell knew Harper was trespassing and didn't report it. You'd think he'd know better than that."

"Yeah, you'd think," I mumbled, pushing my asparagus around in a puddle of hollandaise. I wasn't exactly eager to tell my father that Kevin blamed me for our lack of manpower. Fortunately, Marc seemed disinclined to mention it, too. I'd have to remember to thank him—after I kicked the shit out of him for trying to turn me into a stripper.

"By the way, I told Kevin to expect a call from you, Greg," Marc said. "Very soon."

"Oh, he'll get more than a call." My father's hand paused, his fork halfway to his mouth. "When this is over, he'll get an escort to the Mississippi border and instructions to wait in the free zone until his father decides what to do with him. I'll be on the phone to David Mitchell as soon as we finish here."

At the other end of the table, my mother cleared her throat politely to get our attention. "What about this missing dancer?"

"Her name is Kellie Tandy, and she goes to Tulane on a partial scholarship," Marc said. "A couple of years ago she was looking for a better-paying job to help make up for what the scholarship doesn't cover, and her roommate convinced her to audition at Forbidden Fruit.

"When Kellie disappeared before her second set, her roommate—Ginger—called the police. They showed up at the club a couple of hours later and asked questions, and took a picture of Kellie for their file. But that was it. They seemed to think Kellie would show up in a few hours, and they told the roommate to go back to their apartment and wait."

"I assume she never showed up?" Ethan asked around a mouthful of fish.

"Right. The next day, when the police said they were doing everything they could, the roommate made up the missing person poster on her own and took up a collection from the other dancers and the Forbidden Fruit management to offer as a reward."

"What about her family?" Parker asked. "Can't her parents put some pressure on the cops?"

"She doesn't have any parents," I said, because Marc was busy chewing.

He swallowed and took a drink to clear his throat. "They died when she was sixteen, and she spent her last year and a half of high school in foster care, because her two remaining grandparents were too old to take her in. She's a favorite among the other dancers."

Marc's expression was professionally detached, but I knew him too well to believe what I saw on his face. Hearing about her parents had made Marc determined to find out what happened to Kellie. He had a soft spot for orphans, because when he was fourteen, his mother was killed by the same stray who'd infected him.

"Okay, let me see if I understand everything correctly." My father pushed his empty plate forward and leaned back in his chair. "Kellie Tandy goes missing from Forbidden Fruit in New Orleans on Thursday—the same day Bradley Moore is murdered in Arkansas—but the police won't look for her. On Saturday, Robert Harper is lured out of that same strip club by the rogue tabby, who breaks his neck in the alley and leaves the body buried in garbage. Less than two hours later, Parker and Holden find the body and bring it back to us." He glanced around the table, waiting for a response.

"Sounds right to me," I said.

"Me, too," Jace spoke up, while everyone else nodded.

Except my mother. She pushed back her chair and disappeared into the kitchen without a word. Seconds later she was back with a homemade strawberry cheesecake, which she began cutting on the oak sideboard against one wall.

"So we're just supposed to believe it's all coincidence?" Ethan asked, taking the dessert plate my mother handed him and passing it to Jace, who passed it to Parker, who passed it on to my father. "All this happens at one strip club in New Orleans, but we can't figure out how it's related, if it even is. But it has to be, doesn't it?"

I shrugged, watching as they passed down another plate. "Well, it didn't *all* happen at Forbidden Fruit."

"What do you mean?" Jace asked.

Marc answered for me, placing a slice of cheesecake on my place mat. "Bradley Moore died four miles or so from another strip club in Arkansas. He had a stack of ones in his wallet."

Ethan glanced from him to our father. "So this is about strip clubs?"

"No." My mother set her knife and pie server in the empty half of the glass pie plate, frowning at her youngest son as if he'd just told her the earth was flat. "I would bet the location is largely irrelevant. At least to the tabby. She started in eastern Arkansas—as far as we know, anyway—then moved down to New Orleans, and in both cases she seems to have lured a stray from a strip club to kill him. But why would she go into a strip club? Why would a woman go to a strip club alone? Not just a tabby, but any woman?"

Her gaze swept up and down the table, looking at each of us in turn, including my father. No one answered, and in the silence, the low growl of a car engine rumbled from outside; Owen and Vic were back with the van.

"Faythe?" my mother asked, bringing my attention back on track as she narrowed her eyes at me. Why was she picking on *me?* No one else knew the answer, either. "Why would *you* go to a strip club?"

I frowned, trying without success to follow her logic. "I wouldn't."

"You went to one today," she pointed out, her voice infuriatingly matter-of-fact, as if her statement were perfectly logical rather than a distortion of the truth.

"That doesn't count. I was working. I went in to question the bartender."

She nodded, apparently pleased with my answer, and picked up the silver pie server to gesture with as she spoke. "So you went into a strip club looking for a man?"

"Not like *that,*" I insisted. "I wasn't looking for a date."

"Did these men die of romance?" she asked, mercifully shifting her attention away from me. "Were they killed with too much wine and candlelight?" No one answered, but my father sat back in his chair and crossed his arms over his chest, glowing with pride as he watched his wife at work. "No, because this tabby wasn't looking for a date, either."

"She was working, too," Marc said. "Looking for someone." He was the first to catch on, though my father was nodding, as if he agreed. "Maybe Moore and Harper, or maybe someone else. Either way, she was hunting."

In the foyer, the front door creaked open and Owen's boots thumped on the tile.

Jace glanced from Marc to my mother, lowering his fork to the table with a bite of cheesecake still speared on the end. "She's hunting strays?"

"Not exclusively," Owen said from the dining-room

doorway, his worn cowboy hat hanging from one fist. He leaned against the door frame, and Vic stopped just behind him, his expression grim, his cheek streaked with dirt.

My father pushed his chair back and glanced at his watch. "I didn't expect you back for at least another hour."

"It's amazing how much time you can save by not burying the body," Vic said, pushing past Owen and into the room. "This time she got one of ours. Jamey Gardner. We brought him back for a proper burial."

The dining room erupted into a frenzy of questions and angry exclamations as we vented rage at the murder of one of our own Pride members. My father didn't bother trying to speak over us. He simply stood and walked calmly from the dining room into his office across the hall. The racket around the table faded into silence as we all hopped up to follow him.

Marc and I sank onto the love seat and everyone else settled into place around us. No one said a word. We knew better than to start shouting questions in our Alpha's office, no matter how upset we were. Instead, we listened as he spoke on the phone, hoping the answers to our questions would be revealed in the course of the overheard conversations.

The first phone call went to Michael, my oldest brother. Michael hadn't worked as an enforcer in nearly eleven years, but during times of crisis, my father never hesitated to call him home to help. Michael was a genius at organization and resource management, and much more comfortable than the rest of us were with toggling multiple phone lines and scouring the Internet for information. Having just been made partner in a local law firm, he was also our eyes and ears in the legal community.

The phone call to Michael was predictably short and to the point.

"What's wrong?" my brother asked in lieu of a greeting.

"Call your boss and tell him you need a personal day tomorrow. Then come on over. I'll explain when you get here."

"Give me half an hour."

"Good." My father dropped the phone back into its slim black cradle, then sank into his desk chair, already flipping through his leather-bound address book for the next number. As he dialed, Ethan curled up on the floor at my feet, playing with the frayed edge of the rug, his head resting on my knee. Jace sat on his other side, leaning against one leg of a heavy oak end table.

"Wes? It's Greg." My father leaned forward in his chair, the phone pressed to his ear again. He paused as a disembodied voice greeted him from the earpiece and asked about his health. Wesley Gardner was Jamey's older brother, and Alpha of the Great Lakes Pride. "I'm fine," my father said, staring at his desk blotter as he rubbed his forehead. "But I have some bad news about Jamey."

For a long moment, there was only silence, broken by the occasional crackle of static on the line and the creak of leather as Owen shifted on the couch across from me and Marc, his hat in his lap. When Wes finally spoke, the pain in his voice was obvious, even over hundreds of miles of wire. "How did it happen?"

My father sighed, still staring down at his desk. We all knew how much he dreaded this part of his job, and I was grateful he hadn't delegated the responsibility to one of us. Namely me.

"I'm not sure yet. We got an anonymous tip about a body near Kisatchie National Forest in Louisiana. It turned out to be Jamey. I'm so sorry, Wes. We're doing everything we can to catch the…one responsible."

I glanced at Marc, surprised by my father's failure to mention the killer's gender—the most noteworthy aspect of the case by far. But Marc didn't even seem to notice. Withholding information during an ongoing investigation was standard procedure, but Wes was the victim's brother, for goodness' sake, not some random Pride member.

"How do you want us to handle the burial?" my father asked.

Wes sighed. "We'll come get him. I'll call you back with the flight information once I make the reservations."

"Let me know if there's anything I can do."

"I will. Thanks, Greg."

My father hung up the phone and leaned back in his chair, hands crossed over his stomach, eyes closed. He looked angry. And very, very tired. "Okay, Vic, Owen, tell us what happened."

Vic looked at Owen and shrugged, so Owen started, shifting again on the couch to face our Alpha, who didn't even open his eyes. "There's not much to tell. The body was just where the caller said it would be. He was covered in leaves and loose dirt, so we couldn't see his face at first, but we knew it was Jamey right away. From his scent." Owen glanced at Vic again before continuing. "We could smell her, too. This time we knew what to look for from the scent. And it was fresh."

"Injuries?" my father asked, his eyes still closed.

Owen curled the brim of his hat in both hands. "Nothin' but the broken neck, just like the others."

My father nodded, acknowledging the information, but before he could say anything else, the clicking of my mother's heels sounded in the hallway, accompanied by the rich aroma of good coffee.

Seconds later she appeared in the doorway, carrying a

silver tray full of steaming mugs. Without a word, she crossed the room and set the tray on one corner of my father's desk, then began passing out individual cups.

In that moment, as I accepted a fresh mug of coffee—loaded with sugar and vanilla-flavored creamer, just the way I liked it—I could have kissed my mother. Even though she'd finished cleaning the kitchen before joining the important meeting. Even though she'd just served drinks from a silver tray to a room full of mostly men. And even though she'd done it in a demure skirt and two-inch heels.

At the moment, I was too grateful for the caffeine to ruin her nice gesture by telling her we were perfectly capable of getting our own coffee. So, I just smiled and thanked her. And gave myself a mental pat on the back for passing up an opportunity to argue with my mother and gloat over the fact that I hadn't grown up to be just like her.

"Anything else?" my father asked Vic, nodding at my mother in thanks as he took the mug she offered. She nodded back and accepted the seat on the couch that Parker—ever the gentleman—gave up for her.

Owen nodded as Parker settled onto the floor at his feet. My father's armchair was empty, but none of us would have dared sit in it. "There was a third scent on Jamey's body. A stray. Neither of us recognized it." He glanced around the room, taking in our individual reactions. "I'm sure it doesn't mean anything. He probably just came into contact with a stray at some point today."

Marc frowned and set his mug on the end table to his right. "Are you sure it wasn't Harper's scent?" he asked, and I knew what he was thinking. Instead of reporting Robert Harper's indiscretions, Kevin had helped cover them up, and as much as I hated to consider it, we couldn't ignore the possibility that Jamey had been doing something similar. Maybe that was why my father had withheld information from Jamey's brother.

"We're sure," Vic said. "We all got a good whiff of Harper last night, and this definitely wasn't him."

My father sat up straight, listening to the crunch of Michael's tires on gravel out front. A dark frown settled over his face as he stood and set his half-empty coffee mug on his desk blotter. "This is the third time this rogue tabby has killed someone in our territory in as many days, and now that she's gone after a Pride cat, the council can no longer pretend she's doing us a favor."

He popped the knuckles of his right hand, and the resulting crack seemed to echo throughout the room. "I can get enough votes for a combined effort now. The other Alphas will have to do something to prove they care. But the council will resist being forced into action, and every minute they spend dragging their heels and pointing fingers is another minute added to the tabby's head start. She's hunting in *our* territory, and we can't afford to wait on the council to find her." He took a deep breath before continuing. "So…we're going to apprise them of the situation, as we're obligated to do. Then, while they twiddle their thumbs, we're going after her on our own." He paused, glancing at each of us individually, determination etched into every line of his face. "Does everyone understand?"

Hell yeah, we understood! Our Alpha was going vigilante. As the tips of my fingers began to tingle with excitement, I realized that for the first time in years, I was truly pleased to call myself my father's daughter.

Fifteen

Outside, my father and Michael marched down the gravel driveway side by side, their backs illuminated only by the front porch light because the moon and most of the stars were hidden by a thick covering of clouds. The rest of us trailed behind them. Except for my mother, who'd stayed behind.

Clad in his typical off-work uniform of khaki slacks and a navy polo shirt, Michael listened without a word as our father went over the specifics of the case for him. His pace never slowed, and his step never faltered—until he heard about Jamey Gardner. The instant he heard Jamey's name, he seemed to trip over nothing, regaining his usual grace and poise an instant later. He and Jamey had been childhood friends, not quite as close as Jace and Ethan, but more than just acquaintances.

"You're sure it was a woman?" Michael asked, his stride once again smooth, but noticeably quicker and more determined.

My father nodded. "We have a working description, but no idea who she is or why she's targeting toms in our territory.

Or where she came from, though we're guessing somewhere in South America, based on the scent."

The barn rose before us at the end of the dirt path running down the center of the western field. In my childhood, it had been my secret retreat, but instead of afternoons spent in the company of Oliver Twist and Jane Eyre, I now associated the smell of fresh hay with death and decay, because for the second time in as many days, we were using the barn as a makeshift morgue.

With a stoic heave, and not so much as a grunt, my father pulled opened the big double barn doors. Again. And again we filed in after him. But this time, as Owen and Vic unloaded the plastic-wrapped bundle from the back of the van, my father gave directions to Jace and Ethan, who scampered up to the loft to push down the only three hay bales left over from last season. We weren't going to put the body of a Pride member—a man who'd spent several childhood summers on our ranch—on the floor.

"The most obvious starting point is the unidentified stray scent on Jamey's body," my father said in his Alpha voice, as Owen carefully peeled strips of duct tape from the plastic. "I'm willing to bet this stray is our anonymous informant, and that he saw Jamey with the tabby. With any luck, he'll have some useful information for us—like her name, and where she's going. So the first order of business is to identify this stray."

When the sheet of black plastic draping Jamey's body fell open, a limp hand fell with it, hanging to brush the side of the hay bale. It looked for all the world like an image from a cheesy horror movie, and was every bit as surreal.

Owen clomped forward in his boots to gently lay Jamey's hand over his stomach. As thoughtful as the gesture was, it didn't really help. There's only so much you can do to make the sight of a dead companion easier to accept. Especially under such gruesome circumstances.

My father came forward first, while the rest of us stood watching him with our hands in our pockets. He stood silently at Jamey's side, as if to say his final goodbye, but I could tell by the rise and fall of his chest that he was breathing deeply to take in the scent. He would no more lean down and blatantly sniff Jamey's corpse than he would lay him on the floor. Or leave him exposed as a meal for nature's scavengers.

Finally, he stepped back and shook his head. "I don't recognize the scent, but that's not really surprising. I can't remember the last time I saw a stray in person. A live stray, anyway."

I glanced at Marc in amusement, and he smiled back. My father probably didn't even realize his mistake; he truly never thought of Marc as a stray. He thought of Marc as a son.

Michael came forward next and actually took Jamey's hand in his own. I knew in seconds that he hadn't recognized the scent, because when his breathing resumed its normal rhythm, he didn't offer us any information. Yet he stayed with Jamey for almost a full minute, staring down at his friend's face as if he were lost in some distant memory.

Eventually, Michael shook his head and retreated silently to a spot near the door. To avoid looking at anyone, he cleaned the wire-rimmed glasses he only wore for show. Marc and I stepped into the space he'd vacated. Marc inhaled deeply, and I did the same.

Then I froze.

Son of a bitch! My fingers clenched around Marc's, and his knuckles popped in rapid succession. He yelped in pain and tried to pull back his hand. I barely noticed. When my hand relaxed, his fingers slipped from my grasp. He rubbed his bruised knuckles, smiling broadly at me. He'd identified it, too.

"You recognize the scent?" Michael asked, his voice sharp and clearly skeptical.

I nodded, and Marc's smile widened even further.

My father arched both eyebrows, already impatient with the suspense. "Well?"

"Dan Painter," I said, excitement making a breathless whisper of my voice. Things were finally starting to make sense. *Some* things, anyway.

Ethan shook his head. "What the hell is Painter's scent doing on Jamey Gardner?"

I indulged in a gloating smile, thrilled to be more in-the-know than he was for once. "Clearly Painter is the anonymous informer."

Owen frowned, shifting his hat back and forth on his head. "That's not quite as clear as you seem to think it is, sis," he drawled. "At least not to me."

"I second that." Parker's gaze flicked uncertainly from me to Marc.

"Let me see if I'm understanding this correctly," Vic began, propping one arm on top of the nearest stall door. "Greg's been getting anonymous phone calls, all from the same man, reporting the rogue tabby's kills and telling us where to find them."

"So far, so good." I winked at him for good measure.

"Thanks." He glanced at my father, then continued. "Presumably, this caller has been following the tabby around, watching her. And now you think he's this Dan Painter fellow. The same stray you guys caught and released in Arkansas, what? Three days ago?"

"Right." Marc nodded.

Yet I felt compelled to correct one minor misunderstanding. "Actually, *I* caught Painter. Me. All alone."

Vic grinned. "My mistake." I smiled in acknowledgment, and he continued. "So, we think Painter is spying on the tabby, then ratting her out. But do we think she had something to do with the missing stripper, too?"

"The tabby couldn't have killed her. Or taken her, or whatever," Jace said. "Tandy went missing on Thursday night, around the time the tabby was busy killing Bradley Moore. In Arkansas. She didn't get to New Orleans—that we know of—for two more days."

"So what does the missing stripper have to do with the dead strays? Or toms?" Ethan frowned, looking at the body laid out on the bales of hay. "I guess they're not just strays anymore."

"Maybe nothing," my father said. "But maybe…" He turned to face Michael, tired eyes now bright with unspoken ideas. "When we get in, I want you to do a search for missing strippers in Arkansas and Louisiana. Mississippi and Texas, too."

Michael nodded. "No problem. You're thinking there may be more missing than just the girl from New Orleans?"

"I'm not sure yet, but I think your mother's right. The tabby's looking for something. Some*one*. Maybe she's looking for whoever took Kellie Tandy."

Marc reached out for me, and I let him pull me close. "That would explain why she's two days behind whoever took Tandy," he said. "She's tracking him."

"No way." I shook my head and felt my hair rub against Marc's shirt. "There's no possible way she could have tracked anyone that far." It was *incredibly* difficult for one cat to track another across long distances. In the forest, it wasn't so bad— our ears are very sharp, and the slightest sound can give away your position. However, over long distances, it's virtually impossible. Cats can't track with their noses like dogs can. And even if we could, we'd lose the trail the moment our prey got into his car. "Besides, that doesn't explain why she's killed three toms in less than a week."

My father clasped his hands behind his back, frowning in thought. "No, it doesn't, and such long-distance tracking does seem pretty far-fetched, but without more to go on, I can't see how else Kellie Tandy could be connected to the tabby."

"Well, shi—!" Ethan shouted, snapping his mouth closed abruptly when he realized he'd almost cussed in front of his Alpha.

"What?" our father asked, waving off the social gaffe.

"I just realized that if Marc and Faythe had brought Painter back with them for questioning, instead of releasing him, we'd probably have known who the rogue tabby is three days ago."

Well, hell. I could feel my cheeks begin to burn. Ethan was right.

Excuses tumbled around in my brain, and several jumped immediately into the spotlight, ready for use. But my father beat me to it.

"It's not your fault," he said, taking in both Marc and me with his gaze. "I told you to release him. You did the right thing."

I nodded, thankful for his reassurance, but couldn't help feeling like I'd made a big mistake. *Another* big mistake. Which only reminded me of the one I hadn't yet disclosed to either him or Marc.

"Did Painter say anything…I don't know…*important*, while you were driving him to the border?" Parker asked.

"Um, no." Marc held me tight against his chest. "He was unconscious."

Michael pushed his glasses—which I suspected were just to make him look smarter—farther up on his nose. "Unconscious? How did he happen to lose consciousness?"

"I…kind of knocked him out." I shrugged sheepishly when Michael frowned. "He got vulgar, talking about chasing a piece of…*tail*. So I…" I swung my arm up, in imitation of my prize-winning right hook. But my fist froze in midair and my words trailed off, as what I'd been saying finally sank in.

Chasing a piece of ass. He'd said he was chasing a piece of ass.

"He meant the tabby," I whispered, too surprised to manage any real volume. But it didn't matter. They all heard me. "Painter was chasing the rogue tabby, and I knocked him out before he could tell us about her."

Outside, cicadas chirruped, filling the silence as everyone but Marc stared at me in complete disbelief.

Then Ethan snorted. "Isn't *that* a bitch?" He grinned, his expression one of dark amusement—as if he appreciated the irony—rather than actual anger. But I would have understood anger. I'd screwed up the entire investigation, before I even knew there *was* one.

"I swear on my life that I do *not* do these things on purpose," I said, letting my head fall back to rest on Marc's shoulder as his arms wrapped around me. I hated feeling like my fellow Pride members spent most of their time cleaning up my mistakes. I was better than that, and I wanted them all to know it.

"Of course you don't," Jace said. I lifted my head to look at him, encouraged by the understanding in his voice, and was even more relieved to find sympathy in his eyes. "You had no way of knowing all this was going on. You didn't do anything wrong."

"She didn't do anything right, either," Michael mumbled, still staring at the body of his childhood friend. I wanted to snap at him but resisted the impulse. I wasn't the real source of his anger; that much was obvious.

"Jace is right," my father said, eyeing Michael in compassion, rather than irritation. "She couldn't possibly have known." Bending, he reached for the plastic hanging over the bales of hay from beneath Jamey Gardner's body. He pulled up first one side, then the other, until Jamey was completely and respectfully covered.

Standing, my father headed for the door, motioning for Michael to join him. "You can use the computer in my office to run a search on missing strippers. I want names, locations, dates they went missing, ages, and anything else that might be relevant. Get pictures, if you can find them."

Michael took off through the western field at a jog, headed toward the main house.

"Ethan, you and Jace go fill your mother in on what we have so far, and see if she's thought of anything else we can use."

Ethan nodded, and he and Jace took off down the dirt path, behind Michael.

My father turned to me and Marc next, and my hands began to sweat from dread that he would put us on another plane. Fortunately, he had something else in mind. "Will you recognize Dan Painter's voice if you hear it again?"

"Yes," I said without hesitation. And Marc's chest shifted slightly at my back as he nodded.

"The informant got my machine both times he called, and I saved the messages." My father paused, looking deeply into my eyes to convey the importance of what he was about to say. "I want you two to listen to them and tell me whether or not the voice on the machine belongs to Dan Painter. We have to confirm the informant's identity before we proceed any further, because if he isn't Painter, we're looking at this all wrong."

"No problem," Marc said.

My father nodded, satisfied. "Good. Go."

Marc and I headed toward the house together, while Owen, Vic, and Parker hung back to hear whatever instructions our Alpha had for them. A warm summer breeze blew through my hair as we walked through the field, bringing with it the scent of summer wheat, dirt, and trees. And Marc, because he was upwind from me, though only by an inch or so.

"Jace is right," he said, probably unaware how odd that statement sounded, coming from him. "You didn't do anything wrong. This is not your fault."

"The hell it isn't." I refused to look at him, staring straight ahead at the house, rising slowly from the waist-high field of grass around us. "If I hadn't knocked Painter out, Jamey and Harper would both still be alive right now."

Marc stopped abruptly, turning me by my shoulders to look at him. "Maybe. They *might* still be alive. Or, we might have learned what the tabby looks like, and nothing else. You don't know that Painter could have given her to us. And you don't know that we could have stopped her."

True. I didn't know that for sure. But I felt it with every beat of my heart. I'd messed up. Bad.

I'd made a lot of stupid mistakes in my life—hell, most of them in the past few months alone—but I'd never been responsible for an innocent person's death before. Not even indirectly. And the guilt from knowing I might have saved

Robert Harper and Jamey Gardner was making me sick to my stomach. As in, seriously nauseated.

And unbelievably pissed off. When we found this tabby, she'd get much more than a piece of my mind. She'd get a piece of my fist—right through her pretty little neck.

In the office, Michael sat behind our father's desk, clicking away at the computer with his right hand, and making notes with his left. *Ambidextrous freak.* He nodded at us when we came in, then went right back to work.

I made my way straight to the massive oak desk, while Marc settled onto the leather love seat. "Hey, Michael, where's Holly?" he asked, twisting to face us both.

"Rome, for two more days," Michael replied, without ever taking his eyes from the screen.

"Wasn't she just there last month?"

"That was Venice, in July."

"Oh." Marc winked at me. While most of the other guys were predictably envious of Michael's wife—an actual twig-thin, doe-eyed runway model—Marc let me know over and over again how unhappy he would be with a woman like Holly. She was away far more than she was home, and Michael's career rarely gave him the freedom to travel with her.

Marc liked me exactly where I was—in Texas. With him. Away from the eager eyes of millions of men all over the world.

I tried to take such statements for the compliment he intended them to be, instead of focusing on the underlying hint that my place was at home, with him and our future—thus far purely theoretical—children.

Perching on the edge of my father's desk, I pulled the stand-alone answering machine toward me, noting the blinking red light. Someone had called since we'd left for the barn, and my mother hadn't answered the phone. *Why not?*

Then the answer was there—obvious, in retrospect. She was in the woods. By herself. Again.

"What are you doing?" Michael asked, his eyes moving rapidly back and forth as he read silently from the computer screen.

"Dad wants us to listen to the messages and make sure Painter's the guy." I swung one leg to thump against the side of the desk. "Have you heard them yet?"

"Nope."

"Well, get ready." I pressed the play button on the machine, a digital model that didn't actually take a tape, and was first surprised, then pleased to hear my cousin's voice bubble from the tiny inset speaker.

"Hi, everybody, it's Abby." She paused, then sighed and continued. "My mom said that if I was serious about learning to fight, I should really commit to it, so I was calling to ask what kind of punching bag you guys use. The big heavy one. And I know the school year just started, but we'll be out for fall break in a few weeks, and I'd really like to spend it with you guys, if you don't mind. Maybe Faythe could teach me some more of those self-defense moves. I really want to learn how to disable a guy with one kick…."

I pressed the button to save Abby's message, then began cycling backward through the old ones, glancing at the numbers to eliminate the calls one by one, without listening to them. There was a call from Vic's cell phone, and another one from Ethan. Next was my own number; I'd called from the airport to tell my father I'd gotten his earlier message.

I pressed the button one more time, and a fourth number

appeared on the display. The time and date looked about right for the second message from the informant. So I pressed the play button.

"It's me again. Your friendly neighborhood snitch…"

We listened in silence as Dan Painter—and it was definitely him—told us where to find the body of a werecat near the westernmost edge of the Kisatchie National Forest in Louisiana. "And there's more information where that came from, if you're interested. But I want something in return, so next time, you'd better answer the damn phone."

There was a soft click as the connection was cut, but right before that click there was a single, soft bang, like a gunshot in the distance. And the distinctive air-beating sound of a propeller.

I sucked in a silent breath as my blood seemed to freeze in my veins. I couldn't swear that boom was actual gunfire, but I could swear I'd heard it before. That very afternoon, in the message Andrew had left on my phone.

Fuck.

I told myself it meant nothing. They were two different gunshots, or explosions, or whatever. Dan Painter and Andrew couldn't possibly have called from the same town. It was just a coincidence.

Unfortunately, I didn't believe in coincidence.

Sixteen

"Well, it's official," Marc said, his voice light with relief, because he had yet to notice my sudden panic attack. "Painter's the guy. Our very own overworked, underappreciated anonymous informant. Now we just have to find him."

"Mmm-hmm," I mumbled, still staring at the answering machine.

"What's wrong?" Marc eyed me carefully from the center of the love seat.

"Nothing," I said, a little too quickly. I didn't want to tell him about Andrew until I was sure of what I'd heard on Painter's message. "I was just thinking that the best way to find him would be to start with the number he called from." *Attagirl, Faythe. Stick to the truth. At least, as much of it as you can.*

"Read me the area code," Michael said, the disappointment on his face saying clearly that he wished he'd thought of it first.

Hopping down from the desk, I circled my brother to watch over his shoulder as he opened a new browser window and typed "reverse phone directory" into the Google search bar. When the new screen loaded, I read him the number from the display on the answering machine. Michael added the digits to his search, and sat back while the computer did all the work.

"Did you come up with any other missing strippers?" I asked, watching as a progress bar began to fill on-screen.

"Yeah." Michael extended both hands above his head, stretching like a cat asleep in the sun. "One from Arkansas, and two more from Louisiana." He paused, tilting his head down to peer over his useless glasses at the information now available on the screen. "Here you go." He nodded toward the flat-screen monitor. "Painter called from a pay phone in Leesville, Louisiana."

And though it obviously meant nothing to Michael, according to the on-screen map, Leesville was less than ten miles north of Pickering, where the tabby had left Jamey's body.

"The first call came from somewhere in Arkansas, didn't it?" Marc asked, finally pushing himself off the sofa to join us at the computer.

"Yeah. Um…" Michael reached across the disturbingly neat desk and pulled the huge atlas toward him. It was already open to the Arkansas page, and my father had circled two towns in red ink. One of them was Dumas, the small town just southeast of Pine Bluff, where I'd first smelled, then spotted Dan Painter when we stopped for gas. The other was—

"White Hall," Michael said, finishing my own thought. "Isn't that where you guys found Bradley Moore?"

"And where we buried him." Marc ran one hand up my arm, and I struggled to return his smile. "That makes sense. Moore was murdered in White Hall, and Painter saw it happen, so of course he'd call from there." I twisted in Marc's arms to face my brother. "You said you found a report of a missing stripper from Arkansas…?"

"Yeah." Michael put down the atlas and picked up the yellow legal pad he'd been making notes on. "Amber Cleary. She disappeared on Wednesday night, after her shift at Club Moonlight."

Wednesday night. A full twenty-four hours before Kellie Tandy had gone missing from New Orleans. "Where's Club Moonlight?" I asked, pulling open my father's top desk drawer. Inside, I grabbed a mini legal pad from the top of a small stack and slid the drawer closed. Marc handed me a pen from the jar on the desktop, and I began scratching on the lined paper as Michael flipped through his own notes.

"Um…Pine Bluff, Arkansas."

"Where's that?" Clenching my pen and notepad together in one fist, I bent across the desk for the atlas.

"There." Marc reached around my arm to tap a point on the map, before I'd even found the legend.

I brushed his hand out of the way and focused on the dot his finger had been covering. Pine Bluff, Arkansas, was forty-five miles south and slightly east of Little Rock. And less than ten miles from White Hall, where Bradley Moore was murdered.

I was starting to see a pattern, and it wasn't pretty.

"Okay, this is what I have so far," I said, glancing over the barely legible scribbling on my notepad. "On Wednesday, Amber Cleary disappeared from a strip club in Pine Bluff, Arkansas. The next day—Thursday—the rogue tabby murdered Bradley Moore less than ten miles away, in White Hall. That same day, Kellie Tandy vanished in the middle of her shift at Forbidden Fruit, in New Orleans. Then, on Saturday, the tabby showed up at Forbidden Fruit, where she killed Robert Harper."

I looked up to find both guys watching me. "Am I forgetting anything?"

"Yeah. The other missing strippers." Marc leaned against my father's glass display case as he looked to Michael for confirmation. "Didn't you say there were two more in Louisiana?"

Michael nodded, flipping through his notes again. "Melissa Vassey never made it home after her shift at the Pegasus Lounge on Saturday night. Care to take a guess where the Pegasus Lounge is located?"

"Saturday…" I said, my brain scrambling to assemble a puzzle we didn't yet have all the pieces for. "Leesville, Louisiana. Or somewhere nearby."

Michael nodded. "Good guess."

"How the hell did you know that?" Confused, Marc glanced back and forth between us.

I grinned in triumph. "It fits the pattern. A stripper goes missing, then, a day later, the tabby shows up and kills a tomcat. On Sunday she dropped off Jamey Gardner's body in Leesville, which must mean that on Saturday, a stripper went missing from Leesville, or somewhere nearby." I flipped my legal pad around for him to see. "But the tabby can't be the one taking the strippers. She was busy killing Moore when Kellie Tandy went missing, and she was killing Jamey Gardner when Melissa Vassey disappeared from Leesville."

"So, the tabby's alibi for kidnapping is murder?" A sardonic smile played across Marc's lips. "That's one hell of a defense."

"Not exactly exoneration, is it?" I shrugged. "But it holds up."

"What about Friday?" Marc asked, taking the notebook from my hand.

"What do you mean?"

He aimed one finger at a blank line on the legal pad. "Friday's blank. See? No dead toms, and no missing strippers."

"Damn," I plopped down on my father's desk and took my notebook back for closer study. "You poked a hole in my theory."

"Only a small hole," Michael said. "The third Louisiana stripper went missing Friday night, from a topless bar in Lafayette."

I stared at my brother for a moment, trying to process the new information and fit it into the timeline forming in my head. Then I twisted around and snatched the atlas from the far corner of the desk. "Lafayette." I traced the I-10 to I-49, then north with my finger. "If you stick to the major interstates, Lafayette is on the way to Leesville from New Orleans."

Marc looked from me, to the map, to my hastily scribbled notes, to Michael. "So we have a stripper missing from Lafayette on Friday, but no dead tom. Why?"

Michael shrugged. "We're assuming the tabby's following whoever's taking the strippers, right?"

Unfortunately, we were indeed.

"I'm betting there's no corpse for Friday because she didn't find a tom in Lafayette. There aren't that many of us, and she can't possibly run into a werecat at every gas stop."

Though I'd come across Dan Painter's scent in that very manner.

"Besides, we don't have anyone living near Lafayette, do we?" I asked, glancing to Marc for an answer, because Michael had been out of the loop—for the most part—for the better part of the last decade.

"No. No one with permission, anyway."

In the foyer, a soft click and the squeal of dry hinges signaled the front door opening.

My father stepped into the office doorway and paused when he noticed us huddled around his computer. "Wait just a minute, guys, and let's see what Michael found out."

Michael nudged my hip with the capped tip of his pen, and I slid off the desk and onto my feet just as Vic, Owen, and Parker followed my father into the room.

"Well?" He marched forward to take the position of power: his desk chair.

Michael stood and gave me a shove, and I followed Marc toward the love seat, pausing to grab my notes on the way past the desk.

"I've found three more missing strippers so far."

The Alpha sank into his chair, and Michael finished going over the details, then set his notepad on the center of the desk, where it wouldn't be missed. "We've identified a pattern connecting the murders with the missing strippers."

We've *identified a pattern?* I thought, glaring at my know-it-all older brother.

Marc pulled me onto the love seat next to him, squeezing my hand in sympathy, as if he knew what I was thinking. Hell, he probably did.

Dad scanned the notepad, then stood, motioning for Michael to take his seat. "I want to know why these girls in particular are disappearing. What do they have in common, other than their occupation? Are there pictures? Are they all students, or was Kellie Tandy an exception? Do they all work completely in the nude, or are some of them simply topless waitresses?"

My father turned to Vic, Owen, and Parker as he settled into his armchair. "If you go now, you can catch the eleven o'clock news. I wouldn't be surprised if the missing strippers have made it into the national broadcast."

Vic nodded and led Owen and Parker out the door and down the hall, presumably toward the guesthouse, where three different televisions and two computers were at their disposal, ready to be used for the greater good of mankind. Or feline-kind, in this case.

"Okay…" My father turned back to face the rest of us. "So, we've traced the tabby and whoever she's following, but we don't know who that is, or where either of them are now. Right?"

"Right," Michael said, his fingers clacking away on the keyboard without pause.

Dad closed his eyes, obviously thinking. "So the last known location for the tabby is Pickering, Louisiana, where she left Jamey's body. What about whoever she's tailing?"

"Leesville, which is less than ten miles north of Pickering," I said, glancing down at my notes. Marc shifted closer to me to see them better. "It's where the last stripper disappeared from, and where Painter made his last anonymous call."

"And you're sure it's him?" My father's eyes opened to take us both in from his armchair. "Did you listen to both messages?"

"We only heard the last one, but it's definitely him," I said, annoyed when Dad looked to Marc for confirmation of what I'd said. As if my word alone wasn't good enough.

"So we know who the informant is, and we have a description of the tabby. The only one we know nothing about is whoever she's following."

"Well, we do know *something*," Marc said, glancing at the notebook balanced on my knee. "He's taken a stripper in a different town for each of the past four nights. If he sticks to his pattern, he could be taking another one right now. But we have no idea where he is."

"Okay, so trace his path." Dad templed his hands beneath his chin, his most familiar I'm-thinking gesture. "Maybe we can make an educated guess based on that."

Maybe we can at that. I dropped the legal pad in Marc's lap—in case he needed the cheat sheet again—and stood. My father's gaze followed me as I passed his chair, and I heard the springs creak as he turned to watch me. Stopping in front of the huge oak desk, I spun the atlas around and pulled it close.

"Okay. He drove south from Arkansas, all the way to New Orleans." I traced the interstate down through the state line and into Louisiana. But then I had to stop and flip through the atlas pages to find Louisiana. "From New Orleans, he probably followed I-10 to Lafayette, then went north—not sure how—to Leesville."

My finger hovered over Leesville. "From there, he could go east on Highway 28, or turn either north or south on 171."

"I don't think he'll go back east," Marc said, closing his eyes as he leaned his head back against the sofa cushion. "He seems to be working his way west."

To Texas. I was unwilling to vocalize such a thought, at least until I'd either confirmed or dismissed my suspicion involving Andrew.

"Maybe so." I exhaled deeply to slow my racing heart, then propped one hip on the edge of my father's desk—hoping to look completely relaxed—and pulled the atlas onto my lap. Michael scowled, but went back to information-gathering when I stuck my tongue out at him.

"South of Leesville, there's nothing but more small towns and large patches of forest, until you hit I-10. From there, he

could go back east toward New Orleans—which we all agree
he probably didn't do—or west, in which case he'll wind up
in Beaumont, then Houston."

Marc ran one hand through his dark curls, then leaned his
head on the back of the couch and closed his eyes again. He
looked exhausted. I knew exactly how he felt. "Well, the
closer he gets, the easier he'll be to find," he said.

Oh, shit. I didn't know where the stripper-kidnapper was
going, but I was starting to seriously suspect he was somehow
connected to Andrew. And I knew exactly where Andrew
was headed.

Here.

"Anything new on those dancers yet, Michael?" my
father asked.

My brother nodded without looking up. "Yeah. Just a
second."

Hopping down from my father's desk, I dropped the atlas
on the blotter and headed for the door. "I'll be right back."

"Where are you going?" my father asked, and I heard
springs creak as he stood behind me.

"To the guesthouse for a soda." My sneakers squeaked on
the tiles in a fast, irritating rhythm.

"You need some help?" Marc called. I didn't answer.

At the end of the hall, I pulled open the back door and
shoved the screen out of my way. It slammed shut behind me
as I dashed down the steps, wondering where to go next. The
guesthouse was out of the question; Vic, Parker, and Owen were
in there scrounging up news reports. The barn was a definite
no, too; it seemed very wrong to interrupt Jamey's eternal rest
with my own problem, no matter how serious it was.

At a loss for where to go, I settled for a patch of grass to the left of the back porch, against the rear wall of the house. An owl hooted his greeting as I flipped open my phone, my heart thudding in my ears. I scrolled through the missed calls, thankful for the well-lit LCD screen. It didn't take long to find the voice mail from Andrew. The one I hadn't entirely listened to in the airport.

Not listening was no longer an option. Maybe it never had been.

Holding my breath, I pressed a button and brought the phone up to my ear, my hand shaking. I focused on the tree line ahead, waiting for the message to play.

"I got your message, Faythe. If I didn't know any better, I'd say you—" Again his words were cut off by what sounded like gunfire and helicopter blades—the same sounds we'd heard on Painter's message to my father. "—you don't want to see me. But I'm looking forward to seeing you." More explosions, and blades beating the air. "—take care of something tomorrow, but then I'm all yours. Won't be long now."

Another series of bangs, and this time the beating sound— obviously some kind of aircraft—faded off into the distance over the line. Whatever those sounds were, Andrew was much closer to the action than Painter had been.

"—can't wait to show off my new look. I think you're really going to like it. How could you not, right?"

The message ended with a short buzz of static, a muted click, then silence. Then a soft female voice came on the line, asking if I'd like to save the message. I pressed the yes key and flipped the phone closed, my hands still shaking.

My breath came in quick, panicked bursts, and I leaned against the wall to keep from falling. The fingers of my left hand traced the rough lines of mortar behind me. I focused on the harsh, gritty feel, using it to assure myself that I was awake. That I wasn't in the middle of some terrible nightmare. That I hadn't dreamed the horrible voice mail.

And I hadn't.

Somehow, though he'd been human when I left him, tucked safe and sound among his textbooks, tennis courts, and completely nonlethal lattes, Andrew was now a tomcat. An honest-to-goodness, motherfucking, scratch-fevered stray.

And he was headed my way.

Seventeen

No. I shook my head in denial, though no one was there to see it. *That's not possible.* Yet it was true, nonetheless.

They don't even know about me, do they? You never told them. The words from my last conversation with Andrew played though my head, and they made so much more sense in retrospect. He wasn't talking about our relationship. He was talking about his new *species.* He seemed to think I knew what he'd become, and had been keeping it from my family. But I hadn't known. How the hell *could* I have known?

Chill bumps popped up all over my arms and legs, in spite of the hot Texas night. This couldn't be happening. Andrew was *human* when I left campus. Absolutely, positively one hundred percent human. No fur. No claws. No canines.

So when had that changed? And who changed it? I rubbed both my arms at once, trying to offset the chill spreading over me from the inside out.

Andrew's family was from Tennessee, which belonged to the Midwest Pride, and he went to school in Texas, which was in our territory. So unless he'd been to one of the free zones lately, he was pretty unlikely to have ever met a stray.

That left only one other possibility. As badly as I hated to admit it, he *could* have been scratched by a Pride cat. But the chances were slim. Creating a stray carried an automatic death sentence, and very few Pride cats were willing to take that kind of risk. Very, *very* few.

And it's not like strays could be created by accident. An infectious scratch or bite could only be delivered in cat form, so casual physical contact with humans—such as a rough round of sex or even a fistfight—couldn't possibly result in the creation of a stray.

So where could Andrew have come into contact with a werecat in cat form? *Any* werecat?

I refused to believe that my ex-boyfriend had been targeted by chance; that was like saying Lincoln was just in the wrong theater at the wrong time. Someone had *intentionally* dragged Andrew into werecat business, and whoever the bastard was, his fate would be sealed once we got one good whiff of Andrew. The infector's base scent would be forever threaded through that of his victim—however lightly—just as Marc's scent carried a permanent reminder of the stray who'd killed his mother and infected him.

It was a bitch of a double whammy, and the reason more than a few strays never came to terms with their new identity. But in this case, the scent trail would help us catch the slimy prick who'd put an end to Andrew's human existence. At which point we'd end his own. An eye for an eye.

Tell Marc I'll see him, too. I think he and I have a lot to talk about.

Shit. The very thought of that conversation introduced me to all new levels of stress. And humiliation. And…

An ache began behind my eyes and quickly grew into a searing, throbbing pain and pressure. My right hand clenched my phone, and my left flew up to feel my eyes, which seemed unchanged. For several moments I was blind, dependent on the rustle of leaves in the wind to assure me I still stood in my own yard. Panic set in and I almost screamed, terrified by the claustrophobic sensation of the sudden, nearly complete darkness.

But then the pain subsided, and my vision improved dramatically. Light flowed back into existence rapidly, but gently. I eyed the trees beyond the guesthouse, and saw each leaf in eerily crisp focus, from the thin green veins to the spiked, serrated edges. Cracks in the tree bark seemed surreal in their rough, ragged detail. Every blade of grass at my feet stood out in vivid contrast to those around it, each rendered in a different shade of green as the available light struck them at slightly different angles.

I glanced up, expecting to see the moon breaking free from its cloud cover. But it hadn't. If anything, the clouds had thickened, as forecast by the local weatherman, who'd predicted an unseasonably strong storm overnight. Yet I could see almost as if the sun were up, though my vision was tinted in shades of blue and green.

My eyes had Shifted. I was sure of it, though I couldn't tell any difference in my face without a mirror to stare into.

Though several of our oldest legends hinted at the possibility, there were no other partial Shifts on record, and as far as I knew, I was the only werecat to ever experience one. I'd done it twice before, both during times of extreme stress, yet in spite of several concentrated efforts since that last time, I'd been unable to repeat the feat.

Because of that, the Territorial Council had refused to believe my partial Shift was anything more than the delusion of a desperate tabby in a desperate situation, even with both Abby and Marc vouching for me.

If I go back in now, my father will see, and they'll all have to believe me.

But then I'd have to explain the emotional stress that had triggered the partial Shift, and as badly as I wanted to prove I could do it, I wanted to keep my secret even more. At least until I could tell Marc about Andrew in private. That was the least he deserved.

Gritting my teeth against the pain, I reversed the partial Shift. As soon as my vision was back to normal, I jogged across the yard to the guesthouse and through the door. Parker waved to me from the living-room computer as I headed straight for the kitchen. Then, six-pack of chilled Cokes in hand, I crossed the room again and onto the porch, just in time to hear the screen door to the main house squeal open.

I looked up as Marc stepped onto the back porch. "Faythe?" he called, the concern in his tone contrasting sharply with the bitter anger Andrew's voice had held. "Where'd you go?"

I held up the sodas, trying desperately to regulate my pulse before he heard it racing. "Right here. I'm coming." I took a deep breath, then jogged down the steps and across the soft green grass.

"Is something wrong? You smell…anxious."

"Nope. Just thirsty. What's up?" I asked as I crossed the yard toward him before he could question me further.

"Michael found a pattern with the strippers." I knew from

the grim look on his face as I climbed the steps that I wasn't going to like whatever my brother had found.

We entered the office just in time to hear Ethan tell my father that he and Jace hadn't been able to find my mother. "…but she can't have gone far. Her car's still out front."

"She's in the woods," I said, settling onto the arm of the leather couch as I pulled a soda from the bunch and tossed it to him.

My father nodded, his expression worried but not surprised. He'd known about her solitary treks in the forest. I should have guessed. "She'll be back when she's ready," he said, clearly dismissing the subject. "Faythe, is everything okay?"

"Fine." I popped the top on my own can and downed a quarter of it in one swallow, to keep from having to answer any more questions. For the moment, anyway.

"Good. Michael, repeat what you said about the missing girls, for those who missed it.

"I didn't find any pattern among their personal lives." Michael pushed back the desk and stood, pulling several sheets from the printer tray as he passed it on his way to our Alpha's side. "They range in age from twenty-one to thirty-three. All of them are single except Melissa Vassey, who's married with one child. There's a record of one domestic disturbance at her address, but at this point, I'm thinking that has nothing to do with her disappearance.

"Their educational backgrounds run the gamut, too. One college grad, one still studying, and two with only high school diplomas. As far as I can tell, they've never met one another. So I was at a complete loss for things in common until I did a search for their pictures."

Michael met my gaze, and my throat tried to close when I

saw the dark dread in his eyes, completely unfiltered by his spectacle lenses. He held up the first picture—a black-and-white pixilated image printed on twenty-pound paper—and I frowned, squinting to see it better. I shook my head and held my hand out for the page. Michael handed the first one to me, and another to Marc.

The image was poor quality, but more than adequate to make my brother's point. Melissa Vassey—based on the caption—had long dark hair, just like mine. As did Amber Cleary, whose picture Marc held.

"You can't tell from these, but they both have green eyes. And so does Pam Gilbert," Michael said, holding up one of the two remaining pages.

"Wow," Jace whispered, staring at me openly. "They look like you."

Not quite. Two of the three women in question were quite a bit better endowed than I was—ridiculously so, in Melissa Vassey's case—and no two of us had the same nose. But I knew what he meant. We all had straight, dark hair and green eyes. Not the most common combination of features.

He's making a statement, I thought, stunned to the point of speechlessness. Unable to tear my eyes from Melissa Vassey's face, I slid down from the arm of the couch onto one of the cushions. *Though I'll be damned if I know what he's trying to say.*

The Andrew I'd known could never have taken those strippers. But then, he could never have made those phone calls, either. *He's lost it,* I thought, shaking my head before I realized what I was doing. *Scratch-fever has completely fried his brain.* Why else would he take Amber, and Kellie, and…

Wait. My head popped up and I frowned at Michael. "Kellie Tandy doesn't fit the pattern. She's blond."

Michael nodded. "She has brown eyes, too."

"So she's not part of this?" I asked, my frown deepening. "But we *know* the tabby was in the Forbidden Fruit."

"Show her," my father said.

I glanced first at him, then at Michael, as he held up the last page from the printer. "Forbidden Fruit has a Web site, with a 'cast list,' complete with photographs of the dancers. In costume." He handed me the page, and I took it, dreading what I'd see. "Third from the end."

But I'd already found her. Second row. Kellie Tandy, from the waist up, her ample cleavage bursting from the top of a black leather cat suit, à la Halle Berry. However, the important part, the part that made her fit the pattern, was her hair. She wore a wig—a mass of straight black hair, with pointed cat ears sticking up from either side. She also wore white plastic whiskers glued to her face, on either side of a perfect little human nose. Beneath authentic-looking cat eyes.

They were theatrical contacts. They had to be. But they were eerily accurate, down to the striations in her irises that I was sure were various shades of green in real life, though they were gray in the photo.

Marc took my hand in his, stroking the side of my palm with his thumb, as if to comfort me. If only he knew what an impossibly Herculean task that was at the moment. "We still don't know who the tabby is, or why she's following this psycho from club to club. But we should be able to figure out who *he* is now. Or at least narrow our list of suspects down from 'every cat in the country' to 'someone Faythe knows.'"

"That can't be too hard." Smiling, Ethan dropped onto the

love seat across from me and Marc. "She can't know that many strays. She's been at school for the past five years, and we'd have known if anyone was hanging around who shouldn't have been."

"What if it's not someone she knows, but someone who knows her?" Jace asked, settling onto the arm of the couch on my other side. "Or thinks he does."

"Same thing," Ethan insisted. "Either way, if there was another werecat on campus, we'd have known about it."

Ethan was right. I'd been under constant surveillance by my father's enforcers at school, and if another werecat had shown up, they'd have taken him out before I had the chance to break so much as a nail on the poor bastard. But the joke was on them, because the werecat in question wasn't a werecat at all when we'd been on campus. He was a normal, human math major.

"Enough," my father said. "Faythe, I think Marc's right. The tom in question seems to know you. Or at least know what you look like. Assuming it's a tom at all, and I don't think we should rule out anything at this point."

Well, what do you know? It only took a female serial killer to bring my father into the gender-equal twenty-first century. I'd thought it would take full-scale war.

Closing my eyes, I pulled in a long, slow breath, trying to ignore my galloping heartbeat. When I opened my eyes, everyone was staring at me. "Let me save you all a lot of trouble. I know who's taking the strippers."

"What?" Marc shifted on the sofa to face me, but I couldn't look at him. I watched my father instead, as I said the rest of what had to be said.

"It's Andrew Wallace."

Silence greeted my announcement. Complete and total silence, except for the whispered breaths coming from around the room. And Marc's might not even have been among them. I think he actually stopped breathing.

Michael was the first to speak, from his perch on the arm of the love seat, and I really should have seen that coming. "Andrew? That skinny guy you were sleeping with last spring?"

"Damn it, Michael!" I glared at him from across the rug as Marc tensed on the cushion next to me. "Please don't make this any harder than it already is."

He shrugged, crossing bulging arms over his spotless polo shirt. "I'm just getting my facts straight. So…you're saying you were screwing a serial kidnapper for most of your last semester at school?" He turned then to face our father as my blood boiled. "I'd say that was tuition money well spent."

"Michael…" my father said, his voice thick with warning.

"What? *I'm* not the problem here. *She* is." He whirled back to face me, fury and frustration battling for control of his expression. "Where Faythe goes, trouble follows, and as usual, we're left to clean up her mess."

"You son of a bitch!" My hands curled into fists, and I felt myself leaning forward, ready and more than willing to take some of my stress and frustration out on his face. "Ethan's drilled half the state of Texas, and you've never once thrown that in his face—"

"Hey!" Ethan shouted, eyes going wide as he sat up straight on the couch across from me. "Don't bring me into this."

"—but I have one ex-boyfriend, and you declare me the Jezebel of the county." Blood pounded in my ears, and my fingers tingled in fury, itching for something to beat, or shred. I sprang from the couch, still-human fingers curled into claws.

Michael jumped up from the love seat, hissing at me through bared teeth.

Marc caught me in midair, both arms wrapped around my waist. He spun me around in one smooth, fluid motion and dropped me none too gently in the middle of the couch. "Don't move," he ordered, watching me through the flood of confusion and suspicious anger shining in his eyes.

"Ethan, out." My father was still standing, his arms stiff at his sides, his fists clenched.

"But—" Ethan turned to argue, but the Alpha shook his head.

"Go. And take Jace with you."

Jace stood and shoved his best friend ahead of him. I cringed when the door clicked closed, and all remaining eyes turned on me.

"Is Michael right?" Marc demanded, still standing in the middle of the rug. "Are we talking about *your* Andrew?"

"Well, I wouldn't exactly call him my Andrew…"

"Faythe…" my father said, warning me again. He was making an obvious attempt to calm himself, and I was willing to do whatever it took to help.

I nodded. "Yeah, it's him."

Marc's eyes closed, and his forehead wrinkled. "So we're looking for a human? The tabby's chasing a *human?*"

I shook my head. I couldn't say it out loud.

"He's a stray," my father said, his voice gravelly and almost too low pitched to hear. The attempt to calm himself clearly wasn't working; I'd never heard him any angrier.

"Yes." I met his eyes, reminding myself that I hadn't done anything wrong. Keeping the calls a secret didn't count. I'd had no idea Andrew was involved with the strippers and the tabby.

Marc turned his back on me, heading toward the liquor

cabinet on the far side of the room, opposite the desk. "How?" he asked, glass clinking as he pulled something I couldn't see from the cabinet.

"I don't know."

"Come on, Faythe. You're in too deep to lie about it now," Michael said.

"Fuck you," I snapped. "I'm telling the truth!"

"Marc, make mine a double," my father said, and I glanced up to see Marc pouring himself a glass of whiskey. Straight up.

Marc nodded and got out another glass. "Michael?" he asked, and my brother shook his head. Marc didn't offer me anything.

My father cracked the first knuckle of his right hand against his left palm. It was an overtly aggressive gesture, which made me very, very nervous. "How long have you known?"

"I just figured it out. Maybe ten minutes ago. Outside."

"How?"

"The message from Painter."

Marc crossed the room again, this time carrying two short glasses of whiskey. *Full* of whiskey.

My father accepted his glass and sipped from it, watching me over the rim. "What about the message?"

My hands clenched together in my lap, I watched Marc lower himself onto the love seat across from me, instead of resuming his place at my side. He was mad. And it was about to get worse.

"Andrew's been calling me."

"What?" Marc sat up straight, almost sloshing whiskey into his lap. "Why the hell didn't you—"

"Let her finish," my father ordered, cutting Marc off with one raised palm. He nodded for me to continue.

I inhaled deeply. Then I exhaled slowly. "Those pops, and

that sound like a helicopter's propeller at the end of Painter's call? They were in my last message from Andrew, too. He and Painter are in the same place."

Marc tossed his glass back and got up for more.

"He knows what you are?" Michael asked, just as my father said, "He told you he was infected?"

"Yes. And no." I glanced down at my hands, wishing they were wrapped around a drink, but I knew better than to ask Marc to bring me one. "He definitely knows about me. About all of us. But I have no idea how he found out. And no, he never actually told me he was infected, which is why it took me so long to figure out that he was. And I swear I have no idea how it happened."

My father nodded, as if to say he believed me. But I couldn't help noticing he didn't say it out loud.

"How long?" Marc asked from the wet bar, sipping from his second glass of whiskey. "How long has he been calling you?"

I met his eyes, expecting to see pain and deep, deep anger. I wasn't disappointed. "Once a day since Friday afternoon."

"Three days?" Marc slammed his glass down on the bar and stomped toward me, stopping at the edge of the rug to tower over me. Michael stood, ready to intercede even though he was clearly just as mad as Marc, but a small shake of my father's head held him back. "He's been calling you for three days and you didn't tell me? Why not?"

"Because I knew this would happen." I made myself stay seated, knowing that if I stood, a fight would be inevitable. If I stayed calm—and seated—he might calm down, too. "I didn't know what was going on, but I knew that his calling would upset you, and you'd want to go 'take care' of it. I don't *want* you to take care of my problems. I can handle them myself."

"Clearly." Marc rubbed his forehead with one hand, as if staving off a headache. "You've done such a marvelous job of handling it that he's now waltzing all over our territory, kidnapping strippers who bear a passing resemblance to you. Great job!"

"I didn't know he had anything to do with any of that! I was just trying to avoid…well, *this!* You always do this. You take something small, something that's really none of your business, and you twist it around to make it look like I did something wrong. But this time I didn't. I was under no obligation to tell you anything."

His brows arched high over eyes sparkling in fury. "You think this is *small?*"

"Well, obviously not the kidnapping part," I conceded, shrugging. "But the phone calls were *nothing,* at least as far as I knew. And until I knew Andrew was involved in the rest of this, he was *none of your business.*"

A growl rumbled through the room, extraordinarily low and gravelly. His mouth never moved, but I knew it was Marc. I'd hurt his feelings, and his pride. And I'd pissed him off.

Sighing in defeat, I glanced down at my hands, where they lay in my lap.

"Well, you won't have to worry about my nose in your business anymore."

Movement blurred on the right edge of my vision. I turned toward it instinctively. Marc was gone. I whirled in my seat to see him disappear into the hall, his shirt a black smear passing out of sight beyond the door frame.

I was on my feet in an instant, running after him. My father appeared in front of the door out of nowhere, blocking my path. I ducked to dodge him. One iron-hard arm slid around my waist. He held me back. I kicked and fought, my legs flailing in midair. "I have to tell him I'm—"

"Let him go, Faythe. He didn't mean it. Give him some time and he'll get over it."

"No!"

"Yes." And that was that. My father tucked me under one arm, in the most undignified position I could imagine. He kicked the door shut hard enough to make it rattle in the frame, then hauled me back to the small grouping of furniture, where Michael waited, his eyes wide with astonishment.

My father set me on my feet on the rug and gestured for me to sit on the couch.

I sat. What else could I do?

For a moment, he sipped from his whiskey, while my brother watched me in silence. Then, finally, my father opened his mouth…only to take another drink from his glass. Not a sip this time—a drink. More like a gulp. When he met my eyes again, determination was carved into the firm line of his mouth. "I know you're upset, but we have to go on with this. I have to ask you some questions. Are you ready?"

I nodded. Of course I was ready. I was an adult who'd had a fight with her boyfriend, not a traumatized child.

"Did you ever Shift in front of Andrew, or have any contact with him at all in cat form?"

My jaw dropped. Literally. My mouth hung open, and I stared at my father like a drooling idiot, stunned into silence by a question so serious and insulting it bruised not just my pride, but my heart. I'd expected a real bitch of a question, but not that. Never that.

My father was practically accusing me of infecting Andrew. Of committing a capital crime—one of the most serious we recognized. If I admitted guilt, the council's law required him to have me put to death. Not locked up. Not declawed. Not put on display in front of my fellow werecats with a scarlet *A* on my chest.

Executed.

How could he even *entertain* such a thought? My shock gave way to anger that my own father could know so little about me. That he could accuse me of infecting someone. *Anyone.* Much less someone I'd once cared about.

"Fuck you!" I shouted, jumping to my feet as outrage surged through my veins, a thousand times hotter than blood.

My father—no, my *Alpha*—nodded to Michael, and he stood calmly, crossing thick arms over a broad chest. "Sit down," Michael said. He didn't tell me to watch my language, which said more than I could ever have hoped for.

I hesitated, standing only because sitting would be admitting defeat, no matter how minor.

"Sit, Faythe, and rein in your temper," my father said. He drained the last of the whiskey from his glass and leaned forward to set it on the table at my end of the couch. When he leaned back, his eyes were calm, and still determined. "I have to ask. You know that. So just answer the question."

"Fine, but I'm not going to sit."

He shrugged. "Suit yourself."

Damn it. Standing with his permission didn't satisfy my massive need to piss him off in return for insulting me. *Stupid reverse psychology.* I sank back onto the couch, and Michael followed my lead.

"Hell no, I never Shifted in front of Andrew. And he never saw me in cat form, either. To my knowledge, no human has ever seen…" My words trailed off as I realized

I'd been about to lie. Accidentally, of course, but that wouldn't matter.

A human *had* seen me in cat form once. A hunter, three months earlier. Nothing had come of it, other than a series of Bigfoot-esque news reports on the local stations, but I wasn't about to bring up something I *hadn't* been accused of. No sense borrowing trouble, right? Besides, some of the guys would get into trouble along with me. Ethan, Jace, and Parker had all promised Marc they wouldn't tell.

"No, he never saw me in cat form," I finished weakly, meeting my father's gaze to lend credibility to my statement and distract him from what I'd almost said.

His eyes narrowed, but if he suspected anything, he'd either decided to let it go, or to address it later, because he didn't challenge my statement. "To your knowledge, has Andrew ever come into contact with another werecat?"

"Yes," I said, without thinking. The answer seemed pretty clear to me, but based on Michael's surprised expression, my phrasing needed serious work. "He's *obviously* come into contact with a cat," I amended. "Unless the 'virus' is now airborne, in which case public panic seems inevitable."

My father nodded again, this time with a hint of a smile. That hint—that tiny upturn of one corner of his mouth—set me at ease as no mere drink could ever have done. He would never have smiled if he were planning to have his own daughter put to death.

"Yes, clearly he has come into contact with a cat. I meant to ask if you know the identity of that cat."

"No." I shrugged, rolling my head on my neck to release some of the built-up tension. "I have no idea. And just to speed things up, I'm not intentionally withholding any information from you. Well, no information pertinent to this case, anyway," I corrected myself. And there was that tiny smile again. "I don't know who infected him. Or when or how it happened. Or how long ago."

"And he's called you three times?"

I shrugged, trying hard to appear casual. "Yeah. He was really angry, which I understand now. And he seemed to think I already knew he'd been infected, though I have no idea why he would thi—" My hand flew to my mouth, cutting off my words even as I choked on them. My heart slammed against the inside of my chest as a sudden realization singed through me like an electrical shock, setting off pain sensors I hadn't even known I had. My skin tingled. My head ached. My stomach heaved. I clamped my jaws shut to hold back half-digested halibut and scalloped potatoes.

I knew who had infected Andrew. I even knew how it had happened. He'd only had contact with one werecat.

Me.

Eighteen

"What's wrong?" Michael leaned forward, as if to catch me if I fell off the couch. I barely heard him. I was too busy hearing Andrew.

You didn't tell them about me. Andrew's words played in my head, his voice reproduced in my mind with frightening accuracy. *You owe me, Faythe.*

What I'd said to my father was accurate—for the most part. I'd never intentionally or knowingly Shifted in front of Andrew. But I hadn't meant for my eyes to Shift an hour earlier, either. And they weren't the only part of my face to ever experience an unexpected partial Shift.

My teeth had done it, too.

I'd bitten Andrew's ear the very day I left school, not two hours before Marc had shown up in the quad. I'd broken the skin. Just barely, but enough to draw a single drop of blood. Apparently that was enough.

I'd infected him. I hadn't meant to. I hadn't even known I'd done it. Or that it was possible. Yet I'd accidentally made him one of us, then left him, abandoning him to pain, fear, and incapacitating disorientation during his transition. It was a miracle he'd survived.

Huh. Look at that, I thought, teetering on the razor-sharp edge of hysteria. *I committed a capital crime after all.* No wonder Andrew wanted to kill me. I couldn't really blame him.

"Faythe, say something," Michael urged, and it took me a minute to realize I'd gone completely silent. "If you don't start explaining, Dad's going to draw his own conclusions."

"Too late." My father eyed me with frightening intensity, and it took every ounce of willpower I had to keep from squirming where I sat.

"I think I know who infected Andrew," I whispered. It was the best I could do.

The Alpha sat straighter in his chair, his eyes narrowing in suspicion. If he didn't know exactly what I was going to say, he must have been pretty close. And he was no longer eager to hear it. "What happened?" he said at last. "And consider your words very carefully."

Suddenly the silence in the soundproofed office seemed dangerous, and somehow wrong. I felt compelled to fill it with a blurted confession, followed by babbling apologies and tearful explanations. But I didn't. I wouldn't have shamed myself with such a display before I became an enforcer, and I sure as hell wasn't going to do it now.

But I had to say something.

I hesitated one last time. I'd let my father down more times than I could count, but this was the Big One. This was humiliation, disappointment, and disillusionment all wrapped up together, tied with a big red bow of disgrace. The gift that keeps on giving.

"It was an accident," I said, continuing calmly but quickly, before he had a chance to interrupt. "I didn't understand what happened until just now."

Michael nodded, urging me on. He seemed to be the only one who really wanted me to continue.

My heart thumped painfully, and my hands connected in my lap, my fingers twisting and pulling one another mercilessly. "I bit him. Accidentally." I couldn't help repeating that last part.

"You *bit* him? *Accidentally?*" My father's green eyes hardened. I knew that look. The Alpha had arrived, and he was *angry.* "Explain yourself. Now."

I nodded, grateful for the opportunity in spite of the rage in his eyes. "I was in human form. It should have been safe. I swear I didn't know what was happening." My hands moved wildly, punctuating each sentence, and I couldn't seem to stop them. "At the time I had no clue this was even possible, but now I think my teeth Shifted. They couldn't have changed much, because I didn't notice it, and neither did he. But that's the only way it could have happened."

My desperate, babbling excuses faded into silence, and still my father stared at me. As did Michael. His eyes burned into me, seeing right past my defensive explanation to the truth. The whole truth, which our father obviously didn't understand.

"You bit him in human form?" For one long, torturous moment, confusion replaced the anger in the Alpha's expression. "Why? Why would you bite him?"

Well, hell. He was going to make me say it. *This is* not *a conversation I want to have with my father. Ever.* But it was much too late to back out, so I took a deep breath and plunged forward into the dark abyss. Melodramatic? Hell yeah.

"We were…you know. *Together.*"

"I see," he said, after a long, tense silence. But I had my doubts. He didn't look like he saw.

My father stood, retrieving his glass from the end table, and crossed the room to his desk. As I sank deeper into the couch, he opened his bottom desk drawer and pulled out a half-empty bottle of Scotch. The good stuff.

Seated now, he poured two inches of amber liquid into his glass, hesitated, then poured a third inch. As I watched my father drink, it occurred to me that the testimony I was about to launch resembled a kamikaze's final flight. It would be a sickeningly fast and exhilarating plunge, executed with the greater good in mind. And it was virtually guaranteed to end in death. *Mine.*

Martyrdom always seems so daring and courageous from an outsider's perspective, but from the cockpit of the kamikaze's plane, with the earth racing up to meet you, the view sucks.

My father screwed the lid on his bottle and set it in the drawer. He slid the drawer shut and took another drink. Then he started across the floor toward me, walking slowly, as if he were stiff, or achy. With a deep, weary sigh, he settled back into his chair. His eyes rose to meet mine, and they were completely empty. Blank.

Damn, he's good.

For almost a complete minute, my father stared at me, sipping from his glass. Silence closed in on me, and I wanted to look away from his eyes, but I couldn't. If I broke eye contact, he might think I was hiding something, and I desperately needed him to believe I was telling the truth. Now, more than ever. So we both sat still and silent, ignoring Michael.

Finally, he spoke. "I'm going to give you a chance to rethink what you just told us. That's more than I would give any other cat in the world. Do you understand what I'm telling you?"

I nodded. He was giving me a chance to save myself. To take back what I'd just said. To decide I'd made a mistake—that I hadn't infected Andrew. He was looking for a justifiable excuse to spare my life, at least until after the official inquisition the council would demand if he refused to have me executed. He'd have a good reason for that—if I was willing to lie.

But I wasn't. I *couldn't*. Lying about what I'd done would mean becoming the selfish, heartless monster Andrew must already think I was. The monster who'd turned him into what he'd become, then left him to die.

"Do you want to…*rephrase* your statement?" my father asked. "For the record?"

Slowly, regretfully, I shook my head. It was the single hardest thing I'd ever had to do. Harder than fighting for my life. Harder than leaving Marc years before. Harder than coming home.

But it was *right*. I knew that with every frenzied beat of my heart. In every shadowed corner of my soul.

I was doing the honorable thing. Just as my Alpha had taught me.

"Faythe…" My father's voice shook, in fury and in… *terror*. He was afraid. For the first time in my life, I saw fear in my father's face, lining his forehead, glazing his eyes.

"I can't do it, Daddy. I'm telling the truth. I did nip him, but the infection was an accident. It's not supposed to happen that way. It shouldn't be possible."

My father hurled his glass across the room. The movement was too fast for my eyes to track. I didn't understand what had happened until glass shattered against the wall and the biting scent of Scotch permeated the air. I jumped, whirling to see the wet smear across the oak paneling.

He shot out of his seat. His armchair fell over backward, slamming against the hardwood floor. "I give you the opportunity to save yourself, and you give me this partial-Shift nonsense? Again?" His face was flushed, his eyes blazing.

"It's the truth." I fought the need to pull my feet up onto the couch and curl into a protective ball. "*You* taught me to tell the truth, to take pride in doing the right thing, even when it's hard. And now you want me to lie, because it's *easier?*"

"I want you to *save* yourself, whatever that takes!" He dropped to his knees on the floor in front of me, taking my wrists in his hands. He stared into my eyes from inches away, pleading with me to listen. To understand. "We're talking about your *life,* Faythe. *Our future.* Not who lost the croquet ball, or who broke the antique vase. You're not eight anymore, so don't throw your damned honor in my face. What good is honor when you're dead?"

I swallowed thickly. "What good is the truth, if you only use it when it doesn't matter?"

His eyes burned into mine. "*Damn* it, Faythe!" Dropping my arms, he leapt to his feet, storming past an astonished Michael, who could do nothing but watch. "We all know you went through something horrible in that basement, and you're entitled to believe whatever helps you cope with killing Eric. But now you're taking it too far. This isn't a game. It isn't therapy. It isn't truth-or-dare. It's your *life.*"

"I know," I whispered miserably, wishing I could do what he wanted. Wishing it was that simple. But it wasn't.

"I don't think you do!" He whirled on me from across the

room. "My job as Alpha is to rid the Pride of any threats. But my job as a parent is to protect you at all costs. What am I supposed to do when you *are* the threat? Why are you making it so hard for me to protect you? You have to give a little, Faythe. You have to meet me halfway."

"For the last time, Daddy, I'm telling the truth. The partial Shift is real. Abby saw it. Hell, Marc saw it. You know that."

He shook his head, pacing back and forth in front of the fallen chair. "Abby doesn't know what she saw. It was dark, and she was upset and confused. She said the shadows scared her, for crying out loud."

My palms began to sweat as I realized what an unreliable witness my cousin was. The council didn't really *dis*believe her. They believed she *thought* she saw my partial shift. But they also thought I was responsible for planting that belief in a traumatized, impressionable young mind.

My head spun like a tilt-a-whirl, possibilities flying past too fast for me to catch. "What about Marc?" I asked at last, clinging to the only other witness I had. "He's seen it. Ask him." Surely the Alpha wouldn't doubt his own right-hand man.

My father paused in his pacing to stare at me in surprise. "Marc would say anything to protect you," he said, as if I should have already known that. "He was humoring you before because you were devastated by Sara's death, and this time he'd lie to save your life. Not that I blame him, but the council will never believe him. He's a stray. Half of them think his word is worthless, anyway. If you ask him to back up a story like this, his credibility will be shot for good. As will yours. This Pride can't afford to lose your credibility any more than it can afford to lose you."

No. I shook my head, denying that the council would discredit Marc. It wasn't true. It couldn't be. And even if it was, so long as my father—my Alpha—believed me, the council would have to. Wouldn't they?

And that's when I realized it didn't matter. *None* of it mattered, because he *didn't* believe me.

My head fell in defeat. If my own father didn't believe me, who would? "What do you want from me?" I asked, staring at my hands, where they lay limp in my lap. "You want me to lie?"

My father was in front of me before I could blink. He bent over, his nose inches from mine. His forehead was red and wrinkled, his brows dark and furrowed in fury.

I tried to pull away. He grabbed my chin, squeezing it between his thumb and forefinger. Pain shot through my jaw. Tears formed instantly, blurring my vision. His eyes swam before me, pools of green even brighter than my own, magnified by the lenses of his glasses. I whimpered, too terrified to be embarrassed by the sound of my own weakness.

"Dad—" Michael began.

"I want proof!" my father roared. He actually roared at me. From inches away. My sensitive ears rang from the abuse. My hands shook uncontrollably. I blinked as his Scotch-breath puffed in my face. I'd never seen him so mad. So scared. So *terrifying*.

I couldn't do it on demand. I'd tried—over and over again—but it never worked when I was relaxed and calm, so what were the chances that I could do it now, when I was half-hysterical and scared shitless?

"Do it," my father ordered, giving me a sharp shake with the grip he had on my chin.

My brain rattled in my skull. I blinked, and tears fell from my eyes.

"Show me," he hissed. "Or I swear I'll have you declawed myself to save the council the trouble."

My chin still pinched in his grasp, I closed my eyes. Tears spilled over again, running down my cheeks. He couldn't be serious. He wouldn't have his own daughter declawed. Or maybe he *would,* especially if he thought that would satisfy the council and keep them off my back.

But I *couldn't* lose my claws. Without them, I couldn't defend myself. I'd be dependant on my father and his enforcers for the rest of what passed for my life. And I certainly couldn't go back to school with my deformed, nail-less human fingers.

Panic clawed at the inside of my throat, trapping my breath. My heart raced, and more hateful tears ran down my face to drip on my father's hand. I couldn't live with that kind of damage. I *wouldn't* live with it.

I squeezed my eyes shut as the first lick of new pain shot through my jaw. I recognized what was happening immediately; evidently the list of emotions that could trigger a partial Shift included mind-numbing panic.

Popping sounds filled my ears, my bones crackling like pop rocks. My father gasped, and his hand fell away from my face. I opened my eyes to see him backing away from me, still on his knees. His eyes were wide, his brows arched high in surprise. And in shock.

My gums began to throb and burn. My tongue started to itch. I clamped one hand over my mouth to muffle a moan as the pain intensified. The roof of my mouth seemed to buckle, and I tried to grit my teeth against the agony. But my teeth no longer fit together right.

Michael leaned across the love seat and turned on a table lamp, to see me better. And finally the pain began to ebb, fading from deeply penetrating bolts of agony into a dull ache, with the occasional twinge. When it was over, my partial Shift complete, I let my hands fall away from my face.

I didn't need to see my reflection to know I was monstrous. My father's sharp inhalation said more about my appearance than words could ever have managed, and for a single, completely uncharacteristic instant, his unguarded expression left nothing to my imagination. Michael's choking sound only underlined the point.

Then my father's horror was simply gone, replaced by a professionally empty look, which was especially irritating in that moment, when I would have appreciated a little wonder and amazement in reward for my efforts. Or at least some professional curiosity.

But until he felt like he'd made up for his deplorable loss of control, I would get none of that. At least not from my father. Michael, however, was undeniably impressed. Or maybe disturbed. Either way, he'd taken off his useless glasses and was squinting at me with his bare eyes. But he made no move to come closer. In fact, he might have actually scooted a little farther away. Which was oddly satisfying. Unlike my father's reaction.

"Well? Say something," I demanded. Or rather, I tried to demand. What actually came out was a mutilated string of vowels and sibilant consonants too strange for even me to comprehend, so my father shouldn't have had a clue. But he seemed to understand, anyway.

He squinted at me for a better look. "I'll…be…damned!"

Nineteen

I could count on one hand the number of times I'd heard my father use profanity, and now he'd done it twice in the same half hour. And to my satisfaction, his voice reflected the amazement I'd hoped to see on his face. Yet no regret for scaring the crap out of me.

I wasn't embarrassed to have been afraid of my father. Fear was a perfectly reasonable response to an Alpha's rage. Expected, even. Better cats than I had pissed themselves in terror when an Alpha lost his temper. Fear was normal. And this time, it had also been productive.

He stood and seemed to float toward me, sinking to his knees with an ease and grace he hadn't displayed in years. He took my chin in his hand, gently this time, and turned my face toward the light. His thumb pulled down my bottom lip for a better look at my teeth, which seemed blatantly unnecessary considering that my mouth wouldn't close, anyway.

Or maybe I just resented being examined like a horse on

an auction block. Especially after being forced to perform like a circus freak on display.

"Satisfied?" I asked, nearly nicking one of his fingers.

"That is without a doubt the most…*amazing* thing I've ever seen."

"Um…yes," Michael stuttered. "It's…really something."

I rolled my eyes at him, wishing he'd been shocked speechless. Yes, I was no doubt hideous compared to his classically beautiful model-wife. But I'd like to see Holly rip someone's throat out with those practically worthless blunt porcelain caps.

"So you believe me now?" I asked, turning back to my father.

"Turn a little more to the left." He ignored my question, aiming my head without waiting for me to comply. Maybe he hadn't understood me. Not that it would have mattered if he had.

He squeezed my cheeks until I had to either open my mouth wider or risk cutting myself on my own teeth. "Your jaws are longer, and your teeth are definitely feline," he said, as if making a diagnosis. "Your tongue is rough, too, but your lips are still human, and I see no sign of fur."

"Thanks for the rundown," I mumbled, pulling free of his grasp. I stood and started to brush past my father, desperate for a little personal space after the invasion of my mouth. But before I'd taken even one step, a movement-blurred glimpse of myself in the silver-framed wall mirror stopped me cold. I sank back onto the couch, curling my hands into fists to keep them from shaking.

That one brief, out-of-focus image was more than enough. I didn't want to know what I looked like. Feeling my teeth with my tongue gave me more information than I could deal with as it was. A partial Shift was great when I needed to rip apart a captor, or see in the dark. But proving my father wrong had lost its novelty, and my self-satisfaction was quickly fading into self-loathing. I *hated* looking like a monster. Not as badly as I hated looking like a little girl, but almost.

"If you're satisfied, I'm going to Shift back now," I lisped, as my father settled onto the couch next to me. And he finally looked impressed.

Good for him. I was Shifting back. But not with them watching me.

Over his sharp protest, I stood again, careful to avoid looking in the mirror as I stepped around the fallen armchair. Turning my back on my father and brother, I reversed the process, which was inevitably easier than the initial change, in the same way that the drive home from any given trip always seems to take less time than the torturously slow trip there.

When everything felt normal and I could speak plainly again, I leaned against the desk with my arms crossed beneath my breasts. "Are you satisfied now?"

He chuckled. "I'm much more than satisfied. I'm elated. I'm astonished. I'm relieved." He stopped speaking, and I kept waiting. Surely there was more. But there wasn't. He was done.

"Aren't you forgetting something?"

My father frowned in concentration, clearly searching his memory for the omission. "What?"

Michael wiped his glasses with a white cloth from his pocket. "I believe she's asking for an apology."

"Of course I am. I *deserve* an apology!" I insisted. My father's eyebrows shot up in surprise, and my own eyes widened in disbelief. "You're not sorry for not believing me?"

"Certainly, I'm sorry you had trouble demonstrating your extraordinary new skill, but it would have been foolish of me to believe something so fantastic without proof."

I spoke through clenched teeth. "I trust every word you say. Why can't you give me the same courtesy?"

He frowned. "I've earned your trust. I've never once lied to you."

"When have *I* ever lied to *you?*" Alarm bells went off inside my head, but it was too late to take the question back.

"Half an hour ago, you lied by omission when you avoided mentioning the hunter who saw you in cat form."

Michael chuckled, and I glared at him, my mind racing to figure out how to respond.

Oh shit. Shit, shit, shit. "That wasn't technically a lie," I muttered, already wishing I'd left well enough alone. Why couldn't I stop digging my own grave just once before the hole got too deep to climb out of?

My father's frown deepened, and I felt a lecture coming on. "It's not the letter of the law that matters, Faythe. It's the intent."

Blah, blah, blah. I happened to think that if the letter of the law left room for creative interpretation, it ought to be rephrased, to avoid confusion. And loopholes. Attorneys and accountants were rewarded rather than punished for finding loopholes, so why shouldn't I be?

Because I didn't work for the government, or for Joe Q. Public. I worked for my father.

"How long have you known?" I asked, trying to determine the least incriminating way to find out how much he actually knew.

"Since an hour after it happened," he said. I opened my mouth, but he cut me off before I could chomp down on my own foot. I should have thanked him. "Don't worry, no one tattled on you. I overheard you and Marc arguing about it. You two aren't exactly quiet, you know."

Damn it. No matter how much trouble I went through to cover all my bases, it was always my own mouth that got me into trouble. Literally, in Andrew's case.

"If you knew what happened, and you knew the guys were covering for me, why didn't you say anything?"

My father rose gracefully from the couch, standing to face me. His mouth turned up into a conspiratorial smile, as if he were about to let me in on a big secret. I was curious, in spite of my habitual feigned disinterest.

"I thought about it," he said finally. "I thought about teaching you all a lesson in loyalty and obedience. But then I realized that Ethan, Jace, and Parker were not showing disloyalty to me so much as they were showing loyalty to you and Marc. Their willingness to protect you both, possibly at great cost, shows how devoted they are to the two of you, even though you don't pay them and they haven't pledged anything to you. I can't teach devotion like that, and I'm certainly not going to punish it. Especially since nothing more damaging has come of it than a Yeti-esque article in the paper and some local news reports that make that poor hunter sound like a drunken fool."

I stared at my father in disbelief. Not only was he not mad at us—not foaming at the mouth, like I'd expected—he was actually *pleased* by our conspiracy to withhold information.

Sometimes it scared me that I understood the bad guys better than I understood my own father.

"So you're not mad?" *It might be a good idea to get this in writing, while I'm at it.*

"Not this time." His face hardened and his gaze narrowed, giving me the impression that he saw nothing but my eyes. "But before you decide to keep anything important from me again, remember my willingness to have a second cage installed in the basement. Just for you."

I grinned. "I'll keep that in mind." We were back on familiar territory now. He made threats, and I ignored them. That much I could handle. And now that I was more at ease, it was time to get down to business. "So, about Andrew…?"

"Well, obviously I'm not pleased to find out my daughter infected the stray who's causing so much trouble. But at least now we have a starting point."

Well, that was certainly one way of looking at it, and I wasn't about to complain, considering how close I'd come to a possible death sentence.

"Michael, go find the rest of the guys."

My brother nodded, already headed for the door. "Well, look what I found," he said, and I turned to see him standing in the threshold, doorknob still in hand. In the hall beyond, Owen rose from the floor, where he'd apparently been waiting for the office door to open. And he wasn't alone. Vic, Parker, and Jace filed in behind him, Ethan bringing up the rear. Marc wasn't there.

My father chuckled from his armchair. "You're all fine examples of what curiosity did to the proverbial cat, aren't you?" Parker shrugged, and only Owen had the grace to look embarrassed. Our Alpha waved them all forward. "Come sit down. Now that we have a serious lead, we have a lot of work to do. Was there anything in the news?"

"Yeah. Here." Vic handed him a thin, stapled stack of papers on his way to the love seat, where he settled in next to Parker.

"You want me to go get Marc?" Michael asked as I sank onto the couch.

My father looked up from the reports, and his eyes landed

on me. "No, let's give him a little more time." He scanned the first page, then flipped it over and scanned the second. Then the third and final. "Is this it?" he asked, flipping back to the front of the stack.

"Yeah." Parker ran one hand through a thick head of salt-and-pepper hair. "There were variations of it on a couple of other news sites, but they all had the same information. Which isn't much."

"Okay." Leaning forward, my father slid the packet of papers onto the table by my end of the couch, then leaned back in his chair to address us all. "As I expected, the Louisiana police have connected the missing-stripper cases in their state, and the national news has picked up the story. Fortunately, no one seems to realize yet that the Arkansas stripper is related. But that won't take them long, especially if any others go missing. Unfortunately—" he twisted his arm to glance at the watch on his wrist "—if the pattern holds up, that may already have happened."

Jace frowned. "So the only thing going in our favor is the fact that no one knows about the dead toms. Which is only because we've been burying them."

My father cracked one knuckle as his gaze skipped from Jace to me, then back to Jace. "That's true, but it's not the only thing we have going for us. Faythe, would you like to tell them in your own words?"

Um, no. My words had done enough damage for one night. I shrugged. "Be my guest."

Every eye in the room shifted from me to my father. Though they'd been sitting right outside the office, they hadn't heard a word said inside, thanks to the solid oak door and concrete-lined walls, which gave my father a measure of precious privacy I'd envied on more than one occasion.

"Well, it seems that Faythe's human boyfriend—former in both respects—is somehow involved in the outbreak of stripper disappearances."

I don't know what kind of reaction I expected. Maybe gasps and startled exclamations. But the reality was rather anticlimactic.

"Uh, Ethan already told us that part," Vic said, shooting a sympathetic glance my way.

"Wait," Jace said, and I saw the light go on behind his eyes. He'd been the only one truly listening, because they'd all expected to hear old news. "Did you say 'former in *both* respects'? Meaning he's no longer human?"

I nodded silently.

And *then* came the anticipated drama….

"What the hel—?"

"How is that even poss—?"

"So he knows abo—?"

But it was Parker who hit the proverbial nail on the head. "That's waaay too much of a coincidence. He was dating a werecat, then three months later he shows up as one?" The others stopped talking one by one, now listening to Parker. "Do we know who did it? It has to be someone connected to Faythe. She's the only common denominator."

I'd forgotten how smart the guys really were.

"Yes, we know who did it." My father paused, watching me. "Faythe."

Everyone turned to stare at me expectantly. They thought he was calling on me to answer the question, like a teacher in a third-grade classroom. But he wasn't, and at first no one seemed to understand. And this time, Ethan was the first to catch on.

"Faythe?" He stared at me from his spot on the rug next to Jace, disbelief written all over his face. Then confusion settled in its place. *"You* infected him?"

"It's complicated, and we don't have time to explain right now," my father began. "So let me just say it was an accident, and leave it at that."

"An *accident?"* Ethan obviously had several more questions—as did everyone else—but the Alpha's word was final, so he closed his mouth and frowned. I had no doubt he'd ask me for details later, in private.

One hand on the back of our father's armchair, Michael took over the discussion, to bring the topic back on track. "We're assuming Andrew's actually *responsible* for the disappearances, rather than just involved in them. And while we're outlining worst-case scenarios, I'll venture to guess that the women are all dead."

"Okay," Vic said, jumping on the calm-and-professional bandwagon. "What's the plan?"

"We find Andrew. We apprehend him, subdue him, and find out what he knows about the tabby, if anything. If he *doesn't* know anything, we watch the last strip club he visited and wait for her to show up. Then we take her. Case closed."

"I don't suppose lover-boy happened to mention where he was headed?" Jace asked, tugging on one frayed tassel from the edge of the rug he sat on.

"As a matter of fact…" I smiled hesitantly, and every disbelieving eye in the room focused on me. "He's coming here."

"What on earth *for?"* Ethan asked, just as Parker cried, "Is he sui*c*idal?"

"I don't know." I shrugged. "He probably wants some kind of confrontation with me. Acknowledgment." Which I understood, oddly enough. "Doesn't matter, though. All we have to do is sit back and wait for him. Right?"

"Out of the question," my father said, and the calm finality in his tone took me by surprise. "We are *not* going to let this mess land on our doorstep. We can't afford that kind of attention, either from the human authorities or the rest of the council. We have to find him before he gets here."

Damn. So much for the easy way.

Vic frowned. "Okay, so where do we start?"

"With the phone calls," I said, and my father nodded, showing just a hint of a proud smile. "We know that Andrew and Dan Painter called from the same place this afternoon."

"We do?" Ethan interrupted.

"Yes. Both messages contained what sounded like explosions and propeller noise." I went on, heedless of the confused looks around me. "We also know that Andrew is headed this way from Leesville, Louisiana, where he took the last stripper. So he and Painter—and presumably the tabby—are probably somewhere between here and there, in a town with…a bunch of gunfire and helicopters?" I ended, my pitch rising in question. "Hospital choppers, maybe? Did you guys see anything on the news about explosions?"

Vic, Owen, and Parker all shook their heads.

Rapid-fire tapping broke the silence. "Give me just a minute here…." Michael said, and I glanced up to find him hunched over the computer keyboard again, his head barely visible behind my father's seventeen-inch flat-screen monitor. "With any luck, I'll have a location for you soon…." His words faded away as the clicking got louder.

While Michael worked his computer magic, my father turned back to face the rest of us. His gaze settled first on

Ethan as he seemed to consider something. Then he shook his head and turned toward Owen, on my right. "You and Parker get ready. You leave as soon as we get a fix on Andrew's last-known location, to scout it out and see if he's still there."

"We takin' the van?" Owen asked, already halfway to the door, dusty cowboy hat in hand.

"Yes. And take the full emergency kit, not the trunk version."

I swallowed thickly, unwilling to imagine what use they'd put the emergency kit to when they found Andrew. Yes, by all indications he was no longer the sweet, quiet math major I'd once known. But that was my fault, as was whatever else happened to him. Suddenly I felt sick.

"Faythe?" my father said, and I met his eyes reluctantly, already dreading whatever he would ask of me. "I assume you have Andrew's number, since he's been calling you?" I nodded, and he continued. "If Michael can't find him, I want you to call him and set up a meeting—somewhere other than here. Say whatever you have to say. Agree to anything he wants. If he's really looking for a confrontation with you, he should be eager for this chance."

"Where do you want us to meet?" I asked, my fingers twisting into knots in my lap. I was not looking forward to seeing Andrew again.

"In a park, or campsite. Somewhere that looks open and rural, but that won't really give him anywhere to run. And that will adequately hide the rest of you," he said, glancing around at Vic, Ethan, and Jace. "Give me a minute, and I'll have a location for you. In the meantime…Vic, go make some coffee."

I started to laugh, assuming my father was joking. But then Ethan and Jace followed Vic into the kitchen, without so much as a smile. Evidently "make some coffee" was Alpha-speak for, "It's going to be a long night, folks."

"Don't you think Marc should be here?" I asked several minutes later, plucking at a loose string on the hem of my shorts. As awkward as it would be for me to have my current boyfriend present when I spoke to my ex-boyfriend-turned-psychopathic stalker, it would be worse not to have Marc there.

Michael's tapping paused for an instant, and my father looked up from the atlas, where he'd been eyeing a regional map of East Texas for the past few minutes. "We can fill him in later. You're going to have to give him some time, Faythe. This is going to be very difficult for him to deal with. Parts of it will be impossible. You know that. You know *him*."

I nodded. I did know Marc. That was the problem.

"Coffee!" Vic shouted from the kitchen across the hall. "Get it while it's hot!"

My father scowled deeply, glancing at the open doorway. "He could have at least poured it for us."

I laughed, my mouth already watering from the scent of the gourmet Amaretto-flavored brew now infusing the air. "I think you're confusing him with Mom. We're lucky he even knows how to use the coffeepot."

"All men know how to make coffee," my father insisted, rising to follow me across the room. "It's a survival instinct. I made my first pot at twelve, though my mother wouldn't let me drink any for another four years."

In the kitchen, I padded past Ethan and Jace, who'd come in ahead of me, and stood on tiptoe to take two oversize latte mugs down from the cabinet while my father put spoons out on the counter. I set one mug in front of my father and kept the other for myself, then filled them both.

"Hey, Vic, if I pour coffee for Marc, will you take it to him?" Normally, I'd have told Marc to come get his own damn coffee, but considering he'd just found out that I was secretly still in contact with my murdering psychopath of an ex, I figured I could manage an apology in the form of a simple mug of coffee. Two sugars, no cream.

"He left about an hour ago," Ethan said, pulling a loaf of bread from the breadbox.

"Where'd he go?"

Vic emerged from the fridge with a carton of French vanilla creamer, kicking the door shut behind him. "Don't know. I think he just needed to get away for a while. Don't worry. He'll be back."

I poured creamer into my coffee and stirred, not comforted in the least by Vic's assurances.

"Hey, Faythe?" Jace asked, and I looked up to find him watching me from a stool on the other side of the bar. "How much does Andrew know about us? About him*self?*"

"I don't know." I frowned, sipping from my mug as I considered the question. "He seems to know quite a bit." Which I realized only in retrospect, thinking back over our recent conversations. "He certainly knows what we are, and where we live. And he seemed to know my parents wouldn't be happy about my infecting him." Though I'd had no idea what he was talking about at the time.

"How is that even possible?" Jace pushed his stool back and rose, heading straight for the now nearly empty coffeepot. "I understand how he knows he's infected. I assume that one's fairly self-explanatory. But if you never Shifted in front of him—and I *know* you never told him about any of us—how the hell does he know that you infected him? Or that the rest of us are werecats, too? Or that infecting humans is a big no-no?"

"Actually, I have no idea how he knows any of that." I snatched a slice of ham from the collection of sandwich ingredients Ethan was setting out on the counter. "But that'll be the first thing I ask him, if he answers his phone."

"Well, off the top of my head, I'd say someone told him." Vic blew carefully into his Atlanta Braves mug. "But I'm sure that's much too simple to be it."

My father took another sip of coffee. "On the contrary, usually the simplest possibility *is* the answer, and it stands to reason that Andrew must have had contact with another werecat at some point in the past few months. He'd have to be pretty tough to have survived the initial sickness and first Shift on his own. And while unlikely, it's not beyond the realm of possibility that another stray took pity on him, rather than running him off or attacking him."

My father's response sent one of Andrew's bobbing to the surface of my memory. *You're fucking lying, and we damn well know it.* We.

"Son of a bitch, that's it!" I dropped the spoon into my mug, and several drops of coffee splattered on the counter, but I barely noticed.

"What?" Jace looked up from the ham, cheese, and pickle slices he was layering on a piece of bread.

"Andrew's not in this alone." I plucked a pickle from his plate and gestured with it as I spoke. "New strays don't come out of their initial transition mentally or physically strong enough to pull off the kind of major-league mischief he's been up to. Not on their own."

"You think he's working with someone?" my father asked, green eyes alight with the new possibility.

"Yes." I tossed the pickle into my mouth and spoke around it as I chewed. "I think he has been from the beginning. The same someone who got him through his first Shift and taught him how to survive as a stray."

Ethan smashed his huge sandwich flat with one palm. "The rogue tabby?"

I shook my head. "Couldn't be her. *She's* following *him*, not the other way around."

Vic frowned. "So, maybe she *was* helping him, and he went crazy and took off on his own, and now she's trying to catch him and stop him."

"But she's a murderer. Why would one murderer try to stop another?" Jace argued, voicing a thought we'd surely all had—no one believed we'd find those strippers alive.

"I don't think she wants any part of Andrew's game," I said, stirring my coffee again as I thought aloud. "She's clearly no saint, but look at the *way* she's killed the toms. No slashing, and no biting. No signs of violence of any kind, other than the whole neck-breaking thing. I don't know why she's killing them, but I don't think it's out of rage. But Andrew, on the other hand, is definitely pissed off, and I'd be willing to bet those missing strippers bear evidence of that, wherever they are."

I paused and drained my mug. "And I have a theory about why Andrew's done such a one-eighty. Why he's suddenly so angry and violent."

"Yeah." Ethan shrugged. "He's a stray."

"But so's Marc, and he's never kidnapped anyone. He's completely devoted to this Pride. Loyal beyond all logic. He'd give his life to save any of us, any day of the week."

"Yes." My father nodded decisively. Proudly. "He would."

I smiled at him. "As far as I can tell, the difference between

Marc and Andrew is that Marc has us. He's what and who he is today because you and Mom took him in when he was sick, injured, and newly orphaned. Because you made him one of us and gave him a chance. If the Pride had such a profound influence on Marc, at such a critical stage in his life—his initial transition—doesn't it stand to reason that someone might have had an equally strong influence on Andrew?"

"A *bad* influence, you mean?" Jace said, snatching a spare slice of ham from Ethan's plate.

"Well, yes." I leaned back against the counter, where I could see them all. "I think whoever helped him through the scratch-fever—and taught him what he knows about us—also turned him into what he's become. And I don't think it was the tabby. Based on the way she killed those strays, I don't think she's capable of that much rage."

My theory explained, my opinion given, I poured myself a fresh cup of coffee, waiting for someone to speak.

My father looked impressed but also worried. "So, you think Andrew's still with this bad influence, whoever it is?" I nodded, and he popped several knuckles at once. Then he set his empty mug in the sink and stalked out of the kitchen and across the hall, leaving us all to trail behind him.

In the office, I set my mug on a coaster on the nearest end table and sank onto the couch. Jace plopped down next to me, and Ethan sat by him, still clutching his half-eaten sandwich. Vic settled onto the love seat opposite us.

At the desk, Michael was still clicking away. I leaned back to glance at him and found him chewing his lower lip as he worked. Which meant he was frustrated. Apparently he'd had no luck tracking down the explosions.

"You ready for me to call Andrew?" I asked my father.

While I still dreaded the phone call, I was now eager to get it over with.

"I'm having second thoughts about that now." He frowned, templing his hands beneath his chin. "If Andrew's really working with someone else, I'm not sure I want to grant him this confrontation until we know who we'll actually be facing."

"It has to be someone who knows Faythe infected Andrew," Ethan said, speaking around a bite of ham sandwich. "Otherwise, Andrew wouldn't know that, either. So…who knows you bit him?"

"No one," I said, turning from my father to face my youngest brother. "*I* didn't even understand what happened until tonight. But anyone who smells him will know who infected him—assuming the smeller recognizes my scent threaded through his. So…we're back to someone who knows me. Or at least my scent."

"Exactly," my father said, obviously displeased with the new development. "I think we should put that phone call off for a little bit, until we have a better idea of who he's with, and where they are—"

"Henderson," Michael interrupted, amid another flurry of frantic keystrokes. "Andrew's in Henderson, Texas. At least, he was this afternoon."

"Are you sure?" My father stood to turn and look at Michael, at the desk behind him.

"Pretty sure." Michael nodded, shoving his glasses farther up on his nose. "Those propellers Faythe heard weren't helicopters. They were vintage aircraft from a World War Two demonstration team that did a big show this afternoon in Henderson, as part of the town's centennial celebration. Complete with a pyrotechnic display, which no doubt explains the 'gunfire.'"

"Well, that should make it pretty easy to find Andrew," Vic said, though I could barely hear him over the grinding of gears in my own head. "Henderson's only an hour from the ranch. He could be sitting outside the gate right now."

Ethan choked on the last bite of his sandwich, and Jace pounded on his back. When my brother's throat was clear, he said, "He could have been watching us for hours, for all we know."

"He's not here," I said, surprised to hear how very calm my voice sounded, in contrast to how panicked I actually felt. "Not yet. He said he had something else to take care of first. Apparently I'm not his top priority at the moment."

Out front, I heard the growl of an engine, and I turned toward the door in anticipation. But then I recognized the sound as Owen's truck. *Where the hell had Owen gone?* I'd hoped it was Marc. I needed to see his face, to settle the unease taking hold in the pit of my stomach. I needed to know he'd forgiven me for not telling him about the calls. That we were going to be okay, no matter what happened with Andrew. And considering he still didn't know I'd infected my ex, a good outcome for us was far from guaranteed.

The front door opened, and footsteps clomped on the tiles. Owen was back from wherever he had gone.

"I'm sure you're all going to start yelling at me for this…" Vic began, glancing around at the room in general. "But this may be a good time to bring the council up to speed. We have enough information now that they can't afford to waste time arguing. They'll have to—"

"Absolutely not!" I glared across the rug at him, then turned to face my father when he didn't immediately back me up. To my horror, he sat with his eyes downcast and his hands templed beneath his chin, apparently actually considering Vic's suggestion.

"What are we going to say?" I demanded, already picturing the shocked faces of the other Alphas. "'The council chairman's daughter accidentally infected her human boyfriend during a rough-'n'-tumble nooner, then he followed her home, leaving a trail of missing strippers in his wake.'"

My father released a tired, weighty sigh. "Faythe, they have a right to know. And they can help. The more men we have, the faster we can find Andrew and the tabby, and be done with this whole mess."

My hand clenched the arm of the leather couch, my pulse racing. "Daddy, no! We have to take care of this on our own. If we bring the council in before we get Andrew under control, they're going to want my head mounted on a spike in the front yard."

Behind me, the footsteps stopped. I was already turning as my last word faded into a heavy, tortured silence, and too late, it occurred to me that the clomping in the hall hadn't come from cowboy boots.

Marc stood in the doorway, each arm wrapped around a brown paper bag. Our eyes met. I had a second to register the pain in his. Then the bags thumped to the hardwood floor, and he was gone.

Twenty

Jace and Vic ran after Marc, vaulting over the fallen bags and into the hall. Neither spared me a glance.

I leapt off the couch, a silent scream of anguish splitting my skull in two. On the floor in front of me, a half gallon of triple-chocolate-chunk ice cream rolled across the hardwood, stopping only when it bumped the toe of my sneaker. My favorite flavor. He'd gone out for ice cream, to apologize and make up.

Son of a bitch!

I stepped over the cardboard carton, and my father called my name. I ignored him and took off after the guys, stepping over four more cartons of ice cream, each a different flavor. In the hall, I tripped over a box of waffle cones and had to catch myself against the wall.

As I looked up, Vic disappeared out the back door, Jace and Marc ahead of him.

I ran down the hall after the guys, my sneakers slapping the tile. I called Marc, screaming his name with a desperation that bruised my soul. I knew he could hear me, but he didn't answer.

I was only feet from the back door when someone grabbed my arm from behind. Ethan pulled me backward and stepped in front of me, completely blocking my path. "Get out of the way!" I screamed, trying to bump him aside and run past him. But he wouldn't budge.

"Faythe—"

"Move!"

Ethan held me back, his hands gentle on my shoulders, his eyes oddly imploring. "Give him some time."

"No! The last thing he needs is time to brood and get madder. He doesn't understand what he heard. I have to explain." I shoved him in the chest, but he only bounced back an instant later, wrapping both hands around my upper arms.

"You'll only make it worse."

Fighting tears, I twisted out of his grip. "If you don't want to get hurt, get out of my way."

"I'm trying to help y—"

"I'm sorry." I let my right fist fly. It smashed into his jaw.

Ethan stumbled backward into the wall. "Fine, go make it worse!" he shouted, his hand covering the fresh red splotch on his face.

By the time I made it to the back porch, the guys were gone, having holed up in their overgrown dormitory, surrounded by the staples of masculinity: beer, day-old pizza, and mountains of dirty socks.

Lightning flashed across the sky the moment I stepped onto the grass. For an instant, it lit the entire backyard in a stark relief of light and shadow. The image was still stamped into my retinas when thunder roared across the sky, the ageless creak of ancient floodgates opening. Rain poured from the clouds in a sudden deluge the likes of which Texas—

even East Texas—rarely ever saw. I was completely drenched in less than five steps.

Pushing wet hair back from my face, I jogged across the yard, stomped up the front steps, and tore open the screen door. It flew back to smack the siding. Dripping water onto the porch, I grabbed the front doorknob, already shoving forward as I turned it. Nothing happened. Well, almost nothing. I walked right into the door, expecting it to open. Instead, I nearly broke my own nose.

In my entire life I'd never seen the guesthouse locked. I'd always been welcome. Always. And now Marc had locked me out. Literally.

I did *not* take it well.

"Open the fucking door!" I shouted, pounding on the wood with both fists.

"My dad's not mad at me!" I yelled, straining to be heard over the storm. "Doesn't that tell you anything?"

No response. I glanced over my shoulder and saw my mother's form silhouetted in Ethan's bedroom window. She watched me with her arms crossed over her chest, making no attempt to interfere.

"I can go get a key!" I yelled, turning back to the guest-house door. "You can't keep me out forever. Hell, I'll just kick in the door if you don't open up in the next two minutes." I gave the wood another good pounding, thoroughly bruising both fists, then paused again to listen, pressing my ear against the door. This time I heard results: footsteps clomping down the stairs. So, did I stop and wait patiently?

Hell no. I'd forgotten the meaning of the word patience by then. All I could think about was explaining to Marc what really happened before it was too late.

"I hear you in there. Come open this damn door before I break it down."

"Give it a rest, Faythe." It was Vic, speaking calmly from the other side of the door. The still infuriatingly *closed* door. "You're waking up people in the next county."

"Let me in so I can talk to him." Rain rolled slowly down my spine beneath my shirt, tracing the line of fear building inside me. I had to make Marc understand. This couldn't be the end for us. Not like this. "I can fix this," I shouted, dismayed to hear the edge of panic in my voice. "I swear I can."

"I'm sorry. He'd skin me alive. You'd better give him some time to get over it."

"That's just it." I pounded on the wood again, and Vic swore, then jumped back. Too late, I realized he'd been leaning against the door. "If you don't let me in so I can explain it to him, he's not *going* to get over it. He doesn't understand what he heard."

"I'm sorry, Faythe," he said again. "He just doesn't want to see you."

This isn't possible, I thought, wringing rain from my ponytail. Of course, Marc had been mad at me before. He'd been mad at me for five straight years after I'd broken up with him. But he'd never refused to speak to me. He'd never locked me out. I'd spent holidays with Sammi and her family to escape his relentless pursuit, and still he'd called me at least once a week for three years, baring his soul to my voice mail with so much pain in his voice that I couldn't listen to the messages without tearing up.

When he finally stopped calling, the hush felt strange. It felt like the whole world went silent when Marc did, as if I could see people's mouths moving, but I couldn't hear what they were saying. Like I'd gone deaf.

That emotional silence didn't stop until Marc came for me at school. And it descended on me again as I stood on his front porch. All I could hear was the rain, as if the very heavens were crying for us both.

I glanced at my mother again, only to see her turn away from the window. She looked back once and shook her head. Then she was gone. My resolve strengthened in the face of my mother's desertion. She might or might not know what I'd done, but she believed I'd lost Marc for good. After years of nagging me to go back to him, she'd given up on us.

But I hadn't.

I backed down the steps, facing the front door as I descended into the rain. Water poured down on me, replastering loose strands of hair to my cheeks and forehead. I wiped my face with both hands, blinking rain and tears from my eyes as I assessed the door. It was solid, and strong in spite of its age. But so was I, in spite of my youth.

And anyway, the frame would break long before the oak panel would.

I pushed back my hair one more time and ran up the steps. At the top, I grabbed the support post for balance and kicked the door as hard as I could, concentrating the blow just below the doorknob. Wood splintered, and I smiled in satisfaction. I grabbed the doorknob and shook it with both hands. Nothing happened. It didn't even budge.

Damn it!

Fingers appeared in the window, pushing aside a set of cheap white miniblinds to reveal a pair of dark blue eyes and a lock of brown hair. "Faythe, what the hell are you doing?" Jace yelled through the glass. His face disappeared and the steel chain rattled as he tried to unlock the door. But then something heavy hit the wood, probably someone else's hand.

Vic laughed. "That's not Faythe," he said. "That's the Big Bad Wolf, come to blow us all away."

"She's gonna get in one way or another," Jace said.

Vic laughed again. "She's gonna *try.*"

"You bet your ass," I shouted, and kicked the wood again. More splintering this time, but still the door wouldn't budge. However, this time the problem wasn't the strength of the door, but the strength of the guys holding it in place from the other side.

For a long moment, no one spoke. I was almost convinced they'd gone out the back door when Parker said, "Okay."

"What? No!" Vic insisted. "He doesn't want to see her, and that's his choice."

"I'll take the blame," Parker said, and the chain rattled again. "Get out of the way." The dead bolt slid back and the door opened just wide enough for me to see his face. Parker's eyes were hard, his brows furrowed in unease. "I'm going to let you in here on one condition."

"Fine. Anything." I was perfectly willing to behave myself in exchange for admission. I could break open the door, but I couldn't keep them from holding it in place. And if I went through the window, I'd be lucky not to bleed to death before I got to Marc.

"I'm letting you in to keep you from breaking the door, not so that you can break everything else in the house. No damage. Not to *our* stuff. Not to *his* stuff. And not to *him.* You go make it better, not worse."

"That's all I want. You should know that by now." But I saw

in his eyes that he didn't know that. He didn't trust me not to hurt Marc. After all, I'd done it before.

I closed my eyes and smoothed my hair back, trying to get hold of myself both physically and emotionally before I went inside.

Parker pulled the door open and I stepped over the threshold, dripping rain on the scarred hardwood floor. Jace and Vic stood side by side at the foot of the stairs, blocking my way. Their arms were crossed over their chests, forming a physical barrier, another wall to knock down.

I wasn't up to it. Not anymore. Outside I'd had strength. I'd been willing to tear down the whole house to get to Marc if I had to. But now I was almost there, and I was tired. I was already sick of fighting, and I hadn't even reached the ring.

"Come on, guys," I said as I approached them. "Give me a break. Please."

The conflict on Jace's face was torture to see. I knew how he felt about me, but I hadn't really considered how he felt about Marc until I saw how far he was willing to go to protect him. From me. Even from me. If he could, Jace would take me away from Marc. But he wouldn't let me hurt him.

I met his beautiful cobalt eyes and nodded. It was the best I could do at the moment to acknowledge his pain and the awkwardness of the situation. Apparently it was enough, because he stepped aside.

Vic didn't. My shoulder brushed his bicep as I walked past him and up the steps, still dripping, and now shivering from the air-conditioned breeze on my drenched skin.

The lights were on downstairs, but the upstairs landing was dark. If not for a bright flash of lightning through a rear window, I might have tripped over the throw rug at the top of the stairs. As it was, I had to feel my way past the bathroom and the first bedroom—the one Jace and Vic shared—with one hand on the banister. I felt along the opposite wall until I located Marc's door.

My hand found his doorknob, and I hesitated. I let my eyes close and my head fall back as I listened to the rain, wondering how on earth I was going to get him to hear me out. Finally, I opened my eyes—not that it mattered, I couldn't see a damn thing—and let go of the doorknob. I knocked instead. He would only react in kind if I started things off with discourtesy and aggression.

Of course, by being polite, I was giving him the opportunity to deny me entrance. Or to ignore me completely, which was exactly what he did.

"Marc?" I called, knocking again. He made no reply, but a light went on in his room, illuminating my soaked sneakers from the crack beneath his door. "May I please come in? I owe you an apology and an explanation, and I'd like to give them to you face-to-face. Please."

Wood scraped wood on the other side of the door: dresser drawers opening. "Fine," he said. "I have something to explain to you, too."

My pulse spiked. That couldn't be good.

I opened the door slowly, and the first thing I registered was his scent. The entire room smelled like Marc and literally made my heart throb. I swallowed, and blinked tears from my eyes as I breathed him in. He was everywhere. He could leave at that moment and his scent would still be there ten years later.

Marc crossed the floor with a pile of clothes in his arms, and his movement caught my eye as I stood in the doorway, staring into his room. He dropped the clothes into a suitcase open on the unmade bed, balanced half on a pillow and half on a crooked mound of covers.

"What—" My voice croaked, so I swallowed and tried again. "What are you doing?"

"Packing. I thought it was kind of obvious." He walked back to the dresser without even glancing at me. "I'm taking some time off."

"Time off?" I heard myself and regretted the fact that I sounded like a brainless parrot, but I was helpless to stop it. In the nearly eleven years Marc had worked for my father, he'd never taken a single day off. Not one. Which meant he probably had quite a few coming…

I inhaled deeply, preparing to say my piece. To change his mind. "I'm sorry you heard it like that." I tried to catch Marc's eye, but he wouldn't look at me, nor would he stop packing. I cleared my throat and started over, tracking his movement back and forth across the room. "But you didn't hear enough to understand what happened."

"I heard plenty."

"It was an accid—" I grabbed his wrist as he walked past me, another pile of shirts under his opposite arm. He froze in place. His head turned slowly, and finally our eyes met. His were blank. Empty. He jerked his arm from my grasp and continued toward the bed. "Marc, could you please look at me? This is hard enough without you…packing."

"Well then, let me make it easier for you." He dumped the shirts on top of the pile in the suitcase and looked up at me. "I. Heard. Enough. You infected Andrew. Your carelessness— and whatever freaky, furry game you were playing—condemned a man who was guilty of nothing more than fucking my girlfriend to a life of solitude and violence. Even worse, you're responsible for everything he's done. Those missing women are on *your* conscience. That's all I need to know." He flipped the top of the leather bag over and tried to close it, but the zipper resisted.

Furry game? Was he serious?

"That *isn't* all you need to know. Will you—" I grabbed the handle of his suitcase in exasperation and pulled it away from him. Already strained to its limits, the zipper slid back and the suitcase popped open, spewing socks and underwear all over the bed and the floor, like an explosion from a cotton volcano. Marc growled and bent to pick up a shirt. I snatched it from his hand and held it behind my back. "Will you forget about the clothes for a minute and listen to me? Please?"

"Fine." He kicked aside a balled-up pair of socks and folded his arms across his chest. "You want to explain? I'm listening. Explain how you somehow forgot to mention to me over the past three months that you infected your college boy-friend. Explain why you didn't think that was significant enough to bother telling me *before* he started taking his anger at you out on other women unlucky enough to have black hair and green eyes. Not that I blame him for being pissed off. I know pretty damn well how *that* feels!"

Marc picked up his now-broken bag and hurled it across the room. I flinched as it hit the far wall, next to the window, and fell to the floor in a heap of worn leather and rumpled clothing. "You stood me up at our *fucking wedding,* and I begged you to come back. I just rolled over and took it, even though every cat in the country was laughing at me behind my back. But apparently my complete humiliation wasn't enough to satisfy you. So why don't you explain how you expect me to react when the entire werecat community finds out you created a replacement for me out of some preppy, khaki-wearing college boy who's more familiar with waiting in line for his iced latte than with the finer points of self-preservation. Explain to me just what the hell you were thinking, Faythe," he shouted, and I winced with every sarcasm-laced barb. "I think I'm ready to hear that now."

I took a deep breath, doing my best to remain calm and to resist yelling. He had some valid points, after all. "I wasn't trying to replace you. And I didn't tell you because I didn't know what I'd done. I didn't figure it out until tonight. I *did* bite Andrew, but it was an accident. Well, the infection was an accident," I said, my words rushing together as I back-pedaled. "I bit him on purpose. Kind of." I flinched as the last words left my mouth, uncomfortably aware that I wasn't helping the situation.

Marc blinked at me and his expression hardened even more, which I hadn't thought possible. "Do I even want to know why you bit him?"

Heat rushed to my cheeks. "Probably not."

Outside, a sudden gust of wind pelted the window with rain, drawing Marc's attention away from me. When he met my eyes again, his were flaming in fresh anger. "Well, I gotta give college boy credit for *that,* at least," he spat, his tone dripping with enough acid to eat through the hardwood floor. "The way Vic described him, I didn't think he would have the balls to go for any fur-and-claws action, especially considering how much damage you can do with your *human* teeth and nails. And with your damned dagger of a tongue."

Speaking of sharp tongues… I sighed. This was *not* going well. "I never Shifted, Marc."

"What?" Confusion flitted across his face briefly before the angry scowl settled back into place. "Then how the hell did you infect him? Spit in his drink when he wasn't looking? Inject him with your blood in his sleep?"

"Ha, ha." I perched on the end of his bed, dripping rainwater onto his comforter as I wished for my punching pillow. Alas, as luck would have it, there was nothing in the room I could hit without breaking my promise to Parker. Marc sat against the headboard, facing me. He took one look at the grip I had on his comforter and tossed me one of his pillows.

That small act floored me.

Marc was hurt, humiliated, and pissed off. He was madder at me than I'd ever seen him, and he was scared of losing me to either the council or to Andrew. And on top of that, he felt mortified by what he apparently saw as the ultimate act of cuckolding. Yet he knew what I needed and provided me with it without a moment's hesitation, or probably even a conscious thought.

Marc was always there for me, even when he was packing his bags to leave me. He deserved to hear the truth from me, but what he deserved even more was not to *have* to hear it.

"If you'll promise to listen until I'm done, I'll promise not to leave anything out. But please don't go before I'm finished, because I don't want to wonder later whether you left me because of what you heard, or because of what you didn't hear."

He tilted his head and watched me through eyes narrowed in suspicion and dread. "Does that mean there's more to the story than your making Andrew into a stray in some sort of furry freak-fest? If so, you should feel free to leave out the nonpertinent details."

I smiled a little at that. I couldn't help it. "Um, yeah. There's a little more to it than that. And yet a lot *less* to it than that. There was no furry freak-fest, Marc. Just normal, even average sex."

Oddly enough, he seemed pleased to hear me describe sex with someone else as "average," and I wasn't complaining. Whatever made him more open to listening was fine with me.

"Talk. I might as well know what everyone else is going to be whispering about." He pulled both of his legs onto the bed and sat cross-legged, looking amazingly vulnerable for a man of his bulk.

Marc's new defenseless posture did little to make me want to spill my guts. Spew them, maybe. But I'd promised to explain, and I wasn't going to pass up the chance.

"I was in human form when I bit Andrew," I said, pulling my feet up to mimic his pose. "My teeth must have partially Shifted at the…um, height of things. It couldn't have been much of a Shift, because there was no pain that I remember, and I didn't notice anything different." Embarrassed, I glanced at the pillow in my lap and discovered that I'd twisted it into little more than an amorphous bag of feathers. "Well, there was no pain for *me*, anyway. Andrew yelped as if I'd bitten his ear off, but I barely drew blood. Just a couple of drops."

Marc frowned. "So you did break the skin?"

"Yeah."

His arm moved faster than my eyes could follow, and another feather pillow smashed into the window before falling to rest against the broken suitcase. *Good thing that wasn't a brick,* I thought, absurdly.

"How could you even *think* about sleeping with a human?" Marc demanded, and I tore my gaze from the pillow reluctantly and turned back to face him. "There's a *reason* we have the rules we have, and apparently you're it."

I stared at him openmouthed, waiting for him to realize he'd misspoken. My irritation grew with every second that passed without a retraction. "We *don't* have any rules against sleeping with humans," I said, my teeth clenched hard enough to make my jaw ache. "The guys do it all the time. Most of them lost count of the notches on their belts long ago. Hell, Ethan doesn't even bother to learn their *names* anymore." I threw the pillow at him, and he caught it in one fist. "But when I finally get a life of my own—and keep in mind the fact that this was a mutually monogamous relationship—everyone acts like I've committed a cardinal sin."

With every word I spoke, my pitch rose a little, until by the time I finished, I was screaming at him, standing on my knees on the end of his bed.

"The problem isn't that you've been dating humans, Faythe," he said, tossing the pillow aside. "It's that you've been *infecting* them."

Only one of them, I thought, but I knew better than to say it aloud. "How was I supposed to know that was even possible?" I shouted, backing off his bed and onto the floor. "None of the guys ever infected anyone in human form, so how was I supposed to know *I* could?"

"That's not the same, Faythe. You know human women can't be infected."

As a matter of fact, I did *not* know that for certain, and neither did he. But that was another argument entirely.

"I didn't know about the partial Shift, Marc. I had *no* idea this could happen. If I had, I would never have gone near Andrew, or anyone else, for that matter."

"Well, it's too late for regrets now," Marc said, his arms spread to either side of his torso. "In case you don't remember, since you seem to think you're above the council's laws, creating a stray is a capital crime. The council's going to want your life for this. And they're going to want *me* to bring it to them. So you tell me how the *fuck* I'm supposed to deal with that."

Twenty-One

So that's what was wrong with Marc. He thought he was going to have to kill me.

Well, clearly that wasn't the *only* thing bothering him, but we'd finally gotten down to the part he couldn't get over.

"Marc, it was an accident," I said, shifting awkwardly on a twisted lump of comforter. "The council won't condemn me over an accident."

"You said it yourself, Faythe. They're going to want your head on a spike in the front yard."

"That was *hyperbole*. You guys didn't seem to think they'd execute the rogue tabby for *murder,* so why would they execute me for an accidental infection?" I reached out to touch his arm, but he pulled away as if I'd scorched him.

My eyes watered, and I stood to turn my back on him as I blinked away the tears, hoping with each passing moment that he would touch me. I wanted a hug, or even just a pat on the back to let me know he regretted pulling away from me. I would have even taken an apology. But he didn't offer one. Not that I could blame him.

When I turned to face him, still standing in the middle of his room, I avoided his eyes. I didn't want to know what he was thinking, but even worse, I didn't want to not know. I desperately didn't want to see his poker face staring back at me. So I didn't look.

"They're not just going to take your word for it, Faythe," he said. "They're going to need proof that this was an accident, and last I heard, you couldn't give it to them."

Still avoiding his eyes, I crossed the room and righted his suitcase in one rough, angry motion. "Well, I can sure as hell try." Kneeling on the floor, I folded one of his shirts in a series of fuming, jerky movements. Dropping it neatly into the bag, I snatched another shirt from the floor, uncomfortably aware that I was now helping him pack. But I had to do something with my hands. "And even if I can't do it on command, I've already proved it to my father, and he'll speak up for me." For a single heartbeat, I hesitated, my hands pausing in mid-fold. "You could do the same, if you were so inclined."

"Oh, come on, Faythe." On the wall in front of me, Marc's shadow threw up its arms in exasperation. I turned my attention back to the clothes, vowing not to look at his shadow-self, either, as he gestured at me in frustration. "They're not going to believe me for the same reason they won't believe your dad. They'll think we're both lying to save you."

Damn, were he and my father sharing a brain? Or were they just right?

I shook out a pair of jeans, my gaze centered on the worn denim beneath my fingers. If things were normal, I'd have changed out of my soaked clothes and into some of his dry ones, but at the moment, I had serious doubts Marc would want his clothes smelling like me.

"What about Andrew?" I asked, still holding his jeans. "We'll find him and make him testify. Surely they can't think *he* has any reason to want to protect me. If anything, he wants me dead."

Marc walked around the end of the bed to kneel at my side. "What did he say?"

When I didn't answer, he snatched the pants from my hands. Irritated, I met his eyes without thinking and regretted it instantly. I hated that he didn't trust me, even though I knew he had several good reasons not to.

"He congratulated me on a life well lived," I said, my voice heavily laced with sarcasm. Marc glared at me, and I shrugged. "Well, what the hell do you *think* he said? He's pissed at me for infecting him, then abandoning him. He said he has something to take care of tomorrow, then he's coming here for a reunion."

"It's amazing that he survived your bite, you know. Lots of strays die within a couple of days of being infected. I don't think I could have made it through my own transition without your parents taking care of me. I don't even remember being scratched," he added, and I could almost feel my ears perk up, in spite of my self-centered fear. He'd never spoken to me about his attack, guarding his memories like a leprechaun guards his gold. "I just remember seeing my moth—".

He stopped abruptly and stared out the window behind my head, his mouth firmly closed.

"What's the first thing you remember *after* being scratched?" I breathed, hoping that if I whispered softly enough he might mistake my question for a thought from his own head. No such luck.

Marc turned from the window to look at me, a ghost of a

smile haunting the corners of his mouth. "The first thing I remember is you."

"Me?" I frowned, sure I'd heard wrong.

"Yeah. I woke up and saw you standing in the doorway, staring at me with these huge green eyes. You had a headless doll under one arm, and dirt smeared across your forehead. And all I could think about was what a beautiful child you were."

Lightning flashed outside and Marc blinked from the bright light. And just like that, the spell was broken. "Then I passed out again, and when I woke up, your mom was there with soup." He shrugged, and I knew he was finished talking. At least about the past.

"Marc, I'm sorry. I'm so, so sorry." As the last raindrops pattered against the window, I closed my eyes, trying to decide how best to express my own regret. "I never meant for any of this to happen. I really, truly didn't. But I can't change anything now, and I understand if you still want to leave—"

He shook his head slowly, as if in defeat. "I'm not going anywhere. Greg wouldn't let me leave in the middle of an investigation, anyway."

"Really?" I fiddled with the still-damp, frayed hem of my shorts, unable to look at Marc as I offered him a way out. He deserved at least that much from me. "Because Daddy would probably let you go if you push the issue. He always sides with you over me, anyway."

"Are you trying to convince me to leave?"

I glanced up at him, already shaking my head in denial. "No. Absolutely not. But I want you to understand what you'll be getting into if you stay. It's going to get worse from here, not better. We have to find Andrew, which means that eventually you'll have to be in the same room with him. Without killing him, if I have any hope of him talking to the council."

Marc laughed ruefully. "I won't hurt him unless I have to. You've already done enough to punish him for sleeping with you."

I glared at him, my fists propped on my hips. "How many times do I have to tell you it was an accident? A freak accident I probably couldn't repeat if I *tried*."

He held up both hands, as if to ward off a blow. "All I'm saying is that he got more than he bargained for with you."

"I got more than I bargained for with him, too. Much more. I know he's completely different now, but he was really nice and funny when he was human. But apparently his manners didn't survive the transition."

Marc smiled. "Yeah, well, yours didn't survive puberty, so you can't really talk."

I opened my mouth to rebut, but Ethan cut me off, calling to us from downstairs. I hadn't heard him come into the guesthouse, maybe because the rain was too loud. But more likely, Marc and I were too busy yelling at each other to notice. "If you guys have come to some sort of truce, Dad would like to speak to you both in his office. If it's convenient with you, that is."

I laughed. There was no way on earth my father had mentioned our convenience. But sending a message with Ethan was like looking into one of those old funhouse mirrors. Everything got distorted.

"We're coming," Marc called in Ethan's general direction. To me, he extended his right hand. "Truce?"

"Absolutely." I took his hand and shook it, expecting him to pull me into a hug. But he didn't. On the way out of the room, Marc held the door open for me. But he didn't grab my ass as I walked through ahead of him. And though I under-stood his reason, I couldn't help but be hurt that he stayed several steps behind me on the stairs. I was disappointed, but not surprised. I couldn't really expect things to go back to normal just like that. Of course, "normal" for me and Marc was a relative term, anyway.

To say that Marc and I tended to run hot and cold would be like saying it's a little chilly at the North Pole. I didn't know how to deal with Marc's new lukewarm presence. I'd never known him to demand anything less than all of my attention, and I didn't recognize this polite, courteous behavior. It was too distant, too cold. He was acting as if we were strangers. Or worse, *just friends.*

Downstairs, Parker gave me a hesitant smile, and Vic and Jace avoided my eyes entirely. But Ethan had never been one for subtlety. Or for tact. "So, did you guys break up, or what?" he asked, popping the tab on a can of Coke at the kitchen island.

Marc glanced at me with an arched eyebrow and a wry smile. I shrugged. I would have liked to know the answer to that one myself.

"Sounds like you should learn to listen better," Marc said, stuffing his hands into his jeans pockets.

Ethan grinned, unfazed. "Jace'll fill me in later." He was shirtless, as usual, and damp from the rain.

Ignoring them both, I pulled the front door open and stepped onto the rain-slick porch, beyond caring whether or not anyone followed me.

Ethan jogged after me, sloshing soda onto the porch without bothering to clean it up. "Come on, Faythe," he said, throwing one arm around my waist as I stomped through the soggy grass, my newly wet hair already clinging to my face.

He obviously wasn't still mad about my right hook connecting with his jaw. "I've got twenty bucks riding on this. Did he forgive you?"

"That's none of your business." I pulled his arm up by his wrist and ducked beneath it. In one smooth move, as fat droplets plopped down on us both, I stepped behind him, twisting his arm back and up, until his fingertips brushed his own shoulder blade.

Ethan's howl of pain brought a satisfied smile to my face. I should probably have felt at least a little guilty about getting the better of him twice in less than an hour. But I didn't. I still owed him a few hard knocks from childhood.

"Hey, thanks," Marc said, plucking the half-empty Coke from Ethan's free hand as he passed us. He drained the can, then crushed it in his fist, sparing a grin for my brother as he took off toward the main house, jogging ahead of us in the rain.

"Damn it, Faythe, don't make me hurt you," Ethan said through gritted teeth, pulling against me to free his arm.

I tightened my grip. "Who'd you bet against?" I asked, shoving him forward until he had to either start walking or fall on his face in the wet grass. "Jace?"

"Hell no. Leave me out of this," Jace muttered, passing me from the left. "I didn't want anything to do with his dirty money. It was Vic."

I glared at Vic, and he shrugged.

"You're both assholes." I let go of Ethan's arm, and gave him another hard shove, for good measure. "You have no business sticking your noses into our personal lives."

"There's no such thing as privacy around here." Vic stomped off through the rain with his hands stuffed into the pockets of his jeans.

Parker held the door open for us, and we tromped into the house one at a time, tracking water and clipped grass blades onto the tile in the back hall. On the way to my father's office, I ducked into my bedroom to change into dry clothes and towel-dry my wet hair. Then I headed back down the hall.

In the kitchen, the guys—all but Marc—were gathered around several half gallons of ice cream, each shoveling indiscriminately with his own spoon. I smiled at them, then turned toward the office. My fingers had just closed over the doorknob when it turned on its own.

The door swung open and Marc stepped out, his hands curled into fists at his sides and his eyes blazing. He paused just long enough to meet my eyes, then brushed past me and stomped off down the hall and out the back door.

All commotion from the kitchen ceased. Then, after mere seconds of silence, Ethan became the first to break it. As usual. "What crawled up his ass?"

In his office, my father looked up from his desk at the sound of Ethan's voice. But his eyes settled on me instead. "No sense standing in the doorway, Faythe. Come in and sit down." He glanced over my shoulder and across the hall at the guys in the kitchen. "The rest of you put up the ice cream and get in here."

As I plopped on the end of the couch closest to him, tucking my feet beneath me, he stood and crossed the room to his armchair without waiting to see whether or not his orders were followed. He still wore his suit jacket, but his top button was undone and his tie was gone. It lay draped over the back of his empty desk chair.

With the exception of the occasional postbedtime emergency, when my father came to his office still in silk pajamas and a matching robe, I couldn't remember ever seeing him work in less than a full suit. It was disconcerting. And a little disorienting.

"What's wrong with Marc?" I asked, eyeing my father in suspicion.

He watched me for a long moment, his lips pressed into a firm, straight line. "I split the two of you up." He crossed one ankle over his knee, waiting for my reaction. He wasn't disappointed.

I sat up straight and my heels hit the rug a little harder than I'd intended. "You what?"

"Not as a couple," he said calmly, his hands folded in his lap. "As field partners."

Did that mean Marc would be taking his vacation, after all? I wrapped my hands around the scrolled arm of the couch, sinking my fingers into the cool, smooth leather. "Why? We work well together."

"Not on this assignment. You're clearly better equipped than the guys to find and question Andrew, but I don't want Marc anywhere near him. We need Andrew alive, and not just on the off chance that he might be able or willing to testify about his infection in front of the council. We have to know what happened to the missing strippers, and where they are, and we need him for that. Unfortunately, I'm not sure Marc can deliver him intact."

"He promised he would."

"And I don't doubt that he meant that when he said it. But the fact that you needed a promise from him should say something. We can't afford for him to accidentally go too far with Andrew."

"He won't—"

"It's done."

Damn it. But I couldn't help thinking it was a good sign that Marc was upset about being separated from me. If he'd taken it well, I'd have been worried.

Jace sat next to me on the couch, and Owen settled onto the love seat, but I barely noticed either of them. Apparently neither did my father. "When this is all over, we'll revisit the issue."

"Any room for negotiation on this one?" I asked, my voice sounding hopeless and drained, even to my own ears.

"No." He didn't even smile, and with an almost bitter amusement, I realized I was tired of arguing, at least for today. Marc and I could probably handle one assignment without each other. After all, absence made the heart grow fonder, right?

Or was it out of sight, out of mind?

Twenty-Two

"So what's the plan?" I asked my father as Vic and Parker stepped into the room, each carrying several canned sodas.

"Michael wants to go to Jamey's funeral," he said, politely waving off the can Parker offered him. "So, Owen, I'm keeping you here to help me."

Owen nodded, popping open the can Vic handed him.

"I sent Michael to sleep in the guest room. Wes Gardner will be here first thing in the morning, and Michael and Ethan are accompanying him home for the funeral." That was standard practice whenever a Pride cat died. Each Alpha would be expected to send his own sons to represent both the Pride and the family, regardless of the inconvenience it might cause. "Did you hear that, Ethan?" my father asked, without raising his voice.

"Got it," my youngest brother called back from the kitchen, where he was loitering.

"Faythe, when we find Andrew, I'm sending Jace and Vic out with you."

I glanced at Jace, surprised that my father would pair us after the last time we were alone together. But then, this time we wouldn't be alone. Vic would be with us, which brought up another question. Vic and Marc had been partners for nearly a decade before I became an enforcer, so if my dad wouldn't let me work with Marc, why hadn't he put them back together?

"Thanks," I said, accepting one of Parker's Cokes. But before I could question my father's reasoning, Ethan came in carrying a mug of coffee. "Here you go, Dad," he said, extending the mug. My father accepted it and nodded at Ethan in thanks.

Someone was certainly trying to get on the Alpha's good side.

"Ethan, I want you to go to bed. We can't afford for you to be pulled over tomorrow because you were too tired to be careful."

Ethan frowned, scratching one bare shoulder. "You want me to go to sleep *now?*"

My father eyed the wall clock pointedly. "It's almost three in the morning."

"Yeah, but…" He glanced around the room, appealing silently to the other guys. No one spoke. When Ethan finally glanced at me, I popped the top on my soda and smiled at him, then took a long, slow drink. "Fine," he muttered, and shuffled into the hall. Seconds later, he slammed his bedroom door, and my smile widened.

I was the only one who routinely argued with my father, but I wasn't about to stick my neck out for the brother who'd bet twenty dollars that Marc would dump me.

"Michael couldn't find mention of any women going missing tonight anywhere in Texas, Louisiana, Mississippi, or Arkansas—strippers or otherwise. So the last location we have for Andrew and whoever he's working with is Henderson, Texas. I doubt *he's* still there, but if the tabby isn't there yet, I think it's safe to assume she will be soon. So I'm sending Marc and Parker to Henderson first thing tomorrow, to look around and see what they can sniff out."

My father watched Parker as he spoke, leaning forward to emphasize his next words. "You are to bring her in alive, and *unharmed.* We're not sure whose daughter she is yet, and we are *not* going to risk angering the South American Prides by mistreating her without a hearing, no matter *what* she's done. Treat her like she's breakable. Understood?"

Parker nodded. We all nodded. Bringing in a rogue tabby would be necessarily different than bringing in a rogue tom. It only stood to reason. Yet our Alpha continued to eye Parker, as if to further drive home his point. "I told Marc the same thing, but feel free to remind him."

My father took a long sip of his coffee, then addressed the whole room. "We'll spend tomorrow tracking Andrew down. In the morning Faythe will call him and see if she can find out who he's with, where they are, and what business he plans to take care of tomorrow. Any questions?"

No hands went up, and no mouths opened.

"Good. Everyone go get some sleep. But set your alarms. We're getting an early start."

The room cleared quickly, with my father leading the way. He took his coffee with him and disappeared into his bedroom.

I plodded down the hall in a daze, oblivious to the broad shoulders brushing past me and the air-conditioned breeze blowing my hopelessly tangled hair back from my face. I'd finally reached the end of a very long day, and wasn't quite sure what to make of everything that had happened.

That morning, I'd been one of the good guys, traveling to

New Orleans to re-create a dead guy's last hour in order to learn about his killer. I was relatively happy with my life, and proud of the job I was doing.

Sixteen hours later, I'd confessed to a capital crime and become the object of obsession of a psychotic monster of my own making.

But worst of all, Marc and I had… What *had* we done? We'd fought, of course. But it certainly wasn't the worst fight we'd ever had. No broken furniture, and no blood. We were even still on speaking terms. So what was my problem? Why was I so disappointed to open my bedroom door and not see him thumbing through my CDs in a pair of low-slung jogging pants, waiting for me to loosen the drawstring and let them fall to the carpet?

It's not like we stayed together *every* night. So why did I dread going to bed alone this time?

The answer hit me like a punch to the gut, knocking the air from my lungs as I dropped my clothes in my hamper. For the first time since I was sixteen years old, my connection to Marc was undefined. I had no idea where we stood. We hadn't broken up, but we weren't exactly together, either. He was no longer mad, but neither was he *here*.

I took a quick shower, trying to distract myself from thoughts of Marc by planning my upcoming phone call to Andrew. It didn't work. By the time I stepped out onto the mat, I was replaying the fight with Marc in my head, determined to find something I could have said to end things on better, more sure-footed ground. I came up blank.

In my room again, I dressed in a pair of stretchy black boy-shorts and a matching tank top, my preferred pj's. I was running a comb through my still-damp hair when my bedroom door creaked open.

Whirling around, I found Marc watching me, eyes brooding, face somber. He stood framed by the doorway, wearing nothing but a snug pair of jeans. His bare feet were wet, and thin, short blades of grass clung to them. His chest heaved from what I assumed to be a mad dash across the backyard. Droplets of rain fell from his thick, dark curls to run down his torso, crossing the well-defined lines of his shoulders and the clawmark scars on his chest, to roll down his abs before soaking into the waistband of his jeans.

"Marc? What's wrong?" The comb fell from my fingers as he crossed the floor in several long, determined strides. His left hand went around my waist, and his right tangled in my shower-damp hair, tilting my face to meet his.

He kissed me without a word, his lips hard, demanding. He probed my mouth desperately, taking sustenance from my very soul. The fronts of my bare thighs rubbed against his worn-soft denim, and I felt the heat of his skin beneath. My toes barely touched the carpet between his feet.

Suddenly, abruptly, Marc let me go and stepped back, shaking his head in reproach. In denial.

My chest rose and fell, each breath coming hard and fast. Our eyes met, and I gasped at the raw pain in his. "Marc…"

Marc growled fiercely, possessively. He wrapped both hands around my waist and lifted me, biceps swelling with the motion. My legs wrapped around his waist. His arm snaked around my lower back, holding me up. Holding me close. My arms went around his neck.

His left hand slid into my hair, cupping my head. He pulled me down and kissed me again, hungrily. Urgently. He seemed desperate to touch every part of me, to claim my body with his hands, my heart with his eyes, my soul with his need.

He walked us across the room. My back slammed into the wall. I grunted in surprise, but his mouth was there again, cutting off my insincere protest with another ravenous kiss.

Marc's now-free right hand shoved up the black lace hem of my stretchy tank. My fingers traced his scars. His hand cradled my left breast, squeezing. My fingers skimmed down his chest to his stomach, trailing the thin, dark line of hair below his navel. He lifted my breast, lowering his head. His teeth brushed my nipple.

Gasping now, I arched my back, thrusting up for him. He shoved me harder into the wall, and his mouth closed over my breast. His lips were hot on my skin, his tongue hotter still. My head fell against the wall, my mouth open. My fingers combed through his curls, tangling in a mass of short, glossy ringlets. Soft, silken wisps tickled my chin. *Damn,* I loved his hair.

I drew my tongue along his neck, wrapping my legs tighter around his hips. Desperate for more, I ground myself into him, through both layers of clothing.

Marc groaned around my nipple, thrusting up to meet me. "Marc…" I moaned, my voice hoarse with need. His mouth left my breast, and he raised his head to look at me. Not smiling—just watching. Waiting, his hands on my hips.

"Please…" My hands fumbled at the waistband of his jeans. My fingers brushed the flap of material around the button, tugging. The button pulled free of its hole.

Marc growled again, impatience clear in the low, rolling rumble. He found the waistband of my boyshorts. His fingers curled around handfuls of stretchy black lace.

He tugged once. Hard.

Material cut into my skin. Seams ripped. Elastic popped. I gasped. "Hey…!"

Marc stepped back and dropped me on my feet. I stumbled backward into the wall, thrown off by the sudden movement. Lace slid down my legs to puddle on the carpet. He shoved down on his waistband, and his pants hit the floor, black silk boxers still inside.

He stepped out of his jeans, already bending to cup my ass. His gaze never left my face as he lifted me in both hands, supporting me easily. My back slid up the wall. My arms snaked around his neck. His lips found mine again, his tongue plunging into my mouth. He lowered me slowly, sliding inside inch by exquisite inch.

For a long moment, neither of us moved. He pulled away from my mouth and leaned back to look at me. To watch me, as I watched him, knowing we were joined, as close as two people could possibly be. In that moment, that horrifyingly short, perfect moment, nothing else mattered. There was no Andrew, no rogue tabby, and no council. There was only Marc, throbbing deep inside me.

He closed his eyes and exhaled.

And just like that, the moment was over, the desperation back. His eyes met mine, and need crashed over both of us. He pinned me to the wall with his chest, sliding quickly out of me. Then he shoved his way back in, thrusting me into the wall over and over again. I could do nothing but cling to him, ride him, hoping it would never end.

Marc's fingers trailed along my sides, chills chasing them in a cold, tingling trail. His hands gripped my hips, guiding me, molding me, his fingers digging into my flesh.

I moaned and gripped his shoulders, urging him on out of irresistible, undeniable craving.

Leaning down, he nipped the ridge of my collarbone, then

dipped lower. He nibbled the upper curve of my breast. I gasped, pushing him deeper with my legs. He moaned, and shoved into me faster. His thrusts were frantic now. Uncontrollable.

He drove into me again and again, slamming my spine into the wall. His grip on my hips tightened. His nails broke through my skin as he lifted me and shoved me down, grinding me into him over and over.

I gasped, tightening around him as pleasure built, driven by mutual need.

His eyes closed, and he plunged harder, deeper, drawing whimpers of simultaneous pain and pleasure from me. "Marc…" It was too much. I couldn't take it.

He ignored my inarticulate protest. Thankfully.

He trembled, and release came crashing over me, pointing my toes and driving away all thought. My vision darkened. My fingers curled around his biceps. My legs clenched his back. I shuddered around him.

I clasped my jaws shut to keep from screaming and waking the whole house.

Marc's eyes flew open. He grabbed my upper arms and pinned them to the wall, still pumping into me. "Why, Faythe?" he demanded, his eyes swimming with fear and anger. "Why?"

I shook my head, quivering in the aftermath of violent bliss. I didn't understand. I didn't *know* why. As usual.

Marc shuddered one last time, and collapsed against me, crushing me between his chest and the wall. He was still inside me. I still clung to him, terrified for no reason I could name. Something was wrong. Something other than our nightmare of a day.

I inhaled, breathing in the scent of summer rain, fresh sweat, sex, and all things Marc.

He stepped away, lifting me from him to set me gently on the ground. My legs wobbled. I felt empty.

Hollow.

Lost.

Marc turned from me and, to my surprise and confusion, stepped into his pants. He pulled them up and zipped them, and I'd never in my life heard such a horrible, terrifyingly final sound.

Because he had dressed, I followed suit. I tugged my tank top down over my breasts and looked to find him sitting on the floor, leaning against the wall where he'd had me pinned less than a minute earlier.

"What's wrong?" I asked.

He frowned, whatever he'd been about to say lost. "I hurt you."

"No." I shook my head, denying the truth because it no longer mattered.

"You're bleeding." He reached up with one hand and touched my hip, just above the waistband of my snug gray shorts. His fingers were smeared with blood.

I saw four short, deep scratches on one hip, and a matching set on the other side. "It's fine." I crossed the room to my dresser and snatched a tissue, dabbing at the new marks to avoid his eyes. "You're still mad at me," I said, fully expecting him to deny it.

"Yes." His response caught me so off guard I gripped the edge of the dresser for balance. In the mirror, Marc rubbed his forehead, momentarily blocking his eyes from view as he spoke, and my heart threatened to stop beating. "I'm so mad I can barely stand to look at you."

My hand clenched the tissue, and my pulse raged. "So what

was that?" I spun around, gesturing angrily at the wall, still damp with my sweat. "A grudge fuck? One more for the road?"

His hand fell, and his eyes found mine again, searing my soul like a branding iron. "Do you know how many cats I've executed for doing what you've done? Did you think I took those assignments just because your father told me to?"

Unsure how to answer, I said nothing, crossing the room to the end of my bed, where I leaned against the bedpost for support.

"I believe the death sentence is *warranted* for creating a stray. No one should get away with stealing a person's humanity. If Jose wasn't already dead, I would have killed him myself, not just for what he did to my mother, but for what he did to *me*. For what he turned me into."

"Marc, I—"

"Shut up." He leaned forward, his elbows on his knees. "I know you didn't mean to infect him, and I know you can't take it back, so save your breath." He sighed and stood slowly. "I know I don't have any right to be pissed at you, but I can't help the way I feel. Part of me wants to rip this Andrew's fingers off one by one, just because they've touched you."

"Marc—"

"But another part of me wants to congratulate him for having escaped death-by-Faythe." His voice grew cold, his words clipped in bitter anger. "I swear, any man who walks away from you without limping is a lucky man. Just ask Ryan. Or Eric and Miguel."

Stunned, I sank onto the end of my mattress, leaning against the bedpost. That was a low blow. I'd had to bite through Eric's throat to free myself and Abby, and I'd only defended myself from Miguel. And coming from Marc, that statement was more than a little hypocritical. He'd dished out his own serving of justice to Miguel.

And since he was neither dead nor limping, Ryan had little reason to complain about his treatment at my hands.

"Is that what you want to do?" I asked, my hand tightening around the column of wood as I watched the specks of gold glitter in Marc's eyes. "You want to walk away from me?"

"Yeah."

I recoiled as if he'd slapped me, and tears blurred my vision. I should have known better than to ask a question I didn't want answered.

"I'm not an idiot, Faythe." Marc stood, running one hand through his curls. "I know the best thing I could ever do for myself would be to walk out of your room right now and keep going until I get to Mexico. But I can't do that. I couldn't do it five years ago, and I can't do it now. And I don't know why."

My brain barely registered the blur of movement as he whirled around and kicked my desk chair across the room and into the dresser. I jumped, the crash echoing in my head. The chair fell to the floor, miraculously unbroken. Marc turned to face me, sagging against my desk.

"You never admit that you feel anything for me in front of anyone else. Hell, you're only here because you made a promise to your father. If you hadn't, you'd be back at school by now, with Andrew, or some other poor guy too clueless to realize how dangerous you are until it's too late.

"Yet in spite of all that, even though I know you won't stay here a day longer than the time you owe Greg—assuming the council doesn't lock you up—I can't just walk away. And I hate myself for it." Whirling, he slammed his fist against the door, and I jumped again as it rattled in its frame. "You make me hate myself, for not being man enough to say I've had it and tell you to go to hell."

Speechless, I stared at him, grasping desperately for something to say to make it all better. To erase what he'd said, and take back what I'd done. To accomplish the impossible.

"Say something, Faythe," Marc ordered.

My mouth opened, but nothing came out.

"Oh, *now* you have nothing to say." He crossed my room in several huge strides and was in my face before I could even blink. Bending at the waist, he planted one fist on the mattress on either side of my hips, intentionally invading my personal space. "Tell me I'm wrong," he demanded, pleading with his eyes for me to put him out of his misery. Or maybe he was *daring* me to do it. "Tell me I'm more than a convenient body to warm your bed and keep you entertained during your exile from the real world. Tell me you're not just staying here because you have to. Tell me we have a future together. Damn it, Faythe, tell me *some*thing!" he said, turning away from me in disgust.

"Marc, I…I don't know what to say." I stood, searching my mind frantically for something that would make him happy without lying to him. Because the truth was that I didn't *know* whether or not I would stay past the two and a half years I'd agreed on. I didn't know if I had a future with Marc, because I didn't know whether or not I had a future with the Pride, and I knew he wouldn't go with me if I left again. We'd been down that road once before; it led to me fleeing the ranch the night before our wedding, the summer I turned eighteen.

I couldn't do that to him again. Or to me.

"You're *not* just a convenient warm body," I said, moving toward him with my arms open. He frowned in suspicion but let me wrap my arms around him and lay my head on his chest. I ran my hands over him, soothed by the smell of his skin and the feel of his flesh. He relaxed just a little and returned my embrace, his chin brushing my temple. "If that's all I wanted, I'd be with—" I murmured.

Marc stiffened in my arms, and I froze, cursing myself silently. Why couldn't I learn when to just *shut up?*

He stepped away, and in his eyes was a distant, bitter chill. He grabbed my arms in a bruising grip. "What do you want, Faythe?" he growled, all traces of warmth gone from his face. Now there was only anger. "Just this once, tell me exactly what you want from me."

"I want what we have right now," I said, determined not to let on that his grip hurt.

"That's it?" He dropped my arms, gaping at me in suspicion and fresh pain. "You want what we have now?" He repeated my words slowly, carefully, as if analyzing them for hidden meaning. "What if the status quo isn't enough for me? What if I want more?"

"We're perfect together the way we are." I reached for him, staring into his eyes. "Why change anything?"

He captured my wrist and drew my fingers firmly from his face. "*Life* changes things, Faythe. *You've* changed things by infecting Andrew, even if you didn't mean to. You can't expect us to remain the same any more than you can expect time to stand still. You either adjust to the changes and move along with the times, or you get left behind. So which is it going to be? Are you going to let us evolve, or are you going to leave us behind?"

I shook my head, trying to clear it. "I don't know what you're asking."

"Damn it, Faythe, yes you do!" He dropped my hand and turned around, bending to snatch my desk chair from the floor. The wood groaned beneath his hands, and I watched the muscles of his back tense and gather, as he wrestled with whatever he was preparing to say. Finally, I wrapped my arms around his waist and molded myself against him.

He let go of the chair and when he turned, his face was an odd mixture of anger, hope, and determination. "I can't let you team up with Jace without some kind of reassurance."

I blinked. "You can't *let* me?"

"You know what I mean."

Yeah, and I didn't like it one bit. I'd already apologized for bringing Andrew into our lives. And I was more than willing to pamper Marc through a little insecurity. But beyond that, he was being completely unreasonable. None of this had anything to do with Jace. "You don't trust me?"

He arched one eyebrow. "Would *you* trust you?"

Okay, he had a point there. I'd left him at the altar. Apparently I was never going to live that one down. "What kind of reassurance do you want?"

"A promise." Eyes swimming in vulnerability, he dug into his right pocket and pulled out a ring. "Marry me, Faythe. Say you'll marry me."

Twenty-Three

My heart thudded in panic as I stared at the ring. I back-pedaled so fast I fell on my ass beside the bed, and still I retreated, crawling from the shiny silver band between his thumb and forefinger as if it were connected to the pin in a grenade, rather than to his heart.

One was just as dangerous as the other.

"You're overreacting, Faythe." Marc scowled as he hauled me up by one arm. He sat on the side of my bed and pulled me next to him, our legs touching from knee to hip. "It's not an engagement ring. See?" He held it up to the light for my inspection. "It's silver, not gold. And there's no stone. So no one has to know."

I looked. And looked. And still my fear refused to retreat. "I don't understand."

He smiled, and his eyes held so much hope, so much heart-breaking, soul-bruising anticipation. "This isn't for show. It's a private promise, just for me. The ring's sized for your ring finger because that's the only one I knew, but you can wear it on your right hand, if you want. Or on a chain around your neck. I don't care where. And we don't have to tell anyone. Even your dad. I just need to know you're serious about this. About us."

"Marc…" I still stared at the ring, trying not to notice the carving of a delicate ivy vine snaking its way around the band. As badly as I hated to admit it, the ring was…*pretty.*

Damn it.

He sighed. "I'm not asking you to marry me tomorrow. Or even next year. I'm just asking you to tell me it'll happen *some*day. Promise me I'm not just wasting my time. *Show* me. Please."

"I can promise that without wearing a ring," I pointed out, with what seemed to me to be absolutely flawless logic.

His expression hardened, and his fingers closed over the ring.

I frowned, at a loss for how to make him understand without hurting him. Again. "Working apart for a couple of days isn't going to make me forget you. I'm not interested in anything extra on the side, and I'm not going anywhere. But I don't want to get married. I'm only twenty-three. I'm not ready for that. I'm not even ready to *think* about it. You *know* that."

He exhaled slowly, then stood, stalking across the room. "I know. Believe me, I know. But I need this, Faythe. Please."

My eyes closed, my heart breaking in slow, agonizing increments. Then I opened my eyes, praying for the right words to come. "I love you, Marc. I always will. I'm giving you my word on that, and asking you to trust me. No symbols, no complications. Just my promise, which means as much to me as that ring means to you. Right now, that's what I have to offer." I paused, pleading with him silently. Then aloud. "Please tell me it's enough."

Marc stared at me in disappointment bordering on devastation, and in that moment, I came closer to going back on my own word than I ever had. My resolve wavered as my focus shifted back and forth between his face and the fist enclosing the ring. I couldn't stand seeing him in such pain because of me.

"It's not enough," he whispered through clenched teeth, his jaw bulging. "I need to know we have a future together. Here, with the Pride. Where we belong."

"Marc. I can't…" I stood and took a step toward him, but he only stepped back.

Disappointment drained from his features with alarming speed, replaced with anger. Very, very familiar anger. "Thank you, Faythe." He shoved the ring into his pocket, and I shuddered as the gravelly quality of fury in his voice sent tremors up my spine. "You've just handed me back my balls, and given me the resolve to do what I should have done years ago."

In one fierce motion, he pulled my door open without bothering to turn the knob first. Wood splintered as the fragile frame broke and the hinges tore free. The hollow panel fell forward, pulling a thin strip of wood with it. The strip fell to my carpet, and Marc lifted the door out of the way, propping it against my wall. Then he turned left into the hallway without a single glance back at me.

Seconds later, the back door slammed shut behind him, and I flinched.

Marc was gone.

After Marc left, I couldn't sleep. I couldn't do anything but stand in the middle of my room clutching the broken piece of door frame. I still smelled him, no matter which way I turned, and it actually took me several minutes to figure out that his scent was coming from me. From all over me.

Numb, I sank to the floor at the foot of my bed, leaning against the footboard with my knees pulled up to my chest. I held my hands cupped over my face, trying to stop the tears as I breathed in Marc's scent.

Something nudged my foot, and I looked up, hoping to see Marc, even if he was still mad. It was Ethan. He didn't smile at me, and he didn't say anything. He just pulled me up by my tear-damp hands and wrapped his arms around me.

Finally, when I could breathe without hiccuping, he thumped my back twice and let me go. "I brought you something," he said, gesturing that I should sit by waving a hand at my bed. I sat against my headboard and wiped my face on my rumpled comforter before pulling my punching pillow onto my lap.

At my dresser, Ethan turned his back to me, blocking my view of whatever he was doing. I heard a soft scraping sound, like a lid being unscrewed, then the gurgle of liquid being poured. When he turned around, he held a small paper cup in one hand and one of my mother's everyday saucers in the other. The saucer held a single, huge brownie. Double-fudge-chunk, from the looks of it.

"Where did you get that?" I asked, sniffling one last time as he carried the supersize serving of comfort food closer.

"Angela made them. Or maybe Andrea."

"Wow. Thanks."

"Don't mention it." He sank onto the bed next to me to recline on one elbow. "Seriously. They're Jace's, and if he finds out I snatched some of his goodies, I'll never hear the end of it."

"Understood." I picked up the brownie in one hand and took a big bite, closing my eyes as I treasured the perfect,

cakey texture and the smooth, creamy taste of quality choco-
late. The brownie didn't make me feel any better about Marc,
but it got the taste of him out of my mouth. Which was a
mercy, considering.

"Damn, those girls can bake," I said around my mouthful.

Ethan laughed, nodding. "They're majoring in Home Ec.
Or some shit like that."

Ha. Our mother would probably love them.

"You guys will be okay, you know," Ethan said, pressing
the paper cup into my hand. Doubtful, I drank from it without
thinking to ask what it was, and nearly choked on Scotch.

"Is this Dad's?" I asked, still sputtering as I located the
bottle of Scoresby on my dresser.

"You think I've got a death wish?" Ethan asked. "It's mine.
And that's all you're getting."

"It's more than enough, thanks," I said, peering at the two
inches left in the bottom of the cup. I took another sip and
cradled the tiny cup in both hands as I met Ethan's eyes. "I
think he dumped me."

"I think you're right." He pinched a crumb from the corner
of my brownie. "Seriously, though, what did you expect?
How many times can you *not* marry a guy and still expect him
to hang around?"

"You heard us?"

He shrugged. "I couldn't sleep. And it's not like you guys
were whispering."

I set the paper cup on my nightstand and reached for
another bite of the brownie. Of course he'd heard. "You really
think he'll come back?"

"Well, I didn't say *that*. But it's not like getting dumped
is lethal."

I glared at him as I chewed. "Yeah, like you'd know."

"I'm pretty sure none of my exes have died of it," he said. I glared harder, and Ethan smiled in sympathy. "Sorry, Faythe, but you have to admit you kind of deserved it. You *did* stand him up at his own wedding."

"That was five years ago! Whose side are you on, anyway?" I snapped, reaching for the paper cup. I drained the contents in a single, scorching gulp, and Ethan nodded in approval. And a little amusement.

"There are no sides," he said, and I kicked his elbow out from under him. He sat up, smiling faintly. "Look, I'm not saying he won't take you back. I'm just saying it won't hurt you to stew in your own juices until he does."

"Thanks, Ethan. You're a huge help."

"No problem." He crushed the paper cup and tossed it across the room into the trash can by my desk.

From the foyer, the grandfather clock chimed four times, and I glanced at the clock on my radio to confirm the time. Sure enough, it was four in the morning and I had yet to close my eyes for anything longer than a single blink. Wonderful.

"You'd better go get some sleep before you lose your chance," I said, knowing full well that Michael would make Ethan do most of the day's driving.

"Yeah, I guess." He stood, backing toward my nonfunctional door and watching me through eyes just a shade greener than my own. "You okay?"

"Yeah, I'm fine," I said, pulling my covers straight. "I deserved it, remember?"

He grinned. "Yeah, you're the devil's spawn. Really, you're lucky he didn't call for an exorcist."

I tossed my punching pillow at him, and Ethan laughed,

dashing into the hall as the fluffy pink missile narrowly missed his head, bouncing off the splintered door frame instead. Suddenly exhausted, I got up and set my door in place, propping my desk chair against it when it wouldn't stand on its own. I bent down for the pillow, and as I stood, my eye caught my reflection in the dresser mirror.

My face was red and puffy from crying, my hair swept back behind one shoulder, framing the row of crescent-shaped scars trailing up my neck—a permanent reminder of my run-in with Miguel, the jungle cat who'd haunted my nightmares ever since. Miguel was the first stray I'd ever personally seen, other than Marc, and in spite of similar looks and a shared tendency to cuss at me in Spanish, they had almost nothing in common.

Wait.… Miguel wasn't my first encounter with a stray. *Luiz* was. I'd fought him on campus and sent him packing with a broken nose. That was the night Marc showed up to haul me home. It was also only hours after I'd bitten my human boyfriend. If Marc hadn't come for me, I'd have figured out what happened to Andrew that very night. I would have taken care of him. I would never have left him to the mercy of whatever psychotic cat happened upon him first.…

Oh, *fuck*. My eyes closed, and my image in the mirror was swallowed by my own private darkness.

Luiz. There were no other cats on campus, or anywhere near UNT. We'd have known, if there had been. But Luiz was there. He'd been sent to snatch me, and Miguel would not have been happy with his failure. He might even have sent Luiz back for a second shot. Fortunately, I was already gone. But Andrew wasn't. He was sick, and by then likely *reeking* of my base scent.

Andrew's with Luiz. The minute the thought surfaced, I

knew it was true. No wonder they were targeting strippers who look like me. They *both* hated me.

My new theory made perfect sense to me, but no one else was ever going to believe Luiz had been not only alive, but in *our territory* all this time. Undetected. The only way he could possibly have hidden from a Pride of more than thirty cats for more than ninety days was to lie low and stay in one place. But that wasn't Luiz's style. Three months ago, he'd been killing college girls and leaving them exposed, on some sort of assignment from Miguel. If he'd kept up his little project, we would have found him. Shit, even the *police* would have caught up with him eventually, which would have been disastrous.

But since the night I'd kicked Luiz's ass at UNT, we hadn't found a single dead college girl. Or any other sign of Luiz, until the strippers started disappearing. No one else knew he was involved with that yet, but I had no doubt. Was Luiz continuing his "work" with a new set of victims? If so, why the change in MO? And why the three-month hiatus?

Three months. I grabbed the fluffy pink pillow from my dresser and twisted it in my hands, pacing as I worked to piece together the puzzle in my head. The hiatus was Andrew's recovery period. It had to be. Luiz had put his little hobby on hold to nurse my ex through scratch-fever.

But that was oddly altruistic for a jungle cat. Why would he give a shit whether or not one more stray survived?

Because *I'd* infected Andrew. Luiz probably thought he could use my ex to draw me out. It was because of me. He had likely followed Andrew around the day after I'd left, trying to find me, and discovered what I'd done by accident.

I'd not only infected Andrew, I'd led Luiz right to him.

Furious, I threw the pillow at my headboard, irritated with the harmless way it bounced onto the comforter. The whole mess—the missing strippers, the dead toms, Marc's…issues—would never have happened if I'd realized I'd infected Andrew.

I had to tell my father about Luiz. I was already in the hall, the tile cold against my bare feet, before I came to my senses. I couldn't wake my father up after less than two hours of sleep to ramble on about a theory based on a hunch. I needed proof, something to validate what was otherwise merely the instinct of a vastly underexperienced enforcer.

Ryan. I had to talk to the Cowardly Lion himself. He might know something about Miguel's plans and accomplices that would substantiate my speculation. Spinning on one heel, I ran back down the hall toward the kitchen, pausing in the foyer to glance at the grandfather clock. Even with only pale moonlight shining through the front windows, I could read the time clearly. Four-twenty-two in the morning. I probably wouldn't see my bed again before dawn. Which was just as well, because I couldn't have slept, anyway.

In the kitchen, I yawned as I passed the bar on my way to the basement door before my exhausted brain processed what I'd seen sitting on the long white countertop. There, next to the wall, where the guys had clearly pushed it to make room for their ice cream, was a shiny silver tray, on which sat a dinner plate, loaded with baked halibut, scalloped potatoes, and several spears of asparagus covered in cold, congealed hollandaise. Next to the dinner plate lay a linen napkin, a dinner fork, a dessert fork, and a dessert plate, empty but for a crumb of graham-cracker crust and a smear of strawberry. And a glass of tea, into which the ice had long ago melted.

Ryan's dinner. No one had bothered to take it to him. I

shook my head, half in shame and half in frustration. The fact that it lay unnoticed on the counter said that my mother had spent her entire evening in the woods. She made him a tray every night when she cleaned the kitchen, but had consistently refused to take it to him, even when my father had pushed the issue. One of us was supposed to do it, but apparently everyone's least-favorite chore had been neglected in the excitement of the evening's discoveries.

Of course, the ice cream hadn't been neglected, and someone had obviously found time to eat Ryan's cheesecake. *Great,* I thought. *He's going to be in no mood to talk tonight.* If he was even awake. Huffing in frustration, I set the empty dessert plate and fork on the counter, then picked up the tray. I balanced the tray on one hand as I pulled the basement door open, then marched down the stairs, glad the basement light was still on to illuminate my way.

Halfway along the steps, the stench of an un-flushed toilet hit me, no doubt made worse by the stifling heat in the basement, even in the predawn hours.

"'Bout time," Ryan snapped by way of a greeting, sitting up on his mattress. "You guys forget I was alive down here? Or has Dad decided to remedy that?"

"One can only hope." I stopped several feet in front of the cage to stare at him. "And don't blame me for the delay. I spent most of today in New Orleans."

For an instant, his eyes lit up in curiosity. But then his usual scowl slipped into place, and he whipped the conversation back around to his favorite topic: Ryan Sanders. "Yeah, well, someone could have at least emptied the damned coffee can and brought me some dinner. Or has the list of basic human necessities changed since I last saw daylight?"

Frowning, I set the tray on the seat of a ladder-backed chair next to the cage. "You're in the lap of luxury compared to the hell you put me through, so shut up before I flush your dinner down the toilet along with this." Growling, I picked up the foul-smelling coffee can he'd set just outside the bars of his cage and carried it into the bathroom on the other side of the basement, behind the weight bench and stand of free weights. "Why aren't you asleep, anyway?"

"The sound of my stomach growling kept me awake."

My teeth ground together as I rinsed the can in the sink. "Try sleeping through the sound of your cousin crying herself to sleep after being raped." Angry now, I stomped back to his cell and set the can where he could reach it, then returned to the bathroom to wash my hands.

Back at the bars, I picked up Ryan's plate, sloshing hollandaise over the side, and dropped the fork into the middle of his scalloped potatoes. "Step against the far wall and put your hands over your head, palms flat against the bricks."

"Come on, Faythe. Is this really necessary?" Ryan whined, pouting at me as if I gave a damn. I didn't. I'd let go of any familial affection for him the night he left me locked in Miguel's basement to fight off two rapists in defense of my honor. And my life.

I gave him a faux casual shrug. "Fine. I don't give a shit whether or not you eat."

"All right, all right." Ryan turned and pressed the side of his face into the brick wall, in the same position he assumed three times every day. At least, until today. Satisfied, I knelt on the floor in front of a small steel flap at the bottom of the cage, through which I shoved his dinner plate and napkin. Then I reached through the bars to set his glass of tea next to the plate.

As I settled into the wooden chair, Ryan shuffled forward to grab his plate in one hand and his glass in the other, completely ignoring the napkin as he backed toward his bunk, the only place he had to sit and eat.

I folded my arms across my chest, grimacing in disgust as he licked butter and congealed fat from the handle of the fork. "You just gonna sit there and watch?" he asked. Then, before I could answer, he glanced around the basement, as if looking for something on the walls. "What time is it, anyway?"

"Four-thirty in the morning."

He sank his fork into a cold flake of fish. "What are you doing up so early?"

"So late," I corrected him.

"You haven't been to bed?" Ryan asked, not bothering to cover his mouth. My mother would have been horrified. Maybe his deteriorating manners were the real reason she wouldn't come see him. "So what was so important everyone forgot to feed the poor guy in the cage?"

I took issue with the sympathy Ryan seemed to think he deserved, but I kept my mouth shut. The more I pissed him off, the less likely he'd be to tell what I wanted to know. "We've had a very eventful evening." I leaned forward to make eye contact with him, and as I did, I noticed for the first time how much his face had filled out over the past three months. In spite of the lack of sunlight and fresh air, and the recently missed meals, he looked much healthier than he had in June, when our positions were reversed.

The fork paused inches from his mouth, a spear of asparagus impaled on the end. "What happened?"

"You'll have to talk the Alpha into reinstating your security clearance before I can tell you that." We both knew that would never happen, but because I needed information from him, I fought the urge to laugh at the disappointment in his expression. "However, I have a chance for you to earn a few brownie points."

He bit the tip off the asparagus, his eyes narrowed in suspicion. "What do you want?"

"Information."

Ryan smirked as he chewed. "What kind of information, and how badly do you want it?"

"Badly enough to make sure you don't get fed tomorrow if you don't start talking. Right now," I added, my face carefully blank as his smirk drooped into an angry frown. "I need to hear everything you know about Luiz."

Twenty-Four

"Luiz?" Ryan relaxed visibly, slouching against the brick wall as he speared several slices of scalloped potato with his fork. "Why do you want to know about him? He's dead."

"How do you know?" Suddenly, I wished I'd brought a notebook, so I could take notes. Or at least have something to do with my hands.

My brother frowned. He swallowed his bite and took a long drink of not-so-iced tea before answering. "Well, I guess I just assumed he was dead, like everyone else did. Why? Did he show up?"

I ignored his question, wiping sweat from my forehead with the back of my forearm. *Damn, I hate basements.*

"You never met Luiz, right?" I asked, and Ryan shook his head, damp, stringy hair flopping. "Did you ever speak to him on the phone? Or hear Eric or Miguel talk to him?"

He nodded, pushing another asparagus tip around in a pool of hollandaise. "I heard Miguel and Luiz arguing on the phone a couple of days before they brought you in."

"What were they arguing about?"

"How the hell should I know?" Ryan stuffed the bite into his mouth, then spoke around it. "They were speaking Portuguese. It's not similar enough to Spanish for me to catch more than a few words."

My ears perked up, almost literally. "What few words did you understand?"

"Jeez, Faythe," he said, pulling one filthy-soled bare foot up onto his cot. "That was months ago, and I wasn't really paying attention even then. I just wanted them to shut up so I could hear the game on TV."

"Just think about it for a minute," I insisted. He scowled but closed his eyes in concentration.

"They said something like *'mujer,'* which means—"

"Woman. I know." I waved off his explanation. "What else?"

"Give me a minute!" More chewing, and more thinking, and I couldn't be sure which was more difficult for him. "Um. I heard them both say *'humano'* a couple of times. And maybe *'mordedura'*—bite. And I know I heard something like *'mate,'* which means *'kill'* in Spanish, because I remember thinking they might have been arguing about killing me. But neither of them said my name, so that may not have been what they meant, after all."

I nodded grimly, almost certain he was right, though killing Ryan was surely somewhere on their to-do list. It sounded to me like they were arguing about their pet project.

The grandfather clock in the foyer chimed five times, and I yawned into my palm, making a mental note to start some coffee when I went back upstairs. "Anything else?"

"Yeah. Luiz said something about someone's nose. *Nariz.* Then Miguel kept saying something about a university. *Uni-*

versidad. He seemed pretty insistent, and Luiz kept saying no. Yelling it, like he didn't want to go to school. I thought maybe Miguel wanted him to go learn some English. But then, when Miguel said they were going after you, I realized that they were probably arguing over how best to snatch you from school."

I barely heard a word Ryan said after "nose," because that told me all I needed to know about the last things Luiz said before he disappeared. It sounded to me like Miguel wanted Luiz to take a second shot at me, but Luiz wanted nothing to do with it. Since I'd broken his nose, I couldn't really blame him.

"When exactly did they have this argument?" I asked, rising from my chair to pace in front of his cage. "What day was it?"

"Shit, Faythe, I don't know." He grimaced at the last bite of cold halibut on his fork, hovering halfway to his mouth.

"Well, think about!" I demanded, resisting the impulse to rattle his bars. "How long was it between their argument and the day they brought me in?"

"A couple of days. It was right before Miguel and Eric went after Abby." He bit into the fish and blanched as if it tasted bad. But I knew the problem had just as much to do with old, bitter memories as with cold, rubbery fish.

My teeth ground together, and my hands curled into fists at my sides as images of Abby behind bars flashed through my mind. She'd been bruised and in shock when I first saw her there, hiding behind a curtain of tangled red curls. She jumped at every sound from the house above and spent most of her time curled up on the bare mattress in one corner of her cell.

Instead of letting her out, or even sending our father an anonymous tip about where to find her, Ryan had let her— and later me—sit in that basement prison dreading every single second that passed.

"If Miguel made Luiz go back on campus the next day to take another shot at me, he could easily have stumbled upon Andrew in the grip of scratch-fever," I mumbled.

"Who's Andrew?" Ryan asked. I glared at him, irritated to realize I'd been thinking aloud. But then, as tired as I was, it was a miracle I was thinking at all.

"Are you done with that plate?" I asked tugging on the hem of the tank top now clinging to my damp skin.

"Yeah." He drained the last of the watered-down tea from his glass. "You can take this, too. But could you refill my water before you go?"

I glanced at the office-style water dispenser situated close to his cage so he could stick his plastic cup through the bars and get water whenever he wanted. The reservoir was dry, and just noticing that made me conscious all over again of how hot it was in the basement.

"Fine." I removed the upside-down water jug from the dispenser and filled it from the utility sink in the bathroom, then lugged it back across the basement and reinstalled the bottle. Then I picked up the dishes my brother had slid through the stainless-steel flap, and turned to go.

"What's going on up there, Faythe?" Ryan followed me as far as the bars would allow as I headed toward the stairs. "No one's come down to lift weights or spar in days, and now they're letting me go hungry. And you're asking about Luiz. Have they found him?"

I glanced at him over my shoulder, one hand on the make-shift stair rail, a three-quarter-inch iron pipe running alongside the steps. "Nope. To my knowledge, no one's even looking."

"Come on, Faythe!" Ryan shouted as I bounced up the stairs. "At least I kept you informed. I never left you in the dark."

"Actually…" I stood on the top step, my finger already poised over the light switch. "That's exactly what you did." I flipped the switch and stepped into the kitchen, closing the basement door on the heat, the smell, and his protests.

I should have felt guilty as I rinsed his dishes in the sink and started a pot of coffee, but I didn't. I just felt tired. And famished.

If my mother were up, she'd make pancakes, or omelets, or something equally complicated. But I was far too lazy to chop or mix a bunch of raw ingredients first thing in the morning, especially considering I hadn't slept, or had my coffee. So, I settled for French toast. Even I could do that, with minimum effort.

While my coffee percolated, its mere fragrance keeping me upright, I beat two eggs in a large glass bowl, then added heavy cream, vanilla, and sugar, and beat some more. In fact, I beat the slimy concoction for much longer than was strictly necessary, because it felt therapeutic. I needed to pound the living shit out of something, and since I couldn't get past Ryan's bars, eggs seemed to be my only option at five o'clock in the morning.

Mumbling beneath my breath about how I'd discipline Ryan for his crimes if *I* were in charge, I rifled through the cabinet beneath the bar for a flat pan with raised sides, clanging every pot and skillet my mother owned against one of its stainless-steel or Teflon-coated brethren.

"Good morning," my father said from the other side of the bar, startling me so badly that I banged my head against the cabinet. My own racket had covered his approach.

"Daddy, you scared the shi—er…*crap* out of me." I set the pan on the counter between us, rubbing the new bump. "Could you maybe make a little more noise next time you enter the room?"

He walked around the bar and took two coffee mugs from the overhead cabinet. "Could you maybe make a little *less* noise next time you decide to torture your mother's cookware?"

"Sorry." I kicked the cabinet door shut and reached into the bread box for a loaf of presliced French bread.

"I needed to get up, anyway." He poured coffee into both mugs. "Wesley's flight lands in an hour."

I glanced at him as I lined up bread slices in the bottom of the pan. "Oh." Exhaustion settled over me like a literal weight on my shoulders at the thought of Jamey Gardner, still wrapped in black plastic in the barn.

While the bread soaked up egg-slime in the pan, I heated the griddle.

My father set a mug on the counter in front of me. "Why are you up so early?" he asked, flipping open the top on a bottle of creamer. "And don't tell me you felt like making everyone breakfast."

"I haven't actually made it to bed yet," I admitted, and my father frowned. He opened his mouth to start yelling, but I held up my hand to cut him off, desperate for that initial sip of coffee before I could defend myself with any actual coherence.

I smiled as the first traces of caffeine entered my system, and a groggy peace settled into place. "I think I've figured out who's helping Andrew."

My father sipped silently from his mug, calmly waiting for me to continue.

Damn him. I'd stayed up all night and probably lost Marc for all of eternity, though my father seemed to have slept through that part, thankfully. I deserved at least a little excitement from my Alpha, especially considering that the information I'd dug up was part of the job he'd assigned me.

Glowering, I turned my back on him and placed the first four soggy slices of bread on the griddle. My stomach growled as the toast sizzled, the combined scents of butter and vanilla sweetening the entire kitchen.

"It's Luiz," I said, poking angrily at the bread. Still miffed, I didn't bother to turn around, and regretted my decision when my father choked on his coffee in surprise.

I whirled around to see him blotting at an undignified splatter across the front of his royal-blue robe. A grin snuck out from behind my scowl, and I hid it quickly with my own mug when he looked up.

"What on earth gave you that idea?" he asked, already recovering his usual poise.

"A leap of intuition." I flipped the first slice of bread. "And I'm kind of surprised I didn't think of it earlier. Here's the thing. There were no other cats anywhere near the UNT campus. But we *know* Luiz was there, the very day I bit Andrew. He probably saw us together. Then, if he came back the next day, what would happen if he couldn't find me?"

My father sipped from his mug, unresponsive as he watched me.

I rolled my eyes, gesturing with the spatula. "He'd follow Andrew! Right? To get to me? But I was already gone, and my boyfriend was newly infected. He'd be able to smell my scent on Andrew. In his blood. That'd be pretty hard to ignore."

He frowned, and I tried to hide my disappointment in his reaction. I should have known he wouldn't get it. He made decisions based on facts, not fantastic leaps of logic, no matter how well founded they were.

"Faythe, that's an awful lot of ifs, and no real evidence." My father set his mug on the counter with a ceramic-on-ceramic clink, which somehow managed to convey his doubt. "It's going to take something concrete to make me suspect someone who, by all indications, has been dead for a couple of months now."

"He's not dead." I shoved hair from my face and lifted the first slice of toast from the griddle onto a serving platter. "Everyone's *assuming* he's dead because he hasn't shown up in a while. But they're making asses out of us *all,* because he isn't dead. He's just been busy making sure Andrew survived scratch-fever."

"Wait," my father said, and I closed my eyes in dread, sure I knew what was coming. "You think Luiz—a serial-killing jungle stray—stopped slaughtering college girls so he could nurse your ex-boyfriend back to health? Do you understand how…*absurd* that sounds?"

My fist clenched the spatula. "Yes. Believe me, I know."

"And we have no way of knowing that Luiz actually went back after you ran him off."

I smiled to myself as I removed the last of the toast from the griddle. *Time to play the credibility card.* "Actually, based on information from my source, I'm pretty sure he did."

He arched one brow. "And your source would be…?"

"Ryan."

My father blinked at me, and I grinned from ear to ear. "What did Ryan say, exactly?"

I really, really wanted to fudge a bit on the details, just to make them stronger, since Ryan hadn't actually said anything but a few half-remembered Portuguese words. But my father would verify for himself anything I claimed to have gotten from my less-than-trustworthy brother, so I told the swear-on-my-own-life, cross-my-heart-and-hope-to-be-declawed truth.

"He told me what he understood of an argument Miguel and Luiz had the day I kicked his kidnapping ass."

A brief smile slipped past his usual unreadable expression, so I continued, encouraged. "It sounded like Miguel wanted him to go back for me, and Luiz didn't want to go, because I'd broken his nose." I turned back to the stove and dropped a fresh slice of toast onto the griddle, accidentally slopping egg batter across the pristine stovetop. "Now, I spoke to Andrew on the phone the morning after Marc and I got home, and he was already getting sick. I wish I'd realized then that it was scratch-fever. But I didn't."

"You had no reason to," my father said, and a flood of gratitude washed over me at his words.

"Thanks. Anyway, if Luiz went back for me that day, he'd have found Andrew instead."

"But you don't know for sure that he went back to UNT."

I smiled sweetly at my father as I set his plate on the counter in front of him, along with a bottle of maple syrup. "No. But you don't know that he didn't, either."

My father and I ate side by side at the bar, chewing in near silence as he thought over everything I'd said. At ten minutes to six, Michael walked into the kitchen, already fully dressed in jeans and a somber, dark blue polo shirt, no doubt his idea of the travel-friendly wardrobe of a man in mourning.

Ethan followed him five minutes later, wearing only a pair of gray jogging pants cinched at the waist. His thick black hair was still sleep-tousled, and his cheek bore a crisscross of pillow lines. He headed straight for the coffeepot, probably led by his nose, because he couldn't possibly have seen anything through his half-closed eyes.

Yet he was alert enough to snatch the last half slice of toast from my plate as he walked past the bar.

"Get your own," I snapped, but I wasn't able to work up any real irritation after he'd tried so hard to console me the night before. Or rather, three hours earlier.

"You know I don't cook," he mumbled around a mouthful of my breakfast as he poured the last of the coffee into the teacup he'd grabbed by accident.

"Wake up, Ethan," my father said, setting a box of dry cereal on the counter in front of him. Michael added two bowls and a half-empty carton of milk, then dug two spoons from the silverware drawer.

Ethan drained his cup, then stared at it, clearly trying to figure out how he wound up with one of our mother's rose-patterned china teacups instead of his own oversize Cowboys mug. "I'm awake," he said, rubbing the dark stubble on his chin. He poured a mound of Cheerios into his bowl, then doused it in milk and dug in, eating with the appetite of a two-hundred-pound cat. Which he was.

"Wes insisted on driving here from the airport, to save you all a trip to the car-rental place, so if his flight lands on time, he should be here in less than an hour. Make sure you're packed and ready to go. Charge your cell phones and take an extra battery, just in case. And, Ethan, make some more coffee."

Having started his morning off with a list of orders, our Alpha opened the basement door, flipped up the light switch, then descended into the makeshift prison without another word.

When my mother padded in wearing a pale gray silk robe, I loaded my plate into the dishwasher and plodded down the hall to my room, to avoid the sympathetic looks as Ethan spread the news about me and Marc. I collapsed facedown on my bed, on top of my rumpled covers, and was asleep in seconds.

Twenty-Five

I woke up at ten minutes to nine, after almost three hours of sleep, to the sound of someone pounding on my door frame. "I'm awake," I mumbled, raising my face from the pillow just enough to be heard. I had no real intention of getting up until Jace called out to me from the hall.

"Well then, come on out. Your dad wants to see you."

I flopped over onto my back, staring at my ceiling. "Give me a minute to get dressed."

"You're not dressed?"

I smiled in spite of myself at the lighthearted quality of his jest. Until my broken door began to move. "Jace!" I shouted, trying to keep from laughing as I vaulted off the bed and scrambled to stop him. He wasn't seriously trying to sneak a peek; if he had been, he wouldn't have made any noise. But if I let him get away with a joke today, he'd try it for real tomorrow.

Jace yelped as I ripped the door from his grasp and leaned it against the frame. Then he sulked, his eyes roaming just far enough south to see my tank top and shorts. "Liar!" he accused, the smile in his eyes ruining his pout. "You're not naked."

"I meant I wanted to change."

He grinned. "So, go ahead."

"Nice try." I patted his left cheek, smooth from a recent meeting with his razor. The revival of Jace's former easygoing demeanor told me two things without a doubt: he knew Marc had dumped me, and Marc was currently away from the ranch. If either of those statements had been false, Jace would never have indulged in such comfortable, meaningless banter with me. At least *something* good had come out of the previous night's disaster.

"Tell my dad I'll be there in five minutes."

I dressed quickly in skimpy denim shorts and a snug red T. After brushing my teeth and pulling my hair into a quick ponytail, I grabbed my cell and headed for the office, already dreading my upcoming call to Andrew.

My father was on the phone when I arrived, so I sat on the love seat next to Jace. Other than Vic, alone on the sofa, and Owen, at my father's desk, the room was empty. "Where is everyone?" I whispered to Jace, glancing around.

"Michael and Ethan left with Wes Gardner about an hour ago," he said, leaning over to whisper into my ear. His breath against my skin gave me chills, but it also made me think of Marc, and the way he liked to whisper to me in Spanish while we…

My father cleared his throat, and I looked up to see him drop the phone into its cradle. "Marc and Parker arrived in Henderson twenty minutes ago. They're scouting for signs of the tabby."

He didn't mention my fight with Marc, and as badly as I

wanted to tell him, I didn't. Surely he'd heard what happened by then. Surely someone had told him.

He sat on one corner of his desk and fixed me with a hard stare. "What happened to your door?"

Or, maybe not.

"Marc."

"Oh." My father nodded, and that was it. No more questions, at least for the moment. "In a few minutes, you're going to call Andrew and try to find out his whereabouts, and his current company. But first, let me say that I verified the information you got from Ryan, and I think you might be on to something with this theory about Luiz."

Dad sank into his armchair. The white streaks at his temples caught light from the fixture overhead, and made him look tired, and…kind of *old*.

"Who was that on the phone?" I asked, uncomfortable with the thought that my father would ever be ready to retire. He was the strongest, most stable thing in my life—especially now that Marc had opted out of it.

"If you and Jace hadn't been whispering—" his voice was thick with disapproval "—you would already know that I was speaking to my source in Venezuela."

I perked up in spite of the less-than-subtle censure of my familiar manner with Jace. "What did he say?"

"*She* had some interesting information that may or may not be of any help to us." He took a moment to enjoy my surprise over his informant's gender, then carried on. "Camilla doesn't know of any tabbies who have gone missing recently, but she said that four and a half years ago there was a rash of disappearances across the area."

"All tabbies?" Vic asked, and I went still, half afraid I'd miss part of the answer if I moved.

My father nodded. "They disappeared one at a time over a period of six months, from four different countries. For the most part, the Alphas were not on good terms with one another, and it never occurred to any of them to ask for help, or even to alert their neighbors, until it was too late."

"How many did they get?" I asked, my fist pressed into my abdomen as I tried to ease the knot forming in my gut. The connection was obvious. Luiz and Miguel and their recruits had snatched three American tabbies—including me—before we were able to catch them. The chances of them not being involved in an apparently identical plot in their own corner of the world were almost nil.

"Four." My father wore his business face, which told me how bothered he was by the new information. "They got one tabby from Colombia, one from Ecuador, one from Peru, and one from Venezuela." He paused, watching me carefully. "None of the girls was ever found."

For a moment no one spoke, and I assumed that, like me, they were paralyzed by horror and outrage. Four girls taken, and not one of them found in more than four years. Could they still be alive? And if they were, what kind of hell had they endured at the hands of their captors?

I couldn't bring myself to voice the questions we were surely all thinking. I couldn't even see past the black fog drifting around in my brain, obscuring reason and logic in a cloud of rage and indignation.

Jace cleared his throat, and the sound broke through my shock. "Okay, if Faythe's right, and Luiz is still alive, Camilla's information could be pretty important. Although now he's taking human women, not tabbies. But what does any of that have to do with the tabby we're after? I don't see the connection."

I didn't see it, either, but an image was forming in my mind as the fog began to thin. It was still hazy, large parts sketched with a frustrating lack of detail. But one part of the image was clear. "It's Luiz," I said, staring absently at the rug as I tried to organize my thoughts. "I'm not sure how or why, but he's the connection. The tabby's hunting him and killing tomcats along the way. She has to be after Luiz, because I don't see any connection between her and Andrew, but she and Luiz are both from the same area of the world."

Okay, that was a flimsy link at best—just because they were from the same *continent* didn't mean they'd ever even set eyes on each other. After all, how many Canadian cats had *I* never met? But I was more than ready to grasp at straws.

"Maybe she's the mother of one of the missing tabbies, out for revenge," I suggested.

Vic laughed. "Yeah, you gotta watch out for those renegade mommies. They're the worst."

I glared at him. "You ever heard the phrase 'one bad mother'?"

"Let's focus on the topic at hand, please," my father said.

"Sorry." Vic tried to stop smiling but couldn't quite manage.

"We have to find Andrew, before he makes trouble too close to home. It's time to call him." My father frowned, his attention narrowing in on me, and I struggled to concentrate in spite of encroaching exhaustion.

My father cleared his throat to catch my attention. "Do you know what you're going to say?"

"Yeah." I clenched my phone in one fist. "I'm going to tell

him how he was really infected and apologize. If there's any of the old Andrew left in him, he'll respect that." And frankly, I didn't know what else to do.

"If he still doesn't know you've told us about him, don't enlighten him. He'll be more willing to play into our hand if he thinks he can get you alone," my father said. I nodded, and he gestured toward my phone. "Dial."

No pressure, I thought, acutely aware of every pair of eyes on me, ready to judge my burgeoning enforcer skills. My fingers shook as I pressed the appropriate keys. Holding my breath, I pressed the last button and held the phone to my ear. It rang, a synthesized bleating sound that grated on my already-frazzled nerves.

I heard a click, then the soft hiss of an open line when Andrew answered his phone. "I'm going to go out on a limb here and say you're nervous about seeing me again."

It was a typical Andrew-style greeting—not so much as a hello. But that little glimpse of the man I'd known left me hope that there may yet be more of the old Andrew in there somewhere. "*Should* I be nervous?"

"In my humble estimation…yes."

On the couch across from me, Vic rolled his eyes, unimpressed by Andrew's high opinion of himself.

"Why?" I asked, plucking at a thread dangling from my shorts.

Clothing rustled over the line. "We have something special planned for our little reunion."

"We? Who's with you?" I glanced at my father, asking wordlessly for permission to voice my suspicion. He nodded, so I continued. "Is it Luiz?"

I held my breath, fully aware that if Andrew *wasn't* with

Luiz, he would have no idea what I was talking about. But his sudden silence said that I was almost certainly right.

"How did you know that?" Andrew muttered.

My pulse jumped, and I sat straighter, both thrilled and terrified to have my guess confirmed. "Is he with you right now?"

Something crashed over the phone, a sound like wood breaking. "How the *fuck* did you know about him?" Andrew demanded, and all traces of the kind, gentle man I'd known were gone.

Too nervous to sit, I shot up from the love seat and began to pace, uncomfortably aware that my father did the same thing when he needed to think quickly. "Andrew, listen to me. You have to get away from him."

"Why? So you can turn me into some kind of pet on a leash? Don't you already have one of those?"

Suddenly unsure, I paused in midstep, glancing at my father for guidance. "Say something," he mouthed, and from the corner of my eye, Vic used his hand like a talking puppet to reinforce my father's order.

"Andrew, you have to trust me." I started pacing again, fast now, my bare feet whispering on the rug. "Whatever he's telling you, it isn't true. He's lying."

"What, like you did?" His voice was shrill with fury, then for a moment it was gone altogether, buried beneath what sounded like more furniture breaking. "—turned me into a monster, then left me to die. *He* saved my life. He taught me…everything."

"No." I shook my head, though he couldn't see me. "He's using you. I bit you by accident, and didn't figure out what had happened until last night. I swear my life on it. I never meant to hurt you. But he's been using you all this time, lying to you and twisting the truth to get you to do what he wants."

"You have to be in cat form to infect someone," Andrew snapped, his words clipped short in rage.

Okay, that was true. But…

"Which means you did it on purpose."

"No!" I shouted, by then oblivious to everyone else in the room. "There's more to it than that. Just give me a—"

"You *had* a chance to say your piece, but instead you left me without so much as a goodbye. Why should I believe a word you say now?"

"Because I can help you. I *want* to help you." I'd never said anything truer in my life. It was my fault Andrew was…insane. And likely homicidal.

"I don't want your fucking help!" he shouted into my ear, bitterness rendering his voice a mere shadow of what it once was.

Time to change tactics. I took a deep, calming breath. "Where are you, Andrew? Let me come get you. I'll come alone." I crossed my fingers and held them over my head as I paced, for my father's benefit. I had no intention of going anywhere near Andrew and Luiz alone. But they didn't need to know that.

"Where am I?" He laughed, and in that grating, malicious perversion of joy, I heard a faint remnant of the sweet, delight-filled laughter I remembered from the Andrew of old. The man with gentle eyes and slow, patient hands. He was still in there somewhere. He had to be. "I'm in hell, Faythe. And you're going to keep me company."

Grief rolled through me in a wave of private despair. Grief for Andrew, and the man he'd been. I stopped in front of my father's desk, leaning against it, my shoulders hunched in sorrow, and in guilt. If I had taken care of Andrew during his transition, he might have been fine. He might have turned out very much like Marc. But I hadn't taken care of him. I'd left him for Luiz to find, and now the only part of *my* Andrew remaining was a familiar note in the hollow echo of his laughter.

What had I done? And could I possibly undo it?

"I'm so sorry," I said again, hoping to thaw his heart with my penitence. "I would give anything to change it. To give you back your life. But I can't." Pacing again, I reached the corner of my father's desk and turned. "But I can show you how to live the life you have now. Please let me help you."

"Fuck you, Faythe! You'll be begging *me* for help soon."

My breath hitched in surprise over such an overt threat, and I glanced at my father, who looked almost as concerned as he was angry. "Andrew, I'm telling you it was an acci—"

"You can explain it to Saint Peter," my formerly human, formerly kind, gentle, and sweet boyfriend snarled in my ear. "Say hi for me when you see him." The phone went dead in my hand, and I held it in front of my face, staring at the tiny full-color screen, which now read "end call."

"Damn it!" My hand clenched the plastic, and it took several long, slow breaths before I regained enough control to keep from crushing it.

"Wow!" Vic said, whistling between his two front teeth. "That's one pissed-off little stray."

"*Two* pissed-off little strays," I corrected, thinking of Luiz, who was just as much to blame for what Andrew had become as I was. "When we find Luiz, he's going to pay in full for every finger he laid on each of those girls, and for every single lie he fed Andrew." Though at the moment, it was the truths he'd told that bothered me the most. He probably really thought I'd infected Andrew on purpose.

"Indeed," my father said from his armchair, and for a

moment I thought he was reading my mind. "Well, at least we know now that you were right about his involvement."

Yet I found that a small consolation, all things considered.

After that, the day hit a bit of a lull. Marc and Parker had seen no sign of the rogue tabby, and we still had no idea where to find Luiz and Andrew. My father sent Owen, Jace, and Vic out for a run in the woods, ostensibly to burn off some nervous energy and clear their heads for the coming confrontation— whenever that turned out to be. But I think he was actually trying to get them out of his fur for an hour of peace and quiet.

I stayed behind, out of sheer exhaustion. Whether it was the lack of sleep, or the emotionally draining phone call to Andrew, by the time the guys filed out of the office, I could barely hold my head up. So I stretched out on the leather couch for a short nap, just like I'd done as a kid, lulled to sleep by the scratching of a pencil on paper as my father sketched to set his mind at ease.

Sometime later—about an hour and a half, according to the wall clock—the guys woke me up when they filed back into the office like a herd of elephants on parade. Jace picked up my feet and sat beneath them, and Vic and Owen settled onto the love seat across from us. I was still rubbing sleep from my eyes when the office phone rang out, startling in the temporary calm. My father answered it, and the moment the caller spoke, I sat straight up, instantly wide-awake. It was Marc.

"No sign of the tabby yet," he said after a brief greeting. "But we've got Dan Painter here, and he wants to talk to you. He doesn't seem to know anything about the strays we're looking for—" Andrew and Luiz, obviously "—but he says he knows the tabby personally. And he'll only speak to the man in charge."

Twenty-Six

The phone still pressed to his ear, my father arched his brows in surprise and dropped his pencil on his desk. "Oh, really?"

"Yeah!" Painter's voice was soft from distance to the phone and high pitched from stress, but still easily recognizable. "Fucker nearly broke my jaw, but I told 'em I'm only talking to the main man."

"That would be the Alpha," Parker said from somewhere over the line. "And there's no cussing in front of the Alpha."

Yeah, I was still working on that one myself.

"Sorry," Painter mumbled, just as Marc said, "Should I put him on the phone?"

My father closed his eyes, considering the request. Then he opened them and said, "Please." The phone clattered as it changed hands, and then he was speaking to the informant himself. "Mr. Painter? I understand you have some information for me."

"Yeah, but I got a request first. I want in."

My father frowned. "In?"

"Yeah, in. In the pack, or whatever you call it. The group. The in-crowd."

I smiled, as images from high school popped up unbidden, and my father seemed on the verge of a chuckle himself. "Mr. Painter, we call it the Pride. And Pride cats don't act in anticipation of a reward. They act out of honor. Do you understand what I'm saying?"

"Yeah, I get it." Springs creaked over the phone, as Painter shifted in whatever seat he occupied. "You want me to spill my guts for free."

"I want to be sure that your character is up to the standard I require of my Pride cats, and by *volunteering* your information, you'd go a long way toward showing me that."

Damn, he's good. I exchanged a knowing grin with Jace.

"Yeah, I see what you're saying," Painter said. "I tell you what I know, and you'll let me play your reindeer games."

"You have my word that if you help us in this matter, I will give you an opportunity to prove you belong with us. How does that sound?"

There was silence over the line for several seconds, as Painter thought the offer over. Then he sighed. "Fine. You want to know about the woman, right? You call them tabbies?"

"Yes. How do you know her?" My father picked up his pencil and began scribbling as Painter spoke.

"I met her about a week ago, at this club in Mississippi. First girl-cat I ever saw, and I knew what she was right away, even with her walkin' around on two feet." Painter sounded so proud of himself that I had to smile.

My father nodded, still writing. "You've been following her?"

"Shi—er, shoot, no. I've been travelin' *with* her. Keepin' her company. I didn't know she was killin' people, though. I swear I didn't know that until the other day, the first time I called you."

"How did you find out?"

"I followed her. We drive during the day, then check into a hotel. She goes out every night. Alone. One night I followed her. I think she knew I was there, but she let me tail her anyway. She went to another strip club, and about half an hour later she came out with this dude. Another cat. She took him out back, and the next thing I know, she's standing over his body. I nearly pissed my pants, ya know? But she just pulled him over to his car and heaved him into the trunk. Then she drove him to the middle of nowhere and dumped him in a field. I told you guys about that one. Remember? Then I ran into this fu—I mean, this big guy here, and another chick, and she knocked me the fu— Knocked me out cold. First time I ever been hit by a girl."

Jace elbowed me, and I frowned, still embarrassed that I'd silenced our biggest lead before he could tell us what was going on.

"So you've been traveling with this tabby…" my father continued. "Where is she going?"

"Man, I don't know. Somewhere new every night. I think she's following someone. She gets these calls on her cell phone from some guy with an accent. He just says the name of a town, then hangs up."

Son of a bitch! She was getting calls, too. Only I was betting hers were coming from Luiz, rather than from Andrew. What the hell were they doing?

"So she gets a call, you both drive to a new town, where she goes out and kills someone. Then you call us and report the murder?" my father asked, his pencil motionless over the paper. "Why would you do that?"

"I heard chicks are valuable to you guys. Girl cats. I thought you might be interested in this one. Plus, she's kind of makin' a mess in your territory. Thought that information might be worth something to you."

Painter wanted the best of both worlds. He was enjoying his time with the hot young tabby, but snitching to us the whole time, hoping for an invitation to join the Pride. An idiot's version of a double agent.

My father hesitated, then shook his head. "What is this tabby's name?"

"She calls herself Manx. Won't tell me any more than that."

"Where is she now?" My father tapped his eraser on the legal pad.

"Like I told these guys, I don't know. She got one whiff of them and took off!"

A second later, Marc was back on the line. "So, what do we do with him?"

"Does Painter have a car there?"

"Yeah." Marc gave a short, ironic laugh. "We're sitting in it right now, in his hotel parking lot."

"Good. I'm sending reinforcements. Cuff him and send him back with Owen, when the others get there."

"No problem," Marc said.

My father hung up the phone and stood, eyeing the four of us gathered on the sofas. "Go. Now. Meet up with Marc and Parker. Owen, bring Painter back in one piece. I have several more questions for him. The rest of you check out Henderson in teams. No one works alone. If you can't find anything in a quick once-over, I want one team watching the local strip club—Michael said there's only one—for the tabby. The rest of you keep looking around town. Watch the motels, restau-

rants, and grocery stores in particular. They're going to have
to eat and sleep somewhere."

Jace was already in the doorway, ready to go. Vic stood in
front of the couch, looking just as eager.

"Keep in contact with me and with Marc," my father said,
eyeing me in particular. "And we need Luiz and Andrew alive,
if at all possible."

Vic frowned, clearly disappointed. "Both of them? Why?"

"There's still a slim chance Andrew might be able to help
Faythe. He probably doesn't remember actually being infected, but I don't want to execute the best witness on her
behalf, just in case he can vouch for the partial Shift."

"And Luiz?" Jace asked from behind me.

"The missing tabbies," I answered for my father, pleased
that he and I were finally thinking along the same lines. "If
they're still alive, he'll know where they are. And their parents
will want a word or two with him."

My father nodded.

"No problem." Vic dug his keys from his pocket. "Let's go.
I'm driving."

"Go start the air conditioner in the car," I said, glancing
down at myself. "I just have to change into some work clothes."

Vic gave my snug T and shorts a quick once-over, then
shrugged and headed for the hall. Jace and Owen followed
him to the car and I raced toward my room, barely pausing
when I heard my mother's car pull up out front.

I picked up my bedroom door and shimmied through the
gap before propping it back in place. I was going to insist that
Marc fix my door personally. It would teach him a lesson for
making such a mess, and…well, he'd have to actually come
near me to repair the damage.

After changing I met my mother in the hall, looking perfectly composed in white slacks and a blouse the exact shade of pink as her cheeks. She carried a large white leather purse in one hand and an afghan over the opposite arm.

"Where'd you go so early?" I asked, frowning as she stopped to brush a strand of hair from my forehead.

"I had brunch with Mrs. Jennings and her daughter. Look what Natalie made for the silent auction." She slipped her bag over one arm and shook out the red-and-gold afghan. "Isn't it beautiful?"

"Lovely," I said, for lack of a better response.

"Look at the intricate pattern," my mother insisted, bringing a corner of the blanket close to my face. I looked, but couldn't tell one…stitch, or whatever, from another. And what was that smell? It was kind of familiar. I leaned closer to the afghan, inhaling deeply. *It must be Natalie.*

The scent was soft, and feminine, and…full. Or something like that. And definitely human, so I must have been imagining the familiarity.

"You know, Natalie's expecting her second."

I arched my brows at my mother, not following the change of subject. "Second what?" Mortgage? Conviction? Chance at a new life?

"Baby, of course. Her second baby. The doctor says this one's a girl."

I laughed, genuinely amused that my mother thought it should have been so obvious. "Yeah, well, I bet Natalie can't drop a stray with a powerhouse right hook."

"Not in her condition." My mother frowned, folding the blanket into a neat, fluffy square. "Sometimes I worry about you, Faythe."

"Right back at 'cha, Mom." I stepped around her, grateful in spite of my mostly sleep-free night that I had places to go, and werecats to apprehend.

My mother clucked her tongue at me in shame, but I didn't even pause. It would take much more than her disapproval to make me give up adrenaline and exercise for Lamaze and diapers. Much, much more.

Vic gave me another once-over as I jogged down the front steps and veered toward his black-on-black Jeep Wrangler. He frowned, clearly not pleased by my outfit.

Jace was settled into the back with his earphones on. Owen sat next to him, already half-asleep, so I slid into the front passenger seat.

"You might as well have worn plastic wrap," Vic mumbled as he shifted into first gear and pulled out of the parking circle and onto the long, straight driveway.

"And you might as well paint that frown on to save your mouth the trouble," I snapped, turning toward the door to stare out the window. My clothes were perfectly appropriate, even if my jeans were a little snug. Vic could kiss my ass. He was just being snotty because he was Marc's best friend. But I could be just as snotty.

After half an hour spent listening to traffic sounds, Owen's snoring, and the bass-thumping beat leaking from Jace's earphones, I was bored and fighting to stay awake. I couldn't afford to arrive in Henderson groggy and confused, in which case I might as well hand my cuffs over to Luiz and ram my face into his fist.

Finally, barely able to keep my eyes open, I popped open the glove compartment, in search of something with which to amuse myself. Hopefully, something to read.

"Hey!" Vic snapped, sliding his eyes rapidly back and forth between the road and my hands, which were now wrist-deep in his glove box. "Could you please not ransack my stuff?"

"Sorry. I was just looking for a map." I closed the glove box with a sharp click, and he huffed in irritation.

His hands clenched around the steering wheel. "I *know* how to get there."

I twisted in my seat to frown at him. "What's wrong with you? You've been in a pissy mood all morning."

Sighing, he glanced at me, then back at the road, his face drawn tight in not only anger, but grief. Had I missed something?

"What's wrong with me? You're acting like an idiot, that's what's wrong. A selfish, spoiled idiot."

"What the hell are you talking about?" I was more confused than angry, which probably said a lot about how tired I was.

Vic inhaled deeply, as if preparing to say something important. Something he dreaded. *Great.* "With Luiz back, I can't help thinking about Sara and Anthony, trying to make sense of what happened to them. But I can't. It just doesn't *make* any sense."

Ohh. I nodded in agreement, and in sympathy. Miguel had first kidnapped, then raped and murdered Sara, and Anthony had been killed when we tried to apprehend his sister's murderer. Vic was right. There was no sense to be found in his siblings' deaths, or in any random violence. But that was the world we lived in, and even if we could change it, we couldn't bring back Sara and Anthony.

"I guess that's my problem," he continued, glancing at me before turning back to the road. "Life doesn't make any sense, and neither does death. No one expected them to die so young, but it can happen to anyone, anytime, and there's no way to prepare for it."

Okay, he was starting to sound a bit fatalistic. Which worried me. It wasn't like *Vic* was going to die anytime soon. Not if I could help it, anyway.

"Ever since they died, I've been trying to do everything I always said I was going to do. Trying to really live, you know?" His eyes shined with resolve, as if he'd just found the key to life and was determined to use it before someone changed the lock and left him pounding on the door. "I've been reading a bunch of books I've had since high school," he said, staring at the road as he spoke. "I always planned to read them, but never seemed to have the time before. Now I'm making time. I've been calling my brothers more often. And my parents. I've even been trying weird new foods, like sushi and chocolate-covered ants."

"Not together, I hope."

He smiled at my ill-timed joke. A little.

"I'm glad you're broadening your horizons, Vic." Beneath us, smooth blacktop gave way to the rougher surface of a much older road. "But I don't understand what that has to do with your being mad at me."

He sighed in frustration, as if it should have been obvious. "I don't have a sister anymore, Faythe. But I've known you since before you turned thirteen, and I kind of think of you as a sister now. Especially since Sara died."

Understanding soaked into me like water into a sponge, leaving me heavy with heartache. I swallowed thickly and blinked to stop my eyes from watering. I knew where he was going now, and it broke my heart.

"I want you to have all the things she didn't live long

enough to experience. I want you to have a wedding, with a long white dress and a bunch of handsome groomsmen." He grinned at his own joke, and I bit my lip to keep from reminding him that I'd already rejected that particular experience.

"And a honeymoon someplace tropical," he continued, oblivious to my discomfort. "And a family of your own. With Marc." Vic's eyes left the road to zero in on me, pinning me with an almost physical force. This was the heart of the matter. "He's as much a brother to me as my own brothers are. As Anthony was."

I grinned, hoping to lighten the mood. "So the two of us together would be like incest, right?"

He didn't even smile, though he did turn back to the road, just in time to swerve around a series of orange cones set up around some road construction. "I'm serious, Faythe. You and Marc belong together, and it kills me to see you walk away from each other like there's nothing there."

Yeah, join the club. I stared out my window to avoid his eyes. As much as I appreciated Vic's concern, Marc and I were none of his business. We were perfectly capable of screwing up our relationship all on our own.

"When I found out you bit your ex, I thought it was all over between you and Marc. I couldn't believe you'd do that to him, even when you guys were split up. He doesn't deserve any of this." The road construction ended, and Vic pulled back into the right-hand lane. "He went through hell every day you were gone, and now that you're back, he should be happy. But he's not. He's alone and miserable, and you're here—all dressed up—with Jace looking at you like you hung the fucking moon. It's no wonder Marc talked Greg into sending me with you two instead of Parker."

Ahh, so that's what happened. Marc knew he could count on Vic to keep an eye on me and Jace, and to re-create every awkward moment of this miserable assignment, whereas Parker—the Switzerland of the south-central Pride—would have been careful to stay out of our business.

I glanced in the rearview mirror to see Jace with his head back, eyes closed, earphones still in place. Fortunately.

"I'm not dressed up for Jace," I insisted, glancing down at the mid-to-low neckline of my blouse. If anything, I was dressed up for Marc, though I could never have admitted that aloud, unless I wanted Marc to hear about it later. Which I did not.

"Besides, you're missing something pretty important in all this." I turned sideways again to face him, ignoring the door handle poking my lower back. "Marc dumped *me.* Not the other way around. If you want us back together, talk to *him.*"

"I already have." He flicked the left blinker on and glanced back before changing lanes to pass a slow-moving VW Beetle. "Marc would do anything for you, Faythe, and I don't think you understand that."

"Of course I—"

He cut me off, swerving back into the right-hand lane. "He would fucking *die* for you if you asked him to. But that's not good enough for you. You have to have him on your own terms. With no strings. No commitment. But for him, that means no security. No guarantee that you won't just take off again."

"That's not fair." My left hand found the headrest and squeezed out of frustration. "I only left him because he wouldn't go with me. He wouldn't leave the Pride."

"You should never have asked him to. You gave him Sophie's choice, then told him to live with it. *That's* unfair. And now you're doing it again."

I faced forward and let my head fall against the headrest. "I'm not going anywhere, Vic."

"But he doesn't know that. Not for sure. And Marc needs to be sure." He paused, and for a moment there was only the sound of our tires on the road, and the regular rhythm of Jace's sleep-breathing from the backseat. "He told me what Kevin said."

"About wh—" Then I remembered. *Faythe's the only reason you're even here. Without her, you're just another stray cat licking the Alpha's boots, one false move away from the wrong side of the river.*

"That son of a bitch!" I muttered under my breath. Then, aloud, "Marc can't possibly believe that. Even if we never get back together, my dad would never kick him out. He loves Marc like a son."

"Yeah, but what happens when your dad's no longer in charge?" Vic leaned forward to adjust the air vent. "What if you wind up with someone else? The new Alpha isn't going to want Marc hanging around, and even if he did, Marc could never stay here and watch you with another tom. And where's he supposed to go then? What other Alpha is going to want a stray in his Pride?"

I stared out the window to keep him from seeing how shocked I was. I'd never once considered Marc's future without me. Hell, I'd barely considered my *own* future, beyond the two and a half years I owed my father.

The backseat creaked as Owen shifted in his sleep, so I whispered, hoping he and Jace had missed the entire conversation. "I would never let that happen. He'll always have a home here."

"That's what you say now, but a lot can change in a few

years." Vic glanced at me again, his eyes bright, his expression earnest. "Make him happy, Faythe. Take his damn ring and promise him that someday you'll give him what he needs. Knowing that it will happen eventually will be enough for him."

"Vic, I…"

I don't know how I would have responded if I'd had the chance. But I never got that chance, because that's when Vic's cell phone rang.

"Hang on," he said, digging it from his pocket to check the display screen. "It's Marc." He pressed a button on the tiny black phone and held it to his ear. "Hey, what's up?"

I turned to the window, wishing I couldn't hear their conversation. After what I'd just heard from Vic, I doubted the two of them ever discussed anything other than me and what a heartless bitch I was. And hearing it from Marc would be a million times worse than hearing it from Vic.

But as hard as I tried not to listen, Marc's first statement caught my attention. "…spotted the tabby in the strip club just outside of Henderson."

Twenty-Seven

Vic stomped on the brake to avoid a slow car in front of us, and Owen flew forward, whacking his shoulder—or maybe his head—on the back of my seat. "Owww—"

"You actually saw her?" Vic said into the phone as Jace cursed behind him.

"Not me, the bartender." Marc's voice sounded distant, and a little crackly. "Said she was there when they opened, and left about twenty minutes before we arrived. So she's still here somewhere."

I gripped the dashboard to steady myself as Vic swerved in and out of traffic.

"—ow long?" Marc was asking.

"Ten minutes, at the most." Vic honked at a burly truck driver on our left. "We're almost there now."

"Good." Marc grunted. "We'll meet you in the parking lot of the Motel 6, off Highway 259."

Eight minutes later, we pulled into the lot next to my father's old van, against which Marc and Parker both leaned.

In the front seat sat Dan Painter, a fresh bruise developing on his chin, just below the one I'd given him three days earlier.

"Is this the guy?" Owen nodded at Painter as he climbed from Vic's Jeep.

I nodded as Marc pulled Painter—hands cuffed behind his back—from the van.

"Oh, hell no!" Painter shouted, only lowering his voice when Parker punched him in the shoulder hard enough to knock him into the side of the van. "I'm not going *near* that bitch."

I couldn't help smiling. Until Marc opened his big fat mouth. "You've been living with a murderer for the past week and a half, and you're scared of *her?*" He aimed a dismissive gesture my way. Clearly he was still mad.

"Man, Manx is tame as a kitten, so long as you leave her alone. She don't like to be manhandled. That's where those other dudes fucked up."

I exchanged a raised-brow look with Owen, surprised to hear that Painter hadn't touched the tabby. Yet, oddly enough, I believed him. Like Ryan, Painter struck me as the kind of guy who considered his own well-being above all else—even his hormones.

"So, what's the plan?" Jace asked, coming around the Jeep to lean against the passenger-side door next to me. *Right* next to me. His arm brushed mine. Twice.

I rubbed my forehead, fighting the beginnings of a huge headache. This was not going to be pretty.

"Well, I have to get back to the ranch," Owen said, shifting his cowboy hat back and forth on his head. "And Painter's going with me."

"His car's over here." Marc led the way around the van to a dusty white Dodge Daytona parked on its other side. Parker pulled Painter to the passenger side of his own car and shoved him into the front seat. Then he took the cuffs from his pocket and secured Painter's cuffed hands to the handle of his own door.

"You move so much as a finger and Owen will knock you out cold," Marc warned.

Painter rolled his eyes and nodded. "I kinda figured."

Two minutes later, Owen pulled back onto the highway in Painter's car, which smoked and sputtered until it passed out of sight.

Marc glanced around at the rest of us. "We're going to grab a quick lunch, then check out the main streets in two groups. Parker and I have already covered the south side, so you guys take everything east of Main Street, and we'll take everything on the west side."

Vic looked up from the map Marc passed him. "In the car, or on foot?"

"On foot." Marc dug for his wallet. "Hopefully Faythe's the only one either of the strays will recognize, and that's a small risk to take, considering the alternative—we won't be able to smell anything from the car." He pulled two twenties from his wallet and handed them to Jace. "Run next door and get a dozen corn dogs and some drinks. And make it quick."

Jace scowled. But he did as he was told, because Marc outranked him. And clearly wasn't above using his authority to keep Jace away from me.

This is going to get old fast.

"So the tabby was actually in the local strip club?" Vic asked, one foot propped on the curb beneath his front bumper. I smiled at him, grateful that someone was willing to break the tension.

"Yeah." Parker nodded, salt-and-pepper hair ruffling in the

warm wind. "The bartender said she walked around and checked everything out, including both bathrooms, then left, without ordering anything or even glancing at the stage. Said he thought she was looking for someone."

"Could you smell her?" I asked, curious to know if her distinctive scent had been any stronger when it was fresh.

"Only on the ladies'-room doorknob," Marc said, and I pictured the strange looks he must have gotten when he bent over to sniff the bathroom door. "I don't think she touched much else while she was there."

Well, I couldn't blame her for that one.

We stood around in silence for several minutes after that, until Jace emerged from the convenience store with two bulging white plastic bags, and I breathed an audible sigh of relief. If he'd been a minute later, I'd have gone after him myself.

The only thing worse than fighting with Marc was having nothing to say to him. Or having a lot to say, and not being able to say it.

"Here." Jace handed me one of the plastic bags. Inside, I found an assortment of twenty-ounce sodas and five bottles of water. I handed a soda and a bottle of water to each of the guys, while Jace passed out the corn dogs.

"Okay." Marc opened the driver's-side door of the van. "Turn right on East Main Street and park at one of the businesses there. Then start walking. Keep your phones on and your eyes open. And try not to do anything stupid."

He didn't name names, but he was looking right at me for that last part. I knew why he was mad, and I understood. But he didn't have to be such an ass about it. Was he trying to piss me off?

Of course he was.

I'd finished my first corn dog by the time Vic found Main

Street, and I was halfway through my bottle of Pepsi before he realized he was on South Main, rather than East Main. "Why the hell does any town need four Main Streets, anyway?" he mumbled around a mouthful of food.

"There's only two," Jace said, twisting open his water in the front seat. "The directions change where the streets intersect."

Vic drank from his Dr. Pepper and turned right into the parking lot of a local grocery store. "Same thing. You guys ready?"

For the next hour, we walked the mile-and-a-half section of East Main Street, until we stopped to call Marc and Parker. They'd called us half an hour earlier, with no news, and there was none to report from either side during the second call, either.

"Turn around and walk back to your car, then head to North Marshal," Marc said, over the rumble of a passing car's engine. "We'll take Van Buren, then we'll all meet up for something more to eat if we don't find anything this time."

That sounded good to me. A couple of corn dogs hadn't been enough to fuel any of us for a two-mile walk.

Less than half a mile into our return trip, we paused at a crosswalk on Oak Street. When the light read Walk, the small group of pedestrians started forward. But I froze, shocked motionless by the brief whiff of a scent I'd caught.

"Faythe?" Jace frowned, on instant alert when he saw my face. "What's wrong?"

"He's here." My gaze flitted frantically over the sidewalk, searching for long, tanned legs and a familiar head of light brown hair. I was trying to be inconspicuous, but based on Jace's expression, it wasn't working.

"You smell him?" Vic whispered, glancing casually around the crowd of humans.

I nodded. I did smell Andrew—but not like I'd ever smelled him before. His scent was…different. It was still his own, but it was part mine now, too. It was the scent of a werecat. Andrew was a stray.

I'd known the truth in my head. I'd even heard it in his voice over the phone. But I don't think I'd really understood— truly *believed* it—until I smelled his stray-scent for myself.

"Where?" Jace scanned the sidewalk with us now, his nostrils flaring as he sniffed the air.

"I don't know." Cats don't hunt by scent, like dogs do. The equipment is all there, but the instinct isn't. We hunt by sound, and by sight, so anything more complicated than identifying the scent we smelled was very difficult. And unless Andrew had stopped to pee on every light post he passed, we wouldn't be able to track him. So we spread out on the corner, looking through store windows and strolling slowly down the side-walk, trying to be subtle as we searched for the scent I'd barely smelled in the first place.

Finally, just when I was starting to feel weird about loiter-ing on a corner in broad daylight, Jace whispered my name. I turned to find him leaning against the post on the corner, ap-parently waiting for the light to change. But he was actually waiting for me and Vic.

We strolled toward him, and it was an effort not to run. "Where?" I asked, inhaling deeply as I came to his side.

"The button. I think he pushed the button."

Following Jace's eyes, I found the crosswalk button on the pole. If Andrew had pressed it, his scent would linger. At least until the scents of those who'd touched it after him over-whelmed the smell of stray.

Thinking fast, I reached into my pocket and pulled out a

handful of change, most of which I "accidentally" dropped on the sidewalk. "Damn," I muttered, bending to retrieve my money.

Jace snickered, but Vic knelt to "help."

I got a good whiff of the button on my way down, and on my way up. Jace was right. Andrew had pressed the button. Which meant… "He crossed the street."

Shoving the last of the change into my pocket, I studied the storefronts across the road. Fortunately, the corner was now deserted, most of the small lunch-break crowd having already returned to their various offices, so there was no one around to comment on how odd we were acting.

When I couldn't find Andrew through the window of the hardware store, I scanned a quaint local deli. At the counter, an obese woman was paying for what appeared to be a huge loaf of unsliced bologna. Behind her stood a black man in a suit and tie. And in line behind them both was…Andrew. I couldn't see his face, but I was almost certain.

"Guys!" I hissed, my hands finding and tugging one of each of theirs. "That's him, in the deli." I pulled them to a shadowy nook that would hide us.

Jace squinted into the afternoon sun. "Where?"

"Behind the man in the suit. Wearing a white linen button-down and knee-length khakis." It was typical Andrew-wear. If he'd had brown leather sandals and a worn backpack thrown over one shoulder, he could have been a student traveling around Europe—with his mother's credit card in his pocket, of course.

Vic frowned. "Are you sure? I don't remember him being that tall."

"Well, I could go sniff him," I suggested, smiling when he turned to glare at me. "Yeah, I'm pretty sure. He looks exactly the same."

"From the back?" Vic raised one brow at me to drive home his point. "We have to be sure."

I grumbled but knew he was right. So we waited.

The woman left the deli with her package under one arm, and the men behind her stepped forward. The customer in the suit leaned over the counter to point out something in the case, and while he was waiting, the tall man in khakis turned to look around the store, running one hand through familiar light brown hair, kissed with natural streaks of sun-bleached blond. Then he glanced out the window, and we got a clear look at his face before he turned around.

My pulse spiked, and my mouth went dry. My hand clenched Jace's arm. It was Andrew. Without a doubt. The guys had gone stiff on either side of me; they recognized him, too.

"Jace, call Marc," Vic ordered softly. "Tell him where we are, and that we've found Andrew. Faythe and I will go back for the car. You follow him—subtly, please—and we'll pick you up. Call us if you lose him."

Jace nodded, his phone already in hand.

Vic took off down the sidewalk, practically dragging me with him, because I couldn't take my eyes from Andrew as he perused the meat case. It was eerie, how little he'd changed. How could he possibly look so unthreatening, so very human, yet be one of us?

Finally, Vic gave my arm one last, hard tug, and got my attention. We raced to the car, running—at human speed—once we were out of sight of the deli.

At the parking lot, Vic slammed the Jeep into Reverse, and I drained the now-warm bottle of water Jace had left in the front seat. By the time we turned right onto East Main, almost eight minutes had passed, and Pink was singing from my front pocket again. Jace was calling.

Marc and Parker had picked him up, and they were tailing Andrew down Main Street in his silver BMW Z4—the car his parents bought him when he graduated. Both vehicles were heading west. Right toward us.

Vic spotted the Z4 as I hung up the phone. "Duck!" he ordered, but before I could, he put one hand behind my neck and shoved me forward so that I sat folded in half in the passenger seat.

Seconds later, he let me go and the Jeep swerved into a half-empty parking lot. He cut a tight, too-fast circle, then turned back onto Main. Marc was two cars ahead of us, and as far as I could tell, Andrew was three cars ahead of him. A quarter of a mile later, Marc turned on his right blinker. We followed him onto a side street, where the van slowed considerably. There was no one between him and Andrew now, and it wouldn't be hard for even a rookie stray to realize he was being followed by a van full of men he may or may not recognize from his college campus.

After another quarter mile, Andrew turned right. Marc followed him, but told us over Vic's phone—now on walkie-talkie mode—to stay put. "Give me a minute to see where he's going, and we'll—" Marc stopped in midsentence, and a second later, Parker picked up where he'd left off.

"There. He's turning into that rail yard."

Jace's static-fuzzy voice came over the line, along with the squeal of seat springs. "I don't think it's operational."

I squinted out the window on my right, trying to see past a stand of trees in back of some sort of utility building. The foliage was too thick in the summer; I couldn't see anything but leaves.

"Are they holed up in the rail yard?" Vic asked, aiming his question at the phone I held up for him.

"Looks like it." Marc paused, and paper crackled over the connection, probably a map unfolding. "There's a park about a block away. We can meet there and decide how to proceed. I'm gonna call Greg."

"See you in a few." Vic shifted the Jeep into gear, and I hung up the phone. In front of us, the van rolled forward, and we followed it. I watched Marc through the pair of square rear windows.

He'd hung up by the time we turned the corner, and seconds later we rolled over an old, bumpy set of train tracks. On my right was the rail yard, and I saw immediately what Jace had meant by "not operational." It was abandoned. It had to be.

The tracks leading in were heavily rusted. The buildings— some sort of office or station, and an engine depot—were old and run-down, with peeling paint, broken windows, and cracked, crooked steps. Old box cars were scattered across the lot, both on and off several sets of tracks, and the ground was littered with other debris, including a huge gantry crane once used to lift freight.

The rail yard itself had an oddly deserted look to it. It was like looking at a creepy, half-collapsed haunted house surrounded by a picture-perfect, white-picket neighborhood. And something told me that strange noises from the rail yard went unnoticed—or at least uninvestigated—all the time. Lucky us.

Twisting in my seat, I stared at the rail yard after we crossed the tracks, until Vic turned into the park.

In the white-lined lot on the far side of the swings, we parked both cars side by side and got out. Everyone looked to Marc in anticipation of our new orders. "Okay, here's the plan," he said, leaning against the hood of the van. "I'm going to cut across the park and scout things out. When I get back, we'll discuss a specific course of action."

"Let me go in," I insisted, struck by the sudden impulse to prove that my job performance was unaffected by our splintered relationship. That I was still a valuable member of the team, even without Marc attached to my hip. "I'm the fastest."

Marc shook his head, his expression carefully blank. "You're also the loudest. I'd rather get in and out without being detected than have to outrun them both."

"I'm not going to stumble around and—"

"No." Marc frowned. And just like with my father, that was that. I knew better than to press the point past a solid no.

Still glaring at me, Marc took off. At the edge of the park, he glanced around to make sure no one else was watching. Then he vaulted over a chain-link fence and disappeared behind the first of at least a dozen presumably empty boxcars.

The rest of us waited in the parking lot, growing more and more impatient in the September heat.

Ten miserable minutes after he left, Marc returned, issuing orders before he even got to the car. My father would have been proud.

"Parker, you stay with the van," he said, digging for the keys in his pocket. "Spread plastic over the entire floor and cut the rope in the back into three-foot sections. We're hoping to bring them out alive, but they won't be pretty. Wait for my call, then pull into the rail yard from the front entrance. That's the only way in with a car."

Parker nodded, catching the keys Marc tossed his way.

Marc spun on the concrete to face the rest of us, while we stood in a straight line like good little soldiers. "They're in the old engine depot. The windows are all boarded over or blacked out, so I couldn't see them, but I could hear them talking and clanging around."

Blood rushed through my veins, pounding in my ears in a rhythm so frantic and fast I thought I might pass out. But I was just excited, and more than a little nervous. This was the first big assignment I'd been involved in since we'd taken out Miguel, and that one was a bittersweet success. We'd lost a man.

We couldn't afford to lose another one this time. Not even one of the bad guys. Everything had to go according to the plan. Which was surprisingly simple.

"The bay doors are barred from the outside, which leaves only two ways into the depot," Marc was saying, eyeing each of us in turn. "One standard door in front and one in the back. Jace and Faythe, you'll go in the front. Burst in and make some noise to get their attention."

I couldn't help wondering why he'd paired me with Jace instead of Vic.

"Vic and I will pick up a couple of two-by-fours, then come in from the rear when we hear you. The objective is to take them both out with a single blow to the head. Without killing them. So control your force, please," he said, that last part aimed at Vic.

Vic nodded.

"Any questions?"

I frowned, thinking hard. Surely there was something I should ask. It couldn't be that simple. Could it? But I was drawing a complete blank.

"Good." Marc pointed toward the fence at the back of the park, where he'd gained entrance to the rail yard. "We'll go in there, over that last panel. Give us three minutes to get into place. Then make your move. It'll go fast from there. Keep your eyes open and your mouth shut. No argument, and no unnecessary communication. And keep your minds on the job at hand. Understand?" Marc seemed to be looking at me in particular for that one, which pissed me off.

Jace nodded and elbowed me in the arm. I glowered at Marc but nodded grudgingly.

Parker climbed into the van to make the preparations, and we jogged across the park. Sweat was already running down my back and gathering behind my knees. September in Texas was a really rotten time to be chasing bad guys.

We leapt the fence one at a time, then followed Marc, our shoes silent on the hard-packed earth. At the front of the building, Marc pointed to a spot between the huge bay doors and the closed front door, indicating that Jace and I should wait there. He tapped his watch, then held up three fingers, mouthing "Three minutes" as he and Vic picked their way noiselessly around the far corner of the building.

I nodded, already focused on my watch. The second hand seemed sluggish, ticking from number to number with painful lassitude. By the time it completed its first cycle, I was bored, staring around the rail yard at abandoned parts, machines, train cars, oil barrels, and countless other leftovers from the glory days of cross-country freight trains.

On my right, Jace sighed. He inhaled deeply, and I did the same, searching the air for any sign of Andrew or Luiz. I found none. Not even on the doorknob, which they'd surely touched to enter the building. Unless they'd come in from the rear.

If that were the case—if the front door hadn't been opened in years—might it not be locked? And thus difficult to open? *Hmm.*

Catching Jace's attention, I mimed kicking the door open, rather than turning the knob. Jace nodded. Glancing at his watch, he held up one hand, fingers spread. As he met my eyes, he folded down one finger. Then another. I nodded; his message was clear.

"Five…four…" The third finger went down, and I studied the door, trying to decide where to kick. *There, just below the knob.* "…two…one," Jace mouthed. He nodded at me, and I nodded back. My pulse spiked. My heart pounded. My leg flew.

We kicked at exactly the same time, in near-perfect form. My father would have been ecstatic.

Wood splintered. Metal creaked. The door flew open, tilted at a crazy angle. We'd ripped the top hinge from the frame.

For a long moment, we stood still, staring into the building, waiting for our eyesight to adjust to the darkness within. When it *didn't* adjust, I glanced at Jace and stepped into the depot. That's when the figure inside came slowly into focus. The *only* figure. One body. Not two.

Frowning, I squinted at the form standing in the center of the floor, maybe thirty feet away. Something was wrong. The figure was too short to be Andrew, and too thin to be Luiz. And had *way* too much hair to be either of the men in question.

I sniffed the air and found a familiar scent—but *not* the one I was expecting. It wasn't a stray scent. It wasn't even a *male* scent.

"Stop," she ordered, in a beautifully lilting, lyrical accent. And as my eyes adjusted further, I saw that she was pointing at us with both hands. "I don't want to shoot, but I will if I must."

We hadn't found Andrew, *or* Luiz. We'd found Manx. And she had a gun pointed right at Jace's head.

Twenty-Eight

"Whoa." Jace held both hands up in the familiar defensive posture. "Manx, right? We don't want to hurt you. We're looking for someone else." His voice gave no indication of the half truth in his statement. "Probably the same person you're looking for."

Where the hell are Marc and Vic? I stared furiously at a rectangle of light in the dark, the outline of a closed door ten feet behind the tabby. Beyond the door, something moved, blocking part of the light. Marc and Vic were waiting. They'd probably heard the tabby speak and knew she had a gun. Bursting in behind her would only get somebody shot, so they were waiting for a better opportunity to make their entrance.

The tabby frowned at Jace, but her gun never wavered. "I look for no one." Her accent was thick, but her English was perfectly understandable. And her lie was as transparent as a pane of glass.

"We have a common goal," I said, hoping she wouldn't want to shoot potential allies. "We can help each other."

The tabby growled and swung the gun my way.

My pulse jumped and my throat tightened. I took a deep, calming breath, and the tabby's scent filled my nostrils, thick with that odd element I couldn't quite place. My mind flashed back to my mother holding the red-and-gold afghan up for my inspection.

Was I smelling wool? Or cotton? Or whatever the blanket was made of?

"Is your name Manx?" Jace asked louder than necessary, trying to draw her focus—and her gun—away from me.

She hesitated, her gaze shifting between us as she tried to decide who was the biggest threat.

"What's that scent?" I asked Jace beneath my breath. Her scent suddenly seemed *very* important. "She smells weird. What *is* that?"

The tabby's eyes widened in surprise, then quickly narrowed in fury. Her lips pressed together. She adjusted her aim, and my breath caught in my throat.

Gravel crunched behind me. Had Marc and Vic circled the building?

Manx cocked the hammer.

"No!" Jace threw himself in front of me. The tabby pulled the trigger. A blue flash sparked. The blast echoed through the building.

Jace flinched violently, all over. He stiffened, then staggered backward.

"No!" I screamed, tears blurring my vision. I stepped forward to catch him, but a hand grabbed my arm from behind, jerking me off my feet. Jace fell to the ground. The scent of blood saturated the air.

Manx stared at Jace, mouth wide in horror. She dropped

the gun. The door behind her flew open, and Marc rushed into the room, a jagged two-by-four in one hand. The tabby whirled toward him and froze. Vic ran in on his heels, wielding a steel pipe.

So who the hell was hauling me away from Jace? "Let go!" I yanked on my arm, trying to pull free with no success. I whirled around, expecting to see Luiz and prepared to rebreak his nose.

I saw Andrew instead.

Adrenaline shot through my bloodstream like a jolt of electricity. I jerked furiously on my arm. Andrew's sweaty fingers slipped from my skin. His nails ripped my flesh. I hissed in pain and stumbled out of his grasp, already crawling toward Jace.

Jace blinked up at me.

Stunned, I tried to clear my vision.

Andrew leapt into my path. His face twisted into a vicious snarl. He bore almost no resemblance to the man I'd once known. The man whose life I'd ruined.

His fist shot toward me. I ducked, my leg already sweeping toward his. My foot hit his ankle. He fell on his ass, hissing. His fingers brushed the hem of my jeans. I danced away, then turned toward Jace.

Vic knelt at his side, bare-chested, pressing his own shirt against Jace's right shoulder.

A blur of motion caught my attention from the corner of my eye. I turned my head to see Marc swing the two-by-four at Manx, who'd reclaimed her gun and was aiming it at Vic. He hit her right arm with the broad side of the plank. The gun fell from her grip and slid on the concrete. Manx screamed and toppled. But instead of clutching her injured arm, her good hand covered her belly in a familiar protective gesture.

The afghan flashed in my mind again. The one Natalie had crocheted. Natalie, who was expecting her second...*baby*.

"Marc, no!" I shouted. He froze, the board raised high over his head, ready to come crashing down on Manx again. "She's pregnant!"

Shock claimed Marc's expression. He lowered the board slowly, staring at Manx with a look of wonder—or maybe horror—as if she had three eyes rather than a microscopic, parasitic, completely un-infectious invasion in her uterus.

Instead of hitting her again, he kicked the gun. It skittered across the huge room, lost to deep shadows in less than a second. Marc met my eyes, his mouth already open to ask how I'd known. Instead, his brow wrinkled and his gaze shifted to something behind me. "Look out!"

I whirled around, ducking as I spun. My fingers scraped the gritty, dust-covered concrete.

Andrew stood behind me, arms raised. Something heavy whooshed over my head. I buried my fist in his stomach. Air burst from his lungs. He doubled over. Something hard crashed onto my head, then clanked to the ground.

I stood, rubbing the new bump on my skull, and prepared another kick. My foot slipped on the pipe he'd dropped. It rolled from under my boot. I landed on my ass in front of him.

He kicked and I rolled out of the way. I sucked in a quick breath, and with it came dust and a sticky cobweb. Andrew kicked again, and I reached for his foot. My hand closed around his ankle and I pulled. He fell beside me, catching himself on both hands.

I rolled over, and my hair clip slammed into the concrete. It burst open. Thick black hair fell over my face. I pushed it away, freezing in place as a low, unfamiliar roar rumbled from overhead.

Scrambling to my feet, I looked up to find a loft running across the left side of the engine depot. And another on the right. I squinted, trying to see movement in the darkness. But I saw only shadows.

On my right, Andrew lurched to his feet and a growl echoed from my left. Whirling around, I saw a dark form spring from some twelve feet above, taking shape as it neared. The shadows cleared, exposing the lithe, elegant form of a werecat in midleap.

Luiz. He'd hidden in the loft to Shift.

The cat landed gracefully in the middle of the room, on all four paws. Marc faced him, two-by-four held ready in both hands. Luiz considered him for a moment, then turned toward Vic instead.

"Vic!" I shouted. He looked up to see Luiz flying toward him, but had no time to move. The cat landed on his chest, claws bared. Vic screamed.

I was scanning the ground for a weapon, when something hit me from behind. Pain exploded. I flew forward, throwing one foot in front of the other to stay upright. My feet tangled over each other, and the ground soared up to meet me. I caught myself on my left arm. Pain shot through my shoulder, reviving an injury three months old.

Fingers tangled in my hair and pulled. I clenched my jaws against a scream and scrambled to my feet to keep my hair from being ripped out by the roots.

"Payback's a bitch," Andrew whispered in my ear, his voice a bitter echo of what it once was. "But then, so are you."

"Andrew, wait—"

His grip on my hair tightened, and his free fist slammed into my kidney.

Pain ripped throughout my entire body, rebounding for an instant encore. My legs folded and I crumpled to the ground. Tiny popping sounds filled my ear as hundreds of individual hairs were ripped from my scalp. I couldn't breathe, much less scream.

I forced my body into motion, rolling away in spite of the pain. He kicked me in the thigh. Then the blows stopped.

I opened my eyes, and Andrew was gone.

Manx lay unconscious across the room. Parker knelt over Vic, who now lay on the ground near Jace, who was in a pool of his own blood. Beyond them, Marc stood, iron pipe in hand, facing off against the werecat.

Luiz hissed, teeth bared. He lunged forward. Marc swung the pipe. Luiz dodged the blow easily. But Marc had already gotten off at least one good shot; Luiz was bleeding below his right ear.

I sat up, and Andrew stomped past me, headed for Marc. Before I could shout, Parker shoved himself off the ground and snatched the slab of wood Marc had dropped. He swung. The board connected with Andrew's shoulder. Andrew hit the ground, and I gained my feet carefully, wincing at the ache in my spine.

Parker turned toward Luiz. Marc swung the pipe again, and again Luiz dodged it—right into Parker's path. Parker swung, low and arcing, as if the board were a golf club. The two-by-four hit Luiz's back left leg.

Luiz yelped and limped sideways.

Marc slammed his pipe into Luiz's right shoulder. Luiz whined, then growled. He bounded to his left, past Marc and out of his reach. In less than a second, he was gone, limp-running right out the door. Marc took off after him, the blood-stained steel pipe clenched in his fist. "Take care of them," he yelled over his shoulder at Parker. Then he was gone.

Andrew watched them go, his jaw slack with shock, eyes brimming with fury. He'd been abandoned—again.

"Andrew…" I began, hoping he'd believe me now. That he finally understood Luiz wasn't helping him. And that I could, if he'd let me.

He met my eyes, and the pain and loathing in his made me sick to see. He hated me. He wouldn't let me help him. And he certainly wouldn't help me.

"Fuck this," he growled through clenched teeth, looking from me to Parker, then back to me. "And fuck *you*." Then he turned and ran, right for the front door.

I took off after him, without a second thought.

"Faythe!" Parker yelled.

"I've got him," I yelled, already halfway out the door. "Don't you dare let Jace bleed to death."

"No!" he shouted. But he didn't follow me. Jace and Vic needed him worse than I did. At least, I *hoped* I wouldn't need him.

I followed Andrew around the corner of the building just in time to see the door of the abandoned train station swing closed. *Shit.* We didn't have time for hide-and-seek. If anyone had recognized Manx's gunshot for what it was, they'd have called the police. The cops were probably already on their way.

But a glance at my watch told me that—amazingly—less than a quarter of an hour had passed since we'd jumped the fence into the rail yard. Though the fight in the depot seemed to last an eternity, it had only been minutes long. *Thank goodness.*

I jogged up the steps to the rail station. "Andrew?" I called, pushing the filthy glass door open. I was giving away my position, but I didn't care. I hadn't come to fight him; I'd come to explain. And to apologize. "Andrew, where are you?" My eyes skimmed over the room, but I saw no sign of Andrew.

"It doesn't have to be like this. I just want to help you." My boots crunched on broken glass as I moved farther into the room, and I'd gone several steps before I realized I could hear him breathing. Fast and hard. I sniffed the air when my ears couldn't pinpoint his location. His scent was strong, and heavily tinged with anxiety. He was still in the room—somewhere.

Stepping carefully, I headed for a beat-up customer service booth in the center of the main room, the only obstruction in sight. When I rounded the counter, my foot hit a busted metal cash register and I clutched the cracked countertop to save myself from landing face-first in a scattering of shattered window glass.

And there, crouched behind the counter between a metal filing box and the wall, was Andrew, shirtless, his khaki shorts unbuttoned.

He froze, staring up at me with one hand on his zipper. His shirt lay at his feet. He'd been undressing so he could Shift. And kill me. I could see it in his eyes.

I exhaled slowly, devastated by the rage in every line on his face. "Andrew, you have to let m—"

He pounced. In human form, and from a complete crouch, he was suddenly airborne. His shoulder slammed into my chest. My feet left the ground for just an instant. Then I hit the floor, and his weight drove the air from my lungs.

He sat on my stomach, his knees straddling my bruised ribs. My back burned in a dozen places, where each shard of glass had sliced through my blouse and into my flesh. I lay stunned and breathless, wishing I could get to the handcuffs poking me from my pocket.

Andrew snarled, his eyes wide, lips drawn back from blunt, square teeth. He was in human form, but his inner cat had taken charge. And it was pissed.

"Listen to me. You don't want to do this." I wedged my arms between our bodies and planted my hands on his chest. "I can help you. Let me up, and let's talk."

I pushed against him, but he wouldn't move. Andrew wasn't as big as my fellow enforcers, but he still outweighed me by quite a bit. And thanks to me, he had a werecat's strength. I could make him move but not without hurting him, and I wouldn't hurt him if I didn't have to. I'd already damaged him beyond repair.

"I'm done talking to you," Andrew growled, his eyes swimming in rage. His hand grasped my left bicep, forcing it to the floor, and I winced as another shard of glass bit into my arm.

"Well, *I'm* not done talking to *you*." I met his eyes, only inches from mine. His anger permeated the room as surely as his scent did, and it was probably a bad time to insist on conversation. But I *had* to explain. He needed to know the truth. "I never meant to infect you. It was an accident, and I'm trying to make it up to—"

His fist flew, and my cheek exploded. Tears formed in my eyes, and I sobbed out loud, not from pain—though it certainly hurt—but from heartbreak. The Andrew I'd known could never have hit *anyone,* much less me.

I closed my eyes and breathed through the throbbing. "Is this what you did to those women? The strippers?"

"Yes," Andrew spat, and my eyes flew open. He stared down at me, his nostrils wide. "You want to hear about it?"

I shook my head, sucking blood from the new cut on the inside of my cheek. I did *not* want to hear about it.

"We picked them because they looked like you. I got them outside alone. It was easy—evidently I don't look dangerous. How's that for irony? But I'm not harmless anymore." He punctuated the rhetorical question with another blow to my opposite cheek.

More pain, and this time lights flashed behind my eyes. But I didn't fight back. Luiz had made Andrew into the monster he'd become, but *I'd* given him the opportunity. I was *not* going to hurt Andrew anymore.

"You killed them because they looked like me?" I swallowed thickly, and tasted my own blood. "That hardly seems fair."

"We were trying to *infect* them. Death was an unfortunate side effect. And *life* isn't fair. You taught me that. Luiz taught me lessons of a more practical nature." His fist flew again, slamming into my left side this time. I gasped, then bit my lip to keep from screaming.

When I could breathe again, I met his eyes boldly, the first sparks of anger flashing among embers of guilt and grief. "He left you, Andrew. He's gone, but I'm still here. What does that tell you?"

"That you're not as smart as you think you are." His eyes flashed in cruel satisfaction. "He wanted you alive. I don't." Andrew leaned to my left, and his hands curled around the old cash register. The damn thing had to weigh at least a hundred pounds. He'd never be able to lift it.

But he did. He yanked it from the floor, arms shaking with the effort as he lifted it over his head.

"No!" Panic dumped adrenaline into my bloodstream, and I felt the ground for something to use as a weapon. Broken glass bit into my palm. My fingers curled around something long and cold and hard.

Andrew snarled and his arms tensed. The cash register trembled in his grip, directly over my head.

I swung my unseen weapon, trying to knock him off me before he crushed my skull. My makeshift mace thunked into flesh. Blood poured down on me, hot and wet. His whole body jerked. I shoved Andrew backward and lunged to one side. His hands opened. The cash register smashed into the ground where my head had been.

I scrambled across the floor, heedless as more glass sliced into my hands. Andrew sat against the wall, his eyes wide and empty. His hands clawed at his throat, now impaled by an iron railroad spike. I watched in mute horror as blood spurted.

It was over in seconds. His hands went slack and fell into his lap. His gore-stained chest stopped rising. And as his heart stopped beating, the flow of blood slowed to a dribble.

I sat still on the floor, in a hazy beam of light filtered through filthy windows, staring at a widening pool of the blood I'd first contaminated, then spilled.

Andrew was dead. I'd killed him.

And I couldn't feel a fucking thing.

Twenty-Nine

Marc was the one who found us, an eternity later, though he swore it couldn't have been more than two minutes. He burst through the front door, eyes blazing, ready to tear into whichever of us had survived. In a single sweeping glance, he took in the entire room: scattered debris, bloody corpse, and me. He didn't ask me what happened. He just pulled me to my feet and held me, heedless of the blood I smeared all over him.

I remember him asking if I was okay. And I remember not knowing the answer.

"Faythe, I need you to do something for me," he said, wiping a smudge of blood from my chin. "I need you to save what you're feeling now. Put it in a box in your mind, Seal it up and stack it with all your other memories." He took my hand and noticed the embedded splinters of glass, which he began to pull out as he spoke. "Later, you can open the box, and go through what's inside. But for now, I need you to put it away. We have to get everything cleaned up, and get out of here before the police come. Do you understand?"

Still numb, I nodded. I understood. It was time to save the day. Again.

"Luiz?" I asked as Marc lifted my arms and pulled my blouse over my head.

"Got away." He turned me gently by my shoulders and began plucking shards of glass from my back. I thought it would hurt, but I didn't feel a thing. "The park butts up to a swatch of pine forest, and he took off through the trees. I couldn't catch him on two feet, and I couldn't leave the rest of you like this. Don't worry, though. We'll get him."

Sure we would. Just like I'd gotten Andrew.

Vic turned out to be mostly okay. Luiz had clawed the shit out of him, but the scratches, though long, were mostly superficial. He was even able to help with the cleanup, so while Marc got me fixed up and changed into his shirt, Parker and Vic dealt with Manx, who had to be cuffed, in spite of a very swollen wrist, and carried carefully to the van. She was alive but unconscious, and we had no idea how badly she was hurt. Or how the baby was doing.

Jace was shot in the shoulder. He'd lost a lot of blood and was drifting in and out of consciousness, but Parker said it didn't look fatal. He'd already called my father and Dr. Carver, who'd promised to leave for the ranch immediately.

We threw the bloody two-by-four and the iron pipe into the van, then Parker and Marc wrapped Andrew in plastic, held closed with duct tape. I soaked up his blood from the floor with a roll of shop towels, which we then tied in a plastic bag, along with my ruined blouse. The guys poured bleach over the stain, from a half-full bottle found in one of the abandoned bathrooms. We did the best we could with what we had. Hopefully it would be good enough.

Marc drove to the Lazy S, with Andrew's body in the van. Manx lay next to him, bound and still out cold, and the one glimpse I got of her reminded me jarringly of my own recent trip in the back of a strange van, also bound and mostly unconscious. I tucked that thought away in one of Marc's mental boxes. Someday I was going to have to clean out my memory-attic, and it wasn't going to be pretty.

As per our Alpha's instructions, Parker took Andrew's car into an empty field an hour and a half west of Henderson, where Owen picked him up.

In spite of his injuries, Vic insisted on driving his Jeep to the ranch, so I sat in back with Jace, doing my best to keep him comfortable. He lay with his head in my lap. We all three winced over every bump in the road.

At home, my mother disinfected my cuts, clucked her tongue over my bruises, and stitched up Vic's chest, after numbing it with a topical cream. She made Jace as comfortable as possible on the living-room couch, lined in plastic to avoid bloodstains. He woke up shortly after we got home, and I sat with him for nearly an hour. He said he'd thought Manx was aiming at me. Then he joked about how he should have pushed me out of the way, instead of jumping in front of the bullet.

I thanked him for being an idiot. Then I kissed him on the forehead and left him with a bowl of sympathy ice cream.

Manx wound up in the guest room, where my mother spent most of the first few hours after our return waiting for the mystery tabby to open her eyes. She'd been first surprised, then pleased to hear that Manx was pregnant, and she confirmed my amateur diagnosis with one quick sniff. But she grew more worried with each hour that passed without Manx waking up.

I didn't know how I should feel about the tabby who'd

caused so much trouble. She'd killed at least three tomcats in the past week, and shot Jace, though as near as I could tell, she'd actually been aiming for Andrew, who'd snuck in behind me. Still, I had trouble feeling any real sympathy. But the baby couldn't be held responsible for its mother's actions. Even I had to admit that.

While my mother split her nursing duties between Manx and Jace, I spent hours in the office with my father, helping the guys re-create every microscopic detail of our day in Henderson. The box I'd stacked in my mind remained neatly sealed as I filled them in on Luiz's failed efforts to create a female stray and Andrew's involvement in the project. I told them I thought the college students Luiz killed over the summer were part of the same plan. And I told them how I'd killed Andrew in self-defense.

My father was *not* happy. Andrew's death would be one more strike against me, in the collective eye of the council. I'd still have to stand trial, and now there was no witness to testify that the infection was indeed an accident. Apparently killing the human I'd infected didn't get me off the hook for infecting him in the first place. Weird, huh?

His reaction to the tabby wasn't much better. "She *shot* Jace?" No one spoke. None of us knew what to say as my father paced in front of his desk, rubbing his chin furiously. "She was hunting Luiz in human form? With a gun? What kind of tabby *is* this?"

"The pregnant kind." Vic's mouth twitched, trying to deny a full-blown smile.

I watched my father's reaction carefully, and was not disappointed. He wasn't surprised in the least. "You knew!" I accused, jumping off the couch in spite of the pain in my ribs.

"You knew the first time you smelled her scent. Why didn't you tell us?"

"I told you to treat her as if she were made of glass." When his answer clearly didn't mollify me, he went on. "I didn't tell you because I didn't want any of you to let her condition blind you to the threat she represents. So she's pregnant. She still murdered three tomcats, and now she's shot Jace. Speaking of which, where's the damn gun?"

In that moment, I realized how much I truly respected my father. He wasn't willing to let her off the proverbial hook just because she was pregnant.

"I locked it in your bottom drawer," Marc said.

My father nodded his approval and told us all to get something to eat.

Just after 8:00 p.m. Dr. Carver finally arrived to take charge of the patients. All four of us. He declared my ribs unbroken and said I was fit to work, in spite of multiple cuts and bruises. He pronounced my mother's stitches "beautiful," and said that Vic would be fine, and that his recovery would be accelerated considerably if he would Shift as soon as he felt up to it.

With the minor wounds out of the way, Dr. Carver moved on to the living room, where he did what he could for Jace. He sterilized the wound, removed the bullet, and bandaged the hole in his shoulder. Jace's orders were much the same as Vic's: Shift as soon as possible.

Manx worried Dr. Carver the most, because she hadn't regained consciousness. He removed her handcuffs and gave her a full exam, after which he told my mother that the tabby was approximately four months pregnant, and that the baby's heartbeat was still strong. As was the mother's.

The tabby's wrist was fractured from its meeting with

Marc's two-by-four, so the doc put her in a cast. Beyond that, he said, all we could do was make her comfortable and wait for her to wake up. Both of which my mother took an active interest in.

And she wasn't the only one. The guys were completely fascinated by Manx. They all knew she was officially a bad guy, but if anything, that made her even more intriguing.

Parker and Vic stopped in her doorway at random intervals, just to stare at her. Jace would probably have done the same if he could walk. But what they didn't seem to realize—what I was more than eager to tell them—was that based on her slaughter of three toms in almost as many days, it would seem that the jungle tabby didn't have much use for men. Though one had obviously found use for her.

My father and Marc questioned Dan Painter at length about Manx—in the barn, since Ryan occupied the cage— but didn't come up with much of anything new. He'd had no idea she was pregnant and didn't know her real name. He had no clue where she was from. He only knew that she'd been going from town to town in response to a series of very short cell phone calls from a man with a heavy accent. She did not kill at every stop, never touched a human, and only disposed of those toms who "messed" with her. Manx, it seems, did not like to be touched, a lesson Painter apparently learned early, and well. Which was a point in his favor, for me.

After several hours and no new information, my father let Painter go, with the promise that if he could keep his nose clean in the free territory for a year, he could then officially apply for admission into the Pride—an offer I'd never heard him extend before. With that promise, Painter took off for

Mississippi with his tail tucked between his legs and his phone number and address in my father's files.

By Tuesday night, twenty-four hours after our arrival at the ranch, Dr. Carver had made a second round of visits to Jace and Manx, and had gone back to his hotel, for which the Pride was paying. My father had made a detailed report to the Territorial Council, and had called Michael and Ethan to give them an update. Ethan didn't take the news of Jace's injury well at all, and was eager to come home, but my dad ordered him to stay for Jamey Gardner's memorial, to properly represent our family.

By dinnertime, Jace had stabilized enough to be moved to the guesthouse, into his own bed. Parker set up an extra DVD player in the room Vic and Jace shared, and rented him nearly two dozen action movies to help aid his recovery.

After dinner, I sat in the far corner of the guest room, curled up in an overstuffed armchair with the latest Stephen King hardcover. But I couldn't concentrate on the story. Not with Luiz still free and Andrew's blood on my conscience. And the tabby's motives still unknown.

I'd taken to "reading" in what the guys were already calling "Manx's room," in part because I wanted to be there when she woke up. My curiosity built with every passing hour, until I was nearly desperate to find out who she was, and how she knew Luiz well enough to know he deserved to die. Because, frankly, she was right.

But our mutual death wish for Luiz didn't make his enemy my friend. After all, she'd killed three innocent toms, which a couple of my fellow enforcers refused to remember. I stayed in the guest room to make sure that when she woke, there would be at least one person in the room willing and ready to stop Manx if she tried to leave.

At 8:13 p.m., while my mother watered a pot of begonias on the windowsill, Manx finally opened her eyes, after nearly thirty hours of unconsciousness. The very first thing she said, her voice creaky and her accent thick, was "Where is my gun?"

I laughed out loud, and nearly dropped my book.

My mother spun at the sound of the tabby's voice, and set her watering can on a nearby bookcase. "It's locked in my husband's desk," she said, crossing the room gracefully toward the bed. "We can't let you walk around armed and loaded. That would be irresponsible."

"Where am I?" Manx asked, pushing herself into a sitting position with her good hand. I leaned sideways to get a look at her around my mother's shoulder. "Who are you?"

"I'm Karen Sanders, and you're in my home. You have a broken wrist and you've been unconscious for a day and a half, but the doctor thinks you're going to be fine. And so will your baby."

The tabby's uninjured hand flew to her stomach, where no bump was yet visible.

My mother settled into a chair by the bed. "You're about four months along, right?"

Manx nodded, dark curls bouncing around her shoulders.

"Whose is it?" I asked from across the room, and regretted the question instantly when they both tried to incinerate me with flames from their eyes.

Manx clutched her stomach tighter. "He is *mine*."

My mother looked at me coldly. "What's your name, dear?"

I blinked in surprise, my hands clenching my book. *Dear?* As badly as the nickname had always bugged me, *I* was *dear*.

"My name is Mercedes, but I have been Manx for...very

long time." The tabby stared at her hands, fiddling with the seam of her cast.

"Which do you prefer?" My mother took a bundle of yarn and two knitting needles from the nightstand.

Manx shrugged. "They are just names."

We sat in silence for several minutes, until I could no longer stomach all the unanswered questions. "Why were you chasing Luiz?"

My mother twisted in her chair to glare at me, but I ignored her.

To my surprise, the tabby answered, her voice hard with hatred and determination. "He is a monster. I will kill him." She hesitated, and met my eyes, hers accusing. "When I *find* him again."

I huffed. "Join the club."

"You know Luiz?"

"You might say that." I couldn't resist a smile. "I broke his nose."

Manx laughed, and the sudden joyful sound caught me off guard. "So did I."

A grin stole across my face. She could fight. Of *course* she could fight. She'd killed three toms with her bare hands. She probably only carried the gun because—according to my mother—Shifting after the first trimester could be dangerous for the baby.

I eyed Manx carefully, curious in spite of my anger and caution. Who *was* this pregnant woman, this *girl*—because she couldn't be older than twenty—who'd fought Luiz, then chased him all over three states for the honor of putting a bullet through his head? "When did you break his nose?" I asked, more fascinated by Manx with every word she spoke.

"When he took my baby."

"Your baby?" I glanced at her stomach, where her good hand still rested over the white down comforter, nails ragged, fingers callused.

She smiled softly and shook her head. "My *first* baby. I fight him for the child. I broke his nose, and claw his arms. But he took my son anyway." She looked at my mother through haunted eyes. "I need the gun. I cannot kill him without it, and I will *not* be taken alive. Not again." Her free hand caressed her flat stomach and her eyes hardened. "I will not lose *this* baby."

Taken alive?

A sudden deluge of understanding washed over me, and I fought to keep from drowning in it. We'd been so close to the truth.

Manx was one of the missing South American tabbies. She was among the first victims of an ambitious, brutal project intended to provide breed-able tabbies to some jungle cat— likely *several* jungle cats—in the Amazon. Sara, Abby, and I were part of the project. But beyond that, the dead college girls and strippers were also involved, in Luiz's attempts to *create* tabbies, alongside the greater plan to take them.

Somehow Manx had fought free from her captors and was now out for revenge. I couldn't help but respect that.

"You're safe here," my mother said, almost crooning as she stroked the tabby's hand. "We won't let anything happen to you, or to your baby."

But Manx looked skeptical. Downright disbelieving, as if the very concept of trust were foreign to her. Which was understandable, considering that she'd spent the last four years in hell. In a place where every man she saw beat her and raped her. Then one of them stole her child. Learning to trust men again would likely be the hardest thing Manx would ever do. If it was even possible.

And suddenly I understood why she'd killed the toms. I didn't excuse it, mostly because I couldn't picture Jamey Gardner ever hurting anyone. But Manx wouldn't have known that. She would only have known what she'd lived through, and was determined never to go through again.

I opened my mouth, intending to say something brilliant, and comforting and singularly appropriate. But before I could think of a single thing, the screen door squealed open at the end of the hall, and footsteps pounded on the tile.

"Greg!" Marc called, dashing past the guest room in nothing but jeans and a pair of work boots.

I was out of my chair in an instant, running after him in time to see my father emerge from his office, a pen in one hand and a legal pad in the other. "What's wrong?"

"He's here." Marc leaned over, propping his hands on his knees as he caught his breath after what had obviously been a mad race to the main house. "Luiz is here."

Blood drained from my face, and chill bumps popped up all over my arms. For a moment, I couldn't move. Could barely even breathe. Then a slow smile spread over my face. *Luiz is here. On our land. My land.*

There were half a dozen of us, and only one of him. He didn't stand a chance. I was going to get a second shot at him. Or was it my third? Regardless, it would be my last, and when everything was over, there would be one less jungle stray to worry about.

"Where?" my father asked while I crossed the hall into my room, still listening as I prepared for the fight.

"In the woods. Parker and I found his scent on the back edge of the property, just past the stream. It's fresh." The guys had been patrolling twice daily since we got back from Henderson, just in case.

"Faythe!" my father bellowed as I pulled my shirt over my head, stripping in preparation to Shift. It would be suicidal to face Luiz again on two legs.

Still wearing my bra and shorts, I jogged into the office, where Marc, Vic, and Owen stood, apparently waiting for me. My father nodded when he saw me, then turned toward the guys. "Vic, Marc, I want you to Shift, then spread out into the forest with Parker. We're going to search every acre of our woods, and the preserve, too."

He paused, rubbing his temples with one hand as he considered how to continue. "Owen, go to the guesthouse and help Jace over here. Put him in Ethan's bed, then you Shift and join us."

Owen headed straight for the door.

"Move silently and quickly," my father said. "Don't give away your position until you find Luiz, and once you have, roar loud enough to wake the whole damn county. Forget about taking him alive. Manx can tell us what we need to know about her fellow tabbies. We're going to take care of this jungle cat once and for all."

I gaped at my father, a silent thrill coursing through me. He was going hunting, too. For the first time since I'd become an enforcer, I was going to get to hunt alongside my father. My Alpha.

"Faythe?"

"Yes?" I stood ready for my orders, eager for a piece of the action. Luiz deserved to die slowly and painfully for what he'd done to Andrew, to Manx, and to all those other girls.

My father stared down into my eyes, his expression both serious and concerned. And skeptical. *Crap.* "I want you to stay here while we search the forest—"

"Hell no—" I started, but he cut me off with a furious look and a strong, firm grip on my left arm.

"For once, you're going to do exactly as you're told. That's your job. If you can't follow orders, you can spend the night in the cage with Ryan. Is that clear?" I nodded reluctantly, and he continued. "I'm taking the guys with me, so we can cover the grounds more quickly. But I can't leave your mother, Manx, and Jace here without knowing I can count on you to take care of them. To defend them, should the need arise."

A hint of a grin appeared on my face, in spite of my best efforts to keep it hidden. "You want me to protect the women and chil—er, the wounded?"

My father frowned. He obviously had no idea why I found my assignment so amusing. "Well…yes. Can you handle that?"

"It sounds like babysitting to me, and I'd rather go hunting."

"We've all done our share of babysitting recently," Marc said, throwing my time under house arrest up in my face. "Think of it as paying your dues."

I glared at him. But then I nodded. I could pay my dues, even if my father *was* using the lame assignment to keep me safely out of the action.

"Lock all the doors and windows until we get back. And close the curtains, just in case." My father's voice deepened and went gravelly in anger as he uttered what would normally have been a ridiculous order. We'd never needed to lock up before, because we'd never been threatened at home by anyone but our Alpha, who considered it his right to intimidate the living shit out of us on a regular basis.

For a moment, as he watched me, my father looked like he might smile. Then the moment passed, and his expression was unreadable again. "Thank you," he said, and the guys followed him into the hallway and out the back door.

I watched them until they rounded the corner of the house and passed out of my sight. When I could no longer see their afternoon shadows stretching out behind them, I turned and plodded slowly toward the front door, which I closed and locked. I left the back door open for Owen and Jace, then moved into my own bedroom, to start closing and locking windows.

As I flipped the lever to lock the one, high window in my bathroom, I heard the screen door creak open. Owen had arrived with Jace.

"Faythe, is that you?" my mother called as I pulled the worthless lace curtain closed.

"Yeah. I'm just locking the windows." With my room covered, I moved on to Ethan's, where I had both windows secured and covered by the time Owen appeared in the doorway, supporting Jace with one arm around his torso.

"'Bout time," I teased.

"The doctor can only move as fast as the patient." Owen lowered Jace gently onto Ethan's bed. "Will you be okay until we get back?"

"Yeah." Jace nodded. "Just turn on the TV before you go, please."

Owen pressed the power button on Ethan's twenty-inch set on his way out the door, already unbuttoning his shirt in preparation to Shift.

I handed Jace the TV remote and gave him a kiss on his stubbly cheek, then trailed Owen into the hall to lock the door behind him.

For the next few minutes, I went from room to room, locking windows and closing curtains. I felt like a fool. If Luiz was strong and fast enough to get past the guys, a few covered windows weren't going to give him more than a moment's pause.

Which meant—if he made it this far—the only thing standing between the weakest members of the household and a psychotic jungle stray was…well, *me*. And I welcomed the opportunity to kick Luiz's brainwashing, raping, baby-snatching ass. Again.

Thirty

I saved the guest-room window for last, and for a while I stood watching Manx and my mother, marveling at how comfortable they seemed with each other. Manx wore the lacy white nightgown my mother had dressed her in, which set off her cascade of dark curls. Her right arm was in a cast and a sling, and her left hand held a glass of water. She looked feminine and delicate, and incapable of most of the things we now knew she'd done.

"They take four of us, at first," she said, staring into her glass. "They already have Ana when they catch me. They keep us apart, but we can see each other through the bars. She was so young…."

I stepped back to listen from the hall, afraid she would stop talking if I came in.

"How young?" my mother asked, and I knew she was thinking of Abby.

"Maybe, *quince?* Fifteen?"

My mother gasped, and my own eyes closed in horror.

"She cried for her *madre*. I cried for mine, too," Manx confessed quietly. "When I lose my tail. Much pain."

Well, that explains the name, I thought, unwilling to even *imagine* how she could lose her tail.

"How did you get away from them?" my mother asked. "Here, let me refill that for you, dear." Her chair creaked as she stood, and light footsteps trailed across the room toward the master bath. "Faythe, it's rude to hover in doorways."

Well hell. I turned the corner into the bedroom, my cheeks flaming. Manx watched me lock the window, and she cleared her throat as I was leaving the room. "Faythe? You are welcome to stay."

I bristled in irritation. Of *course* I was welcome to stay. It was *my* house. I plopped down in the armchair opposite the door and watched my mother tend to Manx. The pregnant murderer.

"How did I escape?" Manx asked as water ran in the bathroom. "I fight. I finally know that if I do not fight, I lose this baby, too."

Mom crossed the room again and handed the glass back to Manx. "How long ago did you lose the other one?"

"Not one. *Dos.* Two."

My mother made a strange strangling sound, likely choking on her own horror. I closed my eyes, trying to imagine how one woman could come out of so much tragedy with her mind intact. Just because I didn't want my own children yet didn't mean I couldn't understand the loss of one. Or two.

"Luiz took *two* of your babies?" Mom fell into the bedside chair, meeting Manx's deep gray eyes with emotion far beyond mere sympathy.

"He, and others. They pull my sons from my arms at birth and kill them. One—" her voice broke, her eyes filling with tears at the memory "—by one. But not this one. I will keep this one, and I will avenge the others."

"Why kill the babies?" I couldn't resist asking, my fingers playing along the seam in the arm of my chair. "I thought the whole point of taking women was to make more babies and increase the size of the Pride."

"Girl babies," Manx said, her eyes so full of pain that I could hardly stand to look at her. "They have many men. They want only girl babies."

"Did they get one?"

My mother shot me another angry look, but Manx nodded gravely. "Last year. From Ana. She feed the baby for *dieciséis* months. But then they take the child away, because she not make more babies while she make milk. Ana went mad."

"That's unspeakable!" my mother cried. It was the worst word she knew. According to my mother, the list of unspeakable acts included everything from terrorism to genocide. And apparently any crime that separated a mother from her children. But in this case, I had to agree.

"Dan Painter said Luiz was calling you." I stood and approached the bed hesitantly, tired of having to look around my mother to see the tabby. "Where did you get the phone, and how did he get your number?"

My mother scowled at me, but Manx set her glass carefully on the bedside table. The movement made her wince, and she stiffened her injured right arm. "I take phone from the man I kill to escape. Luiz's number is in the phone. I hear men talking before, so I know where he goes. I call him. He tells me where he is, and tells me come get him."

I sank onto the end of the bed, careful not to jar her. "Why the hell would he do that?"

"To take me back."

Of course. Luiz was baiting her into coming after him. She was the "business" he and Andrew planned to take care of before coming for me. Manx knew what he was up to the whole time, and still came after him. That was one ballsy tabby cat, and as much as I wanted to hate her, I couldn't help respecting her courage.

"I try to take Ana with me, but she screams when she is touched. We would not have made it."

"What about the others?" I asked, as my mother leaned down to pick up the knitting bag beneath her chair. "Did they escape, too?"

From Ethan's bedroom, tires squealed, and canned gunshots rang out. I smiled. Jace had found an action movie.

"No." Manx twisted the edge of the down comforter in her good hand, and I briefly considered offering her my punching pillow. "Rosa died in childbirth, two years ago. Another boy. Carmela kill herself when they take her son."

"So now there's only Ana," I said, thinking aloud. *And she's mad.*

"No, they still have Sonia."

"Wait, who's Sonia?" I sat up straight, closing my eyes as I did the mental math. My father's contact had said four girls went missing. Manx was one of them. Then there were Ana, Carmela, and Rosa. "I thought they only took four tabbies," I added, when my mother shot me a questioning look.

Manx blinked up at me, and her gray eyes seemed to see straight through me. "They bring Sonia later. Maybe…eight months ago. She was human. Scratched. What you call scratched cats?" Her forehead crinkled and her eyes closed in thought.

"Strays," I whispered in incredulity. "We call them strays."

"Yes. She was stray. Very scared. Very sick." Manx tapped her left temple. "Like Ana."

My mother's clicking knitting needles paused, leaving a heavy, meaningful silence. Frowning, I scratched a mosquito bite on my foot. The implications of Manx's claim swirled around in my head, making me dizzy. "How the hell did they—"

My mother stood suddenly and blinked, as if that's all it took to clear her mind of unpleasant thoughts. She laid her latest project—a scarf, from the looks of it—on the seat of her chair. "Is anyone hungry? I don't think I ate any lunch today. Faythe?"

I shook my head. Food was the last thing on my mind. We'd already had dinner, and I had more questions for Manx….

"Mercedes, you must be starving, especially with the little one on the way," my mother said, and Manx nodded, caressing her stomach. "I feel like chicken and dumplings. I don't usually make that during hot weather, but some broth would be good for Jace."

"Thank you." Manx smiled. "That sounds wonderful."

"Faythe? Come help me?"

I arched my eyebrows at my mother in surprise. She wanted my help? With *dinner?* I didn't even know where she kept the Crock-Pot—or whatever she used to cook four whole chickens at a time.

Unfazed, she beckoned me with a wave, and I followed her into the kitchen. "That poor girl has been through hell," she whispered fiercely, pulling a massive cutting board from the cupboard beneath the bar. Before I'd recovered from my mother's use of profanity, she continued. "I want you to leave her alone and be nice to her. She'll have to repeat everything for your father, anyway, and I see no reason to traumatize her twice. Hand me the meat cleaver."

Huffing in frustration, I reached across the countertop and pulled the heavy nine-inch meat cleaver from a huge rack of knives, and hesitated only a moment before giving it to my mother. I was *very* reluctant to hand over such a big knife to someone so obviously irritated with me.

I gripped the countertop hard enough to make the wooden trim creak. "First of all, this *is* me being nice to Manx." I hadn't cuffed her. I hadn't thrown her downstairs with Ryan. I hadn't even really questioned her. "And the truth is that I feel damn sorry for her. She *has* been through hell. But she also has information we need about Luiz, and whoever's running this whole operation in the jungle. Not to mention the fact that she's *murdered* three innocent tomcats!"

My mother pulled a whole, plastic-wrapped chicken from the fridge and dropped it on the cutting board, much harder than necessary. "Her experience with men has hardly been positive, Faythe. I can certainly understand how she might have felt threatened by a couple of strange tomcats putting their hands on her."

"And the council may see things your way." Though I had my doubts. "But the fact remains that you can't pronounce her innocent just because you feel sorry for her. It's the *council's* place to try her, not ours." Yet I had the distinct feeling I'd be supporting the other side of that argument when my own time came to face the council.

"I agree with you completely." She lifted her meat clever into the air with both hands and brought it down with a mighty thud, slicing the first unfortunate chicken clean in half, plastic wrapping and all. "Her fate is up to the council. But until then, her well-being—and that of her child—is up to us, and I will not have you upsetting her with questions you have no business asking. Leave the interrogation to your father, and be nice to Mercedes. That's the end of this discussion."

Be *nice?* She wanted me to be *nice* to the serial killer in the guest room? My mother's priorities were *so* screwed up.

"If you're not going to make yourself helpful in here, do me a favor and take your brother something to eat. I don't think he got any dinner, with all the excitement today. There's some leftover stew on the bottom shelf of the fridge."

By the time I'd warmed up what turned out to be a half gallon of very thick beef stew, my mother had all four chickens on the stove, in two huge stainless-steel pots. She washed her hands and left the kitchen, bound for company she obviously found more pleasant than mine.

Still irritated, I grabbed a spoon and slammed the drawer shut, not quite satisfied with the racket when the forks and spoons clanged together. My hand hesitated over a pitcher of tea in the fridge, but then I changed my mind. Ryan had plenty of water, and prisoners shouldn't get sweet tea, anyway. Or silver trays and cloth napkins. So I crossed the kitchen holding only a plastic tub of stew, with a spoon handle sticking out. Just what Ryan deserved.

I smiled, truly pleased for the first time in hours.

Darkness greeted me when I opened the basement door. I flipped the light switch, but nothing happened. *Damn it.* The light bulb had burned out again, and—naturally—we kept the extras in the basement.

Growling in frustration, I stomped down the stairs. "Ryan? You awake, you worthless lump of fur? I have your dinner, because everyone else has evidently forgotten you exist."

He didn't answer. He didn't even move, that I could tell.

The light pouring down the steps from the kitchen didn't reach the cage, and I couldn't see a damn thing beyond the bars. Wonderful.

I set the stew on the bottom step and made my way carefully toward the bathroom, arms out straight to feel for obstructions. But that precaution proved worthless when I tripped over the edge of the exercise mat and fell face-first onto the four-inch pad. After that, I whacked my elbow on the back of a folding metal chair and banged my left shin on what could only have been the leg-press machine. And, as my final feat of grace and balance, I knocked over a card table stacked shoulder-high with a collection of Marc's old heavy-metal cassette tapes, which he listened to while he lifted, much to Ryan's irritation.

Fortunately, the racket they made clattering to the concrete floor was nothing compared to the noise they made coming from the stereo speakers.

Finally, my hand brushed the bathroom door frame. Reaching around the wall, I flipped the switch and a single forty-watt light bulb blinked to life, doing little to illuminate a basement that stretched the entire length of our house. But in the dark, even a little light goes a long way.

"Ryan?" I squinted across the room into his cage to find him sitting on the floor by the back wall. "Wake up. Why the hell are you sleeping on the floor, anyway?" The closer I came, the odder his pose seemed. He wasn't so much sitting as *slouching,* his chin grazing his chest. "What's wrong?"

My heart thumped painfully, and goose bumps blossomed all over my skin. If I'd had hackles, they would have been standing on end. Ryan wasn't moving, and the basement light was broken. Something wasn't right.

Cautious now, I stood completely still and listened. I heard breathing, coming from directly in front of me. Ryan. He was alive, but breathing so shallowly I couldn't see his chest move. What was wrong with him?

Working on instinct now, I inhaled deeply through my nose. *Jungle stray.*

My hands went cold. I would have recognized that smell anywhere, and I knew only one thing to do when faced with it alone and unarmed: run.

I spun and raced for the stairs. My foot hit the first step as my hand grabbed the banister, but I stopped short at the creak of hinges overhead. Slowly, I glanced up, already knowing what I'd see at the top of the stairs.

Luiz.

Thirty-One

I had only a second to process what I saw before Luiz closed the door softly, cutting off the light from the kitchen. But that was time enough to see the small pistol in his left hand.

Damn, is everyone walking around armed now?

My mouth opened, and I sucked in a breath in preparation to scream, but Luiz's hoarse whisper—startling as a clap of thunder in the silence of the basement—made me reconsider. "*Sim.* Yell for help." I recognized his voice, though I'd only heard it once before, three months earlier. "Yell for *mãe.* I take her, too."

I'd intended to warn them to run, not yell for help, but his comment made me realize that would never happen. They would never run. Manx was dying to put Luiz in his grave, but with a broken arm and no gun, she didn't stand a chance. And even if my mother was willing to leave me to fight on my own, she would never abandon Jace, who couldn't run, no matter what the danger.

My teeth snapped together as I closed my mouth, my

decision made. I would fight him alone. Or, rather, I'd dodge his bullets until he ran out. No problem. *Riiight.*

"Good," Luiz said, and I couldn't help but notice how similar in timbre his voice was to Miguel's, though his English was choppy at best. "Only us." He clomped down one step and his gun made an odd slide-click sound. "You kill my brother. Miguel. I make you pay." I wasn't sure what he was doing until his shadow shifted in what little light from the bathroom reached the stairs. He was aiming.

My heart slammed against my rib cage, and I dove to the right. I heard an air-sucking sound and a hollow pop, then something flew past on my left. The bullet thunked into the wall behind me as I hit the floor. My torso landed on the mat, in a broad rectangle of dull light from the bathroom. My right hip smashed into the concrete.

I hadn't killed Miguel. And I certainly hadn't known he and Luiz were brothers. But something told me Luiz was much less interested in facts than he was in revenge.

I hauled my rump onto the mat, and more clicking sounds came from the stairs. *Reloading after one shot?* I didn't know much about guns, but in the movies the bad guys always got five or six shots before their guns clicked empty. So what kind of pistol was Luiz packing?

The next sound—something sliding into position with a decisive clack—came from farther down the steps. I glanced up. He was aiming at me over the iron-pipe stair rail.

I rolled forward, toward the stairs. The gun popped. The next shot went over my back. On my ass again, I spun to look, expecting a huge hole in the exercise mat. There was no hole. There was only a small dart. A tiny hypodermic needle with a feather where the plunger should be.

A tranquilizer gun. That's what happened to Ryan. Luiz hadn't been able to get to my brother through the bars, so he'd shot him with a dart.

Luiz wasn't trying to kill me, at least not yet. He was trying to *take* me. To reclaim me in the name of his twisted project and avenge his brother's death on me every day for the rest of my life, however long that might be.

A shoe shuffled on the steps. I whirled around and looked up. Luiz towered over me, rushing to reload. He kicked, aiming for my head. I lunged to the right and his foot sailed past me. I grabbed his boot in midair. Grunting, I twisted his foot to the left. Hard.

Luiz spun in midfall. His hands flew into the air, reaching for something to grab on to. The tranquilizer gun clattered to the floor.

Bolstered by his loss of the gun, I jerked back on his foot. Luiz fell onto one knee on the step. Only his hands on the concrete saved him from a broken nose.

"Bitch!" he muttered, tugging on his captured leg. I held on tight, pulling in return. He kicked, trying to dislodge my grip. I tucked his calf beneath my right armpit and wrapped both hands around his leather-clad ankle. One bare foot braced against the wall beneath the stairs, I shoved myself backward, dragging him with me. Luiz's knee slid off the step, banging into the wall. From the stomach up, he now lay facedown on the stair riser, growling viciously.

I braced my feet on the ground and pulled again. Luiz turned onto his side and grabbed the rail with one hand. His foot rotated in my grasp. I leaned forward, trying to pull him off the steps.

His boot came off in my hand. I fell on my ass on the mat. Again.

As I scooted backward, my hand brushed something hard, and I glanced down to see the embedded dart.

Luiz dropped onto the floor in front of me. I threw the boot at his head. He batted it away one-handed. I crawled across the mat, headed toward the bathroom. Luiz lunged for his gun at the foot of the stairs.

I scrambled to my feet, glancing around for something to use as a weapon. There was nothing but the folding metal chair and Marc's cassette tapes.

Luiz turned on me, pistol in hand. He dug a third dart from his pocket and bit off the cap.

I backed up, my hand skimming the stack of cassettes to rest on the back of the metal chair.

Luiz popped the gun apart and shoved the dart into place. Sweat dripped from my forehead into my eyes. He snapped the pistol back together and spit the dart cap out. I grabbed the folded chair and swung it up. He pulled the trigger.

The dart clanged into the metal bottom of the seat and fell to the concrete at my feet. If I'd been wearing shoes, I'd have stomped it to pieces. Instead, I stepped over it onto the mat.

Luiz tried to shove another dart into the disassembled gun. It wouldn't fit. He'd forgotten to uncap it, and I wasn't about to point out his mistake. I lunged forward, brandishing the folded chair. Luiz backed up until he hit the side of the staircase. I swung the chair. He ducked. The gun hit the floor an instant before his fist hit my stomach.

I sucked in a painful breath and swung the chair at Luiz again. The plastic-capped foot slammed into his head. He landed draped over me like a blanket, his weight pinning me to the mat. His fingers wrapped around my throat. I clutched at his thumb to keep his fist from closing.

The basement door opened and my mother appeared on the top step. "Faythe? What's going on down there?"

Luiz let go of my neck and leaned to the left for the dart still stuck in the mat. I rolled out from under him, in the other direction. "Mom! Get help! Now!"

"Wha—"

"Go!" I leapt to my feet as Luiz's arm arced toward me. Something sharp grazed my bare calf. I jumped backward. Several drops of my blood dripped onto the mat.

Luiz vaulted to his feet. I backpedaled, glancing at the stairs as I went. My mother was gone, but she'd left the door open. I could have kissed her, thankful for the light.

"Your *mãe?*" Luiz breathed hard as we faced off.

I nodded, wiping sweat from my forehead with the back of my arm.

He licked his lips, circling to my right. "No babies, but much fun."

"You *touch* my mother and you'll never touch anything ever again!" I dodged his lunge, and my hip hit the corner of the card table. My hand fell on a cassette tape in a plastic case. I threw it at him as hard as I could. It hit his nose and, to my surprise, left a tiny cut and a single drop of blood.

Luiz stomped toward me and crushed the tape beneath his boot. I grabbed another. Aerosmith. *Nope, can't throw classic Aerosmith.* I snatched a copy of the Thompson Twins' greatest hits and chucked it at him. One corner of the case hit his forehead. He blinked, and another drop of blood appeared above his left eyebrow.

Fists clenched at his sides, Luiz growled and lunged forward. I hopped back and found myself against the wall. He caught my wrist and jerked me forward. My shoulder popped, and an echo of pain flared to life from the injury I'd sustained at his brother's hands in June.

Twisting, I let my right leg fly, aiming for his side. He turned and shoved me. Hard. I hit the floor again, and his remaining boot slammed into the left side of my rib cage.

I felt several tiny pops. Pain ripped through my side. A scream tore from my throat. Every breath sent fire blazing through my chest.

Luiz pulled his foot back to take another shot. A feline growl rippled through the air behind him. He dropped my hand and froze. Then he turned slowly, backing away from us both as he went.

Smart tomcat. He wasn't going to leave either of us at his back.

I looked at the cat he'd just exposed, fully expecting to see Marc.

It was my mother, her black coat gleaming in the light from the bathroom. Her lips were pulled back from her teeth in a snarl. Her claws were unsheathed, the points pressing little dimples into the exercise mat. She was one mad mother.

My dam padded slowly toward Luiz, and he took another step back. "Good kitty," he said, fear thickening his accent. Sweat beaded on his forehead and dripped into his eyes. He blinked it away but made no move to wipe his forehead. Sudden movements triggered a cat's pouncing instinct, and he knew much better than to risk it.

I scooted sideways, watching my mother advance on her prey. Left hand pressed to my injured ribs, I used my right arm to push myself toward the weight bench.

Luiz bent slowly. His eyes flicked toward the ground. I followed his gaze to the dart that had bounced off the metal chair.

My mother growled. Luiz froze in an uncomfortable-looking half squat. He glanced from my mother to the dart one more time. I pulled myself up using the leg press for balance. Luiz dropped to his ass on the concrete, his hand groping for the feathered needle.

My mother pounced, driving him to the ground. Her claws shredded his shoulders on contact.

He screamed and seized her neck in one hand. His fingers clenched her throat, bicep bulging as he tried to hold her at arm's length. Too late, I saw his other arm swing up, the dart clenched in his fist.

He stabbed my mother in the side with the tranquilizer. She roared in pain, and in fury. Her left claw ripped deeper into his right shoulder. White bone flashed for an instant before blood filled the wound and poured onto the concrete.

Luiz wrapped his other hand around my mother's throat, squeezing harder.

Her eyes rolled up into her head. Her paws went limp. Either the tranquilizer had kicked in already, or he'd actually choked her into unconsciousness. I couldn't tell which, but I feared the worst.

I hobbled four steps to the dumbbell stand, pain shooting through my chest and side with each jarring step. Hissing in agony, I heaved a forty-pound free weight from its groove.

Four feet away, Luiz had my mother on her side. Her tail twitched, and he bled all over her from his shredded shoulders. His right arm hung limp at his side, but somehow his left one still worked in spite of the mauling.

Forcing my feet into motion, I pulled the dumbbell up as high as I could. Two feet away, I swung it forward. Luiz looked up just in time. His eyes widened in surprise, and in sudden fear. The weight crashed down on him, crumpling his forehead with a horrific, wet, crunching sound.

I pulled the dumbbell from the gory wound and Luiz's corpse fell on my mother's torso. My fist opened, and the dumbbell dropped to the concrete. I sank onto the ground, still holding my left side, and used my right hand to shove him off my mother and onto the floor.

My gaze accidentally grazed Luiz, and I closed my eyes to block out what I'd seen. What I'd done to him. He no longer had a face. He had only a crater, with teeth embedded in mutilated, wet red flesh.

My eyes still closed, I ran one hand over my mother, feeling for her chest. I found it, and as my hand trailed higher through her fur, I opened my eyes. Her chest rose once beneath my hand, and air exploded from my lungs in relief. I hadn't even realized I was holding my breath.

Fresh pain shot through my side from the forceful exhalation, but I didn't care. My mother was alive. Sedated, but hopefully okay. I lay next to her on my good side and snuggled into her fur, my tears mingling with Luiz's blood in a puddle on the floor.

That's how Marc found us, bloody and bruised, but alive. Very much alive.

Thirty-Two

"There she goes! That woman never learns." Ethan leaned half off of his chair in anticipation. On screen, Karen White stared into the dark forest, clad only in her nightclothes.

"Yeah, but you'd do the same thing," Jace countered from the living-room couch. "You hear a howl in the woods, you gotta go investigate. It's instinct."

In the chair opposite Ethan, Marc snorted. He didn't have much to say lately, and he seemed reluctant to be alone with me. So I stayed out of his way. For now.

"It's not instinct for humans," Vic insisted from the other end of the couch, twisting to snatch the popcorn bowl from Parker, who sat on the floor at his feet.

I sat curled up in an armchair near the door, watching the guys watch *The Howling* instead of reading the book open in front of me. I'd been on the same page for three days.

"She'll get what's coming to her in the end," Ethan said, eyes glued to the screen. He'd barely left Jace's side since he got home from Jamey's memorial, almost a month earlier. He teased his best friend mercilessly about being seriously injured twice in one season, but he cared for Jace just as diligently as our mother did, placing most of his faith in iPod therapy, rather than in pills and bandages.

Two weeks after Jace was shot, Dr. Carver pronounced him fit to Shift and accelerate his healing. Jace was thrilled. If the transformation was painful for him, he showed no sign of it, enduring the process in stoic silence, monitored closely by Dr. Carver and my mother. Then, two hours later, he Shifted back, apparently pleased with the results.

As the on-screen heroine fled back into her cabin, my mother appeared in the doorway, carrying a plate piled high with double-fudge brownies. She stopped by my chair and looked down at me, frowning in concern. She'd been doing that a lot lately. "I'm making some tea for your father," she said, balancing flawlessly on two-inch heels. "Would you like some?"

"No, thanks. But I'll take one of those."

She smiled and held the plate out to me.

"Thanks." I took several, and bit into the first, watching as my mother carried the plate into the center of the room, to pass out her treats. She and I were getting along better than ever. Fighting side by side had created a bond between us that two decades under the same roof had been unable to. But I'd gained the most from our shared encounter with Luiz. I'd learned that my mother was a badass in disguise. She was Van Helsing in an apron and heels, and—at least for the time being—I couldn't think of a single thing cooler than that. Except having inherited it from her.

On her way out of the room with the nearly empty plate, my mother set another brownie on the end table next to me and smiled. She hadn't actually gotten a full dose of the sedative that day in the basement. Apparently stabbing someone with the needle didn't provide the same force as shooting it from a pistol powered by pressurized air. And, anyway, Dr. Carver had assured me that even an entire dartful wouldn't have been enough to completely immobilize a full-grown werecat. Luiz must have been counting on shooting me twice, as he had Ryan. Mom had actually passed out from being choked.

She dealt with it pretty well, I thought. She wore silk scarves until the bruises around her throat faded completely, and referred to the attack as a "little incident," as if not calling a rose a rose made the fight any less real. It didn't, but hey, whatever got her through the day....

My father couldn't have been prouder of "his women." He regaled his Alpha friends several times apiece with the story of how Mom and I had defeated the jungle stray who'd snuck past an army of enforcers to invade our lives and destroy the facade of security we'd previously enjoyed. Of course, he left out the part where, instead of locking Luiz out, I'd actually locked him *in* with us. I think he was finally starting to understand that there's really something to be said for selective omission.

Unfortunately, that principle could not be applied where Manx was concerned. With Luiz dead, she agreed to a full disclosure, and finally told us her birth Pride and homeland. Mercedes Carreño was from one of the oldest Prides in Venezuela, and as soon as she said her surname, my father's eyes closed in what could only be grief. Or frustration. He obviously already knew what she went on to tell us.

Two years after Manx's disappearance, her father was killed by an ambitious neighboring Alpha, who then took over the territory Manx was born into. Her brothers died in defense of their territory, and her mother died of heartbreak less than a year later. By the time she fought free from her captors, Manx had no home to return to and no family left to care for, other than the child in her womb. So she'd set her sights on revenge, convinced that she could never raise her son in peace while Luiz—the baby's father—still breathed.

While the new Alpha of her old territory would no doubt have taken her in, Manx would no more turn to the man who'd killed her father than she would return to the men who'd killed her sons. So, with no Pride to defend her or demand her return, her fate was officially in the hands of our Territorial Council, which elected to try her on three counts of murder. However, for the safety of her unborn child, her hearing would be deferred until after the birth of her son.

The council was still arguing over what to do with me. My father's allies wanted to let me go with a warning. His enemies wanted to make an example of me. And because of his relationship to the accused—me—my father was not privy to any of the discussions. So we lived in ignorance of the proceedings, waiting for the other Alphas to come to some sort of an agreement. And until that time, I'd been suspended from duty as an enforcer. The closest I could get to the action now was answering my father's phone.

"It's because she's a reporter," Owen said, still watching the movie from the floor at Ethan's feet. "She's naturally curious. She can't help it."

I laughed. It was just like Owen to make excuses for someone else's shortcomings. Even fictional characters. Owen found my tendency to speak my mind "refreshingly honest," and hailed Marc's temper as "a deep protective instinct." He said Ethan "thoroughly enjoyed life," and that Parker "really knew how to have a good time." According to Owen, we were all doing just fine, and all was right with the world. I wanted to share his optimism, but try as I might, I couldn't help seeing things through my smog-colored glasses.

"Hello, Faythe," Manx said, padding into the living room in her bare feet to stand by my chair. Her little baby bulge brushed the end table, and she reached down to caress her stomach through a loose peach maternity blouse. She was swelling every single day, and was more tickled with her expanding shape than I could imagine ever being.

Dr. Carver had removed her cast two days before, and declared her to be in perfect health. He'd reminded her to refrain from Shifting until after the baby was born and to take the prenatal vitamins he prescribed. And he'd promised to come back every month or so and check on her, if she promised to stay out of trouble, and not to leave the ranch. She'd been happy to accept the deal.

Everyone else had been pleased by it, too. Though some of the guys—namely Marc and Michael—were still wary of Manx, none of them would hear of her staying anywhere else until her trial. The company of a pregnant tabby was too special an opportunity to pass up.

"Shut up! This is my favorite part!" Vic cried, reaching for the remote as, on-screen, the camera zoomed in on the couple naked in front of the campfire. It wasn't the sex he enjoyed. It was that first glimpse of Hollywood's idea of Shifting—which just happened to *take place* during the movie's only sex scene. The guys laughed and chewed their brownies, eyes glued to the spectacle of rubber, prosthetics, and what could only be stop-motion photography.

Manx's eyebrows rose as she watched the screen, snacking on a brownie from my dwindling stack. "What is this, *Howling?*"

"It's a movie," I told her, proud of myself for not snatching my treat back from her. I was getting better at being nice to Manx; like everything else, it just took a little practice. And she wasn't that bad once I got used to her. She was a bit of an attention hog, but I didn't really mind, because she distracted a lot of notice from me, which left me free to live my life in relative privacy for the very first time. "They usually watch it with a drink in hand, taking shots every time one of the werewolves howls. If you're not careful, you'll be completely smashed by the end."

"Hey, Manx, come sit!" Ethan called, twisting in his seat to smile at her.

"You don't mind?" she asked, beaming her thousand-watt smile at them as she brushed a tumble of dark curls from one shoulder.

"Of course not." Vic waved her over. "We'll rewind it if you want to watch from the beginning."

Shrugging, Manx walked around the couch into the center of the room. Several of the guys stood, stepping over one another to find a seat for her and make her comfortable. She wound up in the chair Ethan vacated, part of the crowd yet still removed from the pile of warm bodies.

In the month she'd been with us, no one had touched Manx at all, other than Dr. Carver and my mother. With every day that passed in peace, she seemed a little more willing to believe that no one at the Lazy S wanted to hurt her. And every day she smiled a little more.

"Oooh, look out!" Manx cried, in her exotic accent, biting her lower lip as the werewolf on screen lunged for his victim.

"Faythe," my father called out from his office, just as I stuffed the last bite of brownie in my mouth. He hadn't yelled, but the tone of his voice set me instantly on edge. Chewing furiously, I dropped my book in my seat and made my way down the hall to the office. Whatever he had to say would not be pleasant, and I wasn't ready for more bad news.

"Sit down," he ordered from his desk chair, as I padded silently into the room. Marc followed me, and we sat on opposite ends of the couch. My father nodded at Marc, then stood, carrying a plain white business envelope, beneath a sheet of typing paper folded into thirds.

"What's that?" My heart thumped and my palms began to sweat. I was pretty sure I knew what he held, but I refused to believe it until he said it out loud.

"They've made a decision." He dropped the paper on the end table next to me, then sank wearily into his chair. "They're charging you with infecting Andrew, then killing him to cover it up. Two capital crimes. The hearing begins in eight weeks."

Eight weeks? My stomach constricted and I closed my eyes in dread. Manx got four months, and I got eight weeks? So what? Screw 'em. Eight weeks was more than enough time to prepare my defense. After all, I was innocent—mostly.

I took a deep breath, then opened my eyes and saw pure terror in Marc's. Then I met my father's gaze, and for the first time in my life, I couldn't tell which of us looked more worried. Still watching me, he exhaled wearily, and I smiled.

Let the games begin....

* * * * *

*Don't miss Faythe's trial
in* Pride *by Rachel Vincent*

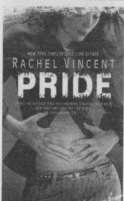

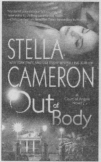